FOR THE DEAD

Also by Timothy Hallinan

The Poke Rafferty Series
A Nail Through the Heart
The Fourth Watcher
Breathing Water
The Queen of Patpong
The Fear Artist

The Junior Bender Series
Crashed
Little Elvises
The Fame Thief
Herbie's Game

The Simeon Grist Series
The Four Last Things
Everything but the Squeal
Skin Deep
Incinerator
The Man With No Time
The Bone Polisher

FOR THE DEAD

Timothy Hallinan

FOR MUNYIN CHOY, ONE MORE TIME
AND TO RALPHIE, WITH THANKS

* * *

DEC 2 2 2014

Copyright © 2014 by Timothy Hallinan

Published by
Soho Press, Inc.
853 Broadway
New York, NY 10003

Library of Congress Cataloging-in-Publication Data

Hallinan, Timothy.
For the dead / Timothy Hallinan.
pages ; cm

HC ISBN 978-1-61695-114-6
PB ISBN 978-1-61695-616-5
eISBN 978-1-61695-115-3

1. Travel writers—Fiction. 2. Murder—Investigation—Fiction. 3. Police
corruption—Thailand—Fiction. 4. Bangkok (Thailand)—Fiction. I. Title.
PS3558.A3923F67 2014
813'.54—dc23
2014019052

Printed in the United States of America

10 9 8 7 6 5 4 3 2 1

Part One
WE ALL FLOAT ...

The River

THE RIVER IS wider than it should be and it's the wrong color. Instead of its usual reddish brown, a gift of the topsoil it steals from the rice farmers upstream, it's a cold, metallic gray-green, the color of the sea beneath clouds. And it runs faster than it should, fast enough to whip up curving rills of white foam where the water quickens over the tops of stones.

Although the sky is a bottomless, unblemished blue, the girl can't find the sun. She sits on the green bank, shadowless, watching the river's flow, not knowing her name and not very bothered by it. Several names come to her, and they all seem to be hers, but she knows she only has one. If she could see her face, she thinks, if she knew how old she is, she'd know which name to accept.

The landscape offers no clues or indications. There's nothing but the stunted forest with its ragged, disorderly trees and waist-high scrub, and the wide gray-green river, flowing swiftly toward her and then past her, leaving her here, a stationary dot on its passage to the sea.

A pale distance away, the river bends to the right and disappears behind a faded green treeline. All that water rounding the bend, resolutely silent, unaware of her. But why shouldn't it be unaware of her? She's barely aware of herself.

Experimentally, she examines her right hand, holding it just above the ground with its tangled green cover. Her hand is so sharp that it seems closer than it is, and she can see the faint blue map of veins beneath her skin pulse with each heartbeat. She feels the blood rushing through them, a tiny river within her, and that thought draws her eyes back to the larger river, and then upstream to the bend where it vanishes.

And she knows—with no feeling of discovery, but as though she has *always* known—that up there, out of sight, on the far side of the bend, the river is bringing something to her. Bearing it, whatever it is, on its unstoppable flow.

And it's something enormous.

She thinks, "I need to talk to my mother." And then the day dims and the girl shivers and realizes that she's grown suddenly cold.

FOR THE THOUSANDTH time since they began to live together, Rose wakes up shivering and asks herself why Poke puts the air-con on high every night, turning their bedroom into a refrigerator, and then steals every blanket on the bed so he can build a fort against the cold he has created.

My mother? she thinks as a tiny scrap of her dream surfaces like a fragment of mosaic and then sinks again. *Why would my mother come to me? Or did she? Mostly, it seems, mostly, it was the river.*

Rose never knowingly ignores a dream. Automatically, she checks the time, which is announced in the sleepy-blue numerals of the bedside clock as 2:46. Too late to call. If something is wrong, there's nothing she can do now. She'll call first thing in the morning, make Poke bring her the phone while his silly, fancy coffee is dripping and the water is heating for her Nescafé.

Still. The dream.

She stretches her arms and her legs and then sits up and reaches for the pack of Marlboro Golds parked permanently on the table, just in front of her big glass ashtray, with this week's disposable lighter lying obediently on top of it. She knows the smoke will wake Poke, so she makes a silent deal with herself. She won't hold the lighter in place when she picks up the pack, and if the lighter falls off she'll put the pack back and go to sleep.

When the pack is in front of her, the lighter is dead center on top.

She palms the lighter and flips open the top of the box, inhaling the rich brown aroma. Even in the dark, the precise white cylinders of the filters are comfortingly clean and—*unused*. They promise hours of solitary pleasure. For so many years, the years when she was dancing in the bars on Patpong, being dragged night after night to hotels by sodden, besotted customers, the moment when it was finally over and she was once again alone—free to breathe again, free to light up a cigarette that belonged to no one but her, to pay attention to no one's pleasure but her own—had gleamed in front of her like a lantern seen through dark trees. It said, *Here you are. Here you can be safe again. Here you can be you again.*

She flicks the lighter and looks down at the cigarette, so secure, so snug, so *right* between her long fingers. There's been one there for so long that she can barely feel it; in fact, sometimes when she lights one it's just because she's become aware of its absence. Smoking this one now is just a matter of inches: inches to put the filter between her lips, inches to bring the flame to the tip. But instead of putting it in her mouth, she thinks, *I need to talk to my mother*, and sees briefly and vividly the river in her dream, broad and gray-green. Breathes in the clean air of the forest.

She lets the lighter go dark and puts the cigarette back in the pack, replaces both objects on the table. The cold presses itself against her. She can feel Poke to her right, can feel, with a mother's ability to penetrate walls, Miaow breathing safely, asleep in her own room. The city outside pulls at her like a tide in her veins, its straight streets deceptively orderly, a reassuring grid imposed on chaos: need, fear, desire, envy, desolation, hopelessness, the invisible web woven by those on both sides of the karmic wheel, those who curse it and the fortunate ones who accept it as their due.

But up here, in the rooms the three of them share, everything is where it should be. Nothing rolls around. The lines between them are straight and strong. Sometimes when she's sitting in her spot on the couch in the living room, she imagines them, each lost in whatever he or she is doing but connected nonetheless by a pale, transparent yellow line, like concentrated light. She can walk through the line between Poke and Miaow and feel it go straight through her, warm as the sun.

Poke, she thinks. *Warm*, she thinks.

She bends down and touches first her left foot and then her right, which may at the moment be the coldest foot in all of Southeast Asia. Poke has his back to her, knees drawn up, the human core of a mountain range of blankets. He sleeps naked, and it's easy, as she slips the foot beneath the blankets, to target the warm bare skin on the small of his back.

The mountain erupts, blankets flying everywhere, and whatever he says, the English is too fast for her to follow it. He sits there wild-eyed, blankets pooled down around his hips, breathing like he's just run a mile, and before he can say anything else, she wraps both arms around his warm neck and pulls him down to her. Says, her mouth inches from his, "Pay attention to me."

For what seems like the second time in an instant, Miaow sits up. The coolness of her forehead tells her she's been perspiring in spite of the single lightweight sheet that covers her.

She hears herself panting. Her heart sounds a quicker-than-normal rhythm in her ears, muffled as a drum in a distant room. But everything she's looking for right now is *here*, it's all here, after all: her dresser, her closet door framing the pale ghosts of her clothes, the rectangular blotches that represent her paintings and drawings. So even though the room is so dark she hates it, hates the paint she made Poke choose nine weeks ago, still, she *is* in her room, which means that she was only dreaming that she woke up before.

When her bed was on the sidewalk. Crowded, like most Bangkok sidewalks, dusk but not yet dark: bat-time, mosquito-time, evening crowd-time, people pushing their way around the bed without noticing what it was, without seeing her as she sat bolt upright with the sheet clutched to her chest. Trying to hide the dirty T-shirt, the ragged shorts, the blackened feet and scabby knees, the grimy nails, dark skin, snotty upper lip, and tangled hair of a street child.

They flowed around her like water around a stone, as though she were something of no value, not worth a glance. But *dirty*. A few women tugged at their skirts or moved their purses from one arm to another, as though they were afraid something might hop on them from the filthy child, lost in the bed in the middle of the sidewalk.

The filthy child. The impoverished, lice-ridden, terrified child she has tried so frantically to leave behind. The child no one at her fancy school knows she ever was.

Miaow realizes she's clenching the bottom sheet in her hand, so hard her forearm is cramping. She releases the cloth, flexes her fingers, and picks up her pillow. She stands it on end in her lap and puts both arms around it, hugging it to her. It's not enough. She thinks about going into the other room to crawl in between Poke and Rose as they mumble permission they won't remember in the morning.

She hasn't done that in *years*.

But she hasn't had this dream in years, either. It's been five years now since she was seven or eight and couldn't read and didn't know her full name, and they took her off the sidewalk and put her in this safe little box eight stories up. Wrapped a life around her, a life she hadn't even known how to imagine.

Why dream it now?

She could talk about it tomorrow at school with Andrew, she

thinks, except that Andrew doesn't know she was ever a street child, and anyway he's so *boy*. Dreams and feelings don't interest him. He lives in that strange boy world where the only things that matter are the things you can see in hard light, the things you can bump into and measure and argue about: "It's not yellow, it's green, and if it were yellow, it would be a statistical improbability." If you said, "It *feels* green," he'd snort. Her least favorite thing about Andrew is his snort.

She has to learn to *manage* him, she thinks, the way Rose manages Poke. Rose has gotten Poke, well, maybe not to *accept* that everything she believes in is real, but at least to acknowledge that it's all in the room with them—the wonderful Rose-cloud of feelings and hopes and memories and beliefs and dreams. The maybes, the what-ifs, the wouldn't-it-be-fines, the ghosts and the spirits of place. If Poke were to draw a map of their apartment, he'd probably find a way to put it in.

And Rose would tell him he got the color wrong.

The same way *she* did, Miaow did, in this room. Picked a color so dark she can barely see her own feet. So here she is, wide awake in a room that's way too dark, and they're in there, sound asleep.

But still, there are walls around them, keeping out everything that's not-them. In a few hours it'll be light and they'll all say hello to one another again and pass one another in the rooms and the hallway, surrounded by the smell of Poke's stupid coffee, and—and—they'll *fuel up* from one another before they go out into the day.

She hugs the pillow closer. Everything is fine. She's here to stay. *They're* here to stay. She's got school, she's got a few friends, she's got Andrew, such as he is. The filthy child has been left far, far behind. Everything is fine.

So why did she have that dream again? Without thinking, she glances at the clock. It's 2:51 A.M.

2

Exquisite Politeness

TWO FIFTY-ONE A.M.

The clouds, lighted pearl from beneath, are impaled like a tent on the tall buildings.

Soft rain creates misty orange halos around street lamps. The narrow *soi* gleams almost empty at this hour except for the two black SUVs following the shining path laid down by their headlights. The leading SUV brakes in preparation for a turn, and almost simultaneously the brake lights blink red on its twin, following three meters behind.

Half a block ahead, to their left, a driveway slopes downward beneath one of Bangkok's newest and most architecturally wrongheaded condominium extravaganzas, an exercise in eccentric, asymmetrical solid geometry clad in a hammer-dimpled shell of titanium. This reflective surface, more than a vertical acre of it, bounces the heat and light from the afternoon sun directly into the shops, offices, and dwellings across the street, making them blindingly bright and raising temperatures into the nineties on the Fahrenheit scale, despite aggressive air conditioning. That entire side of the street had banded together to complain.

That entire side of the street had been told, with exquisite politeness, to stop complaining

As the lead SUV nears the building, a heavy steel accordion

gate at the bottom of the sloping driveway clatters into motion and begins to slide aside. Neither driver signals a turn. The first SUV slows to a creep, the driver trying to avoid scraping the vehicle's undercarriage as it starts its descent. The man in the backseat does not like to hear the undercarriage scrape.

As the vehicle glides into the garage, the lights carve ten thousand ice-blue diamonds from the beads of rain on the polished black surfaces of the roof and hood. The driver has already turned off the windshield wipers, it having been forcefully stated by the man in the backseat that running the wipers inside the garage, when there's no water to remove, creates unsightly streaks of black rubber on the windshield, made of a very expensive polycarbonate compound that can repel slugs fired from a handgun, up to and including a .44 magnum.

The two vehicles coast to a stop near a brightly lighted polished-concrete pillar the size of the average studio apartment that houses two steel-doored elevators beneath multiple security cameras. Upstairs, in the reinforced security bunker behind the door at the rear of the lobby, the SUVs have been visible on wall-mounted flatscreens since they made their turn into the driveway, although neither of the uniformed men in the room has said anything. Now the front passenger door of the second SUV opens, and a man climbs out and moves around the car, glancing in all directions. Another man gets out of the first SUV, dressed, like the first, all in black. They separate, circling the vehicles to survey the garage. Each wears a low-slung holster on his hip, his right hand resting on the grip of an automatic pistol. In thirty seconds, they're back in position, beside the SUVs.

The first man out of the car goes to the elevator and pushes the call button. Behind him, a third black-clad man descends from the backseat of the lead SUV and does yet another visual check of the garage before he joins the others.

The elevator car arrives, and the man standing in front of it steps back and pulls out his weapon. He turns, and makes the *okay* sign: it's empty. He puts out an arm to keep the doors from closing.

One of the two men outside the elevator hurries to the first SUV, pulls open the rear door, and takes a deferential step back. A short, bulky man in jeans and a thin, soft, satin-shiny black leather jacket emerges. He has pitted skin, oiled hair, a wide nose, and the bunched mouth of someone who's just tasted something bitter when he expected sweet. The men with him scramble into a loose formation, one on either side, and the tight-faced man leads them to the elevator. As the doors close behind all of them, the drivers move the SUVs into the shadows.

In the security bunker behind the lobby, two uniformed guards sit in wheeled chairs. On one of the screens they face—more than a dozen of them in all, ranging across the wall in front of the guards— the men from the garage crowd into the elevator. The silence of the security bunker is broken as one of the office chairs slides backward a foot, and the guard who is in it—who had been sitting slumped forward—falls facedown, striking his chin on the edge of the control console. His neck bends bonelessly as his head snaps back, and when he hits the floor, his head is cocked so acutely it rests on his left shoulder. The other guard does not react. The room is silent except for the slow, dripping sound of fluid hitting carpet after it falls from the dangling hand of the seated guard.

Upstairs, the three men in front fan out into the hallway. One of them waits for the man inside while the others hurry to a door halfway down on the right, unlock it, and go in, fast. About thirty seconds later, one of them sticks his head out. "Clear," he says. The sour-faced man and his companion trudge down the hall and into the apartment.

The front door opens into an enormous room, cream-carpeted, that ends in floor-to-ceiling draperies hanging over the external wall, which is all glass. The furniture is heavy and ornate, lots of gilt wood and marble, the kind of decor associated with Saudi royalty.

One of the guards goes toward the back of the apartment. Another remains in the open doorway, and the third trails behind the bulky man in the black leather jacket as he heads for a small flat-screen display on a table against the left wall.

The bulky man says, impatiently, "Come on, come on." The screen fills instantly with an image of the room they're in, from a camera high on the back wall that's pointed at the door they just came through. The bulky man says, loudly enough to be heard several rooms away, "We left at four twenty."

The screen goes dark for a second and then fills again. It looks like the same shot, but there's a time-code in the lower-right-hand corner that reads 16:20. The bulky man watches as the image flickers through almost ten hours of video in a little more than eight minutes. Nothing happens on the screen. No one comes through the door.

The bulky man grunts. His eyes are deeply sunk and rimmed with red from drinking. His oily, black-dyed hair begins well back on his head and ends in greasy curls at the collar of his shirt. The hair frames a smashed nose that looks like it's taken a lot of blunt force, the small, bunched mouth, and three puffy chins. Three steel earrings glint in his left ear.

As the screen goes black, the bulky man turns away. One of the others is still standing in front of it, and another is standing in the door to the hallway. The third is in another room, where he has been operating the hidden hard drive with the security video on it.

"Tomorrow," the bulky man says, his back to the door, heading toward the bar at the rear of the room. "Two o'clock."

The guard standing in the front door opens his mouth wide, throws out one arm, and goes straight down, landing in a seated position and toppling sideways. At the sound of his body hitting the floor, the man standing at the screen turns quickly to see a man in tight black clothes topped by a snug hood that's drawn down over his hair. His face is streaked diagonally with black but otherwise uncovered. He brings up a stubby FN P90 compact sub-machine gun, braces it against his hip, and squeezes the trigger.

The sound seems to tear the room in half. The man in the black leather jacket, who moved very quickly at the first sound, is almost all the way to the bar by the time the man who has been shot crumples to the carpet. He dives behind the bar as the man in the doorway leaps across the room and disappears from sight into the back of the apartment—toward the closet that houses the hard drive. A moment later, the gun rattles again.

Crouching behind the bar, the man in the shiny black jacket yanks out a black automatic. He grips it in both hands and starts to rise, just far enough to get a quick look over the top of the bar, but the man with the submachine gun is back, raking the top of the bar with gunfire. The long white curtains hanging behind the bar are blown backward, and the floor-to ceiling windows behind them shiver into a million pieces and fall into the fog of the clouds. The curtains are sucked through the opening, billowing outward into the mist.

By now the man behind the bar is down on his stomach. He doesn't see the one holding the machine gun go back into the hallway, doesn't see him step back into the room, holding a bottle with a rag trailing from it. The man in the door lets the submachine gun dangle in its sling as he touches a disposable lighter to the tip of the rag. The rag ignites instantly. The man with the gun waits a long, relaxed second and pitches the bottle over the bar.

The space between the bar and the blowing curtains explodes into flame. A bloom of yellow fire rises above the top of the bar, and a hunched form, bent low and burning, charges around the end of the bar and into the room. Half-wrapped in flame, the man in the black jacket has his gun extended, but no one is there. Fire from his jacket licks at his face. The oil in his hair ignites, and he throws himself flat on the carpet, frantically rolling over and over again to extinguish the fire.

He rolls up against something.

It is the foot of the man with the submachine gun. He kicks the automatic out of the burning man's hand and bends down, bringing his face close to that of the burning man.

The overhead fire sprinklers come on. The man on the carpet begins to steam. He and the man with the gun stare at each other through the falling water.

The man holding the gun says two words in Thai, words the burning man sees but doesn't hear over the roaring in his ears. Straightening the gun, the man says two more words and pulls the trigger.

In the guard room, the time-code on the monitors reads 03:09.

3

The Forest

THREE SEVENTEEN A.M.

The buildings are vertical spikes, sharp-edged against a low-hanging sky the color of a scrape of graphite. They're mostly dark at this hour but here and there, high above the street, a yellow rectangle gleams.

The rain has left a shiny line of trickling water in the gutter and puddles half an inch deep where the sidewalk dips. The girl skirts them without a downward glance. The boy stomps through them, trying to splash her. They're small figures, and their clothes are all too big—dark, long-sleeved pullover shirts and loose jeans, handed down apparently by a long sequence of children. The jeans are cinched around their tiny waists with cracked, ratty-looking belts that have dozens of holes punched in them. The one around the boy's waist has been wrapped around him twice. As they pass beneath the streetlight, the dark knitted caps into which they have tucked their hair glisten from the drizzle.

The boy yawns ostentatiously.

"Not yet," the girl says without slowing. Her name is Anchali, and she goes by Chalee, which is what she thinks Charlie Sheen's first name is. She's seen Charlie Sheen on television, and even though she's only heard him dubbed into Thai she admires the way he tells people to fuck off. "There's a dumpster up here. I know a kid who knew a kid who found a laptop in it."

"Working?" The boy's name is Dok, but as long as he can remember, most people have called him Noo, which means *rat*.

"Of course not. But he got nine hundred baht for the battery and the keyboard."

Dok says, "I'm sleepy."

"Poor little baby, up past his bedtime." She is eight months older than he and two inches taller.

"I'm the one who got us out."

The girl wraps her arm around the boy's neck and squeezes, part affection and part threat. "We're going to get caught, that's why we need to find something to take back. How mad can Boo be if we've got something worth a thousand baht?"

"We haven't found anything so far."

"This is the last one."

"Promise?" He holds out a curled pinky.

She hooks her own pinky through his and tugs. "Promise." They separate and she strikes out again, the boy a couple of steps behind. "Some day," the boy says, looking up at the building they're passing, "I'll work in a place like this."

"Not unless your reading gets better."

The boy stops. He's been hungry ever since he slipped part of his dinner into a plastic bag and took it to her after she was sent from the dining room for getting into a shoving match. His stomach growls, and he speaks more loudly to drown it out because he told her he ate his whole dinner and got extra for her. He'd be embarrassed if she knew the truth. "Let's go, then."

To their right the street is a dark river, obsidian, flat, black, empty. To their left, well-dressed women stand motionless behind plate glass like people whose best moment has been frozen for eternity. Carefree and well-groomed and unoccupied by anything specific, they wear clothes that have never shrugged off a wrinkle. Even the soles of their shoes are immaculate. Chalee slows slightly at the sight of a pale yellow sweater with flat pearlescent buttons, but Dok, passing, jostles her shoulder and says, "Come on."

"I just want to look, Dok," she says. "It's the King's color."

Ahead of her, he smiles. He likes that she doesn't call him Noo, even though the other children do.

At the alley, he pauses until she's caught up with him. About halfway down there's a single lamp on a pole, throwing a circle of light that's a weak, corrupted shade of yellow, but there are many dark meters between them and it, and those meters are dim enough to be populated by clouds of rats.

"Last dumpster," she says, passing him.

Dok's terror of rats, coupled with two oversize front teeth, earned him his nickname. He grabs a deep breath and holds it, fighting off the thought of naked tails and clawed skittering feet. Seeking a thimbleful of comfort, he looks up at the ribbon of grayish sky above him. Cool mist sprinkles onto his upturned face, and he's trying to enjoy it as he walks into the girl's back.

Chalee swears with surprising and precocious filthiness. "You made me drop it," she hisses.

"What? Drop what?"

"The lighter, stupid. How can we see anything without the lighter?"

He knows immediately what she wants him to do, and he's not going to do it. "Forget it. We'll go home."

"You made me drop it," she says. "You find it. Find it with your foot. Just stand in one place and feel around with your foot."

"*You* find it with your foot if you're so smart."

"There's nothing to be afraid of," she says. "Look at you. You might as well be a farm kid."

He *was* a farm kid, but so was she, so he lets it pass. "Nope."

"I've walked for hours to get here. I've put up with you. I'm not going back without trying one more time to find something."

The words *I've put up with you* feel like a slap in the face. "Fine," Dok says, turning away. "Do whatever you—" He kicks something small and hard that makes a little scraping noise across the concrete.

"That's it," she says. "How far did it go?"

"Not far."

"Which foot?"

"Right."

"Okay, here's what you do. Bring your other foot up with it, so they're even. Then stick your right foot out just a little and move it side to side, *slowly*."

"Got it," he says. He puts his foot on it so it can't go anywhere and then, with great reluctance, bends, finds the lighter with his fingertips, and snatches it up.

"Don't light it yet," she says. "We're in front of the wrong dumpster. The next one is the one we want." Chalee's hand, warm and soft, lands on his arm. "I'll count the steps, okay? One . . . two . . . three . . ."

Dok likes the way her hand feels. At the count of fourteen, she stops and says, "Okay. Light it."

He flicks the little wheel, and the lighter sparks to life. Two big dumpsters leap out at them, solidified, right-angled darkness, a space of about four meters between them.

"We're in between them," Chalee says. "A little farther."

As Dok steps to his left, holding the lighter, something low and irregular casts a moving shadow in the corner formed by the wall and the first dumpster, which reeks of rotten food. It has no recognizable shape, but it's dark and rounded and almost knee-high. Chalee stops moving, her eyes locked on it, but Dok is the one who says, "What's that?"

HER BODY IS too big for her, too hot for her, too heavy for her; it hangs on her skeleton like a penalty. As cold as she was before, she's hot now. She's dragged herself through the night for weeks, and she knows she's almost finished.

She'd thought the night was *her* time. She'd thought she could hunt in the night, hide in the night. She'd thought nothing could see her. Thought, for once in her life, she'd have an advantage. But the people in the house she'd lived in were just humoring her. They could see her even when she thought she was invisible. The night doesn't care about her any more than the sun does or the rain does. Doesn't care whether she lives or dies. She's just one more weak animal.

And the night is too big and too small. Too big for her to learn its paths and too small to keep her out of the way of the things that want to eat her. She's been running for weeks, lost all the time, hungry forever. Everything she eats out of the big trash cans smells awful and makes her sick. Whenever she rests, they find her and chase her, with their loud voices and their big hands and their awful wet lips.

She had thought she could *laugh* at them.

The forest she's dreaming is dark now and empty, or pretending to be. She's burrowed down beneath a large stone and pulled a mound of leaves and twigs over her. She can sleep here, she hopes, get strong here. Maybe something harmless will hop by and she can reach out, so fast she's invisible, and snatch it up and sink her nails into it and cram it, still living, into her mouth.

She's decided she can eat fur as long as there's meat under it.

But it's rained as she slept and the wet has come down through the twigs and leaves and chilled her. She should move, she knows, try to find a tree with a hollow trunk or broad leaves, but she can't. Her arms and legs weigh too much. She feels as though the weight of her body will push her deeper into the hole she dug, so deep that the earth covers her and she can finally give up and sleep in the dark. Sleep with her mouth open and let the dirt fill it.

She hears a sound, something hard scraping against something else. It's both here and not here. It's on the other side of the world, on the other side of the mound of leaves and twigs. It's on the other side of her eyelids.

It may be the most difficult thing she's ever done, but she opens her eyes.

"IT'S A COAT," Chalee says. "Just a coat."

Dok doesn't like the shape or the size of the thing, but all he says is, "Does it look any good?"

"You're as close to it as I am."

"Old and dirty." He gives it a second look and turns away. "Let's search in the dumpster, fast, and then go."

She makes a quick grab for the lighter and misses. "Maybe there's something in the pockets."

"Fine," Dok says. "I'll be right here."

"I might as well be with a girl," she says. "Give me the lighter."

He says, "Ummmmm . . ."

"I'm going to look," she says, taking it from his hand. She licks her lips and turns to make sure he's listening. "I'm taking three steps closer, okay? One, two, three." She stops. "Now every time I take a step, you take one, too, behind me."

Dok says, "I don't want to."

"Then go away," she says. "Just run away, *Noo.*" She holds the lighter in front of her, a little to the side so the flame doesn't create a halo of darkness, and she takes the eight or ten steps that carry her to the coat.

"I'm right behind you," he says, his ears stinging with the sound of his nickname.

"I'm sorry," she says. "I shouldn't have—" She reaches out to touch the coat, puts a hand on the cloth, then emits a small, high *yip.* She's up in an instant, backing away. "Someone's *in* there," she says, "under the coat, someone is there."

He knew it, but that doesn't mean he wants to hear it. "Are you sure?"

"A shoulder, I felt a shoulder. Or a knee, maybe a knee. And I—I smelled it."

The two of them are standing very close to each other now. The coat is motionless in the corner.

"*Smelled* it? Is it dead?"

"No, it moved. Just a little."

"Big?"

She thinks. "Big? No. Didn't feel big."

"Not big, not dead," he says. "What are you afraid of?"

"What am *I* afraid of? I'm not the one who hid behind a girl."

"Give me that." He snatches the lighter and squats, reaches out for the nearest edge of the coat, pinches the tip of his tongue between his teeth, and tugs the cloth back.

And wets his pants.

A bramble of dark hair. A face patched with black except for a pinkish-white strip across the bridge of the nose and the eyes. As he realizes he's wet himself, the eyes snap open, wide enough to see the whites all the way around the iris, and the lips peel back to reveal gray teeth.

"*Ghost,*" he screams, scrabbling back on all fours like a crab, the lighter going out in his hand. "Ghost ghost ghost *ghost*. Run run run—"

He bumps into something solid. Chalee. He looks up at her and says, "*Black teeth.*"

She reaches down to take the lighter. "It's not coming after you," she says. "A ghost would be eating you by now." She clicks the lighter, looks over at the coat, and sees the dark train of pee leading away from it. A little surge of pity pushes her into action—she needs to do something to make him think she hasn't noticed. "Maybe it's a kid," she says, and with her heart pounding triple-time in her ears, she leans down and tugs back the coat, which has fallen back into place.

Even through the dark patches of whatever has been rubbed into the skin, she can see the delicacy of bone and brow and nostril. A girl. Not much older than they are—maybe one or two years.

She smells terrible. Dirtier than dirty. Very gently, Chalee peels the coat down another few inches and sees collar bones jutting out above a garment that was white once, loose and simple and unbelievably filthy. Chalee has been dirty, too; since her family fell apart after losing their farm, she has learned what it feels like to be so dirty she wants to die, but has never been *this* dirty.

The girl beneath the crumpled coat opens one eye and hisses, and Chalee falls back on her rump. Then the open eye rolls up, and the gray face empties.

Chalee puts a hand, very, very lightly, on the discolored forehead and then snatches it back. "She's so *hot*," she says. "It's a girl. She's feels like she's on fire and she looks like she hasn't eaten in a month. Do you have the cell phone?"

Dok says, "I can't use the cell phone. They'll take it away if they know I've got it."

Chalee turns to look at him. "I think she could die," she says. "So if you use your cell phone, maybe you lose it, and if you don't use it, maybe she dies."

"Yeah, yeah, yeah." He pulls a cheap prepaid phone out of his pocket. "What do we want?"

"We need someone to bring the van," she said. "We'll never be able to get her out of here by ourselves."

Dialing, the boy says, "I really liked having this phone."

Chalee waits until he looks at her, and says, "You're a nice boy, Dok."

NINETY MINUTES LATER, when two boys in their late teens carry the feverish girl into the shelter, they're both scratched and bleeding, and their bundle is struggling helplessly inside the coat, rolled up like a carpet and secured tightly at the elbows and ankles with leather belts. The sounds she makes are almost too high to be heard. Chalee and Dok follow, holding their jeans up with their hands. Their heads hang down. In the doorway they see Boo, the older boy who runs the shelter, silhouetted in the hallway, his hands on his hips, his pose telling them they're in for it.

As they near the entry with its fluorescent overheads, the big patch of urine on the front of Dok's pants comes into dark relief. Chalee twists the top of her beltless jeans into an expert one-handed knot and throws her left arm around Dok, pulling him toward her so he's facing her. She keeps moving, and Dok is now walking sideways, but the wet spot on his jeans is masked by Chalee's body. Boo won't see it.

The smile Dok gives her, with his two big rat-teeth gleaming in its center, almost melts Chalee to the floor.

4

Goop *Is Uninformative*

THE UNPLEASANTLY FULL bowl of breakfast goop that Rafferty has been told will bring his digestive system into harmony and, apparently, allow him to live forever, sends up thick ropes of steam that just add to the morning's humidity. When he cooked it, he'd felt like he was doing a chemistry experiment, fascinated by its sheer, almost gelatinous, viscosity; and when it finally came to a boil, the bubbles had shouldered their way slowly to the surface and then just sat there, unpopped, like gray jellyfish. The pot in which he cooked it will be murder to clean.

Rafferty is beginning to doubt the claims of the Growing Younger Man, an acquaintance from the Expat Bar over on Patpong, who had given him the box of goop. It's hard to see how eating cement will tune up his system or lengthen his life. But, truth be told, he doesn't really care whether the pot will be hard to wash or, for that matter, whether he'll live forever. Right now, he doesn't care about much of anything.

He sighs, something he's been doing a lot of lately, and picks up the big tablespoon he'd chosen to get the goop down more quickly.

Early sunlight peeks over his shoulder at an acute, inquisitive angle, having slipped past the edge of the sliding glass door that opens onto the balcony. The door faces southeast, so the sun is taking its morning bow off to the left, its light and heat hitting Rafferty in the back as he sits at the breakfast counter. The bright light brings into relief a bit of dried something-or-other on the spoon. Rafferty tilts the spoon to see the smudge more clearly, and the spoon's concave surface gathers and focuses the sunlight and beams the flare straight into Rafferty's left eye.

And instantly he's *there* again, ankle-deep in floodwater, squinting against the ravenous brightness of the burning house, seeing both stories reflected upside-down in the water's black rippled surface, seeing the relatively dark rectangle of the doorway and the brutalized child running toward it and through it, straight into the flames. He feels himself leap forward yet again, hoping to do the impossible and splash through the water to catch her, but the house seems to inhale massively, sucking her even further in, and then there's a rush of air and light and heat and sound, and the next thing he knows he's on his back as flaming pieces of the house drift down around him, hissing as they hit the water.

It's been seven weeks since that night, and he still can't find a way around his conviction that he set into motion the chain of events that resulted in that little girl running through that doorway. He's helpless against the memory. The guilt is always just one layer of life away, much the same way the hundreds of thousands of dollars he took from the house are one layer of fabric away from the everyday appearance of things, stuffed into the upholstery of the sofa and the chairs and folded into the pockets of clothes in the closets. Haskell Murphy, the girl's father, is dead, but the evil that flowed from him when he was alive still surrounds Rafferty, pooled and rippling like the water that had reflected the exploding house.

The sun on his back has become unpleasantly hot, so he shifts to the stool to his left and lets it stream past him, into the kitchen.

He sticks the spoon into the goop, with a little more force than necessary. It stands at attention, glinting in the sunlight. Another sigh fills his chest, seemingly on its own, and then escapes.

He can hear Rose in the bedroom, talking to her mother at the extraordinary speed used by women who know each other really well, talking and listening at the same time. Rafferty's been watching his list of fundamental differences between men and women dwindle over the years, but nothing has knocked this one off the page. Most men can't talk like that, period.

There's a silence, and he thinks Rose may have hung up, but after a moment she starts to talk again. He hears the word *dream* several times, the words *frightened* and *river*. She goes on for more than a minute and then falls silent, so she and her mother have moved into a new—and, for them, unusual—rhythm.

Another thing that's unusual. Rose had asked for the phone along with her Nescafé. She normally needs a full cup of coffee to push her way past grunting. But today, a few gulps down, she's rattling away like a tree full of parrots. For a moment, he's tempted to claim some credit. He'd acquitted himself reasonably well last night, he thought, for a man who had been awakened by someone simply stopping his heart with an icy foot. But he knows better. Sex may make Rose purr briefly, but she moved on to the rest of her life the moment she fell asleep. He's the one who painstakingly added the experience, like a bright feather, to his imaginary totem.

He sighs again.

The goop's fragrance stalks him, a little bit like damp paper that might house mice, and he tugs the spoon out, watching half of the stuff pull free of the bowl with a sucking noise. The surface trembles slightly, in a rubbery fashion. If you compressed it into a ball, he thinks, you could drop it off the edge of the balcony and see how many stories it bounces back up.

"Eeeeewwww," Miaow says, coming past him into the kitchen with beads of water on her forehead and the bridge of her nose. They catch the sunlight and sparkle. Her white, short-sleeve blouse and blue school uniform skirt have been ironed until they squealed. She gives the bowl and the upraised spoon a censorious glance. "What's *that?*"

He interrupts his sigh on the inhale, gives her a smile that feels plausible, and pulls himself into the present. "Good morning, Miaow."

"Okay, okay, good morning. What is it?"

"It's my goop."

"Andrew would say that *goop* is uninformative." She pops the refrigerator door open and looks in, with the expression of someone who's getting her first glimpse of the landscape of Mars. Rafferty knows how she feels; Rose constantly rearranges the refrigerator, moving every single thing in it to a new and more counter-intuitive place.

"And if Andrew were here," Rafferty says, fighting his first mouthful, "I'd tell him it's oatmeal-quinoa-bran goop."

"Well, be careful," Miaow says, pulling out a can of caffeinated Diet Coke. "Eat too much of that stuff and you'll be pooping roofing material."

"*Miaow,*" Rose says, coming in wearing Rafferty's newest T-shirt and a pair of white shorts from her infinite supply. Her hair, which falls to her waist when left to its own devices, is coiled up in an improbable structure that's secured with two yellow pencils. "If we have to talk about poop," she says, in Thai, "we don't do it while we're eating."

Miaow says, also in Thai, "Have you seen his breakfast?"

"No, and I won't." Rose turns on the burner beneath her hot-water pot and unscrews the lid on her army-battalion size jar of Nescafé, then licks her index finger and touches it to the side of the teapot, pulling back when she hears it sizzle. "Don't you want your orange?"

"Who can find it?" Miaow says.

"In the fruit drawer."

Rafferty says, in English, "We have a fruit drawer?"

"In the refrigerator." She's spooning Nescafé powder into her mug. "At the bottom."

"I thought that was for your hair conditioner."

"I've got a new one that doesn't have so much papaya in it."

"It wouldn't have spoiled anyway," Miaow says. She chooses an orange, turns her palm to the ceiling, and lets the orange roll down her arm, then straightens her elbow to flip it into the air and catches it without even looking at it.

"I have a refrigerator," Rose says placidly, pouring water into the mug, "and I will put what I want in it." To Rafferty she says, "How can you *eat* that?"

"I can't," Rafferty says, getting up. "But I'm afraid to put it down the sink."

"See what I mean?" Miaow says in her perfect school-English. "If it'll gum up the pipes in the building, think what it'll do to your, you know." She's tossing pieces of orange peel underhand at the sink and hitting every shot. Rafferty is inhaling the sharp orange fragrance and feeling relatively light-hearted for the first time since he got up when Rose says, "Miaow, why do you look so tired?"

Miaow looks as stricken as someone getting bad news from a doctor. "I do?"

"You've got circles under your eyes." Rose blows on her coffee. "Why?"

"I, uh, I woke up last night?"

"Everybody woke up last night," Rafferty says, and Rose laughs hard enough to blow a slop of coffee over the rim of her cup.

Miaow says suspiciously, "Why is that funny?"

"What woke you up?" Rafferty asks, feeling a pinch of guilt; he's been so wrapped up in what happened to another child that he's barely noticed his own.

"Who cares?" Miaow says, in the beginning stages of a retreat he's come to recognize over the past year. "I woke up, that's all."

"Is something wrong at school?" Rose says. "Do you have a problem?"

"*No*," Miaow says, her voice sliding up two full tones. "I just *woke up*, okay?"

"Is one of your teachers—"

"Stop asking me—"

"Or the play?" Rose asks. "Are you going to be in—"

Miaow bangs the side of her Coke can on the refrigerator door and the cola slops on her wrist. "No, I am not going to be in the play." She wipes her wrist on her skirt. "I don't *want* to be in the play, it's a stupid play. Listen, why can't *I* ever decide what we'll talk about in the morning? How come I'm always supposed to stand here while you *question* me? I woke up, so what? Leave me alone."

"All we want to know—" Rafferty says.

"Is everything," Miaow says. "Everything everything *everything*. Where I go, what I do, who I talk to. You know, I took care of myself for *years*. So listen, I woke up because there was a ghost in my room, chewing on my feet, I woke up because I murdered somebody and I have a guilty conscience, I woke up because *I woke up*, is that *okay* with you?"

Rose says, "Did you have a bad dream?"

"I'm *finished*," Miaow says. She tosses the rest of her orange into the sink. She's stalking past Rafferty when something buzzes in her pocket and the long, final, orchestral chord from "A Day in the Life" sounds. She pulls her phone out and runs through the living room and up the hallway to her own room.

"The Beatles?" Rafferty says. "How retro. Gee, I wonder who it could possibly be."

Rose sips her coffee, lowers the cup, and says, with absolute certainty, "She had a bad dream."

"Bad something, anyway," Rafferty says. "How's your mom?"

It takes Rose a moment to respond, a moment she spends gazing down at the surface of her coffee. But then, without looking at him, she says, "Fine." The silence stretches out, and she continues to avoid his eyes. "Just fine."

"THE BUS IS coming," Andrew says, his voice breaking on the word *bus*. "You should be downstairs in six—no, seven—minutes."

"Thanks, Andrew," Miaow says, trying to sound grateful. He's done this every morning for a couple of weeks, calling or texting the moment he sees the bus for their international school shimmer its way through the smog toward his stop, about two kilometers away. She never knows what to say, so she says again the only thing she can think of. "I'll be down there."

"Good," Andrew says. There's a silence on the line, as there is every morning. "Well. See you."

"Right," she says, but he's disconnected. She drops the phone onto the foot of her bed and looks at it as though it might show her a picture of what Andrew's doing, or better still, thinking. It doesn't, so she goes into the bathroom and goes up on tiptoe to study her face in the mirror over the sink. She sees the drops of water on her face and smears them over her skin with her palms, then looks at her eyes. Sure enough. Circles.

And, on her left cheek, a sort of toxic blotch that she can't *not* call a blemish. By noon, she thinks, it'll be as big as a toadstool.

And she's too dark. The skin-lightening cream she keeps hidden from Rose isn't doing anything. She's still too short and too squat and too dark, and now she's got a zit and circles under her eyes, too, like—like a drug addict, but not as interesting. She tilts her head back a bit and lets her eyelids droop, hoping for a kind of elegant wastedness, but all she sees is a dopey-looking dark-skinned girl with circles under her eyes. And a zit.

She has no mystery. She'll never be pretty. If she was going to be pretty, she thinks, it would have started to show by now.

And then there's her hair. The uneven chop that was so daring six months ago now looks like everybody. Three or four times a day, she recognizes herself from behind on the sidewalk. The red dye she's been using looks like rust. She's rusty, she's drab, she has circles under her eyes. Short, dark, ordinary. She could dye her hair purple and tie it in sailor knots and she'd still be short, dark, and ordinary.

She sees again the child from her dream, the filthy child, and she literally shakes her head to clear the image from her mind.

Lately she's been listening to an American band called Fun, and a line from one of their songs suddenly pops into her mind: *We all float before we sink.*

She waves the thought away, a bit anxiously, licks her finger, and draws a wet X across her reflection. Look at Rose, so beautiful, so effortless, so certain of everything. Look at Poke, so—so whatever Poke is. *Surprising,* she thinks. Poke is surprising and Rose is perfect.

Why *wouldn't* they push her bed into the street?

RAFFERTY IS RUNNING water into the bowlful of goop, trying to dissolve it so it won't back up the plumbing for the entire apartment house, when two arms suddenly go around him and squeeze, and his bowl clatters into the sink, and then he hears footsteps and turns to see Miaow vanish around the corner at a sprint.

"You should see your face," Rose says. "Mr. Tough Guy." She sizes him up for a moment and then nods, as though settling something to her own satisfaction. "You were *born* to be a father."

5

One Hundred Twelve Grams

THE BACKPACK FEELS too light.

The bus shoulders its way into a turn as Andrew Nguyen, his stomach suddenly cramped and knotted, hoists the bag again. It's not only too light, it's *precisely* too light. Not by a kilo, not by a half-kilo.

By a much lighter, much more lethal weight. One hundred twelve grams—about four ounces—too light.

Andrew is small for thirteen, narrow-shouldered, with a thin, fragile neck supporting a head that looks like he borrowed it from a bigger boy. Lately, he's been combing his straight black hair forward, feathering it in imitation of a nineteen-year-old American pop singer who changed the way he combs his hair some time ago without notifying Andrew, stranding him once again in the familiar territory between what he thinks is cool and what the world thinks is cool. And, of course, his father, who says Andrew looks like a girl and who doesn't think anything is cool. At the thought of his father, Andrew immediately feels beads of sweat form beneath the still-unfamiliar shawl of hair on his forehead. His glasses have begun to steam up. One hundred twelve grams.

This can't be happening *again*.

He takes a quick, panicked survey of the bus.

It amazes him that no one is looking at him. Not that anyone ever does look at him, but he feels like he's sitting in the center of a red, whirling vortex of anxiety. The whole bus should be staring at him.

Well, one person *is* staring at him—the one who just got on and went past him without a glance—but she looks out the window the moment he meets her eyes.

That's the drill.

Maybe, he thinks desperately, returning to the problem of the too-light backpack, just *maybe* it's not true. Maybe it's a graphic novel that's missing, or something else—anything else—that would equal that weight. The hope that blossoms in his chest flickers bravely as he opens the bag, and goes out the moment he looks inside.

His graphic novel, his spiral notebook, his science text, his bright tin pencil packet (three years too young for him, but it was a gift from his father), the neat little zippered package containing his insulin and the hypodermic he uses to inject it. His calculator, since he tends to quantify things, such as the weight of his iPhone. His wallet, wrapped with a bright red rubber band, still containing the 6,300 baht he started the day with.

Everything except the only thing that really matters. His iPhone. The iPhone 5 with every possible app. The twenty-thousand baht iPhone his father bought him three weeks earlier to replace the twenty-thousand baht iPhone Andrew had lost only three weeks after his father gave him *that* one. Six weeks, two phones, forty thousand baht. Add six thousand more for apps. Forty-six thousand baht.

He is *so dead.*

He pulls off his rimless glasses—less conspicuous at school—and wipes them on the bottom of his neatly pressed long-sleeve white shirt. His glasses, when he puts them back on, are smeared with soap that didn't rinse out of his shirt. The bus seems to have filled with fog.

Now he's wet beneath the arms, too. He thinks about the soap on his glasses and probably saturated in his shirt and imagines suds forming beneath his arms. He'll not only be that weird Viet kid, he'll be that weird Viet kid whose underarms foam.

His father will not replace this phone. He's going to turn its loss into what he calls a "life lesson." Andrew hates life lessons, but even so, he feels a sneaking admiration for his father. Andrew's father is a hard-ass in the great Vietnamese tradition. What other country in the world has defeated the French, the Americans, the Cambodians, and the Chinese?

Only Vietnam. The country of hard-asses.

Andrew supposes that makes him a potential hard-ass, too, but at this stage of his development, he's a five-foot, one-inch, forty-three-kilo wisp of smoke with wet, soapy underarms and a big head. Andrew has researched his physical development, as he has everything that interests him, and he's lagging behind the growth curve.

Dead. He's dead. He'll be home at three and dead by four.

He looks around the bus, which is full of kids from the international school where he met Miaow, and decides that his death is a sufficiently serious issue for him to break Rule Number One. He puts everything neatly back into his bag as his heart pounds in his ears, gets up, and bends forward so he can slide his palms over the cushion of the seat. To the bus at large, he says, "This one has a bad spring. It stuck me," his voice squeaking on the word *stuck* in a way that makes him want to kick himself. He wobbles his way down the swaying center aisle until he can ease into the empty seat beside Miaow, who stares at him with the stone face that means, *What do you think you're doing?*

"Okay if I sit here?" Andrew asks. "The other one has a bad spring."

"It *stuck* him," a girl two rows up says derisively, and there's a ripple of laughter. Miaow's cheeks are flaming. She says, under her breath but with a fierce energy, "This better be good."

"I lost my phone."

The tone of his voice brings her gaze around.

"I must have left it on the bench. After I called you. The bus came, and I guess I got up—"

"Go back and get it." The girl who'd sneered about the spring is looking back at them, and Miaow gives her the Street Eyes that had driven off much bigger kids than she, back when she lived on the sidewalk. The girl whips her head around, but she says something to the girl sitting next to her and Miaow's eyelids drop halfway and she tries to burn a hole in the back of the girl's head.

"It won't be there," Andrew says miserably.

"You don't know that," Miaow says. She's whispering intently, her eyes raking the bus. "But it's *definitely* not going to be there seven hours from now." She gets up. "Let's go."

Andrew says, "You mean—not go to school?"

"What scares you more, Andrew," she demands, "losing another phone or being late for school?"

Andrew goes scarlet. He looks down the aisle, and Miaow knows he's dreading the walk, with everyone looking at him. And she knows just how he feels. But . . .

"I'll go, too," she says, and begins the trek, reaching out to snap her index finger against the ear of the girl who made fun of Andrew. The girl squeals, and Miaow hears Andrew behind her, saying, "Excuse me, excuse me," and she wants to turn and kick him in the shins. She's doing this for *him*, calling attention to herself and pissing the whole bus off for *him*. How dare he apologize? It feels like a betrayal.

But there isn't time to think about that because the bus driver is saying, "Back in your seat."

Miaow says, "I have to throw up."

"Not in here. Wait." The driver, a dark man who's an obvious transplant from the country and who's always been nice to her, signals and fights his way to the curb. The door has opened and

Miaow is partway down the stairs when the bus driver says, "Hey. Where are *you* going?"

Without looking back, Miaow says, "We're going to throw up together."

IT ISN'T THERE. They've searched the bench, under it, and around it. No iPhone.

Now Andrew looks like he really might throw up. He collapses on the bench, puts his elbows on his knees, and lets his head droop into his palms.

Miaow sits beside him. She knows how awful his father can be, but at the same time, she has an obscure urge to slap him. Little rich kid, lost his fancy phone. Within a block there are probably two or three kids with nothing to eat. She says, "How often do they call you?"

He says to his hands, "Huh?"

"Your parents. How often do they call you?"

"Not much."

"Once a day, four times a day? Twice a week?"

He looks at her. He's comfortable with numbers. "Twice a week, on average."

"So if your Dad sees you with the right phone, you'll be okay as long as they don't call."

"Yeah, but—"

"And we'll figure out something about your SIM card later. I mean why your old number isn't working."

"Miaow," Andrew says patiently, "they're not going to wonder about my SIM card. They'll wonder about my *phone*."

"How much money do you have?"

"Six thousand three hundred baht."

Miaow touches her front pocket and says, "I've got some, too. Might be enough."

"Twenty thousand," Andrew says. "*That's* how much is enough."

"We're going to make a deal," Miaow says. "Let's go."

Following her, Andrew says, as though the words are in a new language, "A deal?"

"NOT IN SCHOOL, huh?" The taxi driver has been checking them in the mirror since they climbed in.

"We're on a field trip," Miaow says, seeing, out of the corner of her eye, Andrew's head snap around, feeling his wide-open eyes. It's just possible, she thinks, that Andrew may never have told a lie.

"Yeah?" the driver says. "A field trip? Where to?"

"Our class is, uh, putting together a—a map of Bangkok's used-stuff neighborhoods, you know, the places you can get used whatever. We're looking for phones."

"Good idea for taxi drivers," the driver said. "I can't tell you how many times somebody climbs in, says, 'Where can I buy a used this or that?' How would I know? If I give you my email address, will you send me a copy?"

"Sure." She leans forward. "Up in here," she says. "Anywhere you can stop."

"This is Indians," the driver says. "What do they sell?"

Opening the door, Miaow says, "Whatever you want."

"WHERE ARE WE going?" Andrew had lagged behind to get the driver's email address on a card, which he solemnly hands to Miaow. She drops it to the pavement, and he immediately picks it up. "You shouldn't litter."

"They're up here somewhere. There were four last time I came."

He takes a deep sniff of garlic and marigolds. The people in this warren of alleyways are dark-skinned. "What are?"

"*Phones*, Andrew. Remember phones?"

"They sell phones here?"

"Used ones."

"You mean stolen?"

"Probably. Some of them, probably."

Andrew looks around uncertainly, his eyes slowing at a tiny booth that sells carved wood ornamented with tiny bits of mirror. "How do you even know about a place like this?"

"I spent a lot of time wandering around Bangkok," Miaow says without thinking, and then slams her mouth shut and feels her eyes open wide in panic, but Andrew has come almost even with her, looking interested, and she smoothes her expression.

"You did?" he says. "When?"

"Well, not me, really," she improvises. Andrew knows nothing— no one at school knows anything, and they can't be *allowed* to know anything—about the fact that she was once a street child and a beggar, the lowest caste of all. The filthy child. "I mean, Poke."

"Poke wanders around?"

"Yes. Absolutely. All the time. Wander, wander. And he loses his phone every week."

"But how does he know about this place?"

"Oh," she says, "you know."

"I *don't* know," Andrew says, hauling her to a stop. "That's why I asked."

The ping of irritation she feels at not being allowed to evade the question is soothed by her recognition that this is one of the things she . . . *likes* about him. She does an instant edit on the sentence, deleting the word *loves*, which had shoved its way in uninvited. Yes, it's one of the things she *likes* about him. He thinks in order and in specifics, unlike Poke and Rose and, well, her. Talking with Andrew has a soothing predictability, while a conversation among the members of her family is like a game of Whack-a-Mole: you never know what will pop up, or from which direction.

Up here—right or left? Left.

Since she was abandoned on the sidewalk at the age of two or maybe three, one of Miaow's priorities has been to impose order on the world. When she first lived with Poke and Rose she lined her shoes up every night on the edge of the carpet and allowed a space of exactly three fingers between the hangers in her closet. She ate—she still eats—food in the same order at every meal and resists vigorously the potential anarchy of unfamiliar dishes. Conversation with Andrew is reassuringly orderly, like eating in a restaurant where they've only got hamburgers and fries, and nobody's going to ambush you with polenta.

They turn a corner: more alley, buildings three or four stories high on each side with stalls in front of them, big umbrellas to shade the goods on the folding tables. Women in saris, the occasional man in a turban. It doesn't feel much like Bangkok.

"Poke's a writer," she says as an answer finally shows up. "It's his job to know stuff like that."

"I never see him write," Andrew says. He's glancing around and he looks apprehensive. A child of the diplomatic corps, he moves in a small circle: home, school, the embassy, the homes of a few approved friends. When he shops, Miaow knows, it's in one of the city's many immaculate, air-conditioned malls, nothing like this pungent maze of vendors.

"Me neither, lately," Miaow says. "He came into some money a couple of months ago, and he's been taking it easy."

"How much money?"

She tries not to grit her teeth. *Appreciate* him, she needs to appreciate him. When she'd tried to explain to Poke the way Andrew thought things through, he'd told her there were two kinds of smart people, people whose minds were like a river and people whose minds were like a net.

"A lot," she says. Anticipating the next question, she answers with a lie. "He earned it *writing*, okay?" In an effort to change the subject, she says, "Poke says you think like a river and he thinks like a net."

Andrew lags to watch a woman in a turquoise sari cooking strips of meat over a grill. "What does that mean?"

"People who think like a river," she says, taking his upper arm and dragging him left, into a narrower alley, "go from A to D by way of B and C. They think the world is organized one two three, this and then that and then *that*. People who think like a net believe that everything is connected to everything else, and they might go straight from A to L and then bounce off P before they get to D."

Andrew's lower lip emerges. "It sounds like pachinko. Random and disorderly, with a lot of wasted motion."

"It's just a different approach," she says, feeling defensive.

"Like a bad movie." He turns his head slowly, taking in his surroundings, obviously uncomfortable with what he sees. "Are there really phones here?"

"Just a little farther."

He looks at his watch. "Because we're going to be in trouble if the school calls our parents."

"I'll phone Mrs. Shin and tell her that I got sick on the bus but I'm okay now and we'll be there in a little bit."

"You can really think things up," he says.

"It's hard work," she says, almost snapping. "And I'm doing it for you."

"Right."

They trot on for a few seconds. They're in a section of alleyway that's mostly snack food on skewers and flatbreads cooked over open coals. Here and there Miaow sees a glass display case that's been hauled into the alley, full of small electronics—music players, earphones, GPS units—so she knows they're going in the right direction.

He says, "What about stupid people?"

"What *about* stupid people?"

"What does your father—what does Poke—say about stupid people?"

"He says stupid people's minds are like a big chest of drawers where the drawers change places all the time. Before they can get from A to C they have to search for B, and it's never where they think they put it."

"Huh." He stops, and she stops with him. He blinks several

times, inhales, then exhales, and then says, "I need to talk to you about something."

She looks at him, at his flushed cheeks, and a little worm of anxiety wriggles in her gut. "About?"

"The, umm, the play."

The shift in topic catches her off-guard. They'd met in the school's production of *The Tempest*, but Miaow hasn't thought much about this year's production. "The play?"

"You know, *Small Town*," he says with the weighty patience of someone who's been forced to state the obvious. "Are you going to try out?"

"No," she says. "It's a stupid play, a bunch of white people in a boring little town, not doing anything. There are no wizards or shipwrecks. Nobody in it is as cool as Ariel."

He's looking at his feet. "I guess not," he says. He looks devastated.

Miaow strikes off down an alley to the left, and she hears his feet scuff as he catches up. He says, "But I like the things Julie says about, you know, dying and saying goodbye."

"You like the things *Julie* says?"

"Sure," he says. "You know." He raises both arms, palms up, and declaims: "*One last look, please? Goodbye, all of you. Everyone I liked and didn't like, the people I loved and the ones I fought with—over what? Nothing. The things I cried over. They were tiny. Everything was tiny, and big at the same time. Everything looks so small and ordinary from here and it lasts such a short time, and we make so much of it, and it's all so beautiful. Are we wrong to think it's ordinary, or are we wrong to think it's beautiful?*" He blinks uncertainly, seeing her watching him open-mouthed, and concludes, "*But that's right, isn't it? It wasn't until now that I saw how beautiful it is. Oh, for a chance to do it again, seeing it all this time. I'd see more of it that way, wouldn't I? Wouldn't I?*"

Miaow says, "You *learned* it."

His cheeks two red hotspots, his eyes looking everywhere except at her, he says, "You could play Julie."

"Never," she says bitterly. "It'll be someone *tall*. It'll be Siri."
Siri Lindstrom, the school's acknowledged beauty, played Miranda,
the part all the girls had wanted, in *The Tempest*.

"But Siri can't act," Andrew says, and Miaow's heart suddenly
wells up. "She's beautiful," he adds as her heart shrinks back to
normal size, "but she can barely walk without biting her tongue. *O
brave new world*," he parrots in a flat, uninflected treble voice, "*that
has such creatures in it.*"

"Oh, Ferdinand, *Ferdinand*," Miaow says in the same piping
tone. She's laughing, and Andrew joins in, making sure he doesn't
laugh longer than she does. She sobers and looks around, getting
her bearings, and tugs on his shirt to tow him behind her. "Mrs.
Shin's not going to choose a short Julie."

"I've been thinking about that."

"Well, so have I, and it's not going to happen."

"*Listen*," he says, stopping yet again. She stops beside him,
slightly surprised. He's rarely this assertive with her. He seems
surprised, too. "The school, you know?"

He apparently expects an answer, so she says, "The school."

"Well, about half the kids are Asians and about half of them
aren't, you know?"

She says, "Please stop saying *you know*."

"Well, come on, look at us. Most of the Asian kids are short.
Maybe half the school. And the other half—you know, most of the
non-Asians—they're tall. It's not like a standard distribution,
where there'd be a smooth gradient connecting the extremes—"

"Sorry?"

"*You* know, where you could line everybody up with the tallest
kid on one end and the shortest on the other, and there'd be a
smooth line running from high to low. Look, look, look." He pulls
a folded sheet of paper from his pocket. "Our class picture," he
says, not unfolding it. "What we have is a whole bunch of kids on
the short end and a whole bunch of kids on the tall end with a big
jump in the middle. Like a stair step. It's an anomaly, because of

the racial mix." He's looking a little anxious. "The phenotypes," he says, for clarification. "Nonstandard distribution of phenotypes."

Miaow says, "Okay. So? So some of us are tall and some of us are—"

"Two productions," Andrew says, pushing his way into her sentence. "I think Mrs. Shin should do two productions. A tall production and—"

Miaow gives him a big nod, says, "Oh, *sure*," and starts walking again.

"—and a short production. Some of the best actors are short," he says, a couple of steps behind her. "You're short. I'm going to suggest it."

"There's no way she'll—"

"I'm going to say it'll be discrimination if she doesn't do it."

"*Discrimination?*" Miaow says. "Against who?"

"Whom. Asian kids, short kids. Preferential treatment for, uh, non-Asian tall kids. Look." He unfolds the page, and Miaow finds herself looking at the class picture. A circle has been inscribed around the taller kids, with the words BIG PARTS: MOSTLY ANGLO, while the circle around the short kids says, SMALL PARTS: MOSTLY ASIAN. Beside the picture is a little circular graph, breaking out the heights by racial group.

It takes Miaow a second, and then she starts laughing. She looks at the crowd of people around them, all dark-skinned, and laughs again, "That's totally *on*. They're all crazy about discrimination now. You're really smart, Andrew."

"She'll have to listen," he says triumphantly. And then he adds, talking very fast, "And if you'll try out for Julie, I'll try out for Ned." He stands there, blinking down at the pavement as the declaration echoes around them. He's fidgeting from foot to foot.

She says, "You would?"

"I wouldn't get it," he says instantly. He uses an index finger to blot moisture from his upper lip. "But we could rehearse together before we audition."

"We could," she says carefully. He's given a *lot* of thought to this. Ned and Julie fall in love, but neither of them is going to mention that.

He says, "I already know some of it. Some of Ned's lines, I mean. Not just your—I mean, Julie's—lines."

She leans toward him, as though she's trying to peer in through his eyes, and then she smiles from ear to ear, and he sees the single dimple in her right cheek for only the third time since they met. She says, "I'll talk to Mrs. Shin with you."

"Okay," Andrew says, swallowing between the syllables so it comes out, "Oh kay," and Miaow laughs again and takes his arm.

"Let's get your phone," she says.

6

Going Down

TEN EIGHTEEN A.M.

An apartment house hallway, its sole occupant a silver-haired man in a gray janitorial outfit. He shuffles arthritically, each step an effort, burdened by a big, heavy, open-topped wooden box with a handle, jammed with a jumble of rags, bottles, and jars of cleaning solutions. When he gets to the elevator at the end of the hallway he shifts the case from one hand to the other, lets out a grunt that sounds more like bad temper than exertion, and turns and starts back up the corridor.

This is the third time he's taken this walk since ten o'clock, counting the steps without even knowing he was doing it and then scurrying back in the other direction to be in position if the door should open, which it was supposed to have done at ten.

The man he's waiting for has a reputation for being punctual, and the janitor is growing impatient. This is the last bit before he can leave Bangkok. He and his partners have done everything they've been paid to do, except this, and now the man in the apartment is late.

Of course, the man in the apartment has heard about Colonel Sawat's death by now. He's probably inside on the phone, sweating like a horse, trying to get answers from people at the station, and wondering what Colonel Sawat's death has to do with him. Wondering whether it's the obvious connection. Whether he'll be next.

As the janitor trudges back to the doorway to the service stairs, the elevator groans. Someone coming up.

Moving much more quickly, the janitor covers in a few seconds the seven point three meters separating him from the service stairs, pushes open the swinging doors, and ducks through. He puts a shoulder against the left-hand door and cracks it open half an inch, his eye to the gap.

Two men in brown police uniforms get off. One of them wears dark glasses. He raises them to his forehead, revealing a hard face with a broad, humorous mouth. The cops talk for a second or two and then come down the hall, staying in the center. It's a broad, thickly carpeted corridor with the elevator at one end and an angular floor-to-ceiling multicolored glass window at the other. The janitor will have the cold blue light from the window behind him, which will make it difficult for them to get a close look at him. Not that he needs an advantage.

The officers stop at a door about four meters from the stairway. The one with the sunglasses punches a number into a cell phone and says, "We're here. Knocking now."

The other man knocks briskly, three times in rapid succession.

The cops hear locks being undone on the other side of the door. One of them makes a joke, perhaps about the number of locks, but both men straighten instantly as the door opens. They back off a few steps to allow the man inside to come out.

Inside the stairwell, the janitor peers through the crack between the doors. He sees his man, almost as wide as he is tall, come out of the apartment. The big man nods at the policemen and turns to re-lock the door. Behind him, one of the cops taps his watch: they're late.

The big man is in his early fifties, loose-lipped and red-faced with the spider-veined complexion of a heavy drinker. He has sloping, powerful shoulders, oddly long arms that let his hands dangle almost at his knees, and a relatively small head. His hair stands up on one side, as though he's forgotten to smooth it down after a nap. His white shirt is wet enough beneath the arms to be almost transparent. He pushes between the policemen and trundles stiff-hipped toward the elevator. The cops follow, the one with the sunglasses briefly imitating the wide man's walk.

Looking back, the wide man says, "Something funny?" His voice is unexpectedly high-pitched.

The cop who had been imitating him says, "Got a rock in my shoe." The wide man pushes the button to summon the elevator car.

Behind the swinging doors, the man in the janitorial uniform makes a final check of everything in his case, touches the pockets on his work shirt, counts to three, and pushes through into the hallway.

One of the doors creaks, and the big man and one of the cops turn their heads at the sound. They see a thin, stooped, white-haired man silhouetted against the window's glare, carrying a wooden box clearly too heavy for him. His halting step suggests a limp although it's unclear which leg he's favoring.

The elevator door opens. The cop with the sunglasses steps into the compartment and holds the door for the big man. The other cop and the big man get in.

The janitor calls, "Can you wait for me, please?"

The big man says, "Fuck off" in his high, aggrieved voice and pushes the button to close the door.

The janitor drops the case of bottles with a crash and makes a leap for the elevator. He has an automatic pistol in one hand and a bottle of cleaning solution in the other. The policeman wearing sunglasses makes a snatch at his gun, but the automatic in the janitor's hand jumps twice with a muffled sound like *pfuttt*, and blows a pair of holes in the elevator's back wall. Both cops raise their hands above waist level, the big man screaming for them to shoot. He flails at the elevator doors with small, plump hands, as though he thinks he can hurry their closing.

The janitor reaches the elevator as the doors start to slide shut. He pitches the bottle of cleaning solution, overhand, between the doors. It smashes against the wall, and the hallway fills with the scent of gasoline. One of the policemen tries to force his way out, but the janitor shoots him low in the stomach, and the cop is thrown back against the wall. He slides down into the pool of gasoline on the floor, his hands grasping his abdomen, his eyes wide, his mouth opening and closing. The sunglasses fall off his nose and land in his lap, which is a bright, shiny red. The big man is screaming and kicking at the fallen policeman. The other cop backs to the far side of the elevator as though he's hoping he can push his way through the wall. Just before the elevator doors meet, the janitor yanks a handful of wooden matches from the pocket of his work shirt, strikes them on the zipper on his pants, and pitches them into the elevator, shouting four words as he backs away.

But not fast enough. The plume of flame billowing through the narrow gap between the closing doors is so hot it burns off his eyebrows and eyelashes.

The screams grow fainter as the car descends. The janitor steps back, waving cool air at his face and smelling his own singed hair as he watches the digital numbers above the elevator doors, the remnants of his eyebrows raised in surprise. The elevator compartment obediently carries its burning passengers down five slow floors before the sprinklers kick in and trigger the automatic emergency override.

The janitor goes back up the hall, picks up his case of cleaning solutions, and pushes his way through the door to the stairs. He doesn't hurry on his way down.

7

If You Are Me, Maybe Four Thousand Seven Hundred

THE MAN IN the orange turban is a Sikh. He has the blackest beard and mustache Miaow has ever seen, apparently darkened with eyebrow pencil. His shop is just an overhang of cloth dangling from poles over a scrap of carpet and two scratched and battered glass display cases that look like they fell off a truck. Masking tape runs all the way from corner to corner on the front panel of the right-hand case. Behind the glass is a miscellaneous scatter of cell phones.

When Miaow spotted the shop, there had been two sunburned *farang* tourists, a boy and a girl, wearing the thrift-shop clothes of backpackers. The Sikh had motioned to Miaow to wait, although his eyes kept floating back to her and Andrew as though he expected them to kick in the glass, snatch the phones, and run. After a few minutes of back-and-forth, the tourists leave without buying anything, although Miaow sees the girl slip a phone under her blouse. When she looks up, she finds the Sikh eying her, penciled eyebrows raised. He says, "Watch, small lady."

He lifts his head to look beyond her and points a single finger in the direction the tourists had taken, and two teenage boys take off at a run.

"You think easy, you children?" He raises a finger and wags it side to side. "Not so easy. Maybe two days, that boy walk very bad. Lady have maybe headache." He smiles, and his face is transformed into a wreath of benevolence. "But you children, you good children. Nice clothes. Good shoes." He looks down at Andrew's feet. "Adidas, real, maybe five thousand baht."

"Seven thousand, two hundred," Andrew says.

"Too much," the Indian says in a tone that brooks no argument. "Five thousand, or if you are me, maybe four thousand seven hundred."

Andrew says, "Never."

The Indian says, "You are wanting something? If we bargain we will see who wins."

Andrew says, "Apple iPhone 5."

The Sikh wiggles his head left to right. "Too rich for you. Get nice cheap phone, you don't need—"

"Don't you have one?"

The Sikh pauses, possibly evaluating Andrew's tone, which had bordered in imperious. Then he gives them a shrug. "Of course. Wait here." He goes to the rear of the shop and opens a large cardboard box that's resting on top of another box. Crouching beside it, he says, "I am looking here, but others are looking at you."

Miaow says, "We're not thieves."

"No, no, not," the Sikh says, sorting quickly through the box. "But sometimes we learn things about ourselves, yes? Many phones, man not looking, you very young, you can run fast. Maybe we learn something about you, yes?"

"And maybe you don't have what we want," Miaow snaps. Irritation is a good starting point for bargaining.

"I have, I have." He stands and comes back to the counter with a phone in each hand, and a boy of seventeen or so materializes from thin air and casually puts onto the counter the phone the backpacking girl had taken. "Femily," the man says confidentially, with a gesture toward the retreating boy. "Everything is femily."

He puts the two iPhones on the counter. They look identical to Miaow, but Andrew shoves one aside and says, "Too beat up." He picks up the other one and powers it on. Raises his eyebrows in an expression of approval that makes Miaow want to step on his toe. "Very nice. SIM card?"

The Sikh shrugs, but Miaow can practically see him adding a thousand baht to the price. "If you want."

"Whoever sold this didn't take his SIM card?"

There's a tiny glimmer of humor in the Sikh's eyes. "Maybe he forget."

"It's got all his stuff on it," Andrew says, finger-dancing on the screen. "His phone numbers, his apps, his pictures. Why would he forget it?"

"Pipple," the Sikh says with a shrug. "Everybody different."

"Maybe he stole it," Andrew says severely.

"Maybe," the Sikh says. The dazzling smile again. "Maybe all of these stolen." He looks at the two of them and makes a decision. "You want cold water?"

"Thank you," Miaow says. The man goes to the rear of the shop area again and comes back with a thermos and a stack of paper cups. "Nobody use before," he says, separating the cups into uneven stacks and taking two from the middle. "Very clean."

Andrew puts down the phone and tries to look at it indifferently. He says, "I can pay you—"

Miaow shoulders him aside. "Five thousand baht."

The Indian laughs, although it doesn't disturb the precision of his pour. "You making joke," he says. "My family. My femily, they eat and eat."

Miaow picks up a cup and drains the cool water. Then she says, "Show him, Andrew."

Andrew moves the phone aside and then, as though to make it clear he's not being sneaky, hands it to the Sikh. He pulls his wallet from his backpack, peels the red rubber band off it, and opens it. The Sikh cranes for a look, and Miaow steps on Andrew's foot and tries to put a hand over the wallet, but he ignores her and fans the entire wad of currency. "Sixty-three hundred," he says proudly. He glances at Miaow, and a crafty look comes over his face. She wants to kick him. "But we need to eat," he says. "We need a taxi."

"We have more than one pocket," the Sikh says.

Between her teeth, Miaow makes a noise like frying bacon.

"That's it," Andrew says. He turns his trouser pockets inside out. "I haven't got any—"

"Ahh, well," the Sikh says. "I put back."

"I have three thousand," Miaow says.

"And you keep," the Sikh says. He breathes on the phone and polishes it. "This phone, fourteen thousand eight hundred."

"I have three thousand," Miaow says.

She gets an expressive Sikh shrug. "Come on," she says to Andrew. "We'll get the other one."

Andrew starts to say something but Miaow gives him a look that backs him up a full step.

"Other one where?" the Sikh man asks.

"Not a member of your femily," Miaow says. She grabs the sleeve of Andrew's T-shirt and jerks.

The Sikh tilts the phone so it catches the light. "Fourteen thousand."

"Twelve thousand, five hundred and that's it," Miaow says. It'll mean she has to spend most of her secret seven-thousand, five hundred-baht stash, the money she always carries, tightly folded, in her rear pocket in case she finds herself abandoned on the street again. She gives one more tug, and this time Andrew comes with her, so suddenly she feels like she should hear a cork pop. Over her shoulder she says to the Sikh, "Up to you."

The Sikh says, closing the deal, "Twelve-five."

Andrew, confused, says, "How did we get to twelve-five?"

THE TAXI IS dirty and full of exhaust. Miaow is getting carsick. She and Andrew had to bargain their way down a line of cabs to find one that would take them to school for the amount of money Miaow is willing to pay, so they're enduring what she thinks must be the filthiest, stinkiest taxi in Bangkok, with an actual hole in the floor and exhaust fumes floating through it, like incense with a grudge.

"This is kind of creepy," Andrew says for the third time. He's apparently indifferent to both the taxi and Miaow's reaction to it, his eyes on the screen and his finger doing close-up magic with the icons.

"I can't look." She fans herself with her hand. "If I look, I'll throw up." She looks out at the street and then cracks the window, exposing herself to a stream of hot carbon monoxide with trace amounts of air. She raises the window in self-defense and asks, "Can you turn up the air-con?"

"More air-con, more gas," the driver says. "You're not paying enough."

"How much is it going to cost you to clean this seat if I throw up?"

"Wow," Andrew says, eyes on the phone. "He has *no idea.*"

The driver turns up the air, grumbling, and she points the vent directly at her face and looks out the window again. She unfocuses her eyes and begins to count silently and slowly. At twenty, she feels good enough to say to Andrew, "Get it ready and show it to me fast."

"Okay, okay," Andrew says in the aggrieved tone of someone who's been interrupted, and Miaow thinks, *This is how he talks to his mother.*

"Here we go," he says, holding up the phone.

"Down, down, I don't want to see things moving behind it."

"This is the guy," Andrew says. The phone is on his left thigh, the thigh closer to Miaow. She leans forward, turns the vent toward her face's new location, and looks down.

It's a man in his hard-used forties, thick-waisted and frog-faced, with rough, damaged skin and a bunched, unpleasant mouth, the mouth of someone who doesn't hear "no" much. On a sidewalk somewhere in Bangkok. Three-quarter face, not looking at the camera. Wide shoulders and a small paunch. Black oily hair, combed straight back from a low hairline, a triangular face that narrows toward the top, with the base formed by a broad frog's jaw that's slowly sinking into fat. The kind of guy, Miaow thinks, she'd cross the street to avoid.

"Here's another one," Andrew says, swiping the screen. "And another. Tell me what you think."

There are seven pictures of the man. They're taken from different angles, the man never looking toward the camera. Miaow knows what Andrew means by *creepy*: the man had no idea he was being photographed.

"This is kind of icky," Andrew says.

"It's sneaky." She has a furtive feeling, not entirely unpleasant, as though she's spying: it feels grimy but a little bit thrilling, too. And then there's the man himself. He's what some of her school's popular girls would describe as nothing to skip lunch for. He looks as if he might be bad to bump into, as though he's made of something heavier than whatever goes into most people. *Brutal* is the word that comes to mind.

"Look at these," Andrew says, pointing the tip of his little finger at the man's head. Gleaming in his left ear are three heavy looped earrings.

"He's too old to wear those," Miaow says. "He's older than *Poke*."

Andrew says, "I've seen him before, I think. Somewhere."

"*I* haven't seen him," Miaow says. "And I don't want to. He's scary."

Andrew nods just as Miaow looks up, on the verge of getting sick, and sees that the driver is pulling to the curb. She puts a hand on the door handle.

"Wait," Andrew says. His hand lands on her arm. "You've got to look again. You haven't seen the fat one yet."

8

You Can't Live for the Dead

ARTHIT HAS BEEN trying for half an hour to smile through the abdominal cramps that announce that he's once again followed his head without consulting his heart. The cramps already feel like snarls of the purest anxiety, but when he opens the door to the small closet, they take a leap in intensity that almost folds him in half.

He *hasn't cleaned it out.* He remembers now, cataclysmically, that he postponed it out of cowardice. He'd managed to get rid of her shoes and her fancy things—not that her family had let her take many of them when she left to marry him—but he'd told himself not to rush things when it came to her everyday clothes, the clothes he could have recognized a block away on a crowded sidewalk. The clothes that would have made him smile on sight.

So they're still hanging here.

And they *smell* of her.

She might as well be standing in the closet, looking at him. Noi. His dead wife, the woman who had been the center of his being for almost fifteen years.

"This is the last one," Anna Chaibancha says, tugging a black, many-zippered suitcase through the door. Her face is shiny with sweat; Arthit has a lower-back spasm to go with his cramps, and Anna insisted on toting her things into the house. All morning Arthit has been holding a silent negotiation with Noi's ghost as he distributes Anna's things here and there, trying to find places where they'll look natural, where they won't spring at him every time he comes into a room. *Is it all right if I move this?* he asks the air as he places on the living-room table a photo of the son whom Anna's rich former husband rarely permits her to see. With a quick apology he slips into the table's single drawer the picture of him and Noi, beaming into the sunlight beside the climbing rose she'd planted. "You never liked this vase," he whispers as he replaces it with a plastic trophy from Anna's son's school, almost the only token she seems to have of his present life.

Finding places for the cooking implements Anna loves, pushing aside Noi's old spatula, Noi's old rolling pin, Noi's favorite carving knife, Japanese and rusting now because Noi didn't believe stainless steel took an edge. Anna had looked at it and wrinkled her nose, but Arthit said, "It gets sharper than you can believe." Her glance had been as sharp as the knife.

But he's gotten through it by telling himself, *It's not Anna's fault, it's not anybody's fault. You can't live for the dead.* Over an hour or two, the argument has condensed itself into the single sentence *You can't live for the dead.* Noi wouldn't have wanted him to live for the dead. The phrase has taken on the properties of a spell, a talisman against the dull edge of sorrow that keeps sawing away at him.

But it's not powerful enough for this. Not for these clothes that she once filled with her body, that she had bought and modeled for him, looking for his approval and laughing when he couldn't simulate it. The clothes he'd seen each morning, the clothes she'd been wearing when he came home. The scent that welcomed him back.

He can't let Anna see the clothes. It would put her in an impossibly awkward position.

She's hauled the suitcase to the top of the bed and stands with her back to him, unzipping it. Her head is down, baring the pale neck beneath her efficiently blunt-cut hair, so thick, so different from Noi's flyaway hair with the curl she kept trying to comb out of it. It amazes Arthit that Anna hasn't felt something of his . . . his panic or desperation or whatever it is that's threatening to bring him to his knees in his own bedroom.

He pushes the closet door closed, grateful for once that she can't hear it, and crosses the room. As he's about to touch her arm she senses him and turns to him with a smile that doesn't quite reach her eyes, and he realizes she *has* sensed something, and all he can think to do is open his arms.

The smile goes the rest of the way home, and she embraces him, actually rocking him back and forth. She's short but solid, much stronger physically than Noi had—

Stop that. You can't live for the dead.

She steps back and looks at him more closely. Her eyebrows contract, and she reaches up and brushes the pad of her thumb over the skin below his right eye. He blinks quickly, several times, fighting a surprising surge of irritation, and nods. "Yes," he says. "I'm tired."

She lets her hands drop and busies herself smoothing the thighs of her linen pants, wrinkled with the heat. She says, in the atonal voice of those who have been deaf since birth, "What can I do?"

"Coffee," he says, feeling fraudulent to the soles of his shoes. "A cup of coffee. Would you like one, too?"

She nods, lowering her eyes, and turns to leave the room, but he touches her arm. "The good coffee," he says when she's looking at him. "Grind the beans. Is that all right?"

"If you want," she says.

"It would be better," he says.

Anna hesitates, as though waiting for more, and then turns away. Arthit watches her as she turns right in the hallway to the kitchen. The moment she's out of sight he grabs the partially open suitcase and puts it on the floor and yanks the bedspread and blankets all the way to the foot of the bed. Within a few seconds he's pulled the top sheet off, dropped it onto the floor, and put the covers and bedspread back on. He takes an extra moment to straighten the pillows and chase some wrinkles to the edge of the mattress with his palms. Forgetting his back, he bends to pick up the suitcase. When he lifts it, it feels like pliers closing on the base of his spine, and he can't stand completely upright.

He drops the bag on the bed and uses his foot to kick the sheet on the floor open until it's almost full-size. Then he stands there, leaning forward with his hands on his thighs, panting, feeling like he's going to burst into tears. He bends his knees more sharply, trying to stretch through the pull in his lower back, wrenches himself upright, and yanks open the closet door.

Her scent billows out at him, a kind of pale lavender shimmer with a hint of the talcum she used to dust herself with in the hottest months. He spreads his arms wide and pulls the clothes together into a bundle, but instead of removing them, he stands there with his arms wrapped around them, almost hanging on them, swaying back and forth and breathing deeply through the cloth. With a grunt he lifts it all, until the hooks on the clothes hangers clear the horizontal rod they're hanging from, and he swivels to pull them, sideways, through the door so he can drop them onto the open sheet.

It takes one more fragrant armload to empty the closet. Once the clothes are gone, he goes on tiptoe, not even feeling the pain in his back now, and sweeps his palm across the high shelf to make sure there's nothing there, and when his hand comes down he's holding a tiny white purse, covered in something that sparkles, a purse he hasn't seen since the day they were married.

He can't keep himself from opening it. The scent swims out at him even before he sees the pressed tuberose, a clipping from her bouquet.

And he's lost, standing there open-mouthed and loose-limbed, completely adrift in the moment, with the weightless, brittle, faded flower in his palm.

The coffee grinder whirs into life in the kitchen.

He eases the flower into the purse and pats it goodbye, then places the purse in the center of the bright sundress on top of the pile. With an old man's grunt, he drops to one knee and lifts the bottom edge of the pile of clothes and folds them in half, and then he wraps the sheet around them neatly, like an enormous cloth envelope. He compresses it with his hands until it will fit beneath the bed, and then shoves it out of sight. With his hands flat on the floor and his cheek against the side of the mattress, he lets himself breath deeply four or five times, repeating to himself, *You can't live for the dead.* And then pushes through the spasm in his back and stands upright, and there it is in front of him: the whole room and everything in it, from the color on the walls to the pattern on the pillowcases: it's all Noi.

He puts his face in his hands and says her name three times aloud, a supplication of sorts, a plea to the only person who always helped him. Then, making a mental list of the things in the room he'll have to replace, he turns to the business of the living.

Most of Anna's clothes are hanging neatly when she comes into the bedroom with two cups of coffee in her hands. She hands him one and raises her own cup until he lifts his and toasts her, and then she looks at the closet and goes to it, running her hand over the hanging clothes.

"You are the sweetest man," she says. When they first met she'd been reluctant to speak aloud, insecure about her voice, but now she almost never uses the pale blue pad she'd written everything on during those first days. She gives him a smile that ties his heart in a knot and takes a deep breath. "It smells so good in here."

At the precise moment his words desert him, Arthit's cell phone rings. He smiles at her and puts it to his ear. His lieutenant, Kosit, says, "You'd better get in here. Last night someone killed Sawat and three other guys."

"It was just a matter of time," Arthit says, feeling Anna's eyes on his lips.

"Well, your boss is completely crazy, and two of the three who were killed were cops."

9

Flat as Buttons

THE ROOMS THROUGH which Arthit hauls himself, his back still in spasm and arguing against every step he takes, are oddly quiet. Here and there, cops gather in tight circles. Faces are stiff and voices are low. One of Arthit's friends meets his eyes, points up toward the floor claimed by the brass, fills his cheeks with air and blows it out, and shakes his head.

Meaning, *rampage.*

Well, fuck him, Arthit thinks. By "him," Arthit means his immediate superior, Thanom, a man who has painstakingly squandered every bit of trust any of his subordinates were ever misguided enough to offer him. He's a fifth-rate cop but an Olympic medalist at riding the ever-shifting updrafts and occasional tailwinds of political favor. Kosit, Arthit's closest friend on the force, once said, "He's never missed an ass he tried to kiss." Thanom has survived the rise and fall of prime ministers and police chiefs. He's weathered the intricate, Machiavellian backstage minuets of the *princelings*—the third and fourth sons of old families, assigned to stratospheric ranks in the police because their older brothers have already claimed positions in government and the military. Once embedded, the princelings seize territory, inhale departments, and double-cross each other in the perpetual struggle to dip into the wide, endless river of graft.

Thanom *should* be upset about this, Arthit thinks. He should be scared bloodless.

Kosit materializes out of a doorway. He says, "You look a hundred."

Arthit says, "Thank you for reminding me."

Kosit slows to Arthit's pace. They walk side by side, eyes straight ahead, trying not to look like they're having a conversation.

"He wants to keep it in this department," Kosit says, barely moving his lips. He waves at someone as they pass a door.

"Sure, he does. He's got to be soaking wet and stinking by now. This will splash all over him."

"The Dancer? He'll shimmy out of the way. He did before, didn't he?"

"Just barely," Arthit says. "Sawat reported to him. It was a miracle he didn't go down when the story broke."

"You mean, just because one of his very own, hand-chosen, hand-promoted officers was running a murder-for-hire ring, using other cops to kill people? Little thing like that's not going to bring down the Dancer. Barely scratched his finish."

They make a right and go up a flight of stairs, Arthit feeling the cramps in his stomach having a tug-of-war with the ones in his back. "Who were the cops who got killed?"

"Didn't recognize the names of the active cops, but the other guy got kicked out same time Sawat did. Worked under Thanom, too. A real low-forehead, first name was Jian."

"Don't remember."

"A head-cracker."

"Good company for Sawat." They reach the top of the stairs. "You know," Arthit says, "if you think back to high school, a lot of the people who became cops were tough guys. You looked at them then and you thought, fifty-fifty which side they'd wind up on. Could have been kicking heads in for some godfather or carrying a gun and a stick and kicking heads for mom and country."

"That was me," Kosit says, his leathery face wrinkling in a grin.

"What brought you to the side of the angels?"

"The cops usually won," Kosit says as Arthit goes through the door with a grunt as his back muscles find a new way to squeeze. "And then, of course, there was the shining example of men like you."

Arthit laughs, but his laughter stops when he walks into the low-walled cubicle occupied by the dragon who heads the group's secretarial pool, and receives a look that's simultaneously frayed and rattled. Arthit can't remember the dragon ever being rattled.

"He wants you," she says the moment she spots him.

"He'll wait."

She shakes her head, picks up a phone and punches a double-digit number. "He just walked in," she says. "He'll be right up."

Arthit says, "Traitor."

"This is no time to demonstrate how independent you are. I've been here forty years, and it's never been like this." To Kosit, she says, "Drag him up there."

Kosit says, "Come on," and snags Arthit's arm, pulling him around toward the door and wrenching a groan from Arthit as his back clenches like a fist. "Be a big boy," Kosit says, hauling his friend along, "and later you can have some ice cream."

"Wait," says Thanom's secretary as Arthit comes in. Kosit had peeled off at the last moment like a booster rocket, his work done.

"He wants me."

"He wants everything," she says. "But most of all he doesn't want anyone going through that door until he says it's all right."

Arthit lifts both hands and lets them fall, just an acknowledgment that neither of them is in charge of anything.

She punches a button and says, "The Lieutenant-Colonel is here." She winces at the response and replaces the phone very gently. "Go right in. You might want to straighten up a little."

"If only I could," Arthit says. He goes to the door, grabs a breath, and pushes it open.

"Why aren't you in uniform?" Thanom demands. He's behind his desk, his face as impassive as always, the black eyes flat as buttons, the long upper lip with its suggestion of chimpanzee as rigid as ever. Offhand, Arthit can't remember ever seeing his superior's upper teeth.

There are dark rings under his arms and damp handprints all over the glass on top of his desk. Thanom is no one's idea of an expressive man, but he actually smells of anxiety, strongly enough to cut through the sneeze-provoking scent of the air freshener plugged into the wall outlet behind him.

"I'm off today," Arthit says.

Thanom blinks. "Is that right? Thanks for coming in."

This is new territory. Thanom has never thanked him before. Arthit says, "My pleasure," hoping it sounds more sincere than it feels.

The full colonel's three stars glitter on Thanom's uniform. He uses his cuff to blot his upper lip. "We've got a situation."

"Sawat."

Thanom looks up quickly. "Is the news out?"

"Only in the building."

"Well," Thanom says, "that won't last." He pauses and leans back in his chair. "I have a very special assignment for you."

Arthit waits. The phrase has something truly awful about it.

Thanom takes a deep, rasping breath and drops his eyes to the surface of his desk. Whatever's coming, he can't hold Arthit's gaze. "I'm not always properly appreciative," Thanom says, and Arthit forces his eyebrows back down, but not fast enough to miss Thanom's quick glance. "I know," Thanom continues, talking to the desk again. "I don't always demonstrate my—my esteem, but I think of you, you personally, I mean, as one of my protégés."

Arthit says, "Really." Something more seems to be called for, so he says, "I'm surprised."

Thanom clears his throat and has the grace to blush. "Because of that," he says, plowing along, "because I trust you, I'm going to ask you a favor."

For the first time all day, Arthit feels like laughing. Even his back eases a bit. "Anything I can do."

"Good. Good." A few things on Thanom's desk—a memo pad, a sleek little laptop that makes Arthit's look like a museum piece, the old-fashioned intercom that links him to his secretary—seem to be slightly out of place. When he's rearranged them, he tilts his chair back, his eyes on a spot floating in the air a few feet to the left of Arthit's head. "The killing of Sawat—"

"And the others," Arthit says.

"Of course, the others. Policemen, some of them, and a former policeman." He grimaces and sucks air through his invisible teeth. "It—it—well . . ."

"Awkward," Arthit volunteers.

"Yes, awkward. Doubly awkward, because Sawat apparently had policemen working for him even now. But most of all, there's all that other business, that . . . unpleasantness from a few years back. All that will get raked over again."

"Bad for the department."

"Terrible. A ring of hit men in uniform. Even though we managed to keep it out of the courts, it took years to put it behind us. Careers were ruined." He tugs down on the front of his shirt, smoothing it over his belly. "Even some of those who kept their jobs have a black mark in their files. A *do not promote* mark."

Thanom is one who has been promoted since the story broke, even though he was Sawat's immediate superior and the obvious place for blame to land. The betting pool, down at Arthit's level, was four-to-one in favor of Thanom being forced into early retirement, but he somehow managed to zig when a zag would have put him on the street, and he's been zigging ever since. The Dancer.

"Well, we did avoid the courts," Arthit says with a certain amount of enjoyment. "Both the judiciary and the police board decided that it didn't make sense to reopen the cases—"

"Yes, yes, yes. But the newspapers, television, the new Prime Minister's party. It's all going to get raked up again, by people who don't sympathize with us. The only thing to do is deal with it swiftly."

"Decisively," Arthit says.

Thanom's flat black eyes come up, and Arthit thinks he's pushed it too far. Thanom waits, expressionless as a shark, until it becomes clear to him that Arthit isn't going to look away. "Of course," Thanom says. "And, as smart as you are, you've already spotted the central problem."

"Finding someone you can trust," Arthit says. "There are people here who might leak to the papers or the government. Putting favors in the bank. And then, on the other side of the issue, Sawat obviously was still connected to people in this building, and they're probably afraid they'll be exposed. In fact, one of them might have killed him."

"He was a nasty piece of work," Thanom says. "And, as you say, connected inside the department." But his heart isn't in it, and he lets it trail off. Then he sits forward. "This is the confidential part. Before I go any farther, I need to know this is between us."

"If you're uncomfortable with it—" Arthit begins, but Thanom lifts a hand and brings it down onto the top of his desk with a flat *smack*.

"Of *course*, I'm uncomfortable with it. But if I'm going to make any progress, I need allies. I need confidants. And you and I—well, we've never gotten along very well, but I've observed that you have a code of ethics. If you give me your word, I'm going to take it."

"Well, then." Arthit pulls a chair up to the desk and sits. "Since we're being so frank with each other, how do I know you're not setting me up? Here I am, Mr. Trusty, poking his nose into everything, acting on your secret orders, and everybody's staring at me because I might be incriminating them or shielding myself. And you suddenly have no idea why I got involved in the first place."

For a tenth of a second, Thanom's eyes connect with Arthit's and then bounce off, so quickly it's almost audible. "You want candor? There are a hundred ways I can fuck you over, whether you help me or not. But instead here I am, telling you I need your help. So here's what I'll do. I'll write a paragraph, right now, in longhand, explaining that I asked you to work on this. Undercover. Would that satisfy you?" He hasn't raised his voice, but his face is a deep, almost arterial red.

"No need," Arthit says. Thanom's right; he can destroy Arthit any time he wants. "I'll trust you."

Thanom draws a deep breath, and the corners of his long upper lip pull up in an expression he probably wants Arthit to interpret as a smile. "Only a few people know about this: we have video. From the security cameras in the building."

"I see."

"And this is where you begin to help me." Thanom leans back in the chair again and swivels to his right so he can look out the window. "I need to limit the number of people who see that film."

The muscles in Arthit's back extend their grasp practically all the way up to the base of his neck and yank. He sees it coming, and it's not good on any level.

"Your friend," Thanom says. "That woman."

Arthit says nothing.

"The deaf one," Thanom says with an edge on his voice. "I need her to look at it." He drifts around in the chair until he's facing Arthit again, and this time his eyes find Arthit's and hold them. "And I need your word, and hers, that what she sees will be between her and me only. Is that clear?"

"She's working," Arthit says.

Thanom says, "Is she." It isn't a question. "This is how we begin being honest with each other?"

Arthit starts to lick his lips and thinks better of it.

"Somehow, in that very obscure scuffle a couple of months back with your *farang* friend," Thanom says, "she got on the wrong side of Shen and his national security ghostbusters. As I hear it, they got her fired from the school she worked at. Am I wrong?"

"No, sir. But she's been looking—"

"I'm sure she has." He lifts the corners of his mouth again. "And maybe we can help her. There must be other schools for damaged children. A word from us could do wonders, don't you think?"

Arthit feels like he steered off the curve. "Yes. Of course. Sir."

"So get her in here for me. I need her here in half an hour. Agreed?"

"How could I not agree?" Arthit says, just barely not snapping it.

He stands and turns to go, but the buzzer on the desk rings, and Thanom says, "One minute." He picks up the phone, and his face drains of color. When he hangs up, he says, "Thongchai's been killed. And two active cops. Just now." He grabs hold of his hair and yanks. "They just killed *three more*."

10

I Feel Like We Should Take Care of Her

THEY'VE BEEN IN the room for almost an hour, Dok and Chalee, and the girl on the bed hasn't moved. She's on her back. The top part of the bed, with its flat, hard-looking pillows, has been cranked up a few degrees, so they can see her face. Handcuffs clamp her wrists to the steel railings alongside the narrow mattress, and a thin transparent line snakes from the plastic bag hanging two feet above her head and ends beneath a bandage on the inside of her right elbow. The drip apparently contains a sedative, because Dok and Chalee's conversation, which began in whispers, has progressed to a normal tone of voice, and there's nothing to suggest it reaches the girl on the bed.

They're on metal folding chairs, cold when they first sat down. Chalee has a book in her lap, something big that's covered with stupid-looking color pictures for little kids, turtles with hats and some kind of dog-looking thing with a red tail. Dok had sneaked several glances at the pictures before Chalee put the stack of paper on top of it. The paper, printed on one side with words and numbers but blank on the other, is donated to the Center by businesses. Chalee, as usual, has snatched a stack about thirty sheets deep. Her eyes flick back and forth from the paper to the girl on the bed. Dok watches the face emerge from the pencil's tip. The eyes of the girl on the bed are closed, but in the drawing they stare back at Dok.

"She's so pretty," Chalee says, and when Dok looks over at the bed again he sees that she's right. It took four people to do it, but the girl has been scrubbed clean and her tangled hair not so much combed as pressed into a semblance of symmetry. The face the hair frames looks immensely fragile, as though the bones beneath the skin are eggshell-thin and would cave in if they were blown on. The girl's skin is paler than Dok's and Chalee's, her nose narrower and higher-bridged, the hair curlier and shaded toward auburn, with a hint of red. Chalee is working on the nose now, and it's giving her trouble; she's making a quiet little clicking sound with her tongue.

Dok says, *"Hasip-hasip?"* Fifty-fifty?

Chalee rolls the tip of the pencil lead against the side of her thumb and then uses the thumb to rub a shadow down the right side of the nose, making the bridge jump out. She squints at it, licks the thumb, and wipes it on her jeans. "Sure."

"If she's got a *farang* parent, why was she starving in an alley? *Farang* are rich."

"Not all of them," Chalee says, the pencil moving quickly, shaping a cheekbone. "We had one in my village. He showed up one day, drunk and crazy and dirty, just came out of the woods. He smelled *awful*. The cops came to get him. If he was rich, it wasn't in his pockets."

Dok lifts his chin toward the girl on the bed. "Do you think *she's* crazy?"

"She had such a high fever, who can say? Maybe she saw things we didn't." Chalee glances toward the ceiling and then back down at her drawing. "Once when I was sick, when I was little, I saw the spirits in the corners of the room."

Dok feels his mouth fall open. "What did they look like?"

"Like smoke. Like cobwebs." She takes the eraser to the center of an eye, making a tiny circle with it, and when she lifts it, there's a pinpoint of light reflected in the dark iris. "I could see through their faces. They looked sad, like they wanted to say something but they knew we couldn't hear them." Chalee's hand pauses just above the paper's surface. "Maybe she sees them. Or maybe not. Maybe someone was terrible to her." She begins making very light, very short lines that, as Dok watches, become eyelashes. "Maybe she's just frightened."

Dok considers the alternatives, a little envious that Chalee saw a room's spirits. "Who do you think she is?"

The pencil stops, its point describing little figure eights just above the page. "Maybe a bar girl's daughter."

Dok shoves his lower lip out and tilts his head to one side. There's something in the girl's face—something fine, he thinks—that doesn't say *bar girl* to him. "She looks like a princess," he says. "Why a bar girl?"

"Because she's beautiful. So are bar girls, right? That's their *job*. And if her mother wasn't a bar worker, then she would have married her *farang* and this girl would have a family to live with instead of wandering around sick and starving. I think maybe a bar girl who uses drugs. Maybe she overdosed and left her daughter alone. Poor baby. Shhh for a minute." She holds her arm out in front of her, the pencil vertical in her fist, sighting past it at the sleeping girl. Then she closes one eye, opens it, and closes the other.

"Why do you do that?"

"I saw someone do it on television. I've been trying to figure out why."

"Why do you *think* they did it?"

"Because it looks good. Watching someone draw is boring."

Dok says, his face warm, "I'm not bored."

"No," Chalee says, "but that's because you're sweet."

The inside of Dok's chest goes all fizzy. *Sweet* is so much nicer than *ratface*. "We found her," he says, just to keep Chalee talking. "I feel like we should take care of her."

Chalee says, "Awwww." She does something to the hair over the girl's forehead, lifts the pencil, and sticks it behind her ear. Pursing her mouth critically, she stares down at the sketch. "What do you think?"

Dok leans over, inhaling the smell of soap that always seems to surround Chalee. Even with its open eyes, the face on the page is sealed and mysterious, like a dream seen from outside. The lips are parted slightly, as though preparing to form words that might explain everything. "It's beautiful," he says.

Chalee makes a *psssss* noise and says, "It's okay."

"Have you always been able to do that?"

"I drew pictures of everyone in my village. Everybody—" She swallows and breaks off.

"I'll bet they liked them," Dok says.

Chalee nods, her eyes on nothing much, a point a few inches above the top edge of the page. Swallows again.

"Me," Dok says, suddenly terrified she's going to start to cry. "Could you draw me? I've never had a picture of me." Chalee doesn't speak, and he says, quickly, "Probably not. Why would you want to draw—"

"Sure," Chalee says. It's mostly breath. She says, "Sure," again, and then she clears her throat. She's clenched her right fist, and she knocks her knuckles rapidly on top of the stack of paper, and Dok doesn't think she knows she's doing it. She says, "Here." She riffles through the sheets of paper in her lap, and pulls one out. "This is my sister," she says, pushing the paper at Dok. "Sumalee, her name is Sumalee."

"*Sumalee* like the flower?" Dok says. Sumalee is pretty, but not—in Dok's eyes—as pretty as Chalee. She's twelve or thirteen, wearing shorts and an oversized T-shirt with some kind of picture on it, lost in the folds and wrinkles, and she has a village schoolgirl's chopped hair, a big accidental-looking split like an upside-down *V* in her bangs. There's an open window to her left, so that the right side of her face is in shadow. Dok runs his fingertips very lightly over the surface, afraid he'll smudge it. "It looks like she's coming out of the page," he says.

"I worked hard on that," Chalee says. "Sumalee hated to sit there. She had too much energy."

He lifts an edge of the paper, crisp and new. "It looks like you just drew it."

"I did. I've drawn it a hundred times."

"Sumalee," Dok says, memorizing the name. "Where is she now?"

Dok watches Chalee put the drawing back on the bottom of the stack, and there's the face of the girl on the bed again, back on top. He counts to five silently, and when it's clear that Chalee isn't going to answer the question, he says, "What about those things on her nose?"

It seems to take Chalee a moment to hear the question, but she looks from the picture to the sleeping girl and says, "What things?"

"Here." Dok touches his finger to the bridge of his nose several times, as though he's making little dots. "These things."

Chalee sits way forward in her chair and crinkles her eyes, staring at the girl on the bed, and Dok wonders whether she needs glasses. She says, "I don't see—"

"Sure," Dok says, and then they're both up, Chalee heading to the left of the bed and Dok going right. Dok says, touching his nose again, "Some *farang* have them. You know, priggles or something." He puts a knee on the bed, below the rail with the girl's hand cuffed to it, trying to get closer.

"Freckles," Chalee says in English, bending down, and as Dok's weight pushes into the bed, the girl's eyelids flutter and then open, and she looks straight at Dok's rat-teeth, only a foot or two from her face, and screams a shredded sound that seems to bring part of her throat with it, and then she's yanking frantically at the cuffs and banging her head up and down on the hard pillows and flailing her legs to kick the blankets off, and she turns her head and sees Chalee and the dangling tube at the same time. Chalee leaps back as the girl's head lunges toward her, mouth wide open and all teeth, but what she does is clamp them on the tube and jerk it out of her arm with a spray of droplets, and then Dok's running for the door as though the world's biggest, angriest rat is snapping at his heels.

* * *

BY THE TIME the girl who has some training as a nurse arrives with a replacement IV kit, Chalee is sitting halfway down the bed, lightly caressing the back of the girl's hand where the cuff scraped it, and Dok is patting the other hand, although from quite a bit farther away. The girl is making short, broken sounds, not quite sobs, that seem to come all the way from her stomach, and there are shiny tracks down the sides of her face. She's staring a hole in the farthest wall.

"Did she say anything?" the almost-nurse says, coming in, and the eyes of the girl on the bed widen at the sight of the IV bag.

"Maybe in Lao," Dok says.

"Do you speak Lao?"

"Not enough."

"It wasn't Thai," Chalee says. "She was crying and yelling, so it was hard to understand her, but I don't think it was Thai."

"It was Lao," Dok says, surer of himself.

As the almost-nurse approaches, the girl on the bed begins to scrabble with her legs and pull against the cuffs again, but Chalee puts her palm on the girl's forehead, barely touching her. The scrabbling stops, although the girl's eyes stay on the IV in the almost-nurse's hand.

"It's okay," Dok says, using the English word. "It's okay, it's okay." He thinks for a moment and then gets down off the bed and holds out his arm. To the almost-nurse, he says, "Stick it in me."

"I can't do that," the almost-nurse says. She's only about nineteen, and she looks very uncertain. "The needle has to be sterile."

"Look at her," Dok says, tugging the sleeve of his T-shirt all the way to his shoulder. "She's so frightened. You won't even get the needle into her arm."

"But I can't—"

"Okay, okay, okay," Dok says very fast. He licks his lips and glances at the girl on the bed for a second. "Then do this. Take the needle out and aim it at my mouth and squirt some into my mouth." To the girl he says, in one of the English phrases all Thais know, "No problem, look, look."

"I don't know," the almost-nurse says.

"Well, I do," Dok says. He opens his mouth wide, the two big teeth in front gleaming, and closes his eyes.

"Look at her," Chalee says, and the almost-nurse takes a quick, timid look at the girl on the bed, who is watching the almost-nurse's hands very closely. "She wants to see."

"You don't tell anybody," the almost-nurse says. She slips the needle out of its sheath, positions it about six inches from Dok's mouth, and squeezes the bag. A thin stream of clear fluid snakes into Dok's mouth, and his eyes pop open, very wide, and a look of dismay seizes possession of his face for a second, but he banishes it and makes a great show of swallowing, and then, with another quick look at the girl on the bed, he opens his mouth again. This time, he lets the stream flow for a few seconds and then raises a hand. When the almost-nurse pulls the needle back, he turns to the girl on the bed, swallows hugely, makes a painful smile, and nods. The moment he looks at her, her eyes dart away.

"Good," he says, and then he shudders.

Chalee says to the almost-nurse, "Does it have that sleeping stuff in it?"

"I don't know," the almost-nurse says, sounding surprised. "The doctor left three of them last night. All I do is put them in."

Dok displays his arm to the girl on the bed, tapping his finger on the inside of his own elbow and then pointing at hers. "Okay?"

The girl closes her eyes and moans, but she lets her right hand fall open. She bares her gray teeth when the almost-nurse pulls off the bandage, and she turns her head to the left, toward Dok, when the needle goes in. But she doesn't resist.

"Thanks," the almost-nurse says to Dok, once the bag is dangling from its spindly metal stand. "I don't know how I would have done it. Boo should know how much you helped."

"She's just frightened," Chalee says. Dok pats the bottom of the bed, and when the girl's eyebrows contract he points at his chest and then the bed. She doesn't respond, so he slowly climbs back up onto the bed and begins to smooth her left hand again. Chalee pulls her chair up to the right side of the bed and when the girl turns to regard her, Chalee holds up her sketch and widens her eyes in a silent question.

But the girl doesn't look at the drawing. Instead, she studies Chalee's eyes for a moment and turns slowly back to Dok, up on one elbow on the bed beside her, his hand on hers. Chalee watches the two of them for a few minutes, and then Dok's eyes grow heavy and close, and he puts his head down on the bed. The girl looks down at him, so emptily he might be a mile away, and then she begins to blink slowly, and her eyelids come up a little less with each blink and then close again.

Except for one short, rubbery snore from Dok, the room is completely silent. Chalee gives them a few minutes to slide more deeply into sleep, then gets up and tows her chair to the other side of the bed, where she can see both of them. With their eyes closed and their lips parted they look like they've gone somewhere together. She begins to draw.

11

Human Fractals

THE MONEY IS driving him crazy.

Rafferty has never thought much about money, aside from wishing for more of it. Now that he has more than he knows what to do with, he thinks about it all the time.

When he's not thinking about that girl running into the burning house, that is. Or when he's not thinking about Miaow.

He doesn't know which event comes as more of a surprise: that he's suddenly swimming in money—money that he can't, in good conscience, spend—or that Miaow has become so paralyzingly difficult.

He's long been aware, as a matter of information, that children go insane when they become teenagers. But it's one thing to know that and to sympathize politely with people whose kids have suddenly ceased to be conventional, predictable beings and turned into human fractals. It's another to deal with it day by day in your own home, when the child who's bewildering you is the one you love. And Rafferty loves Miaow with a love that seems to flow through him rather than from him, because, he thinks, he couldn't possibly hold so much. He'd have run dry years ago.

His laptop screen goes dark, a reproach for how long it's been since he touched the keys. Not that he has anything to write, anyway. He's making a second try at fiction, and the people he makes up seem much less interesting than the people he knows.

The coffee in the kitchen, his nose tells him, is burned. When Rose drifted in there half an hour ago, on her way out of the apartment, he'd asked her to turn off the pot and she'd said she would, but what he's smelling right now is fried coffee. He gets up from the white hassock, now stuffed, like practically everything else in the apartment, with Haskell Murphy's money, and goes into the kitchen. The little red light glows reproachfully on the coffeemaker and the stink is so thick the air should be brown. He snaps the hotplate off and totes the carafe to the sink, where he runs cold water into it. The pot makes a loud high clicking sound like teeth slamming together, but when he pours out the water, it's intact.

"If I were broke," he says to it, "you'd have split in two."

After Miaow left, towing most of Rafferty's heart behind her, Rose telephoned half a dozen of her confidantes from the bedroom, showered and dressed, and then gave him a distracted kiss on the head, forgot to turn off the coffeemaker, and left to meet one of the crew—probably Fon, her first friend in Bangkok, back when she was new to the bars.

Rafferty is halfway through filling the grinder with beans before he realizes he's making coffee in a sort of automatic chain of actions that began when he rinsed the carafe. He glances at his watch: 2:30 p.m., and decides to finish the job. He'll have time to stop jittering before Miaow comes home.

She's wrapped herself in some invisible parent repellant. For the first four years they lived together, she told them everything, even if she told most of it to Rose, but now she gets upset whenever she hears a question mark. She lives with them like a spy in deep cover: she spends hours online but doesn't talk about it. She goes to school but doesn't talk about it. With a little cramp of anxiety, he acknowledges that he knows why: she's told too many lies there, beginning with her first name. In the biography of Mia Rafferty she's created, she was never a street child; Rose comes from a rich family somewhere up north; he, Poke, is a famous writer. Mia is practically an aristocrat.

And then, of course, there's Andrew. Miaow talks to him and texts him endlessly and spends three or four afternoons at his parents' apartment, but never talks about it. Asked what they do, she says, "Stuff."

Rafferty supposes he should take *some* comfort from the fact that Andrew is so unthreatening, that he's—well, a geek, a father-dominated Vietnamese geek with a big head on a narrow neck and no social skills at all. But Andrew will never be permitted to enter Poke's Circle of Trust for the unarguable reason that he's a boy, and Rafferty remembers, with eye-stinging clarity, what he had been like as a boy. At Andrew's age, which is to say thirteen, Poke was already pushing his way into the deeper sexual thickets, with no regard at all for the girls who kindly showed him the way.

If Andrew ever treated Miaow the way he, Rafferty, had treated Sophie and Kim and Lita and—what was her name?—Trinity, and what *had* her parents been thinking?—if Andrew treated Miaow that way, Rafferty and Rose would be picking up pieces of her for years.

He pours water into the coffeemaker, thinking that he could tell her *so much* about what she should avoid, beginning with boys like the one he used to be. But it's out of the question. She's got an alert system like those outdoor lights that go on whenever anyone moves, and before he could mouth the first syllable he'd be blinking helplessly against the glare and the whoop of sirens, and she'd be half a mile away and running full out.

And he knows what Rose will advise. She'll say, *Leave her alone.* And she'll say it with such serene superiority that he'll have to bite his tongue to keep from saying something *really* stupid.

He yanks the pot from beneath the steaming stream of coffee and slips his cup in. Somewhere in this irritable near-teen with her hacked, badly-colored hair is the little girl he met and befriended when she was selling gum all night in the entertainment district and whom he and Rose ultimately decided to adopt—the little girl who had never been in control of anything in her life. To whom every kindness they showed her was a gift. When Rafferty looks back, it's easy for him to identify the time when she began this appalling metamorphosis: it was the day she stopped parting her hair. And now, here she is: impossible. It's as though a butterfly had spun a cocoon and come out as a carnivorous caterpillar.

Three or four mouthfuls have dripped into the cup so he reverses the swap, slipping the pot back into position and wandering into the living room. The apartment's space seems to him to be surprisingly elastic—small, even crowded when they're all there, but large enough to echo when he's alone in it. They've been amazingly happy here, he thinks, despite all the drama the rooms have hosted. One woman dead, another attacked with a knife, a destructive explosion of fury from a street child named Boo—the child who'd rescued Miaow when she was first abandoned on the sidewalk and given her a home and a band of friends, of sorts, before burning himself almost into invisibility in the fire of amphetamines.

And what *is* Boo up to now? he wonders. The kid's been off drugs for a few years. Last time Rafferty saw him, he was working, a bit uneasily, with a pair of crooked cops in a scam to rip off tourists who tried to pick up children. Rafferty thinks the kid could probably succeed at anything he wants to do that doesn't require formal education, but doubts he would stop working with homeless kids. Especially not now, with thousands of them flooding into Bangkok as Thailand's rural farming communities break down.

He gulps the coffee and lets his eyes wander the room, seeing Murphy's money everywhere: stacked beneath the cushions of the hassock, inside the couch, running all the way around the edge of the room beneath the carpet in stacks of hundred-dollar bills. Back in the old days, he'd felt flush if he had forty or fifty thousand baht stowed in the safe hidden in the headboard of his and Rose's bed.

But, of course, this money isn't really his. He doesn't even know whether the person to whom it actually belongs is alive.

In all, the apartment has a little less than half a million dollars in it, jammed into every piece of furniture, in empty cereal boxes in the kitchen, in weighted baggies in the toilet tanks. He knows it's silly to salt it everywhere like this—when he took it from a burning house eight weeks ago, it had fit very snugly into a single large briefcase—but he can't bring himself to keep it all in one place. Given the number of unpleasant people who have come unbidden through their front door and the ease with which they've done it, it's always possible there will be another, so why make it simple by putting all that money in one place? This way, at least the son of a bitch will have to work for it.

At times he wishes he could throw the money off the balcony. He can't bank it because he can't explain where he got it, and in Bangkok a large sum of money emits a fragrance that can penetrate the thick walls of banks, all the way to government and law-enforcement offices. The ones in uniform would give him a few memorably bad moments and take it all.

Here's *another* reason he wishes he could just call Arthit. As a cop, Arthit probably knows how crooks hide the huge sums of illicit money the papers are always talking about. But he and Arthit—perhaps the best male friend he's ever had—haven't spoken comfortably since Arthit announced, in a brusque, awkward phone call, that Anna—Dr. Chaibancha—was going to move in with him.

Poke and Dr. Chaibancha have a wary non-relationship. She had been an acquaintance of Arthit's now-dead wife, Noi, but when she knocked on his door to re-establish her friendship with Arthit, it was under false pretenses: she had actually been sent by Thai security police in the hope that she would learn, through Arthit, where Rafferty was and pass the information back to them. The cops had lied to her, appealed to her patriotism, but he still doesn't trust her, and she knows it, and it can't be paved over. The memory of her treachery, a little less than a couple of months ago, stands between him and Arthit like a wall.

The cup is empty. Rafferty shifts his weight from foot to foot in the middle of the living room, wishing he had work to do, wishing he knew how to talk to his daughter, wishing he could call his best friend, wishing he wasn't burdened with all that money. Wishing he weren't haunted by the image of a girl running into a burning house. Wondering how someone who has everything in the world that matters to him could be so deeply and so completely discontented.

12

Home

ARTHIT SAYS, "SAME man?"

Anna nods. She won't speak aloud in public. They're in the back corner of a restaurant just far enough from the station that it's unlikely a familiar cop will wander in—and if one does it'll confirm his belief that Thanom is going to keep an eye on him and Anna for a while, if only to know whether they met immediately after Anna looked at the surveillance videos. Arthit is certain he wasn't followed from the station, so if anyone was, it's Anna.

He looks around the restaurant again, sees no one who seems to be paying attention to them. He says, "Only one man."

That I saw, she writes on one of the blue cards she carries.

"Kosit figures there were at least three. The security men in Sawat's condo were killed with knives. Had to take two, at minimum. The man who shot Sawat and his guards was waiting upstairs in an unoccupied unit. So he thinks three. How do you know it was the same man on both tapes?"

He sips his iced coffee, keeping half an eye on the food cooling in the center of the table. She's too busy writing to eat, and he feels a twinge of guilt and puts his hand over the pad. With his other hand, he indicates the food.

Anna pushes his hand away. *He made his hair gray the second time and he walked like an old man, but when he moved fast, it was easy to see it was the same one.*

"What kind of gun? In the second video, the killing of Thongchai."

She shakes her head and shows him the palms of her hands.

"Not a big one, like the first time."

Another shake of the head.

Arthit takes the pen and draws two crude guns, one a revolver with its curved lines, and the other a boxy automatic. Anna taps a fingernail on the automatic and holds up her index fingers, about seven or eight inches apart. She waits, and he nods.

"You could see what he said after he threw in the match?"

She scratches her head and then wiggles her hand from side to side, meaning, *sort of*. Then she begins to write again. *I think he said, Two children. One woman.*

"And when he killed the first men," Arthit says. "He said, 'Two women, three children.'"

She nods.

"Victims, probably," Arthit says. "Sawat and Thongchai murdered a lot of people. These killings were probably revenge for the dead." He rubs the bridge of his nose between thumb and forefinger, and says, "Children."

Anna drops her gaze to the tablecloth. Without looking at the blue card, she folds it in half and then in half again. She uses her thumbnail to sharpen the creases and looks up as he taps the tablecloth.

"So first you looked at the video from last night, where he killed Sawat and the other three, and then someone brought in the second tape."

Anna nods.

"And what happened to the cop who brought the tape into the room?"

She makes a brusque, shooing-away gesture, flapping the backs of her hands toward him.

"Thanom told him to leave. And Thanom's reaction," Arthit says. "When he saw the face on the second tape, the face of the fat man, how did he look?"

Anna unfolds the creased card and writes on the blank side, *Like he went to the bathroom in his pants.*

Arthit surveys the restaurant again and sees no one to worry about. He has a *thousand* things to worry about, but none of them seems to be present. He says, "Do you want to take the food home?"

She nods, gathering up the blue cards and stacking them, evening their edges so she can put them into the compartment in the front cover of the pad, where she keeps the ones she's written on, and he motions to the waiter and makes a box in the air with his hands, miming shoveling the food into it. Anna breaks into laughter. She writes, *Talking to me too much,* and he joins her, although the laugh has to push its way past something squatting in the center of his chest.

The killing of Thongchai, Arthit thinks, will be very bad for Thanom. Thanom barely dodged the hail of institutional bullets when Sawat's murder-for-hire scandal broke, and several innocent men went down in his place. Thongchai was Sawat's lieutenant and accomplice. These killings will raise all the old questions again, and someone—finally—will have to take the blame. The question is, who.

For Arthit, one fact is inescapable. Thanom *knows* Anna will tell him about all this. The talk about respecting Arthit, about Arthit's *ethics,* isn't worth the breath Thanom used to pronounce the words. Ethics are the last thing Thanom's interested in. So what's he really up to?

He touches the back of Anna's hand and forces yet another smile, in a day of forced smiles. "If you're not going to eat, I need you to do something. I want you to leave by yourself. Go left on the sidewalk and don't look around. Go two blocks down to the little *soi* that's got all the pharmacies on it."

She nods.

"Take the *soi* all the way to the boulevard and then flag a cab. Go to the house, go anywhere you want. I'll see you tonight at home."

Her eyelids drop for a second, and when they come back up, her eyes are an open door, completely unguarded. She says, out loud, "Home."

The word on her lips blindsides him, and he hears what he just said. Part of him wants to push his chair back and run from the restaurant, leave her there with her life and her ruined career and the son she never gets to see, and part of him wants to put his arms around her and tell her everything will be fine, although "fine" feels miles and miles away.

He can't hold the smile, so he brings up his hand and brushes the backs of his fingers over her cheeks, then he nods, a tiny nod, less than an inch, that means something enormous. She puts her hand on his and presses it to her cheek. For a moment, that's all there is.

After she's left, Arthit follows his watch's second-hand around the slow circle of a minute and then tracks it another thirty seconds for safety's sake. Then he gets up, his back still stiff, and picks up the white plastic bags of food.

He sees no one obvious on the sidewalk, so he picks up his pace, a man in a hurry, and when he gets to the little *soi* with the pharmacies on it, he drops a bag of noodles.

Crouching on the pavement to pick up the food as people side-step him, he sees Anna, almost all the way to the next block, and ten meters behind her, measuring his stride to hers, her follower.

Thanom, he thinks. *Children*, he thinks.

13

Door Number Two

R AFFERTY SAYS, IN Thai, "I don't know what to say to her."

"Then don't say anything," Rose says, in English. Two hours have passed since she returned from her mysterious errand. They're on the living room couch, a litter of takeout boxes and paper plates on the table. It's been dark for almost an hour, and Bangkok glitters like costume jewelry through the glass door. Rafferty loves to sit with Rose and watch the night slide in.

Music, muted and tinny, floats in from Miaow's room, the door to which is closed and guarded, in Rafferty's imagination, by a pair of fire-breathing dragons.

"Mrs. Shin said they were almost two hours late for school."

"I'll ask her about it," Rose says, from the center of a cloud of remote serenity that puzzles and irritates him at the same time. She smells like limes, the result of having scrubbed the backs of her hands with them. She thinks it lightens her skin. Since they sat down, she's been gazing through the glass door at the city as though this evening it's assembling itself differently than usual.

"Andrew, Andrew, *Andrew*," Rafferty says, the words pushed out of him by a surge of irritation.

"They got to school, didn't they?" Rose says. "That should make you happy. When she starts not going to school at all, *that's* the time to worry."

"I don't know," Rafferty says. A wave of moroseness makes

him slump until he's sitting on his spine. "What do I know about girls?"

"Everything that matters," she says, patting his hand comfortingly.

"I knew this had to happen eventually. I mean, in theory."

"Nothing is happening," Rose says, sounding a little too patient for his taste. "She has a friend. The friend is a boy. They were late to school one day, that's all. Her body is changing, and she's hiding it, and she doesn't—"

"Her body is changing?"

"It's confusing for a girl when—"

"Her *body* is changing? Where have I been?" *Outside that burning house*, he answers himself silently.

"Why do you think she wears your shirts all the time? Look at you, you're like a guard dog, with your ears pointed up. You should be chained to the wall."

"I'm not ready for this. I mean, I knew it would come sooner or later, but I voted for *later*." He sits there without doing anything for a minute and then says, "Poor kid."

"She'll live through it."

"Do you think she's hungry?

Rose says, "She said no twice."

"Maybe I should ask again. If she's growing and all—"

"The hall is only seven meters long," Rose points out. "She's capable of walking that far, even if she's weak from hunger."

Poke subsides for a few heartbeats and says, "She's *twelve*," as though the number were a crushing argument.

"Maybe thirteen," Rose says. "Considering all this, *probably* thirteen." She's wearing cut-offs and one of Poke's white shirts, and she smoothes her thighs with her palms as though she enjoys the feel of her own skin. Rafferty watches enviously.

"Are you calmer now?" Rose says.

"I've been calm the whole time," Rafferty says, trying to sound calm. "Just because I'm concerned, that doesn't mean I'm not—"

He breaks off as Miaow trudges by, looking persecuted, to disappear into the kitchen. By the time Rafferty has thought of something to say so she won't think she interrupted something he didn't want her to hear, she's come back out with a can of Diet Coke and a plastic bag filled with slices of sour green mango with chili and salt that Rose bought from a street vendor. She holds it up, more as a point of information than a question, and disappears again. Sure enough, she's wearing one of the loose, shapeless shirts she borrows from Rafferty after school.

"It's a good thing I've got a lot of shirts," Rafferty calls after her, getting three or four muttered syllables in response. "I probably shouldn't talk about that," he says to Rose. "Or should I? What's the protocol?"

"Mmmm-hmmm." At long last, Rose looks at him, but she's giving him the glassy eyes that mean she's thinking and he knows she's not listening to him. Then she focuses on his face and says, "I want a TV."

Rafferty says, "Excuse me?"

"A television," Rose says. "I want a television."

"Me, too," Miaow says from the hallway.

"Are you listening?"

"No."

"Good, because I'm not buying a—"

"*Everybody* has a TV," Miaow says, coming into the room with the plastic bag looped over her index finger and a piece of red-dipped mango in her other hand. Rafferty's shirt hangs loosely enough that, he thinks, Andrew could fit inside it, too.

"Obviously, everyone doesn't have a TV," Rafferty says. "You don't."

Miaow gives him what the Thais call small eyes. "That's not an answer."

"Television is evil." Rafferty is thrilled they're having a conversation. "Tiny spores fly through the screen like gnats and go right through the bones in your skull and sit around laughing as they eat your IQ. Next thing you know, you like Simon Cowell."

Miaow's brow wrinkles. "Who?"

"The things I've spared her," Poke says to the air.

"How am I supposed to be an actress if I can't watch acting?"

Poke says, "I thought the play this year was stupid."

Miaow opens her mouth and closes it again, apparently surprised to be reminded that she's actually discussed something with them. "It is."

"What is it?"

"Something *old*," she says witheringly. "*Small Town*."

"Really?" He sits back in surprise. "When I was in high school, I was in *Small Town*."

"That's what I mean. It's old." She licks some of the chili-salt mix from the mango slice. "Who were you?"

"Ned."

"Gooey gooey. Mushy. Ned and, uh—"

The way she's looking at him, he knows she knows the name, but he says "Julie."

"Julie," she says. Then she looks at the floor.

"You'd be a great Julie."

"I'm too short for it."

"Well, then." Rafferty starts to say something more but realizes the Miaow is still talking. She says, "But Andrew—" She breaks the sentence so abruptly she might as well have snapped it over her knee.

"Andrew?" Rafferty says innocently.

"He has an *idea*," Miaow says.

"To make the play less stupid?"

Miaow shrugs, and suddenly she seems farther away.

"To make you taller?"

Rose says, "Poke."

Miaow says, "To make Mrs. Shin do two shows. One tall and one short."

"But," Poke says, and stops. Whatever he thinks of Andrew, the kid's not dumb.

"It's discrimination," Miaow says. She pulls Andrew's chart from her pocket and unfolds it. "Most of the Asian kids are short and the Anglo and *farang* kids are tall. So he's going to say—"

She stops because Rafferty is laughing. "That's great," he says. He snaps the picture with his index finger, making a satisfying *thwack*. "Of course, it's discrimination." And then he's laughing again.

Miaow almost smiles, but instead, she says, "So I need a TV."

"Pretty good," he says. "But not good enough for a TV."

"Okay," Miaow says, going for Door Number Two. "Then how about a piercing?"

Two minutes later Miaow is back in her room, listening to Tegan and Sara, played at the limit of the speakers on her laptop. Rafferty says, "It isn't fair. This is like a miracle, right? I mean, my little girl is, you know, she's, um, she's—"

"Becoming a woman?" Rose supplies, and then bursts into laughter. "The things you don't *know*," she says.

"She won't even talk to me."

"She talks to you when she wants a TV. And, in case you've forgotten, I want one, too."

The doorbell rings.

Poke waits until it rings again and it becomes apparent that no one else in the apartment has any intention of getting up. "Don't bother," he says loudly enough to be heard in Miaow's room. "I'll get it."

He opens it to see Andrew in his after-school clothes: knee-length black T-shirt celebrating a local thrash band called Drool, a pair of jeans that were undoubtedly distressed by puzzled Chinese who'd been proud of the way they looked the first time, and black-rimmed spectacles, more conspicuous than the rimless ones he wears to school. He looks stricken, like someone who's just barely escaped a fight with a bunch of bullies who are waiting outside. He's clutching a tightly folded newspaper under his arm as though he's afraid it will escape.

"Hello, Mr. Rafferty," he says without visible enthusiasm. He peers around Poke and his face lights up. "Oh *hi*, Mrs. Rafferty. Is Miaow home?"

Rafferty says, "What's it worth to you?"

From Miaow's room, the volume of the music drops and she calls, "Is that Andrew?"

"Seems to be."

"Poke," Rose says between her teeth, "let him in."

Rafferty opens the door the rest of the way, and Andrew sidesteps him as though he might bite. Rose gets up from the couch, says hello to Andrew, and goes to the counter between the living room and the kitchen to get her purse.

"Come on back to my room," Miaow calls.

"No problem," Rose says, raising her voice for Miaow. "You can come out here. We're going out."

Rafferty says, "We are?"

"We are," Rose says. She glances at the door to the bedroom. "Bring your wallet."

Rafferty says, "How are you going to get home, Andrew?"

Miaow says, from the hallway, "*Dad*. He just got here."

"My father's driver," Andrew says. "He's waiting."

In the elevator, going down, Rafferty says, "I forgot. His father's driver."

"He's a nice boy," Rose says from inside her infuriating bubble of peace.

Rafferty says, "*Andrew*." He scuffs the heel of his shoe over the linoleum floor and says, "I'll bet he wants to play Ned." He has memories, vivid even now, of hours spent alone with the girl who spelled her name Suzi and played Julie opposite him in high school. "This is all happening too fast."

MIAOW OPENS THE refrigerator and withdraws another Diet Coke, then turns to see Andrew shifting from foot to foot as though he hasn't gone to the bathroom for a week. She stands there, the chill of the refrigerator flowing down her left side. Andrew blinks heavily a couple of times and says, "You have to look at this. You, uh, you have to." He puts the newspaper on the counter, opens it, flattens it with both hands, and then steps away from it as though it were a snake.

The unopened can of Coke icy in her hand, Miaow comes around the counter and looks down. Her spine snaps straight, as though it had been yanked from both ends, and her jaw drops open.

A dark-haired man glares at the camera, dead-center on the front page, his hair oiled and combed back. The same man whose face she saw for the first time eight hours ago on Andrew's new phone.

The word beneath the photo is MURDERED.

Beneath that, in smaller type, it says: DISGRACED POLICE COLONEL SHOT TO DEATH.

14

Fifty Inches Is a Swimming Pool

"FORTY-EIGHT THOUSAND BAHT?" Rafferty regards his wife as though she's just told him he's about to be struck by a meteorite. "That's fifteen hundred dollars."

Rose shrugs as if to say *small money*. "We're rich. It's a good one. Look at it, very pretty." The other customers in the store haven't had time to get used to her yet. She's still drawing stares, as befits the owner of the longest legs in Southeast Asia.

Rafferty says, "She just wants to watch acting, right?" he says. "She can do that on a little one. Hell, for fifteen hundred dollars, I can have actors come up to the apartment."

In Thai, Rose says, "There's me, too."

"Sorry?"

"I've been very good about this, even though—are you still going to love me if I tell you this?"

"No promises," Rafferty says, "But try me."

"I *like* television. I like turning it on and watching people move around. When I was living in the village, there was only one TV, and since I was so tall, they made me sit at the back of the room, and I couldn't really see anything because I'm near-sighted—"

"I've actually heard all this, and it's heartbreaking all over again. There should be music, or maybe boxes of Kleenex everywhere so we could—"

She's already talking again. "But I even liked it *then*. And I've lived with you for years now, and never asked for one." She adds, in English, "I am *soooo* nice. TeeWee help me with my Englit." She's leaning on the accent pretty hard.

"Great. You can learn to sound like you grew up in an American trailer park. In New Jersey."

"You're a snob," Rose says in Thai, but using the English word. To the salesman, who has been orbiting her in disbelief for four or five minutes, actually sniffing the air, and who looks to Rafferty like he might be in the opening months of his fourteenth year, she says, "What really worries him is that he won't be able to figure out how to make it work."

"My father's the same way," the salesboy says, looking helplessly at her knees. "Older people just can't—"

"There's no point in you two talking to each other," Rafferty says. "I have the wallet."

"That's a fifty-inch screen," the saleschild informs Rose for the second time, shifting to his left to talk past Rafferty. He wears black slacks and a blousy white shirt, and he's as narrow as his necktie. "Good size for an apartment. Ten-eighty resolution, backlit, 240-hertz engine, smart screen, built-in wi-fi, six HDMI inputs, and we'll throw in a set of gold cables." He stops and fidgets, obviously wishing he had more to say.

"All of that?" Rose says, giving him a smile that adds an inch to his height. "What's the best discount?"

Poke says, "Fifty inches is a *swimming pool*—"

The saleschild throws him a tolerant nod of the head that says, *isn't he cute?* and says to Rose, "For you, I can take off ten percent. Cash or charge?"

"Cash," Rose says. "My father is rich. For cash, twelve percent."

"Twelve," the boy says. "So, forty-two thousand, two-forty."

Rafferty says, "We're letting a scourge into our lives."

Rose puts a hand on his arm. "Don't you think Miaow has talent?"

"Don't I think—of *course*, I think she has talent. But she'll be watching Korean music videos."

Rose says, "And I'll be watching it a lot, since I'm going to be home more." She says to the saleschild, "It's difficult for him to let go of money. He was very poor as a boy."

Rafferty fishes a wad of thousand-baht notes from his pocket and counts out forty-three of them for the boy, who wheels away as though he's afraid Rafferty will snatch it back. "You're going to be home more?" he asks, watching his money walk away. "Why? Is business slow? Are you and Peachy having trouble finding jobs for your clients?" The clients of the domestics agency Rose runs with her partner, Peachy, are mostly former sex workers trying to get out of the game by cleaning house.

"Not exactly," Rose says. Her tone brings him around to face her. She seems to sharpen her focus, and Rafferty has the feeling she's looking right through his face, to something he didn't know she could see, something that might even be behind him. She regards him that way for a long moment and then says, "Business is fine."

"Then why—"

There's a tug at the tiny muscles around her eyes; it's almost a wince. Her eyes skitter past him and then come back, and she says, "I'm," and stops. She takes a breath and says, "I'm pregnant."

For Rafferty, time goes all *bent* somehow, as though it's curved itself to stretch around something massive. The room brightens and a tone in his ears slides up the scale until it's a high hum, and the store wavers once or twice like something seen through ripples of heat, and he blinks it away and all he can see is Rose.

Rose says, "Are you—I mean—are you happy?"

Squinting at her as though she's standing in front of a bright light, he sees the glint of water in her eyes, sees a pulse of uncertainty flicker in her face, and then there's water in his own eyes and he sniffles, hard. He reaches for her, gets one hand on her shoulder, and pulls her to him, squeezing her until she says, "Oof," and he panics and steps back, keeping a tight grip on her hand as though she might bolt and run, and then he turns after the retreating salesman and says the thing he'll later remember with shame as the most *guy* remark of his life. He says, "Hey, hey. *Hey.* What about that sixty-inch?"

T H E Y   R I D E   I N a bell of silence in the back of the cab, her head on his shoulder. At one point, she turns and flutters her eyelashes against the side of his neck, and he feels the hair on his arms stand up. She laughs softly and resettles herself.

"How long have you known?"

"I had a dream last night," she says. "Don't get crazy, it's not just the dream. I'm a month late, and I'm never late. The dream was— well, it was a message. Telling me to start to take care of myself."

"One month?" Rafferty says.

"*And* the dream. And my mother, when I talked to her this morning, she said she's been thinking about me and a baby. She saw a girl carrying a baby in the village a week ago, and for a second it was me. The month, the dream, my mother. Poke." Her voice when she says his name is almost all breath. "Poke. I'm going to have a *baby.*"

He presses his cheek against the top of her head, not trusting his voice.

"I hope I'm this happy when I die," Rose says. "I have everything now."

"But—but what do you *need?*" He finds himself in planning mode. It's more familiar than being happy. "And what should I do? You know, to get things ready."

"Be nice to me. And get the TV set up."

"But I mean, taking care of you—"

"Find something to do. Surely, in this big city, you can find a problem."

"I'm not going to—"

"Well, something that will keep you busy. If you don't, you'll be *home.* You'll be looking at me all the time, trying to bring me tea when I need to pee from all the tea you've already brought me, asking me if I want to prop my feet up every time I get comfortable, covering me with blankets when I'm hot. Standing in front of the television. Go out and do something. Make friends with Arthit again." She touches the tip of his nose. "But first, we have to solve a problem."

"I can solve anything," Rafferty says. "What is it?"

Rose says, "How we're going to tell Miaow."

15

Something Outside Herself

THERE'S ONE STAR that doesn't move. It's yellow and dim, but even when her head is spinning, which it does quite a lot, the star stays still. She spins and spins, but it remains fixed, giving her something outside herself, something she can cling to.

Only—

It's a light bulb.

It's not a star. It's a light, high on the wall at the other end of the world.

Her mouth is dry. She's dizzy. Whatever they're giving her, it makes her dizzy.

Against the wall beneath the light, on the folding metal chairs, the girl and the ugly boy are asleep. He's fallen sideways with his head in her lap, and her head is tilted back, against the wall. Her mouth is open.

She doesn't know how long she's been here. She can't tell whether it's day or night. That light is always on. She slips in and out of sleep all the time.

And they're always here.

She's never known people her own age. It was always her father, the maids, the ghost of the woman who used to be her mother, her face half-buried in a glass of something that smelled so sweet that even now the memory of it makes her stomach shrivel.

I'm not hot any more, she thinks.

She shifts her shoulders against the pillows that prop her up. One door. No windows. One bed, two chairs. That boy and that girl.

The line going into her arm.

She looks down at the steel cuffs that fasten her wrists to the frame on both sides of the bed. Her wrists look very thin.

With her eyes on the boy and the girl, she brings her right wrist closer to her, hearing the grate of the metal cuff as it slides over the rail. The frame rests on an upright, just about where her waist is, so she can't bring the cuff any closer than that.

But she can sit up.

Slowly, quietly, she pulls herself up until she's sitting almost vertically. A whirl of dizziness stops her, and she holds still, breathing through her mouth and keeping her eyes on the light, until the dizziness passes. She's sweating, but it's not the sour, sick sweat she had before, when she felt like she was on fire.

She's gotten stronger.

It takes her a minute or two because of her dry mouth, but finally she works up some spit. When she thinks she has enough, she leans forward and spits on her wrist.

The spit feels cool. It's slick. She pushes her wrist into the cuff to get the metal wet and then, slowly, rotates her arm, trying to spread the wetness over the entire assembly. Then, very deliberately, she pushes her hand forward, brings her fingers tightly together, straight, with her thumb tucked against the center of her palm, and begins to pull it back.

Pulls it all the way to the base of her thumb.

The boy murmurs something, his big front teeth gleaming beneath the light on the wall.

She ignores the pain and pulls very, very slowly. Feels the cuff slide *almost* over the knuckle at the base of her thumb. The widest part.

She can do it.

Just a little more spit, just a little more hurt.

The boy says it again, the same sound, and the girl beside him, without opening her eyes, lets her hand drop on the boy's shoulder. The hand rests there, thin-fingered and dark against the boy's T-shirt.

Her hand slides out of the cuff.

The boy moves his head slightly, back and forth, just getting more comfortable on the girl's lap.

On the bed, not far from her left ankle, is a rectangle of white. There she is, in pencil, looking up out of the page. Beyond the drawing, on the hard metal chairs, the chairs she knows are uncomfortable, are the sleeping girl and the boy with the big teeth. They've stayed there. With her.

Without making a sound, she begins to weep. She leans back and lets the tears come, not sobbing, not even sniffling, just weeping with her mouth open and snot running down her upper lip. When whatever it is has cried itself out of her, she pushes her hand back into the cuff.

She leans back and closes her eyes.

Part Two
. . . UNTIL WE SINK

16

Allergic

"TURN IT OVER," Andrew says in a no-nonsense voice. "The sun will fade it." He's in the lead today. He'd taken off at a brisk pace the moment they got out of the cab. Although he'd been tightlipped on the ride over, she thought he'd slow down to walk next to her, but he hadn't. Saturday morning, she thinks, and he's not skipping school, so he's confident.

"It won't fade," Miaow says to the back of his head. She likes the way it curves down into his slender neck. "Or did you print it in invisible ink?"

"Ha, ha, ha," Andrew says. "Why don't you let me boss you around once in a while?"

"Why should I let you—" She sees his back stiffen and says, "Look, look, I'm turning it over." She turns the picture over so the image faces down. "The sun *is* pretty bright."

Andrew says nothing. His shoulders are high and tight, and his neck looks rigid enough to break if he were to turn his head.

Miaow trots to catch up. Andrew's little bag with his diabetes kit in it hangs from her shoulder, and it slaps against her side. "What's wrong?"

"Nothing." The alley is intersected by another, and he turns right. Miaow has already started left, which is the correct direction.

She runs through three or four possible approaches before she asks, "Are you sure it's that way?"

"I give up," Andrew says, coming to a stop. "You go the way you want. I'll just tag along."

She tries to meet his eyes, but he's looking past her. "Are you mad at me?"

Andrew's gaze falters, and he looks down at his feet. "No," he says. "I'm sorry. It's not your fault. I'm just—I feel like—" He screws up his face, relaxes it, and returns her gaze. "I've never done anything like this before."

She says, "I'm sorry."

"No," Andrew says, "*I'm* sorry."

The two of them stand in silence for a moment, both of them looking at his feet. Then she says, "We don't have to do it. We could just give the phone to Poke."

"I'm not *frightened*," Andrew says.

"I didn't mean you were—"

"*We're* the ones who found it," he says, as though she's arguing. "It's a clue, right? It's got pictures of the man who was killed last night and, and another man, and pictures of two other guys in a hotel room. If one of the men in that room is the man who sold the phone, then he might be the guy who killed that old cop. We'll have found a suspect, and *then* you can tell Poke."

"Okay," Miaow says, without much force.

"My father," he says. "My father would never think I could do anything like this. Help the police like this."

Miaow has no idea what to say.

"I'm not afraid of *him*, either," Andrew says.

"I know."

Andrew's shoulders ease a little. "Okay, you know where it is. You take me there." Blushing furiously, he holds out his hand.

"Sure," she says around the hard little stone in her throat. She transfers the photo to her other hand and takes his. It's very smooth and a little damp, and it feels as delicate as a bird's nest. She wants to squeeze it, but she knows he'll grab it back if she does, and anyway it seems too fragile to squeeze.

They go back the way they'd come and start the curve to the left. Miaow can hear Andrew's breath, and she has a sudden, unexpected urge to lean over and sniff it. The very thought heats her face. She's thinking about fanning it with her free hand when she hears Andrew gasp. He's stopped cold.

He says, "Whoa."

The little shop where they bought the phone looks like a car has been driven through it. The glass in both display cases is smashed. Bits of telephones are everywhere, gleaming among the shards of glass, all afire with sunlight, in the absence of the awning, now ripped down and left to dangle from its poles.

The Sikh, his head sloppily bandaged, is pushing the wreckage around with a broom, creating piles of devastation. The linen wrapped crookedly across his forehead has a red stain on it. The blood hasn't even had time to dry.

"Okay," Miaow says. "Let's go home."

"No way," Andrew says. "We came all this way, and—"

"This, uh, *this*." Miaow says, lifting her chin toward the ruin of the shop. "This has got to have something to do with the guys in the pic—"

"Maybe not," Andrew interrupts. "Maybe it's those *farang* who stole the phone when we were here yesterday. Or maybe he cheated somebody and they got mad." He's already walking, and once again Miaow has to hurry to catch up to him.

When they're a few feet away, the shop owner hears them and looks up from his sweeping. His eyes widen in a way that makes Miaow want to turn and run, but Andrew bulldozes forward.

"What happened?" he asks.

"Problem," the Sikh says. "Small problem." He shakes his head as though to clear the pain. "You go," he says. "Come back in three days, four days." He's looking past them, scanning the area for someone. She tugs on Andrew's shirt.

Andrew shrugs her off. "Is this the man—can I have the *picture*, Miaow? Is this the man who sold you the—?"

"Go," the Sikh says, his eyes all over the place. "Go now, or—" He sees whatever he was looking for, and his teeth click together.

Miaow looks over her shoulder and sees two men in T-shirts and jeans, both of them familiar from the photos in the phone. One is short and dark and heavy, and the other, staring directly at her, is tall and lithe, with golden skin.

His eyes are fixed on her. He has a hand on the back of the smaller man's neck, the way someone might rein in an attack dog before letting it fly.

Without moving his lips the Sikh says, "Go now, go fast, go."

"Andrew," Miaow says, smiling up at the Sikh. "When I say *now*, you are going to run as fast as you can. To our left. Do you hear me?"

"Yes, but why—"

"Do you hear me?"

"Uhh, sure."

"Yes, child," the Sikh says, smiling back. "Fast *fast.*"

"Good," she says to the Sikh. "Thank you. You've been very nice and I hope your head feels better soon." She gives him another big smile and says, "Andrew. *Now.*"

THE FIRST SURPRISE is how quick he is.

He leaves her behind in just a few steps. In a burst of panic, she forgets about the men behind her, focusing only on one terrifying revelation: *He's abandoning me.* His legs seem to stretch elastically in front of him, and the distance between them lengthens although she's already running as fast as she can, past a blur of stands and open-air restaurants, through the smells of frying food and spices and exhaust, and a glance behind doesn't lessen her fear: the shorter man is pounding along behind her, T-shirt flapping, and behind him, loping easily, like a big cat that's preserving its strength, is the tall golden man.

He's got *lots* of speed left.

A couple of meters ahead, Andrew risks a look back and slows, extending a hand to her as though she were on skates, as though he could whip her around in front of him. Then he sees the men behind her and his eyes go wide, and Miaow realizes he was only running because she told him to, and he's got energy in reserve. *Well,* she thinks, *at least one of us will get away.*

The long curve of the alley comes to an end. To their right is the straightaway, a narrow passage between shopfronts, that leads to traffic and taxis and policemen. Miaow gasps as Andrew takes the wrong turn, a turn that will lead them farther into the maze, and she manages to grab the back of his T-shirt and yank. It almost pulls both of them off their feet, but he turns to her again, a wild-fire of confusion in his face, and she points toward the boulevard and takes off.

She hears his sneakers slap the pavement behind her, coming up fast, and then in front of her she sees another short dark man, this one with a brutish, heavy face, standing dead center in the passageway, arms spread and knees bent to lower his center of gravity. At that instant a new, even narrower alley opens up to her right, and she shouts Andrew's name and makes the turn.

She bangs the top of her head against an umbrella, earning a shout from the vendor, and she sees that this passageway is all umbrellas on both sides, put up to prevent sun-faded merchandise. *We're short,* she thinks with a thrill of recognition; this is a street-kid tactic—use your pursuers' height against them. An adult will have to edge his way through. She bends at the waist and motions behind her, patting the air palm down and exaggerating her stoop, and she hears one umbrella go over. When she looks back, she sees Andrew leaning down just enough to clear the umbrellas and gaining on her.

And then one of the short men charges into the alley and knocks over two umbrellas.

The day shimmers and brightens as Miaow realizes that she knows where she is.

Or *used* to know. It's been six years.

But what's the alternative?

She risks a look back to find Andrew on her heels, close enough to touch, his eyes tiny and his lips drawn back with effort and fear. Eight or ten yards back, she sees the closer of the short guys trying to hop through a tangle of fallen umbrellas as a couple of shop-keepers grab at him, shouting.

"Up here," she says to Andrew, "to the right, to the right, follow me." And she takes off again, part of her looking for the turn and part of her listening for the sound of his shoes.

"Faster," he gasps behind her. She manages to force out a tiny bit of additional juice, and she almost overruns the alley.

It's too narrow to be an alley. It's more like a space between buildings for air conditioners to drip into. Even now, even running for their lives, she's stunned by how filthy and smelly it is—was it like this before? What will Andrew *think*, her dragging him into a place like—

And there it is, the chain-link fence.

Without even knowing she's doing it, Miaow looses a yell from deep in her chest and launches herself, arms spread, from five feet away. She lands about a third of the way up, fingers shaped into claws, the toes of her sneakers jammed into the diagonal openings. The strap with Andrew's insulin kit slips from her shoulder, and as she grabs at it, the fence bounces like a trampoline, nearly shaking her off, announcing Andrew's arrival. She starts up again and feels the fence shudder as he climbs, and then he's passing her. His mouth is pulled tight and he's squinting like someone facing into a sandstorm.

"Over?" he pants.

"Over."

On the other side, visible through the wire, is a weedy field, and in the center of it is a chunk of concrete blight, the asymmetrical ruin of an abandoned hotel that was partially demolished and left to mildew in the rain seven or eight years ago. As she swings a leg over the top of the fence, she hears the men shouting behind her.

She shoves herself free, lands loosely, rolls, and comes up running again, with Andrew right beside her.

"Those men—" he says. It's all air.

"Yes. The last few pictures on the phone. The ones in the hotel room."

"Where to?"

She risks a glance back and sees the two short men struggling to climb the fence. "There," she says, indicating the ruined hotel. "Come on."

Andrew ups the pace just a bit, but she stays with him, the weeds whipping at her legs. The men are shouting to each other, but then, suddenly, she and Andrew are at the hotel, and she leads him around the shell and through a gaping wall into the ruin of a lobby that's been stripped to the concrete. Across the room, a long rectangle cut into the gritty tiles shows where the reception desk once stood. Beyond that a dark doorway leads to the offices. At either side of the lobby, corridors lead right and left.

The last time she was here, it was dark, but she remembers, *left*, and she grabs hold of Andrew's slender wrist and charges into the corridor as fast as she can haul him, and then he's even with her and pulling his hand free so he can pump both arms.

Miaow says, "Room one-sixteen," and breaks off, almost stumbling as she sees that there are no room numbers. They've been stolen, pulled off, put to use elsewhere. Gone.

She slows, time stuttering to an end. Without the room numbers to guide her, the hallway is a dead end. She's led him into a dead end.

Andrew says, "Ummmmm," looking behind him, almost dancing in his eagerness to move, and Miaow spots the ghost of a number on the nearest door, just a shadow where the paint beneath the missing number hasn't faded. It says *107*.

"That side," she says, pointing at the opposite side of the hall. She points at the door almost directly across from 107 and guesses, "One-oh-eight, come *on*," and they're hurrying together.

"One-ten, one-twelve, one-fourteen, one-sixteen." She stops and peers at the ghost number, not really readable, and pushes the door open anyway, and there it is: at one corner of the empty room, a hole kicked in the wall to the right, a jagged frame of plaster surrounding darkness.

She motions Andrew into the room, hearing the men's feet scraping over the lobby floor like grit between teeth. One of them calls out, the words distorted by echo, and is answered by a voice she somehow knows belongs to the golden man. There's the sound of running feet, which she places in the lobby, and then nothing.

The men have fallen silent, and the silence is more frightening than the noise.

Andrew stands loose and bewildered in the center of a room that was once white, but now is the faded pale of long-exposed bone, its cracked windows milky with dust. A heap of plaster and small floor tiles at the door to the bathroom announces that the toilet and sink have been pulled out and hauled away.

Miaow is listening so hard she can hear the thin whine of her blood. From the direction of the lobby, shoes scuff on the gritty floor. Two, as far as she can tell. Getting nearer.

Without a word, she puts an arm on Andrew's shoulders and pulls him toward the hole in the wall. Then she drops to her hands and knees, thinking, *What if I don't fit? What if I've gotten too big?* Andrew, still standing, is looking down at her, his glasses askew, his eyes so wide she can see white all the way around the irises. He shakes his head, *no.*

She whispers fiercely, "Yes," and crawls in.

It feels much smaller than it did before. She's shaped differently, wider in the hips. Her hips brush the walls on either side of the air duct and her spine touches the top. Andrew's zipped kit hangs down from her neck and drags over the grit. *It's too tight,* she thinks, but when she tries to move forward, she discovers that she can. There's enough light coming through the hole behind her that she can see that the duct seems not to have rusted, even though it's filthy and cobwebbed and pebbled with rat shit and smells like the bushes near her apartment where all the cats piss. But at least it doesn't feel like the bottom will disintegrate beneath her weight. She crawls forward, listening for Andrew, and hears him suck in his breath in what sounds like disgust. Then his hands slide over the floor of the duct and his knees announce themselves with soft thumps.

She freezes as an adult male voice echoes down the duct in front of her. No, she thinks, he's just in one of the rooms between them and the lobby, one of the rooms this duct serves. The ducts carry sound, making it important that she and Andrew move silently. There are at least three ducts on this floor, she knows, and each of them branches off into multiple rooms.

But this is *her* duct.

About two months before she met Poke, this duct had probably saved her life. The man who'd been chasing her then, through a moonless Bangkok night, had been crazed on amphetamines and trying to do something to her she couldn't even imagine.

The men who are after Andrew and her may not pay attention to the hole in the wall. The man chasing her hadn't noticed it at night. But even if these men *do* see it, they'll never be able to fit. And they'll have no idea where the duct comes out.

All she needs is to do the disappearing trick once more: to vanish from room 116 and then move invisibly until she emerges into the light on the far side of the building.

She's crawling again, coming up on the first turn, and she's soaking wet. The sudden perception of danger, the chase, and now the fear, purifying and reducing itself into something like terror: *Andrew* is in danger, too. She can smell herself even over the stink of the duct. She slows and stops until she knows that Andrew is right behind her. Then she whispers, so softly she can barely hear it herself, "It's going to get dark."

"Where are we—" Andrew begins, but she shushes him and begins to crawl again. She reaches the four-way intersection and starts to take the left turn; straight ahead leads to other rooms, and the branching to the right leads to a gentle drop down to where the heating unit once stood in the basement. The turn to the left, assuming the bottom hasn't rotted out of the duct and that the metal rods that secure it to the floor above them haven't pulled loose, will lead to a venting grill at ground level.

She *can't get around the corner.*

She's too big now, she's too wide, she's too long. She gets part of her torso angled for the turn, but there isn't room for her to crawl all the way in. Her spine won't make the turn. She can't work her hips around the sharp angle.

A drop of sweat runs down her forehead and into her left eye. Suddenly the duct seems to be smothering her, swallowing her, suffocating her. What she wants to do—what she *needs* to do—is crawl backward into room 116 and take her chances with the men.

But Andrew's behind her. *She* might be able to deal with them; she dealt with terrible people all her years on the sidewalk. But Andrew, with his big glasses and his tiny neck and his protective parents and his spotless blue apartment, Andrew is as defenseless as whipped cream.

She reaches back with her foot and finds Andrew's arm, taps it twice. "Back up," she whispers, barely a breath, but the duct will carry it to him. "Just a little."

Andrew whispers, "I need to get out of here. I'm going to be sick."

"We're going to get out. I just need a little space for a second."

He doesn't say anything, but when she explores his space with her shoe, there's nothing but air.

"It's a corner," she breathes. "You're skinny, you'll be able to get around it, but I can't."

"What do you *mean*, you—" On the one word, his voice breaks through his whisper.

"I can, I can. For you, no problem. Don't worry, we're almost out."

Hating to do it, she lowers herself all the way down onto her stomach, the dirt going ropy beneath her hands as she slides them forward. She turns on her right side and pulls herself, forward, facing left, the direction she wants to take. When she's pulled herself far enough forward, she bends her waist and then drags her legs behind her, still lying on her side. Once she's around the corner, she rolls back onto her stomach and up on hands and knees again, saying to Andrew, "Okay. Just follow me. Left, left."

But now, with the turn behind her, cutting off the light coming in through the hole in the wall, it's completely dark.

Her T-shirt and jeans make a raspy whisper as they slide over the metal sides of the duct, and she can hear Andrew's breathing, fast and shallow. She wonders whether the men can hear it, too, through the vent in whatever room they're searching, and realize that she and Andrew are on their way out. Their only hope is to get out of the building and well away while the men are still searching inside.

A spider web plasters itself on her face and its occupant, feeling as big as her hand, scuttles over her cheek and down her neck and—she's going to *scream*—inside the opening in her T-shirt and up her shoulder toward the center of her back. She stops and says, "Guuhhh," and tries to swat at it, and can't get her arms up, but the scratchy feeling of its legs scrabbling over her skin is all she can think about, so she twists and smacks her side and back against the wall to smash it, hitting the wall harder than she'd realized, and suddenly the entire duct is trembling, swinging back and forth very slightly and making a deep creaking noise.

Even her heart stops. She's completely immobile, no longer feeling the spider, no longer hearing Andrew's breathing, doing nothing at all except willing the duct's supports to hold, praying to the spirit of the duct not to let it fall and trap them deafeningly in a crumple of metal with no way out.

It's impossible for her to estimate how long she's been motionless when Andrew whispers, "Please, gotta get out. Gotta get out. Please."

The duct stops moving.

And Andrew sneezes.

It's an explosive sneeze, enough to set the duct vibrating beneath them, and it's *deafening*, and then he sneezes again, and again.

It's shockingly loud. The duct is all metal, and it grabs each sneeze and amplifies it, bounces it back and forth, drapes it in echo, and broadcasts it to the world. He sneezes a fourth time, and a fifth, and Miaow is scrambling forward now, not bothering to feel her way, not trying to be quiet, just moving as fast as she can, trying to get the two of them ahead of the sound.

Then the sneezing stops, and the two of them are clawing their way like crabs through the dirt and the darkness and the rat droppings, trying to get as far as they can, and Andrew whispers, "Allergic," and he's sneezing again.

The darkness seems to solidify just in front of her. She puts a hand in front of her as Andrew stops again. She feels the end of the duct wall, and there's a slight flow of cooler air from her left.

"Turn left," she says aloud. "Put your hand on my foot and turn where I do."

His hand touches her ankle gently, and she suddenly envisions his face, the crooked glasses and skinny neck and the eyes that have never seen any of the world's bad things, and she feels like weeping. He sneezes once more and whispers, "Sorry," and she says, "We'll be fine" in a sharp whisper, and starts crawling again.

This time the turn is only 45 degrees and she slips around it easily. A moment later, Andrew says, "Okay," and she thinks it's good she hasn't got room to turn around because even in her panic she wants to kiss him for that single word. She says, "One more turn," and a moment later she reaches it, a zigzag right, another 45-degree angle with pale gray light coming through the shaft, and she hears Andrew draw the longest breath yet—he's been panting between sneezes like a dehydrated dog—and without willing it, she begins to crawl even faster.

Then he's sneezing again, even louder than before, it seems, but at the same time the light brightens, and then at what must be the end of the duct there's a glare that hurts her eyes, squares of light like a quilt, that resolve themselves into the openings in a grate, square holes about an inch on a side, small enough to keep out rats. The two of them will come out, she knows, on the other side of the building, with the fence they climbed far behind them, facing a weedy stretch of open ground and another fence they'll have to navigate before they're someplace with a lot of people, someplace where they might be able to flag a taxi or hide in a restaurant and call someone to come get them.

As she nears the grate, she slows to listen, but Andrew knocks urgently on the sole of her shoe. His breathing has quickened again, hot-sounding, shallow, with a kind of ratchety wheeze as though his throat is closing up.

It makes her hurry. She puts an eye to the grate and looks as far left and right as she can, sees no one, puts both hands against the inside of the grate and pushes. It resists, sealed by a layer of rust, but the fear inside her crests and breaks, and thinking *Andrew*, she puts all the strength she possesses into it, and the grate gives way with a squeal and falls out onto the dirt. Miaow squirms, gasping, out of the duct and into the brightness, and instantly a hand is clapped over her mouth and an arm goes around her throat and she tries to kick the hotel wall in warning as Andrew crawls out, wet and wheezing, right into the arms of the golden man.

17

You Can Come Back Now

"How did that make you *feel?*" Rose says out loud. Then she says it again, a bit differently: "How did *that* make you feel?"

The American man on the television, a doctor of the head, according to Poke, looms vividly on the huge screen standing in front of Poke's poor little desk, now completely hidden from view. The doctor seems to like that question. This is the second time he's asked it, and when he does, he leans forward, blinking through his squarish eyeglasses. Rose knows what the question means, but she doesn't understand why the doctor asked it, since the woman he asked has tears rolling down her face.

If the doctor had asked Rose, she would have answered that her day so far was making her feel very good indeed.

Rose says, "Wery good," and then overcorrects to, "Vvvvery good," pushing her front teeth deeply enough into her lower lip to make a dent.

The woman who was asked how she felt is wiping her cheeks with a ragged tissue. She's in a big room full of extremely orderly women sitting in rows of chairs. They peer at the weeping woman as though she might disappear at any moment, like a ghost.

There's something extremely comfortable, Rose thinks, about sitting on your own couch with a plate of leftover green mango slices, watching someone else cry. Wearing one of your husband's best shirts, one he pretends he doesn't know you wear when he leaves. With the apartment empty and all yours as the day outside passes noon. With America on your big television.

With a baby growing inside you.

She puts a flat hand on her flat stomach, trying to find a little spot of extra warmth. She knows she won't find it and she doesn't, but the act of looking for it makes the day even better. It makes her want some Nescafé.

She gets up and says in English, "Excuse me, I come back" to the crying woman on the television, laughs a little at her village-girl joke, and pads barefoot to the kitchen. She pauses before she steps into the gleaming kitchen, just to take in again—perhaps for the fourth time today—how clean Poke left it. He'd gotten up long before she did, and when she went in for the day's first cup of coffee, she'd smelled chlorine and had spent an anxious moment looking for the source until she discovered that he'd scoured the sink, getting rid of the map of ancient coffee stains and the pale brown spots where wet tea bags had sat for hours. The stove had been scrubbed and the refrigerator door had been sponged, Miaow's handprints wiped away. He'd also rearranged the refrigerator's contents into tidy, logic-free rows. It had taken her several minutes to find things she could usually touch blindfolded.

The *floor* was clean.

He'd even filled her teapot with bottled water, ready to be heated. When she'd picked it up, the unexpected weight almost made her drop it on her foot.

She turns the knob on the stove, waits for the reassuring blue poof of flame that tells her they're not all going to die of asphyxiation or in a terrible explosion, and pulls the jar of Nescafé crystals from the cabinet above the rice cooker. Poke had placed it right on the edge of the shelf, within easy reach, as though going up on tiptoes might damage the baby.

How long will this last? she asks herself. Nothing good lasts long.

And how will it change when Miaow learns what's happening? Miaow had fled through the front door a little after ten in the morning, not even waiting for the television man to finish setting up the big screen and turn it on. Maybe Poke is right. Maybe the attachment between Miaow and Andrew is deeper than they had thought.

A little blister of anxiety forms in the region of her heart. It makes her want a cigarette.

The pack of Marlboro Golds is right where she left it, next to the bed. The lighter is still on top of it. It's been there all day, sending out the occasional siren call, and every now and then she's had to fight the impulse to grab it and light up.

She hasn't gone back into the bedroom since she got dressed.

Thinking about the cigarettes, she slides her hand over her stomach again, but this time she doesn't know she's doing it.

Miaow, she thinks. The throw-away child, tossed onto a sidewalk. As tough as she tries to seem, Miaow worries about everything. She double-checks everything. If she were hanging over a cliff, held only by a knotted rope, she would try to improve the knot. She has no idea how remarkable she is, how smart, how decent, how much she's loved. Somewhere in the center of her being, Miaow is still the short, dirty, dark-skinned, frizzy-haired, unloved reject who tried to sell chewing gum to Rafferty on his second night in Bangkok.

The baby—Poke and Rose's *own* baby—is going to shake Miaow to her core. She's going to feel like unwanted furniture. They're going to have to be very careful about how they tell her. They're going to have to love her extra-hard.

Rose jumps as the teapot shrills. She turns off the gas and realizes she hasn't even opened the jar of coffee.

"How did that make you feel?" she asks herself, trying to sound American. Then she says, "Make me feel stupid," and unscrews the jar. The teaspoon that she thought she'd already taken out is still in the drawer. "One, two, three," she says, focusing on opening the drawer, pulling out the spoon, and ladling a little mountain of Nescafé into the cup. A couple of brisk, businesslike stirs, and the spoon, with its clot of undissolved coffee, clatters into the bottom of the sink.

She takes a gasping-hot mouthful and forces it down. To the baby, she says, "Get used to it," and the people in the living room laugh appreciatively. Maybe that woman has stopped crying. For some reason, the laughter makes Rose feel guilty about staining the sink. She puts the cup back on the counter and runs water over the spoon, rinses the bottom of the sink, and dries the spoon on her shirt.

She says, "Aiya," drops the spoon to the floor, and grabs the bottom of the shirt, Poke's shirt, Poke's *favorite* shirt. "No, no, no," she says. There's a smear of brown on the tail of the shirt.

She runs hot water over her fingers, touches the tip of the dish detergent bottle to her index finger, and rubs at the smear, making it bigger. She takes the dishtowel, a fresh clean one Poke put out to replace the mottled, malodorous rag that had been on duty for a couple of weeks, drips water on it, and scrubs at the smear. The dishtowel gets browner but the shirt doesn't get whiter.

It's *coffee*, she thinks despairingly. The only way to get rid of a coffee stain is with a pair of scissors.

She knows it's not really a problem, knows he's aware she wears the shirt, even knows that it's not actually his favorite shirt. All this is just a game they play, one of a thousand games they play, about tiny things at the edges of their lives, things that don't matter. They build the games because they can *make* the tiny things matter. It's a way of reminding themselves how blessed they are.

So he won't actually be mad. But it will spoil the game. One of the secrets she pretends to keep from him will be gone.

She wipes at the shirt again and then takes it off and puts the stain under the faucet, working detergent through it with her fingers. Keeping the non-secret a secret is suddenly important to her. And she knows it's because of the *real* secret, the secret Poke doesn't even suspect.

The baby she lost.

Someone's baby, she has no idea whose. Some drunk's baby. There were always customers who refused at the last moment to use condoms, who didn't have one and wouldn't take the one she tried to force on them, who made it clear that they weren't going to let her leave the hotel room until they were done with her. There was the occasional broken condom. In the month before she was late for the first time in her life, there were four or five times like that.

Four or five long-forgotten possible fathers. A whore for a mother. Why would that baby want to be born?

And it hadn't been.

She drops the shirt into the sink, the gleaming clean sink, sucks in all the air her lungs will hold, and spreads both hands on her bare belly, barely touching her skin. *This* baby. This baby will be strong. *This* baby has a father who will love her. This baby isn't coming into the world of a bar girl, a girl who won't be able to take care of it, who'll just park it up north in a leaking hut with her mother and her drunken father. Go see it on Buddha's birthday, when the bars are closed. Bring it bright toys so it won't cry when it sees the strange woman leaning over it.

That was her dead baby, not this one. She's been living part of her life for her dead baby ever since . . . ever since. Now she won't have to. This baby will have a good father, a happy mother, a smart sister. This baby will have no reason to decide not to come into the world. Ignoring the coffee cooling on the counter, the water running over Poke's shirt, she closes her eyes and sends a prayer to her dead baby, and is startled to hear herself say, in her mind, *You can come back now.* Her eyes pop open, and she stands there, looking at nothing. She says, "You can come back now. You can come back now."

A bolt of energy runs down her arms all the way to her finger-tips. Moving briskly, she takes the rough side of the sponge and scrubs the stain on the shirt into another world. She hangs the shirt to dry on the handle of the refrigerator door, squares her shoulders, and goes into the bedroom. When she comes back, she has the package of cigarettes in her hand. The water is still running, and she holds the package under the faucet and then tosses the sodden mass into the trash.

She says fiercely, "You can come back now."

18

The Fence

THE THING IS, they're going to have to climb a fence and cross a sidewalk.

The golden man had barked into his phone, ordering the car to be brought around, probably by the other dark man. She thinks, *he'll bring the car to the street at the front of the hotel.* There's a chain-link fence there, with a gate in it. In the old days, sometimes the gate was open. The last time Miaow was here someone had removed the metal U that snapped down over the upright pole to lock the gate in place.

If the gate is open, she thinks, she and Andrew haven't got a chance. But that was a long time ago. For all she knows, the whole thing has been stolen by now, and they might be able to walk straight through and they'll *really* be screwed. If not, she'll have the fence.

Her karma will give her the fence.

If she were alone, the fence would be all she needed to get away. She can scale it and jump down from it much faster than they can. She could be a block away by the time their feet touched the sidewalk.

But there's Andrew, who's still wheezing and coughing.

The golden man and the short one with the red shirt have hauled them into the destroyed lobby. The golden man has the neck of Miaow's T-shirt twisted in his fist, and the man with the red shirt leans against a peeling wall with one foot braced against it and his arm around Andrew's throat, its elbow pointed at Miaow. It looks like a wrestling hold. He's smoking a cigarette. Andrew is dead white, white as paper, his face dripping sweat. His eyes are unfocused and there's something empty about his body, as though its spirit has fled it.

The golden man says to Miaow, "Is he all right?"

"I don't know," she says. She remembers the little zipped bag hanging from her shoulder. "He has diabetes," she says, holding the bag up as evidence.

"Boy," the golden man says. "Boy, are you sick?"

Andrew makes an *o* with his lips, then licks them, and his eyes come to Miaow's and she sees the terror in them. "No," Andrew says, and then he coughs. His voice seems to come from far away.

"Loosen your arm," the golden man says to the short man. "Boy, did you take your medicine before you left your house?"

Andrew shakes his head *no*, and then nods *yes*. Nods again.

"You'll be all right," the golden man says. "We just need the phone, and then you can go."

Miaow says, "Give it to him, Andrew."

Andrew says, "I don't have it."

The golden man says, "Careful, boy."

"It's at home," Andrew says. His voice is all tremor; if she couldn't see him, Miaow wouldn't recognize it as his.

The short man gives Andrew a shake. "Why would you leave it home?"

"It doesn't—doesn't have my SIM card. If my parents call and I don't answer, I can say I forgot the phone."

"Check his pockets," the golden man says, and the short man clamps his arm more tightly around Andrew's neck and pats the boy down, then shakes his head.

"Sorry, girl," the golden man says, and quickly slaps her pockets. He feels her phone in her jeans and says, "Take it out."

She holds it up for him. It's an iPhone 4, black like Andrew's, and his eyes widen and then slide away, rejecting it. He nods at the bag hanging from her shoulder. She puts the phone back and unzips Andrew's case to show nothing but his diabetes kit.

The golden man draws a long breath, and Miaow can feel heat coming off him. He says to Andrew, "Who is at your house?"

Andrew's blinking fast. "My—my father. It's Saturday. And my mother, she's sick, so she's always home."

"I'm sorry," the golden man says, and Miaow feels a cold needle of fear pierce her stomach. She knows instinctively why he's sorry, and it isn't because Andrew's mother is sick. She knows, as sure as she's standing there, that they're all as good as dead.

"It's not your fault," Andrew says, and Miaow wants to hug him just once, hug him as hard as she can, hug him until he squeals. She should have hugged him months ago.

The golden man's phone rings, and he listens and says, "Good." He hauls Miaow across the lobby. "Take her, too. I'll go ahead. I'll be on the other side of the fence. You stay back until I wave you to come." To Miaow, he says, "This man will kill you if you fight him."

The short man knots her T-shirt in his fist.

"Look for me," the golden man says. "I'll wave you out. If they have to go over the fence, they'll come one at a time." He looks from Andrew to Miaow. "Him first. If I've got him, she won't go anywhere. Three minutes." He gives Miaow a last look, his eyes lingering on her for a second, but then he shakes his head and turns and lopes out of the lobby, toward the fence. He runs, Miaow thinks, as naturally as most people breathe. If they have to outrun him, they have no chance.

But, of course, no matter how fast he is he can only chase one of them. If Andrew gets his courage back, he can outrun the short man. So the thing is, if it comes down to being chased, she has to make the golden man chase her. Even though he's faster than she is.

She tries to catch Andrew's eye, but he's staring at the wall. He seems even less substantial than he had before; it's as though tiny bits of him are flaking off and rising into the air, as though he's dissolving in front of her and in a minute she'll be able to see through him. She scuffs her foot loudly on the floor, and the man holding her shirt shakes her like a puppy. Miaow coughs, and Andrew's eyes come to her. She holds them, willing him to understand that he's to follow her lead.

He glances away, and she thinks, *Look where following me got him*. But she can't allow that, she can't allow anything that might make her hesitate. She knows what will happen at Andrew's apartment.

The fence and the sidewalk. It has to be the fence and the sidewalk.

The feeling comes upon her the same way it used to, when she was on the street. Time almost stops, except for the rhythm of her breath. Her vision sharpens and there's a sparking in her core, the surge of extra life that always came to her rescue in the old, chaotic days. She'd thought then that it made her—for as long as it lasted—more alive, faster, smarter, than the people who were after her. They didn't stand a chance.

She hasn't felt this in a long time.

Andrew is looking at her again, and he seems puzzled. *It's showing*, she thinks, and she pushes it down, coiling it inside her so it can explode when she needs it. She looks at his eyes, then drops her own eyes to her feet, then repeats the pattern, hoping it means to him what it means to her: *follow me*. But his eyes drift up, probably to the face of the man who is holding her, and then down to the floor again.

Miaow's silent count has reached 200 by the time the man in the red shirt says, "Now" and tugs on her shirt. She needs Andrew to be ahead, so she stumbles and falls to her knees, and then lags back, limping, as they enter the weeds that surround the hotel, waist-high on her, thigh-high on the man.

Everything looks so *normal*: the sun is high, and dust from the weeds billows into the air and glints yellow in the light. The shade beneath the trees has bright spots in it where there are holes in the canopy. She can hear traffic noise from two directions: from her left and from the boulevard in front of them, six lanes wide, on the other side of the chain-link fence.

That either will or won't have a gate.

Miaow prays for the gate to be there.

And sees it. Closed. She can't tell whether it's locked, but her pulse accelerates slightly.

A woman walks by on the other side of the fence with a bulging white plastic bag dangling from each hand. Free to keep going, to go home and be with her children, released from school on this sunny Saturday, free to nap or cook or do nothing at all. Free without giving it a thought.

Seeing that she's looking at the woman, the man hauling them twists the neck of her T-shirt, as though he's afraid she'll cry out, then raises the near leg and brings his foot down on her instep.

She yelps and then goes still. No point in fighting him. She could get free, but there's Andrew to think about.

Cars go by on the other side of the chain-link.

They're about five meters from the fence now, standing in the weeds with the ruined hotel behind them. Miaow squints at the gate. The stolen U-joint has been replaced with a new one, and a padlock holds it in place.

At the moment she accepts the lock as a joyous certainty, the golden man comes into sight from the left, probably from the spot where the car is waiting at the curb. He gives them a fingers-curled come-ahead sign and then stands there, looking left and right as a couple of teenagers go by on bicycles. The moment their backs are to him, he holds up a single finger and points at Andrew.

The man holding them begins to move, hauling Miaow along, and Miaow pushes the dangling bag behind her so she can get to it without it being visible to the golden man on the other side of the fence. She drags her feet as the three of them wade through the weeds.

The golden man looks left again and gestures for them to stop. One more glance in each direction and he waves them forward. A moment later, they're at the fence. The man shoves Andrew toward the chain-link, holding him by the hair, and the golden man gestures for Andrew to climb.

But he doesn't. He shrinks back and then he's clawing at the man's hand and screaming for help. The man yanks Andrew back, against his own body, and knees him hard, in the middle of the back, and Andrew sags. The man knees him again, and Miaow slips her hand behind her onto Andrew's little leather case. Deliberately, giving it one hundred percent of her attention, she unzips it and withdraws the hypodermic, bringing it up to her face and using her teeth to pull the sheath off the needle. As the man wraps the neck of Andrew's shirt in his hand and lifts him from the ground, Miaow drives the needle deep into the knuckle at the base of the man's index finger, where it's knotted around her T-shirt.

The hand snaps open and the man screams hoarsely as Miaow yanks the needle free, and as he bends down, still roaring, to grab her, she aims for his eye but misses, the needle going instead into his cheek and hitting the cheekbone. He screams again and backs away, letting go of both of them and grabbing with both hands at the injury, and as Andrew leaps back, looking stunned and disbelieving, Miaow reaches the man in one leap and buries the needle in the side of the man's neck.

She grabs Andrew's hand, and the two of them are running, running the length of the fence to their right, away from the injured man on their side of the fence and the golden man on the far side— but now, six or seven long steps behind them, the golden man is starting to run, too, and Miaow knows he's faster than they are and she calls to Andrew, "At the fence pole, *go over*," and she takes her own leap at the fence.

Scaling it faster than she's ever climbed anything in her life, she feels a quick grasp and jerks her foot away from the man below. He's left holding her flipflop. She's free but the golden man is coming, and she feels the fence vibrate as Andrew hits it and she scurries the rest of the way over and jumps, jarring onto the pavement only a few steps in front of the golden man, and as Andrew tops the fence a couple of meters farther down, she pulls out her iPhone, her fingers covering its distinctive screen, and waves it in the air as she runs, and the golden man instinctively starts after her. Instead of running away from him, she reverses and runs *toward* him, her one bare foot hot on the pavement, sees him stop, off balance and confused, and then, hearing Andrew's shoes slapping the pavement behind her, going in the other direction, she feints left, as though she's going to try to get between the golden man and the fence but goes right instead, bolting between two parked cars and into the first traffic lane, just avoiding, by a few inches, being run over by a motorcycle policeman.

19

An Empty Envelope

DR. RATT SAYS, "She's hopeless."

He and Rafferty are standing on the sidewalk in front of the apartment house that shelters, temporarily, Rafferty's latest good deed gone awry. With them is Hwa, the maid who's been caretaking the addict upstairs.

"She want to go home," Hwa says.

Hwa is Vietnamese, slender and small-boned, Chinese-featured, with hard, tired eyes, her gray-streaked hair pulled tightly into a no-nonsense pony tail, nothing cute, just an announcement that she declines to put up with any interference from her hair. If there's a soft side to her, Rafferty hasn't seen it, and she certainly takes a hard line about her charge, the woman named Neeni for whom he rented and furnished the apartment upstairs.

Neeni is, Rafferty thinks, what's left when someone who had nothing but beauty is no longer beautiful. She's a faded photograph, an empty envelope, something that could be blown sideways by a window fan. Dr. Ratt has just come from his third monthly visit to evaluate Neeni's withdrawal from the mixture of whiskey and codeine-laced cough syrup that she'd lived on for several years before Poke pulled her and Hwa out of a burning house and drove them through a flooded Bangkok toward a different life.

A life Neeni is apparently declining.

"Has she been good?" Dr. Ratt asks Hwa.

"Can't be bad," Hwa says. "Nothing here for her to take, and can't go out. I don't let. Tranquilizer finish three week ago."

"She looked quite tranquil," Dr. Ratt says.

"She lively today," Hwa says. "Eye open, everything. All she want is go back to village in Laos and start again." Hwa knows Neeni better than any of them. For years, in Haskell Murphy's dreadful household, Hwa had made sure Neeni had her medicine at hand, didn't set fire to things, and kept out of her dangerous husband's way. For the past seven weeks, on Rafferty's orders and in exchange for the promise of some of the money Rafferty took from Murphy, she's been playing nursemaid again.

Dr. Ratt says, "Neural damage. You can only make them misfire for so long before the paths get worn away. A lot of the connections you and I take for granted aren't there any more. Her brain is an erased blackboard. Some of the paths are still there faintly, some are just gone. If she's sober for years some of them might come back, but she'll never be who she was."

Hwa says, "Wasting time, you wasting time here."

"Yeah." Rafferty wipes both hands over his face like someone who's just waking up. Neeni sucks the energy right out of him; ten minutes with her, and he's exhausted. "But look," he says. "Neeni's probably still got a daughter. Treasure is somewhere in Bangkok. What happens if—"

"What *happen*." It's a scoff: Hwa's lips are curled, the corners pulled down. "Maybe Treasure burn too bad, maybe die somewhere else."

"I don't think she was burned," Rafferty says. "I think Treasure ran straight through that house and into the yard and that room she made in the hedge. At least, I hope so. The hedge wasn't burned."

"House—*boom*," Hwa says.

"Treasure's little room was fine." Rafferty glances to Dr. Ratt, looking for support. "You saw it."

"I did. Of course, the fact that the room was intact doesn't mean she was in there."

Head cocked on one side, Hwa says, "You see room?"

"He took me," Dr. Ratt says.

"Soft heart," Hwa says to Rafferty, and it doesn't sound much like a compliment. "But, you know—this girl crazy."

"A gift from her father. But yeah," Rafferty says, feeling like he's admitting something he hasn't wanted to acknowledge, "it's hard to imagine her making friends."

Hwa puts her hands near her ears and makes scrabbling motions with her fingers. "Crazy. If she not dead, maybe live near river. In hole, like animal. Before, at house, she catch things every night. She *baba-bobo*"—Vietnamese slang for "crazy."

"The issue," Rafferty says, hearing the total hopelessness of it in his ears, "if she's alive, I mean, is what happens if we find her. Whether she can be helped. I'm keeping money for her to get help—the money I took from Murphy's. But the question is, does she still have a mother?"

"*That* woman?" Hwa says, lifting her chin toward the apartment several stories above them. "You see. What you think?"

"But if she goes home, to the village. Maybe you could go—"

"No." Hwa's face softens. "Cannot, you know. Cannot help everybody. Neeni will drink. Treasure crazy. Sometime—" She makes a gesture, a fluttering, falling leaf, with one delicate hand. "Must to let go."

Dr. Ratt says, "She's right."

"*I* know she's right," Rafferty says. "Fucking hell, I know she's right. I just hoped—*keep* Neeni here, let Hwa help her, maybe she'll—"

Hwa says, "No."

"Right." Rafferty scuffs his shoe over the pavement. "Can you take her home?"

"Can," Hwa says. "Then I go my house."

Rafferty says again, "Right. What about the money?"

"You give me."

"I mean, for her. I've got, I don't know, a lot that really belongs to her."

"A little at a time," Dr. Ratt says. "Give her too much, she'll be dead in days."

"I'll work it out. A hundred a week or something."

"Give the rest of it away," Dr. Ratt says. "Give it to Father Bill." Father Bill Chandler runs a school and shelter for Bangkok's street children.

"Maybe," Rafferty says. "But I should keep it for Treasure." He rattles the five-baht coins in his pockets without even hearing them. "Treasure," he says. "Who the hell knows."

"I'll set up the money," Rafferty says after Hwa has gone back upstairs to see whether Neeni is trying to smoke the sofa. "Hwa can make the travel arrangements."

"Hwa can do just about anything," Dr. Ratt says. "They should make her prime minister."

"I had really hoped . . ." Rafferty's voice trails off.

"Life goes on," Dr. Ratt says. "Even when it doesn't."

"Speaking of that," Rafferty says, feeling the lift in his heart, "speaking of life going on, Rose is pregnant."

"No. What can I say?" Dr. Ratt is not normally a demonstrative man, but he spreads his arms. "Come here." He hugs Rafferty, American-style, and then lets him go. "Is this her first?"

"Jesus," Rafferty says. "If it's not, I don't know it."

"I'll have Nui call her. She's had three in her spare time. Nui can be her guide. Where's Rose's mom?"

"Isaan. They've been on the phone all day."

"Well, until her mom arrives, she can talk to Nui. Nui will love it. I'm so happy for both of you. Does Miaow know?"

"That's sort of the problem," Rafferty says.

Dr. Ratt sorts through the ring of keys in his hand. "I've been through it. Our first one was six when Nui got pregnant with her little sister. She went completely nuts, breaking things, threatening to run away." He chooses a key and pushes a button, and something chirps behind Rafferty.

"What did you do?"

"We made her part of it. Nui didn't want stretch marks, so Lala got to put lotion on her mother's stomach. We put her in charge of Nui's naps. She drew signs to keep me quiet." He turns to go. "But the most important thing we did was to let Lala name her. That made the baby Lala's, too."

"And it worked?"

"She was seven when Sorn was born, and she was that baby's second mother. Even now, eight years later, she's Sorn's best friend and substitute mother."

"Let Miaow name her," Rafferty said. "That's great."

"Have you told Arthit?"

Rafferty says, "Ummmmm," and his cell phone rings. He pulls it out and sees ARTHIT. With a certain amount of foreboding, he says, "In the darkness fate moves its heavy hand." He shows the phone to Dr. Ratt, and says, "Hello."

"Poke," Arthit says. "You need to come down to the station, now. You need to come get your daughter."

20

And a Few Who Want to See It Worked Out Wrong

"SHE GAVE THEM my name," Arthit says. He and Poke are in an empty office: metal furniture, last year's calendar, a linoleum floor. There's a circular smear of hair oil, like a permanent halo, on the wall above the office chair behind the desk. Arthit is sitting on a corner of the desk behind a couple of official-looking forms, and Rafferty is fidgeting just inside the door, which Arthit left ajar behind them. "The moment they took her into the station, she told them to call me. I had them bring her up here."

"What happened?"

"She ran in front of a motorcycle cop. There was a guy chasing her into the street, and another one on the other side of a fence. What she says is that she and her—companion, I guess—"

"Andrew."

Arthit glances at one of the forms, but not long enough to read anything, so it's just discomfort, the same discomfort Rafferty feels. "Andrew Nguyen."

"Boyfriend."

"Really." Arthit's eyebrows go up, and even in his agitated state, Rafferty feels a sense of loss. In the old days—seven, eight weeks ago, before Anna—he and Arthit would have talked about Andrew for hours. "Well, what Miaow and Andrew say is that the men chased them through the Indian section, and the kids hid out in the old Indra Siam hotel but when they came out, the men grabbed them. The men were trying to get the kids over the fence and into a car when they got away. Your daughter, according to Andrew, stabbed the men who were hanging onto them with his hypodermic needle. Andrew's a diabetic."

For a split second, Rafferty feels like he's going to grin. Instead, he says, "She hasn't lost it."

He sees his suppressed grin appear in Arthit's eyes. "Not only that. She led them into the hotel in the first place because she knew an escape route through the ventilation ducts."

Rafferty says, "And she's *still* as fragile as glass. What about the men?"

"Gone. The one outside the fence took off in a car driven by a third man. The other ran back toward the hotel. They had plenty of time. Our cop was trying to keep Miaow from charging straight into traffic since he had no way of knowing she can probably run between raindrops, and Andrew—to my personal surprise, now that I've seen him—came back to see whether she needed help."

"That's right," Rafferty says. "He probably would, despite the way he looks. I forgot that you hadn't met him."

"No," Arthit says, lining up the forms side by side. "Haven't had the pleasure."

In a brisker tone, Rafferty says, "Why were the men chasing them?"

Arthit says, "The simple answer is, an iPhone. Andrew apparently lost an iPhone 5 his father bought him, and his father is, I have to say, a hard-ass of the old school. So your daughter, like a good street child, showed him where to buy a stolen one until they could come up with an explanation for Andrew needing a new SIM card." He eases himself off the desk and sits in the chair behind it. "Sometimes I regret not having children, and sometimes I'm delighted."

"So? So they bought a phone. Who was chasing them, and why?"

Arthit swivels the chair right and left. "This is where it gets complicated. I'm not sure I can tell you everything."

"What you're not sure you can tell me, Arthit," Rafferty says, just barely not between his teeth, "is it the explanation for why those men were chasing my daughter? Is my not knowing likely to put her in danger again?"

Arthit's mouth tightens at Poke's tone, but he closes his eyes for a moment, and when he opens them, he takes a slow breath and forces a smile. "I doubt it. We should be releasing the news that we've got the phone later today, and that will take the heat off."

"Releasing the news," Rafferty says slowly. "That the police have recovered a stolen iPhone. A bulletin to the breathless millions. What have I missed? Are we in a news-free week?"

"Andrew had left the phone at home. The men were going to force him to take them there. Miaow says she thinks they were going to kill everybody in the apartment once they had the phone."

"Kill four or five people for a phone."

"It obviously wasn't the phone," Arthit snaps. "It's what was on it." He rubs his eyes, draws a long breath, and says, "You don't know any of this, not from me."

Rafferty thinks about it for a second and says, "Okay."

"Close the door." Arthit waits until he hears the latch click and says, "You remember Sawat?"

"Sure. The cop who was running an expensive murder ring. In the police department, no less. He just got killed."

"Fat Thongchai?"

Poke has to rummage for a minute. "The lower-ranking guy who tried to cover for Sawat."

"Thongchai was killed yesterday morning, although we haven't released that yet. Same way as Sawat, shot and burned. Same guy." Arthit wipes his palm over his forehead as though he's perspiring, although the office is cool. "Both victims' pictures," he says. "They were on the SIM card in the iPhone Andrew bought."

"Two murdered guys," Poke says. "Why would their pictures be on the phone?"

"This is conjecture," Arthit says. He looks past Rafferty to the door for a moment, then comes back to him. "To be precise, it's *my* conjecture. Both Sawat and Thongchai were photographed without their knowledge. On sidewalks, mostly. They never saw the photographer. There were several pictures of each of them, and then two of a couple of men in a hotel room. My conjecture is that it was murder for hire, which has a certain poetic symmetry to it, and the phone was given to the killers, maybe the men in the hotel room, so they'd shoot the right guys."

"The phone Andrew bought."

"Yes. And my guess is that the murderer was supposed to toss the phone into the river but looked at it and thought, *here's another few thousand baht*, and sold it."

"It wouldn't connect him to the murders?"

Arthit shakes his head. "The last two pictures taken, of the two men in a hotel room, were probably taken by the third murderer, as Shakespearean as that sounds, and he was the one who sold the phone. There might be prints, but there might not be, too. Or there are but they're not on record. Or they're on record in some dirt-road station where our computers aren't connected. Other than that, there's no reason the phone would incriminate him. He certainly didn't buy the phone or the SIM card and he's not in the pictures. There weren't any outgoing calls, and all the incoming calls come from anybody-phones, the ones you buy for eight hundred baht in cash. I'd say he felt free as a bird when he sold the phone."

"But then," Rafferty says.

"But then his friends went to give the phone back to whoever hired them, as they'd undoubtedly been ordered to, and he didn't have it. So they went back to the booth to get it, and they were there when Miaow and Andrew arrived." He spreads his hands. "Bad break."

Rafferty says, "I should really go talk to Miaow."

"Let her wait," Arthit says. He leans back. "This might as well be a learning experience."

"Then can I have that chair?"

Arthit says, "Sure. I was just sitting in it." He gets up and wheels it around to the side of the desk.

"I need it more than you do," Rafferty says, sitting. "So, Andrew and Miaow buy the phone and all of a sudden these guys are chasing them."

"No," Arthit says, reseating himself on the desk. "It's *much* stupider than that. Andrew lost his own phone yesterday morning. That's when they bought it."

"Skipping school," Rafferty says. "That's why they were late."

"And Andrew went through the shots on the phone in the cab on the way to school. Yesterday afternoon, he saw Sawat's picture in the *Sun*, and he did what any good citizen would have done. He took the paper to your apartment and showed it to Miaow."

"My daughter," Rafferty says, "is not boneheaded enough to play amateur detective."

Arthit says, "Boneheaded?"

"I do *not* play amateur detective." He realizes he has leaned forward and uses his feet to push the chair back a few inches. "Or if I do, it's because I have to because the professional detectives are either not disposed to help or are, umm, constrained—"

"That's a nice way to put it. *Constrained*, as opposed to corrupt or scared of running up against someone bigger than they are who might sympathize with—or be on the payroll of—the other side."

"It's hard to be a cop here," Rafferty says. "An honest one, anyway."

The two men look at each other across a few years of shared history, and the moment makes Rafferty ache. Arthit breaks the silence. "So Andrew was going to be a hero. Go back this morning and find out whether the men in the pictures were the ones who sold the phone in the first place. And then he was going to go to you with Miaow at his side and give you the phone to give to me, along with this red-hot clue. And that would make his father ease up on his heroic son for having lost the phone in the first place."

"It's enough to make you cry."

"But the bad guys are right there, and you have the chase and the hotel and all the rest of it."

Rafferty says, "And the murderer?"

Arthit says, "Pardon?"

"The one who killed Sawat and Fat Thongchai. You said they were hit by the same person. That suggests to me that you have a visual of that person. Was he one of the men chasing Miaow?"

"I don't know that. Not for sure."

Rafferty holds his friend's gaze.

Arthit puts up a hand and leans back, breaking the connection. "Look, here's what you're really asking. Is the murderer, the *murderers*, likely to come back for them? Think about it. Until they chased the kids, no one had seen them. The phone was the only visual link. But now a dozen people, including a Bangkok cop, can ID them. They can't kill everybody."

Rafferty spins the chair around.

"Listen," Arthit says, "if I get any sense at all that I'm wrong about any of this, although I can't imagine how I could be, I'll see that Miaow's covered night and day."

"She got a really first-class look, didn't she?"

"Poke. They wanted the *phone*, the pictures of themselves. We have those pictures now. We have surveillance video—you didn't hear this from me—of the one who did the killings. The world will learn all of that tomorrow morning, so there's no need for them to go after Miaow and Andrew again. It would expose them to risk for nothing."

Rafferty says, grudgingly, "Okay."

"And I can tell you that for some people in this department, figuring this whole thing out is the most important item on our agenda. You've got to remember that Sawat and Fat Thongchai were a disgrace to the department. This building, all our buildings, are packed with people who need to see this worked out, and worked out right."

"And a few," Rafferty says, "the ones who covered for Sawat, who probably want to see it worked out wrong."

Arthit says, "I'm going to talk to you like a cop for a change, Poke. Stay out of this."

"And I'm going to answer you like a father, Arthit. I need to know that my daughter isn't in danger." He gets up. "Where is she?"

Arthit stands, too. "I'll take you down there." He puts his hand on the doorknob but doesn't turn it. "Tomorrow is Sunday," he says. "She doesn't go to school. Keep her home, keep an eye on her. Give me tomorrow to think about it. If I decide you're right, or if something happens here that seems, I don't know, off-color, I'll think about putting someone on her. Anand or someone, someone too young to have had anything to do with the original case."

Poke says, "Thank you, Arthit."

Arthit says, "We should have a drink some time."

Poke says, "We will." He hears the hollowness of the reply and sees Arthit hear it, too.

Turning away, Arthit says, "You can take her home. We don't need to talk to her any more." He opens the door, and Poke follows him down the corridor, seeing for the first time the stiffness in his friend's back. The weariness in his shoulders.

21

You Don't Know Anything

M IAOW WON'T LOOK at him.

He's followed Arthit into the small room where she's waiting, just a table and two chairs. Someone, probably being thoughtful, has brought in a little television and plugged it in, but Miaow hasn't turned it on. She's filthy, her arms and face streaked with dirt. She smells of sweat and rat urine. There are white tracks down her cheeks, where tears washed the dirt away.

The door closes behind him and Arthit, but Miaow sits in the molded plastic chair and looks at her feet, one of which is bare. All Rafferty can see is the back of her neck, her shoulders, her blackened knees, and her hair, which has cobwebs and plaster and God only knows what else in it.

He says, "Hello, Miaow."

She doesn't move.

"What happened to your shoe?"

"What shoe?"

"Do you want to go home?"

In a voice so low he can barely hear her, she says to the floor, "Who cares."

"It's over," he says. "You were brave. You saved Andrew. You're all right now."

He doesn't think she'll reply, but she says, "You don't know *anything*."

"Well," Rafferty says, shooting Arthit a glance, "why don't you wait in here while I learn a little."

Arthit says, "Do you want something to drink, Miaow?" but Miaow doesn't acknowledge the question. Rafferty opens the door and holds it for Arthit, and after a moment's pause, Arthit passes through it.

Arthit leads him two doors down, out of earshot, and then turns, his arms folded. "Okay," Rafferty says, "is she just being dramatic, or is there some personal tragedy I don't know about?"

"The kid's dad," Arthit says. "Andrew's dad. We called him first because we wanted the camera, and it was at their place."

"Wouldn't have anything to do with his being a diplomat."

Arthit's face flushes. "Even if it did," he says, "you know I wouldn't make that decision. If you don't know that, you should."

"I'm sorry, Arthit." Rafferty swivels his head, and his neck cracks like popcorn. "There's a lot going on right now."

"The father heard the story, and he was pretty rough. Said they wouldn't be seeing each other any more. Asked what kind of a girl knows about ruined hotels and old ventilation systems. What is she, he asked, a street kid? I thought Miaow was going to kick him, but it was worse than that. She just sort of disappeared. Pulled way, way inside herself, while he ranted on. And this, of course, was the girl who just saved his son's skinny, helpless ass."

Rafferty sags against the wall. "Oh, no." He looks down the hallway, at the door Miaow is behind. "For her, for Miaow, this is about the worst thing that could have happened."

Arthit pulls his head back in surprise. "Are they that serious? They're pretty young."

"It's just infinitely complicated. Yes, it's that serious, at least for her. He's all she thinks about. She barely talks to us any more, it's just Andrew, Andrew. But I don't think it's all just romance. It's like the fact that he cares about her makes her interesting, makes her into somebody else, someone who's not a worthless street child pretending to be someone who matters. That sonofabitch really nailed her."

Arthit is looking down at the floor, but his head is slightly cocked and Rafferty can feel his attention.

"And Andrew goes to her school, so she's probably terrified about word getting around. Arthit, she's invented up a whole different *person* for school. Her name is Mia, her mother is rich, her father is famous. She talks differently there. She's spending most of her allowance on whitening creams. She's bought little lifts for her school shoes to be taller. You've seen her hair. She's twelve, thirteen years old, and she hates every inch of herself." He massages the back of his neck, pushing back against his own hand. "Andrew is a nice enough kid. I like him, and she likes him, too, but I think, for her, he was partly proof that it was all working, that she was becoming someone—better."

He breaks off, squeezes his eyes shut and opens them again. "Hell, I don't know, maybe I'm wrong, maybe he's really her first love. Maybe that's all it is, she's just brokenhearted instead of feeling exposed and dirty and terrified that this is going to get out at school, and everyone will be pointing at her. Looking at her like she needs to wipe something off her upper lip. Like she's street trash. She's been pretending to be a white-shoe rich girl. And here she is, someone who knows every filthy short cut in the asshole of Bangkok. So, no, I don't think it's just teenage heartbreak."

Arthit says, "I'm so sorry."

"And it had to happen now, of all the times, it had to happen now."

"Why is that such a problem?"

Rafferty says, "Arthit." He feels like he could weep. "You should have been the first person to know this. I have no excuse for not having told you. It's Rose. She's pregnant."

"*Poke*," Arthit says, and for a moment, he sounds like himself. "That's—" He breaks off, and then he says, "Oh."

"Yeah," Rafferty says. "In that regard, it's just awful."

They stand silently for a moment and then Arthit says, "Walk with me," and he puts his hand on Rafferty's upper arm and they move down the ugly hallway, Arthit limping slightly against the muscle spasm in his back. "You have to keep these things separate, right? If there's one thing I learned after Noi died, it was that problems aren't really knotted together, they just seem that way. If you tangle them up they'll paralyze you, they'll get too big to see around them, to where the solutions are. So even though I don't know much of anything, even though I may be making a huge mistake in my own life right now, let me talk for a few minutes, okay?"

Rafferty says, "You have no idea how much I want you to talk to me."

Arthit squeezes his arm. "Okay, so here goes. First, you've been blessed. You have a wife you love, you've got a brave, resourceful, good-hearted daughter who just saved some little geek's life, and now your beautiful wife is going to have a baby. There will be four of you, Poke. That's where you're actually standing right now. Does that sound about right?"

"It sounds wonderful."

"Well, hang on to that. Okay, one thing at a time." He stops where he is and taps his hard, round little belly a few times, not even aware he's doing it. Rafferty has seen him do it a dozen times when he's thinking. The dark-skinned face with its broad nostrils and downturned mouth is tilted toward the floor and he's wiggling one foot side to side on its heel, another signal that he's working something through. He looks up at Rafferty and starts to walk again. "First, don't worry about the thing with the guys who wanted the phone. I'll work on it all day tomorrow, and stay on top of what's happening in the department, and I promise you, Miaow will be protected if it seems even halfway necessary."

The hallway branches left and right, and Arthit takes them right. "Now. Andrew."

Rafferty says, "Maybe Nguyen will back down. Maybe he'll let them—"

Arthit says, "Not quickly, he won't. He's got a whole tree up his ass. But maybe, just maybe, Andrew is stronger than you think he is. Maybe he'll defy his father. There's no love sweeter than the Romeo and Juliet kind."

"But remember, this whole thing started because he's afraid of his father. That's why they bought—"

"That was *stuff*, that was a phone, that was something Andrew's father could *buy*. This is Miaow. I'm not trying to sugarcoat anything, Poke, but she's not like anyone Andrew's met in his protected little life. Two fences, a hypodermic, and an air duct? In about *fifteen minutes*? And she did it for him, you know. Without him, she could have been halfway home by the time they started chasing her. Do you think he doesn't know that?"

Rafferty says, "Okay."

"So let's say that the love tragedy is something you just park for now. Love your daughter, stay out of her way unless she wants you in it. Wait for the phone to ring, wait for them to reach out to each other again, wait for her to come home from school looking happier. And in the meantime, here's what you do about the baby. Nothing. You don't tell her about it."

Rafferty says, "I've missed you."

"Let's not get all teary. We've still got a problem between us. It's Anna. She's moved in with me."

"You know what?" Rafferty says, "That's great. Do you love her?"

Arthit says, "Maybe I do."

"Then I'll learn to love her, too."

"Okay," Arthit says, blinking fast. "Let's get all teary."

"I'd hug you," Rafferty says, "but we're in a police station."

"Aaaaahhhh," Arthit says, and they hug each other, and then Arthit steps back. "While I still have some reputation left," he says. He rubs his eyes with his sleeve. "The thing to do with Miaow is to be infinitely patient. And don't *understand* her too much. Kids hate that. Not that I'm an expert on kids. But *I* sure hated it."

"Got it," Rafferty says. "Love her, don't over-understand her, and wait for true love to find a way. Cross my fingers that word doesn't get out at school. And keep quiet about the baby for the moment."

"Until Rose just can't hold it back any more."

"Should I talk to Andrew's father?"

Arthit says, "Do you think it'll do any good?"

"Probably not."

"Well, then, sure," Arthit says. "Odds like that, you've got to try."

"Thanks, Arthit." Rafferty throws an arm over his friend's shoulder. "Let's go get my daughter."

22

The Opposite of a Cover-up

IT'S GOTTEN DARK out, but not so dark that the cabbie doesn't turn his head, his eyes wide, as Miaow climbs into the backseat. She startles Rafferty by baring her teeth and growling, and the cabbie's head snaps forward.

He lowers his window against the smell.

Miaow has her door halfway open before Rafferty can reach past her and slam it closed again. She says, "Let me out."

"Soi Pipat," Rafferty says.

The driver, his eyes on the mirror, says, "She wants to get out."

"Well, she's not going to. Let's go."

The driver says, "No. Here's what. You both get out." He thinks for a second. "Or *you* get out and I'll take her where she wants to go. For free, if I have to."

Miaow says, "It's okay."

"Is he trying to take you someplace you don't want to go?"

"I don't want to go anywhere," Miaow says. "But I might as well go with him."

The driver says, "I don't do that."

Miaow says, "Look at me, please. In the mirror." She waits until his eyes are on her, and then she makes a *wai*. "Thank you for being worried about me. I've had a very bad day and I know how dirty I am, and I'm sorry for being in your cab, but this is my father, and he just wants to take me home."

"Yes, Miss," the cabbie says, and Rafferty finds himself staring at Miaow. She's never stopped surprising him, but this is a voice he hasn't heard before. He thinks, *This is who she is at school.* And he wants to put his arms around her.

She won't look at him. As the cab pulls away from the curb, she sits with her knees pressed together and her hands folded tightly in her lap, presenting the smallest possible amount of surface to the world. Her eyes are open, and she's staring directly at the back of the driver's seat, as though she thinks it's the direction bad news is least likely to come from.

"Do you want me to get your mother out of the way so you can clean up before she sees you?"

"Doesn't matter," Miaow says.

"It might matter to your mother."

"Up to you." She turns away and looks out the window of the cab.

"Okay, then I'm deciding. You wait outside for a minute and come in when I tell you, and then you can go get in the shower or whatever you want."

"Whatever I want." She puts nothing into the words.

"Okay, what *I* want," Rafferty says. "And that would be a shower."

"You already won," Miaow says.

Rafferty says, "I have to say this, even though I know you don't want to hear it. I'm so proud of you I could burst into tears."

She doesn't turn to him, but she swipes the back of a filthy hand across her cheek. "Well, don't."

"I won't," Rafferty says, wiping his nose. "I'm a grownup. I'm even a man. We don't cry."

The cabbie is looking at him in the mirror, and when Rafferty catches his eyes, he gives a little shrug that Rafferty reads as, *Oh yeah?*

"If it's all right with you," Miaow says, "I don't want to talk."

"No problem."

She starts to cry. He puts a hand on her shoulder, but she pulls away from him and brings up her knees, turning herself into a ball of knees and elbows, and she sobs as though something much bigger than she is, much too large for her to contain it, is trying to force its way out.

In the mirror, Rafferty and the driver share a glance of helpless complicity.

THANOM, WHO HAS worked all day Saturday, has not been asked to change his uniform, and he feels the slight the moment he steps into the high, airy entry hall. Through the wide archway to the left, the room glimmers with medals and jewels, the rainbow of the women's clothes and the white dress jackets, glittering with decorations, of many of the men. Thanom stands there in his wrinkled day uniform and feels his face burn.

He hears music: a string quartet, not a recording. This is the life he's always wanted, and he's being reminded forcefully that he doesn't have it.

The servant who opened the door and left him standing here is better dressed than he is.

People glance at him but their eyes keep moving; he's no one worth looking at.

So he looks at the floor, his hands clasped tightly together in front of him, until the servant reappears and says, "Please follow me," and leads him away from the big bright rooms and the music, *Mozart*, he thinks, since he always guesses Mozart, and he cringes internally at his own pretentiousness. Showing off for *himself* and failing to impress.

Up a short flight of stairs to a landing. The servant stops at a closed door, knocks once, indicates with a gloved hand that Thanom is to open it.

Thanom waits until the servant is partway down the stairs. Then he pushes the door open and enters the room.

"Close it, please," says the man behind the desk.

Thanom's heart suddenly pounds in his ears. He's never exchanged a word with this man before, and up until this very moment he hadn't realized he should have been grateful for that fact.

"Sir," he says, his back to the closed door.

"So," the other man says. "This Sawat situation won't go away, will it?" He's slender and fair-skinned, black hair cut medium length, parted on the left and trained to fall casually over a scholarly forehead. He wears a pair of rimless glasses with slightly smoked lenses. There's something ascetic about him, although rumor says he has women stowed in apartments all over Bangkok. He's younger than Thanom—early fifties—but every cell in his body seems comfortable with the disparity in their stations. He should be, since he's a princeling, presently the highest-ranking princeling in the department, the third son of a family that misses being ancient but has, for several generations, been very, very rich. The room is lined with books, with a gleaming ebony desk and a dark, thick carpet. The only spots of color are four framed photographs on one wall, formal portraits of two boys on the verge of becoming teenagers.

Thanom says, "We're making progress, sir."

"'Progress' is a strong word for 'accident,'" the other man says. Thanom can't see his eyes through the gray lenses.

"We have descriptions and photos now, of both of them."

"No," the younger man says. "You already had, on videotape, the one who committed the murders. The other is just hired street muscle." He waits, but Thanom says nothing. "I'd like you to tell me what you saw on that phone."

Thanom masks his surprise at the question. "Photos of Sawat and Thongchai, several of each, and two pictures of two of the men who chased those children."

"Is that all?

"Yes, sir."

"Nothing or no one else?"

"No, sir." He can actually feel his blood pressure mount. "Although the phone was only in my possession for a few hours."

An economical nod. "That's correct. And you won't be seeing it again, either. You'll also find that the copies of the photos you put on your office computer have been deleted."

"Sir. I'm supposed to be leading this investigation."

"Well, no one will know otherwise unless you tell them, will they?" He slides a palm over the surface of the desk, as though he's seen some dust. "In fact, you will be working quite closely with me."

Thanom says, "Yes sir," keeping his voice flat.

"And since you'll be helping me, tell me something. At the moment, what should our objectives be?"

"I'm writing a report—"

"Don't." The slender man makes a graceful side-to-side motion with his right hand, a polite discouragement. "I know your first impulse, *everyone's* first impulse, is to write a report, but don't. Just *tell* me. Give me a sense of your prioritizing skills. What are the two things we need most to do?"

Thanom feels his face heat up and hopes he's not about to break into a sweat. "To find the person behind the murders, and to stifle speculation about the department's involvement in what Sawat did all those years ago."

"That's good, Colonel. I'd put them in the opposite order, but that's a quibble. Please," he says, pulling out the chair behind the desk and sinking into it, "sit down."

"Thank you, sir." Thanom sits in one of the two plush chairs set in front of the desk.

"Don't lean back," the slender man says. "You've had that uniform on all day."

"Yes, sir." Thanom indulges a brief mental image of leaping across the desk and twisting the other man's head off his neck.

"And, of course, those two objectives are related, aren't they? Or perhaps *tangled* would be a better word."

Thanom has no intention of volunteering anything in response to this remark, so he says, "Sir?"

"Our first objective," the slender man says, raising his eyebrows in assumed surprise, "in the order you assigned them, was finding the people who killed Sawat and Thongchai, right?"

"Yes. Sir."

He nods, waiting. When Thanom doesn't continue, he says, "Let's think this through together, shall we? Just who in your department do you trust to help you find those people?"

Thanom weighs it for a moment. "Almost no one."

"There we are. Finally." He slides the lamp a few inches closer to Thanom, as though to see him better. "You're going to need to be more candid with me if we're going to get anywhere together. To move things along, I'm going to speculate about the reason you don't trust anyone." He places two fingers against his cheek, his thumb beneath his chin. "Will that be all right?"

"It will be fascinating."

"This is all hypothetical. It's not as though I actually know anything. Are we clear on that?"

Thanom shifts in the chair. His back is getting tired. "Yes, sir."

"All right. There are two groups of people who are most likely to have killed Sawat and Thongchai, aren't there? The first are the friends or relatives of their victims."

"Yes," Thanom ventures. "The things that were said on the video, the count of women and children killed. That says *grudge murder*."

"And the second group," the slender man says, "are cops. High-ranking cops. We've all assumed since the beginning that Sawat had help from higher up and that he was sharing his very extravagant murder fees in exchange for that help. There was quite a lot of discussion about who that help might be, if you recall."

Thanom forces a smile. "I do."

"I'd be surprised if you didn't, since, when the story originally came to the public's attention, you were pretty directly in the line of fire."

Thanom feels a flare of anger in the center of his chest. He says, "Quite a few of us were."

The slender man ignores the response. "Fast forward to today. Both Sawat and Thongchai had expensive lifestyles. Security alone, for Sawat, cost tens of thousands of baht a month. And they were running out of money, or at least Sawat was; I hadn't been paying attention to Thongchai. Assuming that the speculation was true, that higher-ups *had* been profiting from what Sawat was doing, those high-ranking cops would be the people Sawat would approach for money."

"Absolutely," Thanom says.

"Making it a difficult issue to probe in the department, since you have no way of knowing who, if anyone, it was."

Thanom says nothing.

"Now, what's the third possibility? It will make me very happy if you don't disappoint me here."

"A combination," Thanom says. "Sawat hit up his former superiors for money, and the former superiors pointed the survivors of a few of Sawat's murder victims at him."

"So two out of three of our hypotheses involve someone—"

"Or several someones," Thanom says.

The slender man puts one hand on top of the other, ostentatiously waiting to see whether Thanom has another interruption in mind. "Let's not get ahead of ourselves," he says. "If we find one, he will certainly give us the others. But now you know why I said our objectives were tangled: solving the crime may cause a new scandal in the department, making the *stifling* objective, as you termed it, impossible. The last thing anyone wants."

"The best thing," Thanom says, volunteering the one thing he's certain of, "would be to wrap this up very quickly, before the press and the politicians can build momentum."

"I'd say we're forty-eight hours away from the first editorials and the first speeches calling for everything to be reopened. And it would be even less if this weren't a weekend."

Thanom says, "That's very much on my mind."

"I was sure it would be. But I don't like to take things for granted." The slender man turns his head slightly to the left, as though listening to the music, and Thanom hears the string quartet, too, and knows it isn't Mozart.

The man in white looks back to him, seeming almost surprised. "I'm sorry," he says. "Would you like something to drink?"

"No, thank you," Thanom says. "I still have work to do."

"I'm glad to hear that. Coffee, then?"

"I don't think so."

"Fine," he says. "We need to wrap this up quickly. First, catch the murderers of Sawat and Thongchai. That should be fairly easy, since they gave us details about the crimes they were avenging, and we've got their photos. I'd like you to handle that end of things."

"Yes, sir."

"Within the department—well, that's more delicate. So now you're going to learn why I took the camera and deleted the photographs you copied. When I asked you whether you saw anyone else in the pictures, you had a moment of doubt, didn't you?"

"I only got to look at them three times."

"Well, imagine how much doubt there will be among those who haven't seen them. So I'm going to set up a trapdoor spider."

"Ahh," Thanom says. He has no idea what a trapdoor spider is.

"I'm putting the pictures on the department computer, behind a password. Beginning an hour from now, I'm going to give you lists of officers who were plausibly close to Sawat, five at a time. You're going to circulate some sort of summary, on an eyes-only basis, of what's going on—just the boy, the girl, the iPhone, things that are already scuttlebutt—and you'll include the password somewhere in the document. If anyone is interested enough to log in to look at the pictures, the trapdoor will open and the spider will scuttle out and grab the identifying data from that computer."

Thanom says, "Some people might look just for curiosity's sake."

"I know that," the slender man says, and the sudden rigidity of his face reminds Thanom forcefully that he's not accustomed to being questioned. "We'll get some false bites," he says. "But do you think anyone who actually was involved could resist it?"

"Probably not."

"So those who *do* resist it—we'll be able to eliminate them, won't we?"

"Yes, sir. Very clever, sir."

"But? I can hear the *but*."

Thanom takes a deep breath and dives in. "But even those who do look—it won't prove anything."

"Maybe, maybe not. Worst case? Half the department looks at the pictures, you catch the murderers, and they have no idea who hired them, they were hired through a go-between, and we're at a dead end." He leans back in his chair and folds his hands over his flat stomach, an oddly vulnerable position, Thanom thinks. "But here's the bottom line, Colonel. No matter what happens we will solve this within seventy-two hours one way or the other, and if it proves to be *the other*, I need to know now that you're with me." He lowers his head and gazes at Thanom over the gray glasses, revealing eyes that look as though they've seen everything a thousand times, and with very little interest. "If we must, we will arrange a solution."

"We," Thanom says, "meaning you and I."

"Is the department worth protecting?"

"Yes, sir."

"Does it seem to you that working with me on this might actually be—helpful to your career?"

Thanom isn't sure he'll survive the collaboration, much less benefit from it. "I haven't thought about it."

"Really. If that's true, I'm dismayed. But now that I've raised it, what do you think?"

"A mentor is always helpful," Thanom says neutrally. "But how could I assist you?"

"There's an odd bit of synchronicity here, isn't there? One of the people who had the phone is the daughter of a good friend of an officer in your department. An officer who was positioned perfectly to have helped Sawat six years ago. An officer at whom some fingers were actually pointed back then. That's the kind of thing I'd call interesting. *And*," he says, the eyes over the top edge of the glasses fixed squarely on Thanom's, "an officer who was able to manipulate the, um, department so that the lip-reader who saw the surveillance tapes was his, his—whatever she is to him. Quite a *lot* of synchronicity when you think about it."

Thanom feels an unexpected pang for Arthit. "I suppose it is. But people know how the little girl got involved—"

"Details," the slender man says. "Details are infinitely elastic. This officer was there when Sawat and Thongchai commissioned the original killings, he's here now, and he has connections with the phone that could be made to look like more." He spreads his hands, a man who is saying something that should be self-evident. "Certainly the best way for the department to deflect inquiries would be to offer up one of our own as a responsible party. Fall on our own swords, so to speak. The opposite of a cover-up."

"Yes, sir."

"Do you think you're likely to need more guidance?"

"I know what to do. Try to find the men in the photos, circulate your memos and then stand back, if necessary."

"Good, then." The slender man stands. "You'll be wanting to get back to work now."

23

Sunday

ALL NIGHT LONG, as he tries to get to sleep, Rafferty hears Miaow.

Hears her door open and close. Hears her footsteps. Hears the toilet flush, the water run. Hears the tinny voices of some cosplay drama she follows on YouTube.

Keeps listening for the ringtone of her phone, Andrew sneaking a call in the dark.

Just before he finally drops off, around four, he sees the hallway light go on, a yellow strip beneath the door. He holds his breath, hoping she'll come in, but a moment later the light goes off again, and then he's asleep.

So by the time he gets up, about eight A.M., Sunday already seems a week long.

He wraps himself in his ratty robe, laundered until it has holes in it, and goes to Miaow's door to listen but hears nothing. There must be something he can say to her, something that won't just be cosmetic. *Cosmetic*, he knows from five years' experience with her, won't fly. Moving lightly, he heads for the kitchen, where he tosses the Growing Younger Man's box of goop in the trash and takes advantage of temporarily being able to find everything to make pancakes, which are the only things, other than an orange and a Diet Coke, Miaow will eat for breakfast. He creates an especially high stack, centers it on a plate, drenches it in syrup, goes down the hall, and knocks very lightly on her door.

Miaow says, "I don't want any." She sounds sniffly.

"Well," he says. "You know. If you get hungry or anything."

"If I get hungry," Miaow says through the door, "I'll phone you."

"Okay," he says. He's halfway down the hall when he hears something hit the wall in her room.

In their bedroom, Rose is deep in the special sleep that Thai women invented and own exclusively, a sleep so deep Rafferty believes he could change the sheets without disturbing her. He sneaks a kiss and goes back out into the living room, once again unaware that he's sighing. The huge dark rectangle of the television screen dominates the room; it's like waking up and finding a car parked in front of the couch. His little desk and chair seem to be hiding behind it, as though he's been banished from his own living room. He briefly considers sulking at his desk, but instead he pulls out a stool at the kitchen counter and eats Miaow's pancakes.

The second time he fires up the coffee grinder, Rose pads out of the bedroom, her hair a tangle so glorious it suggests to Rafferty some new and alien mathematics governing physical reality. She says, in her unused morning baritone, "Is my water hot?"

"Half a minute," he says, turning on the burner and feeling useful at last.

There are mornings, Rafferty thinks, that Rose is actually still asleep for the first ten or fifteen minutes she's moving around. This seems to be one of them. She rests one hand on the counter, dead center in a spill of maple syrup, her eyes half closed, just staring at the teapot. As he measures out the Nescafé, he sees her lift her hand from the counter, look down at it, sniff her fingers, and then lick the syrup off them.

"Pancakes?" he says.

She says, "Coffee."

"Got it." He pours water in, gives it the approved triple-stir, and hands it to her.

She says, "Miaow?"

"In her room."

"Mmmmm," she says, but it's in response to the taste of the coffee. She blinks a couple of times, swallows again, and says, "She'll come out."

"Women are harder on women than men are."

"I won't argue with that." She looks down into the cup, says, "More, please," and drains it. When he's taken the cup from her hand, she trails an index finger through the spill of syrup, licks it again, and says, "I'm going to whisper now."

"Hang on." He's scooping the spoon through the Nescafé again. "Either that or come over here and whisper."

"I'll wait here."

"You sure you don't want to try my coffee?"

"How long have we been together?"

"Five years? Six?"

"Have I ever wanted to try your coffee?"

"No."

"Well," she says, "thank you for thinking I'm capable of changing."

He hands her the cup. She takes a long pull, squinting at him through the steam, and whispers, "We need to get a bigger apartment."

"For whom? Is your mother coming? I'll sleep on the couch."

"Not for my mother. For—" She pats her belly.

He says, "That's nine months—wait. Are you seriously telling me you're going to sleep in a different room from—you know, the, ummm—" He puts a palm on her stomach, and she covers it with her hand and presses it gently against her, and his knees go a little rubbery. Her skin always seems to him to be a different temperature than anyone else's.

"No," she says. "But you may want to."

"I'm probably flattering myself," Rafferty says, sliding his hand over the smooth plane of her belly, "but I think we're in this together."

"And then, later," Rose says. She takes his hand and lifts it to her face and presses her cheek against his palm. "We're not going to put the baby into Miaow's room."

"That's *two years* from now."

"And we have all this money," Rose says. She nips the tip of his little finger with a sleepy amusement in her eyes that suggests they might be a moment or two away from going back to bed.

He's leaning forward to kiss her when Miaow comes out of the hallway, glances at them the way Rafferty might locate something he doesn't want to trip over, and opens the refrigerator.

"And," Rose says in a normal tone of voice, "the television is too big for this apartment."

Watching Miaow's rigid back as she pulls out a can of Diet Coke, Rafferty says, "Then let's get rid of the television."

Miaow leaves the kitchen with the refrigerator door wide open. Her bedroom door closes.

Rose gives the refrigerator door a push and says, "She's definitely going to want her own room."

Rafferty's cell phone rings on the counter. A man's voice says, "This is Nguyen. We need to talk."

ANNA IS MASSAGING Arthit's back on the bed, using her left elbow to torment one of the muscles that's in spasm, when the phone rings. Grateful for the interruption, he starts to get up.

"Where are you going?" she asks.

"My phone."

"Let it ring."

"It might be something important."

"Your back is important," she says.

"It'll wait." The phone is on the dresser, and the display says THANOM.

"Yes, sir."

"Sorry to bother you on the weekend," Thanom says.

The new Thanom, equipped with apologies and what seems

like a genuinely uncertain tone, makes Arthit uneasy. "Not a problem."

"I need to put you on identifying the killers. The men on the phone."

"I haven't seen the men on the phone."

"Doesn't matter. I want you to work back from the victims."

Arthit says, "Which victims?"

"The victims the killer described in the video. The ones he was avenging."

Arthit allows himself to grin at the phone. "I don't know what he said."

"You don't? You mean Dr.— Dr.—"

"Chaibancha."

"Yes, thank you. Dr. Chaibancha didn't tell you what he said?"

"You ordered her not to."

Arthit can almost see his boss glaring at the phone, chewing on his lower lip and weighing the probability that he's being made fun of. "I order people to do a lot of things," Thanom finally says. "That doesn't mean they do them."

"Well," Arthit lies, "she did."

"What he said to Sawat was 'Two women, three children.' And the second time, to Thongchai, he said, 'One woman, two children.'"

"Women and children. Got it."

"I want you to find those murders in the database. There can't be many with that precise victim count. You'll probably know them when you see them. They'll have something in common, something that points at Sawat."

"Right." Anna, who has been smoothing the covers on the bed, makes a rolling gesture with her hand that means *hurry up*.

Arthit holds up a hand. On the other end of the line, Thanom hasn't even paused. "I'm arranging for you to use the computers at a station outside Bangkok. It's a few hours' drive, but no one will be looking over your shoulder. I'll email you the information."

Anna is watching him, her forehead furrowed in what looks like puzzlement. He feels the same expression on his own forehead and smoothes it out. "Yes, sir. Tomorrow?"

"First thing. And you'll communicate with me only directly. No emails, no voice mails except to tell me to call you back."

"Yes, sir."

"Thank you."

As Arthit puts the phone down, Anna tilts her head slightly, a question.

"I have the feeling," Arthit says, "that I'm being gotten out of the way."

BOO'S OFFICE OCCUPIES a windowless corner in an unpainted concrete building that adjoins Father Bill's First Home center for Bangkok's homeless children. The office isn't much—its third and fourth walls are a pair of white screens loaned by the same hospital that furnishes the hospital bed and the almost-nurse—but there are still days, after all his years on the street, when he can't believe it's his.

He has a small desk and three chairs—reserving the comfortable one for himself—plus an ancient, cracked-screen laptop and a broken table fan that he keeps on top of the desk because he thinks it makes him look prosperous. Behind the desk is a wheeled whiteboard that's supposed to be filled with to-do lists, but kids come in when he's not here and decorate it with doodles.

He's no longer the sullen, amphetamine-addicted street child whom Miaow dragged home to Rafferty, trying to repay him for having protected her when she was left on the sidewalk to live or die. He's tall and handsome now, with shining shoulder-length hair and an effortless air of competence. After years of commanding street gangs and then helping other street children escape the sidewalks, he's now—at the age of sixteen—been given probationary control of a rundown, dirty, badly ventilated building, two stories high and swarming with mice, that adjoins First Home, a substantial shelter and school that feeds and educates Thailand's poorest children.

Father Bill, the priest who runs First Home with Old Testament firmness, regards Boo as an experiment, the goal of which is to find a way to open his sanctuary to some of Bangkok's more dangerous street kids—kids who have stayed alive by committing occasionally violent crimes. In the ten months Boo has been here, he's had as many as thirty kids sleeping in the building at a time, boys downstairs and girls on the second floor. So far only nine of them have made it into First Home.

Boo worries about the kids, but he's worried about himself, too. A couple of years ago, he rescued a 17-year-old girl named Da who had been put on the street by a high-ranking gangster to beg. At the last moment, the gangster had handed Da an infant—women with babies earn more—so when Boo snatched her from the gang, he took the baby, too. And now, he supposes, they've become a family. He's being paid almost nothing at First Home, but he and Da and the child need every penny of it.

Which makes him even more anxious that in the ten months since Father Bill gave him the space and the opportunity to prove himself, more than half of the kids Boo has lassoed into staying there have melted back onto the streets, and most of the others have accepted the meals and the bed but declined the school and the other activities that the priest regards as minimum commitments for formal admission to First Home. Sooner or later, these kids disappear, too. Boo is on trial.

And now this.

The young black American woman sitting opposite him is not coping well with the heat; the underarms of her short-sleeved blouse are soaked, and a bead of sweat wobbles at the tip of her nose. Boo wouldn't dream of laughing at her, though; he admires *Khun* Katherine far too much for that. She came all the way from America to work with Father Bill's castaway kids, and no one puts in longer days than she does.

"She's out of danger," Katherine says in her slow, careful, badly pronounced Thai. He could speak English to her, but she insists on Thai, and she's gotten better even in the time Boo has been here. She's taken the chair closest on the other side of the desk, having been in the office often enough to avoid the one that wobbles. "Her fever is gone, her vital signs are good. She might even have gained a little weight. If she'd chew and swallow something, we wouldn't have to keep her attached to the IV. There'd be no reason for her to stay in that hospital bed."

"Except that there's nowhere else," Boo says.

"You can't keep her sedated and handcuffed forever."

"She's tried to harm herself. And *has* hurt others. She gouged the faces of the two guys who brought her in."

"I walked her to the bathroom this morning," Katherine said.

He blinks. "You should have asked me."

"She had to *go*, Boo. The boy was there, so I couldn't give her the bedpan."

"What boy?"

"That sweet little one with the awful teeth."

Boo thinks for a moment. "Noo."

"That's not what his girlfriend calls him. Noo? You mean, like *rat*? What a terrible nickname."

Boo puts his elbows on his desk and rubs his eyes. There's no point in pretending he understands anything she's saying. "His girlfriend?"

"The one who was with him when he found the patient."

"Chalee," Boo says. "She calls him Dok. So, you couldn't use a bedpan because Dok was in the room. Why were Dok and Chalee in—"

"They're always in there."

"They've been skipping school?" Classes are offered six days a week, including Saturday.

"They take turns. The one who goes catches the other one up. Did you know that Chalee can draw?"

"What? Who cares?" He pauses. One of Katherine's responsibilities is the relationship between Father Bill and the hospital that donates medical supplies and the beds; there's no point in alienating her. "Has—has she talked to them?"

"No. But she likes them."

"You don't know that. All you know is that she hasn't tried to kill them yet."

"She lets Dok sleep on the bed."

Boo brings his palms down on the desk. The noise is louder than he expected it to be. "Why don't I know about this?"

"They've been with her practically ever since she—"

"They're spending the *night* in her room? I do a bed check every night, and they've been here."

"You thought they were here the night they found her, too," Katherine says, and then she laughs, and, after a second, Boo joins in.

"They're with her now?"

"Always," Katherine says patiently. "That's why I couldn't use the bedpan. And I wanted to take her for a walk."

"So you unhandcuffed her, too. She might have hurt you."

"She was calm," Katherine says. "She's better with women."

"She's better with women," Boo repeats mechanically, but he's thinking, *She was calm?* "You talked to her?"

"Sure. All the way to the bathroom and back. All she did was look around. She sniffed the air a few times, like an animal."

"And then you handcuffed her again. She didn't fight you?"

"She put her arms on the railings of the bed and looked at the ceiling. She doesn't need to be in a hospital bed, although she won't want to part with Dok and Chalee."

"But she won't *eat*. And how can you be sure she won't hurt herself?"

"Boo, we need that bed. We have two sick kids inside the compound. I know you hate to lose any of them. But this girl is twelve or thirteen. She's not an infant who can't meet her own needs, she's—"

"Meet her own needs? She won't even eat."

"She can't get the care she needs here," Katherine says. "Maybe she should go to an institution."

Boo says, "I thought this was an institution."

"Where she can get medical help. Emotional help. She hasn't spoken a word, she won't meet your eyes, she's borderline suicidal, which is probably why she won't eat. These aren't the normal street-kid problems."

"I've had kids almost this bad before," Boo says, although it's not actually true. "The best help for kids is other kids. She'll stay here." Katherine mops her forehead with the tail of her blouse, which is already soaked, and Boo watches her suffer the heat with a tiny bit of satisfaction. "But she needs the bed just a little longer. I can't trust her around the other kids yet."

"She's getting along with—with Chalee and Dok." Katherine puts her hands on the arms of her chair. "Come on. She's awake now. The kids are with her. Just come take a look."

Boo gets up unwillingly and follows her through the gap in the partitions that defines his doorway and across the boys' dormitory—empty in the daytime and with blankets and sheets on only a melancholy seven cots—and out of the building. They're no sooner in the blinding sunlight than Chalee almost runs into them, Dok hurrying just a few steps behind her.

"Boo, Boo," Chalee says, grabbing his wrist and practically swinging from it.

Dok says, "She *said* something."

"What?"

"Not Thai," Chalee says. "Sounded like—" She closes her eyes to concentrate, but then she opens them again and waves Dok to her. When he's next to her, she whispers in his ear. Dok screws up his face, his rat-teeth gleaming in the sun, and shakes his head. Chalee stamps her foot impatiently and whispers again into Dok's ear, and Dok gives her a huge smile.

Proudly, Chalee says to Boo, "She said, *Poke*."

* * *

ANDREW'S FATHER WEARS slacks and a long-sleeve knit shirt, buttoned almost to the neck, and he manages to make it look like a uniform. His receding hair is combed back and wet-looking. Even standing in Poke's doorway, he has the bearing of a soldier.

His face is uncomfortably stiff. Poke thinks, with a sinking feeling, *He's embarrassed.*

"Mr. Nguyen." He steps aside without actually inviting Nguyen in, and after an awkward moment, Nguyen comes through the door.

He lets his eyes travel over the living room, tiny compared to the Nguyen apartment. His gaze pauses at the enormous television set, which in Poke's class-conscious imagination, screams *nouveau riche*, and halts when it settles on Rose, immaculate on the couch in a long-sleeve coral shirt that gives her the blush of a nectarine.

Nguyen bows slightly. "Mrs. Rafferty."

Rose says, to Poke, "Will this take long?" From Rose, that's breathtakingly rude.

Small red spots bloom on Nguyen's cheekbones.

"Will it?" Rafferty asks.

"I wanted to apologize—" Nguyen begins.

"Ahh, well, if *that's* why you're here, let's get the person you owe the apology to." He raises his voice. "Miaow. Andrew's father is here."

They hear her bedroom door open, and a moment later she's standing at the end of the hallway. Her hands are clapped to her sides like those of someone standing at attention. Her lips are pressed together so tightly they look like they've been sewn shut, and the tilt of her head has something imperious in it, but her eyes are the eyes of someone expecting a slap.

"I'm here to say I'm sorry," Nguyen says. "You have to believe that I admire your courage, young lady, and that I know—because Andrew has made certain that I know—that you saved him from something dangerous yesterday." He stops, looking like he's lost his place.

The line of Miaow's mouth hardens in a way that doesn't suggest that she appreciates the sentiment, but her eyes don't waver.

"I spoke to you yesterday in a way I shouldn't have. I owed you thanks, not rudeness. I apologize for that."

Miaow says, "*But.*"

Nguyen holds her gaze. Miaow's head still tilts upward as the silence stretches out, but then she brings up her right palm, brusquely wipes her eyes with it, and turns and goes back down the hallway.

Rafferty hears the phone in her bedroom play the final chord of "A Day in the Life." Miaow accelerates, but not much, and closes the door behind her.

Rafferty and Nguyen look down the hallway. Rose leans her head back against the wall behind the couch and closes her eyes.

Rafferty says, "But."

Nguyen says, "Andrew is my only child. His future is more important to me than my own." He puts his hands in his pockets and immediately takes them out again. "He needs to be around girls who are—"

"Upper class," Rafferty suggests.

"Vietnamese," Nguyen says.

"Right," Rafferty says. "Well, now that you've soothed your conscience—"

"I'm an only son," Nguyen says. "Andrew is an only son. That's a burden for a Vietnamese family, especially one like mine. If he had an older brother, if—if—" He waves the thought away. "And we're only going to be stationed in Bangkok one more year . . . They'd have to separate then, anyway. It's probably better that they say goodbye now, before they grow—fonder of each other. It could be very difficult for both of them, if they—"

Rafferty jumps at the *bang* of the door to Miaow's room being thrown open, hard enough for the knob to punch a hole in the wall.

Miaow marches into the living room and past Nguyen to the door as though the room were empty. She opens the front door.

Rafferty says, "Where are you going?"

She says, "Somewhere else," and slams the door behind her.

Rose says to Nguyen, "Are you finished?"

He says, "I *am* sorry."

"Wait," Rose says. "Only one elevator is working. She doesn't want to be with you."

In the bedroom, Rose's phone begins to ring. She gets up, and Nguyen's eyes follow her as she leaves the room.

"Count of five," Rafferty says. "One. Two." He goes to the front door. "Three. Four." On "Five," he pulls the door open, looks out, and says, "Coast clear. Goodbye."

Nguyen nods and goes out into the hallway, and when Rafferty closes the door and turns around, he sees Rose, her hands tight on the phone.

"It's my mother," she says. "I haven't talked to her today, so she didn't know we weren't going to tell Miaow about the baby."

Rafferty says, "Oh, no."

"She called just now to ask Miaow if she was excited about being an older sister. Miaow hung up on her."

Rafferty says, "Where would she go?" With a cold spasm of panic, he remembers Arthit saying to keep her home on Sunday, and on the kitchen counter, his phone rings.

"She could be anywhere in Bangkok," Rose says. "You'd better get that," and Rafferty skids across the floor to pick it up. It says ARTHIT.

"I think we need to talk," Arthit says. "They're sending me out of Bangkok, and I haven't heard anything new about the phone."

"Arthit—" Poke begins, but the phone bleats to announce a call waiting. An unknown number. "I'll call you right back." He touches the screen to accept the call.

"Mr. Rafferty?" says a voice Poke hasn't heard in more than two years. "This is Boo."

Part Three
DROWNING GIRLS

24

One Girl Down There Somewhere

VIOLET SKY TO the west. To the east, the hard white diamond of the evening star, punching a hole in the dark. The tatter of bats in flight. The same sky that's hung above this swampy bend in the Chao Phraya River for hundreds of thousands of years.

On the curving banks of the river, a city that's been the capital of Thailand under several names, most recently, *Krung Thep Maha Nakon*, known to the world as Bangkok. Like the ever-expanding boundaries of the town, the city's history has been fluid and often directed by its sheer, obliging adaptability; the name *Bangkok* has no clear meaning in Thai and may have been adopted formally as the city's name simply as a convenience for the foreigners who misheard and mispronounced one of the town's colloquial names, *Bang ko*. The town exploded in an influx of foreign money in the 1980s, and exploded again more recently as poverty and the breakdown of community structures in the countryside have swelled the population to an estimated ten million, and as many as twelve million at the peak of the workday.

Ten to twelve million people. A thousand miles of sidewalk beneath the bat-specked, purpling sky. One girl down there somewhere.

* * *

RAFFERTY AND ROSE are in a cab, heading for Arthit's house, when Rose says, "Call Boo back now. If anybody can find her, he can."

Rafferty says, "I'm not thinking clearly," and hits *redial*.

WHEN ARTHIT OPENS the door, Rose hugs him so hard he huffs like someone who's been hit in the stomach. She lets go of him and steps back, blinking tears away. Rafferty throws an arm around Arthit's shoulders, and Arthit turns to lead them into the house.

"Boo might be coming, too," Rafferty says, and then they're in the living room, and in its dead center, standing very straight, with her hands crossed formally in front of her, is Anna. She's wearing business clothes: a jacket and matching slacks, every crease sharp, and Rafferty understands immediately that she's dressed up for this meeting. She looks at Arthit as though seeking reassurance and then blinks heavily and directs her eyes to Poke.

But Rose takes control of the moment, saying, in Thai, "Hello. I'm Rose." She looks around the room and says, "You've made this room even more beautiful."

Anna, her eyes sharp with the embarrassment of speaking aloud, says, "Thank you."

Now that Rose has opened the door, Poke can say, more or less naturally, "Hello, Anna."

Anna keeps her hands in front of her and makes a very small bow, almost Japanese-style, from the waist, and then opens her hands and lifts them in a *wai*, just beneath her chin. Rafferty sees it as a request for forgiveness, or at the least as a plea for him to pretend forgiveness.

"We're all friends," he says. "It's good to see you."

The four of them stand there for a moment, Arthit shifting a bit, and Rose says, to Anna, "Our daughter has run away." Her tone is light enough to draw a glance from Rafferty.

"She's been through a lot," Rafferty says.

Anna reaches into the pocket of her jacket and pulls out the familiar pad with the blue cards, writes quickly, and shows it to Rose. *My son is difficult, too.* Then she says aloud. "Please. Sit down."

"How old?" Rose asks.

Anna practices the word silently once, lips only, and then says, "Twelve."

"Then you know all about it. I don't want to trouble you, but I know Poke would like some coffee," Rose says. "Poke always wants coffee. Maybe I could help you?" She loops an elbow under Anna's arm and more or less hauls her into the kitchen. A moment later, Rafferty hears Anna laugh.

"Rose is surprisingly light-hearted," Rafferty says.

"You have no idea how she's feeling," Arthit says. "Right now, she's being an angel and making friends with Anna."

"Still, she's pretty chipper, considering what we just went through." He tells Arthit about Nguyen's visit and the call from Rose's mother. "I suppose I should be grateful Miaow just left, instead of jumping off the balcony."

Arthit sits on the couch and waits for Rafferty to settle himself into his usual chair, and then he says, "I don't know how I can help you. I mean, I could give you the children-are-resilient speech, but I have no idea how resilient children are or aren't."

"Well, I'm not really looking for parental guidance."

"So here's the other bad news. I don't think we should involve the cops."

"Really," Rafferty says, his heart sinking at Arthit's tone. "Tell me about that."

"Things feel bad." Arthit puts his hands palm-to-palm and squeezes them between his thighs, rocking forward a little as though he's cold. "Thanom made a big deal out of pulling me into what was supposed to be a tight little circle of people who would be involved in this case. And now he's sending me hours away to look into the murders the people who killed Sawat are supposedly avenging."

"Maybe he's just worried that it'll leak if you're doing it closer to home."

"No one has seen the surveillance tapes. They've vanished. That means that almost nobody knows what those combinations of murdered women and children mean. I could search for them all day long, and not even someone who looked over my shoulder would know what I was working on. And now he's quarantined Andrew's iPhone, too."

"What does that mean?"

"It means that it's essentially vanished, just like the tapes. This isn't about keeping the investigation tight, Poke, it's about controlling it. And from the moment I learned it was Sawat who'd been killed, I've been waiting for Thanom to get yanked off the case."

"Why?"

"Because he was Sawat's and Thongchai's boss. And they were both dirty. So how does it look from outside that Thanom's been put in charge of the investigation?"

"Like a fix."

"Doesn't it." Arthit sits back, closes his eyes, and massages the bridge of his short, wide nose. "How much do you know about what Sawat was pulling?"

"Murder for hire. It happened just before I got here."

"Let's pretend you don't know anything, and I'll start at the beginning. It'll explain why I don't want to get the department involved in looking for Miaow." He opens his eyes and looks around the room as though he's surprised at how much it's changed. "You *are* going to find her, you know."

"Actually, Rose thinks she'll come home before we do. I'm not sure enough of that to relax. But how could the thing with Sawat affect Miaow?"

Arthit raises a hand. "Give me two minutes to sketch the background. Beginning about twelve years ago we had a spike in murders of people with a lot of money. It continued for roughly five years. There were ten murders—ten that we identified, anyway. A statistically unlikely increase, since most murder victims tend to be lower income."

"All right."

"A couple of other things were statistically unlikely. First, the solution rate was one hundred percent. For another, they were bang-up, textbook-perfect cases. We had eyewitnesses, we had arrests, and we had confessions. And finally, one cop solved a remarkable number of them. Sawat."

"I missed most of this. He got fired but not brought to trial."

"The cases were closed, officially. And he was sort of a hero at the time. You wouldn't know it to look at a recent picture, but he had a great smile. Sherlock Holmes, with good teeth. He got fan mail."

A coffee grinder makes its gravel-chewing noise in the kitchen, and Rose laughs.

"So we had a hero cop, and that caused a certain amount of jealousy. Two officers who felt resentful, or saw their careers endangered, started looking at a few of the cases more carefully. And they found a couple of very interesting things. First, two of the people convicted of these murders got released quite early, four or five years into their sentences, and they seemed to have a surprising amount of money. Second, it turned out that one of the eyewitnesses was being booked for a minor crime at the time he was supposed to have seen the killing."

Poke says, "That's embarrassing."

"And these cops told some reporters. The reporters investigated further and their editors went to the opposition politicians they supported, and between the newspaper stories and the opposition's calls for an investigation, it took about three weeks for everything to fall apart. Speaking privately to us, the people who had been convicted admitted they'd been paid to confess, the witnesses said they'd been threatened or paid to testify. Even a couple of prosecutors admitted they'd been given what they called 'special preparation' by Sawat and his men."

"Full-service package."

"That's why it cost so much. You paid for the hit, you paid for the witnesses, you paid for the person who got convicted. And, of course, you paid for Sawat and Thongchai, who handled the cops who actually did the killings. Still, at two to three million baht for each killing, you got your murder done and it looked safe as a glass of milk. Case closed. No questions, ever. And he pulled this off ten times that we know of, so we're talking about more than twenty-five million Baht."

Rafferty does the math in his head. "Around three-quarters of a million dollars."

Arthit looks past Rafferty, as though embarrassed. "And we shut it down internally, no trial, just fired Sawat and Thongchai, in disgrace, with nothing proved. That took a lot of muscle from someone, but it was worth it because *obviously*, other cops were involved, some of them considerably above Sawat in rank. One unavoidable suspect was Thanom. But he dodged it—and now they're leaving him on Sawat's murder. And that suggests one of two things: first, that someone higher in the department than Thanom, who has a low opinion of his skills, ordered the murders of Sawat and Thongchai—maybe got to the grieving relatives and gave them the phone somehow—and he feels safe with Thanom in charge."

"Why kill Sawat?"

Arthit shrugs. "Because he was getting out of line? I don't know. He didn't go to prison, impossible as that may be to believe. Maybe, all these years later, he was demanding money or something, threatening to reveal just who actually kept the lion's share of the fees. And that person is actually running this investigation and he's leaving it with Thanom because, well, he's Thanom, and he's not very capable. Or—and here's the other interpretation— Thanom has been assigned to handle it this way because he's being set up for it. He's the perfect fall guy for the whole thing. The plan is probably to catch the guys who chased Miaow and Andrew and kill them, and then promptly arrest Thanom and say look, we've handled everything. Case closed, Big Bad Wolf pinched."

Rafferty says, "It's like the Kremlin. I don't know how you work there."

Arthit leans forward for emphasis. "Same reason as a lot of cops. Once in a while, you get to do the right thing."

The kitchen door opens and Rose and Anna come through. They're holding hands, although Anna looks slightly startled about it. Rose says, "Coffee in a minute. Solving anything?"

"We're just trying to get our arms around it," Rafferty says.

"And to continue with my larger point," Arthit says. He squeezes his eyes shut and blows out some air. "I do *not* think it's a good idea to get the department involved right now. I don't know how Miaow might figure into the plans of whoever is running this. The phone has disappeared, and she and Andrew are the only people outside the department who saw the photos. If this is a cover-up, and it looks like it, the two of them are loose ends."

Rose drops Anna's hand.

"That's what I needed to say," Arthit says. "But I don't want to get you any more worried than you need to be."

Poke says, "I don't think I *could* be more worried."

25

I've Changed, But I Haven't Changed Into Anything

THE CURB FEELS different than it used to. And it's not solely
because she's bigger, although she'd been surprised, when she first
sat down, by the fact that her knees folded so sharply and were too
high for her to cross her arms on, the way she used to do.

The pavement is harder, too. Even though she's gained all
the weight that almost trapped Andrew and her in that air
duct, the concrete presses uncomfortably on her sit-bones.

It's not exactly a surprise that she doesn't fit here any more.
Where in the *world* did she think she was going when she made
her grand dramatic exit? What was she expecting? Gasps? Horri-
fied protest? Two minutes later, Rose was probably imitating her.

Did she think she was going back onto the street? To some
friend's house? The only friend she's really made in the whole
world is Andrew, and she doesn't fit at Andrew's house, either.

And she won't fit at school, not that she ever really did. He'll
talk about this sooner or later, she's certain. It's the most exciting
thing that's ever happened to him, judging from the stories he's
told her about his life. So he'll talk about it and there won't be any
more Mia Rafferty.

Mia was obviously a pretty thin mask. But it was the one she made
and forced on people, and she's stuck now with what those people see
when it slips off. Someone who isn't good enough to be herself.

A bus roars by, less than half a meter from her feet, and she pinches her nose closed and breathes through her mouth in self-defense. No, she's definitely not who she was then, back on the street. *That* girl breathed exhaust like fresh spring breezes. That girl could have taken care of herself out here.

She thinks, *We all float until we sink.*

She doesn't even have her secret money. After paying for Andrew's stupid phone and a few other things, she's got only about 700 baht. She's blinking against the bus exhaust, and then she realizes she's not blinking against the exhaust at all, and she just lets herself cry. She's quiet about it, no loud, gulping sobs that would get the attention of the people crowding by on the sidewalk behind her, but crying nonetheless, until it seems to her that all she's done recently is cry, and that's about enough of it.

She wipes her face with her forearm, hoping it looks like she's mopping sweat, and instantly thinks, *No one is looking at me. No one ever looks at me. If I'd just realized that, I wouldn't have pretended to be someone else.*

But now she's stuck with all those lies. Stuck with being Miaow.

Stuck with being a big sister to a baby. Poke and Rose's *real* baby. She's wanted a television forever, and they bought it for a baby who's not even here yet.

She thinks, in so many words, *I'm feeling sorry for myself.*

The world flickers and blinks on. She's sitting on a curb on Sukhumvit, between the tented tables of two vendors. Their fluorescent tubes have buzzed into life, putting a sparkle on the cheap watches and the cheap clothes, picking out the names of the cheap generic drugs from China printed in faded ink on the cheap boxes, brightening all these useless, ugly things.

And creating a pool of relative darkness for her to huddle in. Behind her, tourists push up and down the sidewalk, speaking every language in the world and probably saying nothing. There are a lot of Arabs in this area of Sukhumvit, both immigrants who have opened shops here and tourists staying at the nearby Grace Hotel with its Arab clientele. The men are either fashionably three-day unshaven or bristling with assertive facial hair, the women like black cut-outs, the little boys acting like emperors in spite of their big, soft eyes.

She doesn't think she'll lose Poke. She knows that the baby won't change Poke. He'll go on loving her because he told her he would when he took her in, and he always does what he says, the chump. The problem is Rose, Rose who is growing her own child inside her own body, and what love could be stronger than that? It will be in there for months, sharing Rose's blood and breath, assembling itself from her beneath her skin, beneath the caressing palms of her hands. As long as it lives, it will be someone made of Rose. How could Rose's feelings *not* change? And it's been mostly Rose's love that she's been basking in all these years. Now she'll be the ugly step-sister, the one who's always so hateful in the fairy tales. There will be the real baby—the one Rose made herself—and the one she found in the street. The other one.

And when were they going to *tell* her? If they hadn't known it would hurt her, they would have told her right away. For all she knows, they found out *weeks* ago. They lied to her because they knew the news would make her feel like the unattractive, not-very-smart girl they adopted before they found out they could have their *own* children.

The sound level from the sidewalk drops. She smells cologne.

She turns her head as little as possible and looks at the brown-clad legs of a policeman. Her stomach clenches instinctively, but she forces herself to look up. He's probably there to write some foreigner a 2000-baht ticket for dropping a cigarette on the sidewalk. She's expecting him to wave her away, but he just nods down at her and goes back to looking at something on the opposite sidewalk.

Automatically, she reaches up to smooth the hair on either side of her part, and is startled to feel the stiff, uneven chop. *If I needed any more proof that I'm not who I was,* Miaow thinks, *this cop would be it.* She's no longer the girl a policeman would automatically chase away unless he'd been bribed by some godfather to let her beg or sell flowers. For years she had either run away from the cops or paid the crooks.

It's my clothes, she thinks. But what she's wearing is ordinary enough, a pair of jeans and a T-shirt with an angry duck on it. A street kid could wear these clothes. But they probably wouldn't be so clean. And her shoes are new, sort of.

So what? Even a street kid could steal a new pair of shoes. *I have changed*, she thinks, *but I haven't changed into anything. I'm halfway between this and that. I'm not really anything.*

The evening is still hot, but she feels cold. And small and dark and forgettable. Someone who isn't anybody, who may never be anybody.

It was *stupid* to walk out of the apartment. Now she'll have to slink back in, and they'll act like she just went out for an ice cream, and so will she. Nobody will tell the truth.

Her cell phone vibrates in her pocket, and she grabs for it. It can't be Andrew, she knows, he doesn't have a phone now, but still—

It's Rose.

A little bubble pops in the region of her heart. Poke has called twice, but this time it's Rose. It's *Rose*, calling her.

She's on the sidewalk, feeling lighter than air, weaving between people, before she realizes she's even gotten up. Stepping down from the curb at a corner, she automatically registers that she's crossing Soi 7. Cars are at a dead stop on Sukhumvit, and motorcycle taxis thread their way between lanes. By the time the light changes up there, there will be a herd of motorbikes, maybe a hundred of them, racing their motors in front of the cars. Poke had used that traffic pattern once to explain to her how sediments form at the bottom of the ocean, with the smallest particles filtering down through the bigger ones to form clays, just like the motorbikes weave between . . .

How much time has Poke spent explaining things to her?

She should call Rose back. But not yet.

Stepping up onto the curb on the far side of Soi 7, she gets a little itch between her shoulder blades, an itch that makes her want to look behind her. So she's been wrong. Her instincts have dulled. Someone *is* looking at her.

Just to her right, bathed in a chalky fluorescent glare, is a booth selling bootlegged DVDs. Colored sleeves for the current titles are thumb-tacked to the back wall. Hundreds of others are clipped together into thick stacks for customers to flip through.

She stops and begins to leaf through one of the binders, turning just enough to be able to look from beneath her lashes in the direction from which she came.

Waves of people push toward her. There are a lot of what Rose calls "Pattaya executives," sunburned, unshaven, often-unwashed males in sleeveless T-shirts, arms festooned with tattoos. In their proximity, the conservative Arab women, wrapped in black like night on the move, seem like aliens. She wonders what they think, snatched out of their protective societies and plopped down here among these rampant males, on a street where every fourth booth is selling counterfeit Viagra. Rose says the Viagra is because the men get too drunk. Twice, when Miaow was on the street and men were after her, their drunkenness was the only thing that saved her.

That's something she's never talked about with Rose or Poke.

Looking back down the sidewalk, she realizes that some of the Thai women she's passed are working the pavement, their eyes glancing off those of the oncoming men. Here and there, people stand still, snagged by something or someone for sale. She sees no one she recognizes. No eyes find and then release her.

There's a tightness in her chest and she can feel her pulse tapping against the skin of her throat, as though demanding her attention. The sidewalk seems to brighten very slightly. Her energy, kicking in.

Something. But she can't pick it out.

She waits until an Arab man approaches, trailing three women behind him, walking side by side like a platoon. Miaow puts down the stack of DVD sleeves and steps in front of the man, no more than two feet ahead of him, adjusting her speed to his. She knows she's invisible to anyone behind the group, but also that whoever is back there will see instantly that she's no longer at the DVD booth. What she needs right now is an inconspicuous way to get off the sidewalk.

On her right, another opening, just wider than her shoulders, separates two booths.

The group of Arabs continues to clog the traffic. When Miaow slants right, she'll be in plain sight for a moment. She cuts in front of a skinny, jittery-looking *farang* and slips into the dark space between the booths, meaning to scoot straight through it to the curb and hurry back on the traffic side to put herself behind whoever is back there.

But she can't. There's a web of black electrical wires, eight or nine of them, hanging parallel to one another like a fence, connecting a line of booths to a single bootlegged outlet. If she snags them as she tries to get through, lights will blink off on either side, and her follower will be right on her heels.

Her heart pushes her like a drumbeat as she turns around and threads her way back into the crowd, hoping not to shove up against whoever it is.

Coming up on the left is Soi 7/1, now essentially a one-block red-light district. A Coffee World on the corner lends it a patina of respectability that vanishes the moment the rest of the street, lurid with pink neon and girls in short skirts, comes into view. The sidewalk in front of her is a dense press of people, but the *soi* will give her room to run. She goes into the Coffee World, angles through it quickly, and comes out the side entrance, directly onto the *soi*, which looks like a dead end but actually ends in a U to the right, an unpaved, usually muddy passageway that leads back to Sukhumvit. She takes one look behind her and breaks into a run.

I'm not as fast as I used to be, she thinks. Still, she outran the darker of the men who chased her and Andrew, and that thought gives her an extra burst of speed. Just as she thinks she'll be all right, she hears running feet behind her.

Instead of looking over her shoulder, which on this uneven street could put her flat on her face, she pushes herself to her top speed, hearing the slap of shoes and then a disorganized crumple of noise and a shout, and she slows just enough to glance back and see a *farang* sitting in the road yelling at the man who's just knocked him down—the man who had blocked her and Andrew's path to the boulevard when they were being chased from the Sikh's booth. The man who was knocked down is young, strong, and angry enough to be slightly drunk, and Miaow sees him as a weapon and angles right, all the way to the curb, and then turns left and left again, making a fast U-turn that puts her running at full speed back the way she came. She pushes her way through a startled covey of miniskirted girls who are trying to wave customers into a massage parlor.

Her pursuer slows and stumbles, his mouth wide and his eyes blinking in uncertainty. Recovering his balance, he tries to edge left fast enough to intercept Miaow as she emerges from the group of masseuses. She sees the silver glint of a knife and she screams the highest, shrillest sound she can force out, just squeezing past the man with the knife and grabbing onto the one who had been knocked down, wrapping her arms around his waist and shrieking for help.

The *farang* shakes her loose as Miaow's pursuer slows and then stops, and then the *farang* makes a leap toward him, calling him *motherfucker*, and the dark-haired man takes a single swipe with the knife as girls on both sides of the *soi* back up onto the sidewalk, clucking like chickens, and then he turns and runs away, toward the bottom of the U, and within two or three seconds, Miaow is back on the Sukhumvit sidewalk, edging between booths and flagging a motorcycle taxi.

The moment she's onboard, the driver peels into traffic and shouts, "Where?"

Miaow says, "Anywhere." Changing her mind, she leans forward and says, "Klong Toey near the river."

26

Her Mother Was Beautiful

"SHE'S NOT ANSWERING," Rose says. "Her phone must be off."

Rafferty says, "Or something has—"

The doorbell rings, and Arthit gets up. When he comes back in, he's ushering a slender young man in a yellow linen shirt. Rose, who stood the moment the bell rang, runs to him and takes both of the young man's shoulders to look at him. "You're so *handsome*," she says. "How are Da and the baby?"

Boo ducks his head, embarrassed by the praise but grinning. "They're fine," he says. "Baby is—" He holds his hands two feet apart and spreads them wider, then does it again. "Too big," he says. Rose finally gives Poke a turn with him, and a piece of paper in Boo's hand crackles as the two of them hug. Poke steps back, looking down at the page. Boo turns it around to display a pencil sketch of a young girl, and Poke has the sense that his entire world is drawing in around him, past and present, and from all directions, all at once.

He takes the drawing and shows it to Rose and says, "Treasure."

THE LITTLE GIRL is pretty in an angular, mischievous, fox-faced way, and the little boy would be handsome if it weren't for his protruding front teeth. They're both sidewalk-thin and dumb-struck by the array of adults facing them. Rose has gone home so she'll be there if Miaow shows up, but Arthit and Anna occupy the chairs in front of Boo's desk, with Boo behind it and Rafferty sitting on one of its corners. In addition to Dok and Chalee, three other kids have drifted into the room, so Boo enlarged the office by pushing back two of the partitions. With a quick glance at Anna, he'd also erased a mildly pornographic cartoon someone had drawn on his white board.

"She was sick," Chalee says defiantly. "We wanted to help her."

"We know you were helping, Chalee," Boo says.

"It was my fault we were out on the street when we found her," the boy says.

"It's good that you did," Rafferty says. He holds up the drawing. "Which one of you made this?"

"I did," Chalee says.

Rafferty says, "You have talent. I recognized her instantly."

"She's in a hospital bed," Boo says. "She's been handcuffed and sedated because—"

"I can imagine," Rafferty says.

To Rafferty's surprise, Anna lifts her free hand; she's writing with the other. Then she holds the card up to Boo: *Is she a danger to herself? To others?*

"We don't know," Boo says as the children stare at Anna. "What do you think?" he asks Poke. "You're the only one who knew her before."

"I didn't *know* her," Poke says. He blinks away the recurring vision of the burning house. "I met her once, when I sneaked into her house. She was—she is—damaged. Her father, he—he hit her a lot. He tried to make her into someone like him."

"Like him?" Boo says.

"He was a violent man." He looks up at all the eyes fixed on him. "I don't know how she'll feel when she sees me. I helped to kill him."

"You *killed* him?" Dok says.

Poke jams his hands into his pockets, trying to decide how to approach it. He decides on details. "About eight weeks ago, as I said, I was inside her house. Here, in Bangkok. There was an explosion. He was killed. I thought she'd been killed, too, but I was wrong. I don't think she's ever been outside the walls of that house before." He turns to Anna. "So, actually, I don't know whether she's dangerous."

Dok says, "She lets me sleep on her bed."

Poke says, "You two are probably the first friends she's ever had."

Anna holds up a hand again as she writes. The card says, *She's socializing. That's a good sign.*

"But I don't know what she'll do when she sees me," Poke says.

"You're the one she asked for," Chalee says.

"I'm surprised at that, too," Rafferty says. "But as—as odd as it sounds, there were a few minutes there when we almost made friends. I listened to her. I don't think anyone had listened to her much. When she got nervous about me getting too close, I made a game out of it. I mimed a big plate glass window between us, and then I pretended to walk into it and bump my head." He rubs his forehead and looks up to find everyone in the room staring at him, although no one is staring with more intensity than Anna. "I played with her," he says. "It made her laugh."

Chalee says, "Did she talk?"

"Sure. She asked me about my daughter." Poke stops at the thought of Miaow, still out there somewhere, then pushes forward. "She wanted to know whether—" He swallows. "Whether I liked her. I mean, if the question is, can she talk, the answer is yes."

Boo says, "How did she respond to her father's death?"

"When he got shot—" He feels the children's eyes on him and sees that their mouths are hanging open. "Jesus, what a conversation. When he got shot, what she said was, 'Do it again.'"

The room falls into silence, no one really looking at anyone else. Dok is the one who breaks it. He says, "I know lots of kids who would say that."

*   *   *

EVERYONE BUT POKE stops at the door. Dok is ready to trot in, but Chalee yanks his arm, practically pulling him off his feet, and Poke goes in alone, the key to the handcuffs in his palm.

A few steps in, he stops to take in the small, dim room, the two metal chairs, the narrow bed with its fever-creased sheets, the gleaming IV stand. From the far end of the bed, her gaze hits him like a stream of cold air.

He goes only halfway to her. "Hello, Treasure."

She looks at her lap.

"I'm so happy to see you." It feels trite, but it's what he means. "I've been worrying about you." He's speaking English, her father's language, as he had when he first met her. She hasn't looked back up at him, and he takes a couple of slow, careful steps closer. "I went back the next day," he says. "The day after everything happened. Into your room, in the hedge." She remains still. "Looking for you."

He tries not to hover over her, tries to let the silence lengthen until she decides to break it. He fails. Says, "I'm here. You asked Dok and Chalee for me, and I'm here."

Silence stretches emptily between them. To Rafferty, who can feel his heartbeat's muffled thump against the skin on the inside of his wrists, the silence almost has a weight to it. As he's about to speak again, she says hoarsely, "Dok."

"Your friend," he says. "Dok. And—and Chalee. Treasure. Can I come close enough to take those handcuffs off?"

She tugs against the right cuff and says, "I can't fight."

"You don't need to," he says. "All you have to do is say no. Do you want to say no?"

She turns her face away.

"They only put them on you because you were so sick and they were afraid you'd run away. Do you want me to take them off?"

She says, "Look." She sits forward, just far enough to spit on the back of her left wrist. A moment later, she holds up her hand, leaving the cuff dangling from the rail. She turns to look at her hand, and her eyes meet his for an instant and dart away again.

"You could have gone," he says. "Any time."

Now she brings her eyes to his and holds his gaze. She says, "Where?"

The word hits him like a slap. How could he not have seen it coming? He says, automatically, "You're going to be fine."

Her hands are clenched so tightly that her knuckles are white. Two knuckles on the hand she tugged free of the cuff are bleeding. She breathes deeply and says, "My—my—my—"

"He's dead," Rafferty says. "You know that."

"And my mo—my—Neeni, *Neeni.*"

"She's—Neeni. You know how she was, and she's still like that. Let me unlock the other one, you've hurt your hand." Holding his breath, he moves to the side of the bed and very slowly bends over her arm. Not touching her skin, he angles the cuff upward until he can work the key into it and turns the key until he hears the double click and it springs open. "There," he says.

She works her wrist back and forth, wincing slightly, and then holds up the arm with the IV in it, extended and palm up, the pale elbow open to him "This," she says.

"I can't take that out," he says. "I'll—I'll faint. Needles make me—" He makes a little cyclone spiral with his hand.

"That's silly," she says, and she begins to peel off the bandage.

"No, no, wait. Wait, wait, wait." He turns to the doorway. "She's going to pull out the *drip*," he says, hearing the panic in his voice, and then he hears something that sounds like a hiccup, and then another hiccup, and he turns back to the bed.

She's laughing. She's laughing at him. She's beautiful.

TEN MINUTES LATER, the drip has been pulled while Rafferty has his back turned. Dok has claimed his place on the bed, sliding the empty handcuff up and down the left-hand rail, making a skin-tightening sound until Chalee, sitting on one of the metal chairs at the bedside, slaps his hand.

The sound of the slap brings Treasure's head around, fast, but when she sees Dok shaking his hand in the air, her face relaxes. She looks down at Dok as though he's something new and unexpected, something that sprouted up through the blankets and into the light.

Chalee says to Poke, "She's so pretty."

"Her mother was beautiful," Rafferty says as Treasure's eyes come to him. He's on the metal chair Dok vacated when he climbed onto the bed. Treasure didn't seem to be paying any attention to him; her hand was only an inch or two from the edge of the bed, and when he sat down she hadn't pulled it away. He feels its presence as though it's throwing off heat, knowing it's costing her something to leave it there. Slowly, he puts his hand beside hers, and she doesn't move away. "She's still beautiful," he says.

Treasure lets the remark float past her as though it were in a language she doesn't understand but then, very slightly, her chin dimples. She puts a hand to her face as if she could still it that way.

Boo and Arthit had seemed to make Treasure nervous, so Rafferty and Dok are the only males in the room. Chalee is drawing again, a picture of a young girl sitting in a dim room, the light coming from a window to the girl's left. She works with little attention to the task, as though the lines are already faintly sketched on the paper. Leaning against the wall at the end of the bed, her arms crossed across her chest, Anna regards the group at the bed with, it seems to Rafferty, the kind of dampened regret she might feel toward a picture that's emerged inaccurately from memory. The peculiar focus Rafferty felt from her when he described his first encounter with Treasure has lessened but not disappeared, and Rafferty knows she's watching the lips of everyone who is facing her.

"Who is that, Chalee?" he asks.

She keeps drawing for a long moment, and when she looks up, it's not at Rafferty but at Treasure. "My sister," she says. "Sumalee."

"How old is she?"

Breaking her gaze on Treasure, Chalee begins erasing fiercely. "She's dead."

Treasure's eyes remain on her, and Chalee raises her head again. To Treasure, she says, "She killed herself."

Treasure says, "Your—your father?"

"No. Well, yes, but no." Chalee glances at Rafferty, just an instant, as though she would rather he weren't in the room. In a mixture of Thai and Lao, she says to Treasure, "We were—rice farmers, in Isaan. We didn't have money. He, my father, borrowed a little every year from a bank—no, no, not a bank," she says, squinting toward the memory, "a *trust*. Farmer's Trust, something like that. And he trusted them, like their name said, but then they took the farm and the house. My father was going to sell Sumalee to get the money, but she ran to our old house and threw a rope over the beam in front of the window." She and Treasure look at each other as though no one else is there. "She told me she was going to leave a present for the Trust," Chalee says. "I didn't know what she meant."

Treasure pulls her feet up and pats the covers on the bed, and Chalee puts down the stack of paper and crawls up as Dok slides over to make room. There's a moment of silence, and then Chalee starts to cry. A second later, Dok sniffles.

Anna stands suddenly and waves Poke out of the room. As he goes through the door, his phone rings: Rose.

"Now I *am* worried," she says. "I called Nguyen, and Andrew is there, but they haven't seen her. I searched her room, hoping she'd left her phone, but it's not there. Poke, I'm getting frightened."

He tries to think of something worth saying and can't. "She'll be fine. I'm sure she will."

"But why hasn't she called? Why hasn't she answered?"

"She's hurt. She thinks we lied to her."

Rose says, "That's probably it." There's a moment's silence, and she disconnects.

"Sure," Rafferty says to the dead phone. He turns, not certain whether to leave or go back into Treasure's room, but Anna makes a noise like steam, *Sssss-sssss-sssss*, a demand for his attention.

She's writing on one of her blue cards. Impatiently, she pulls it free and hands it to him and begins to write on the next one.

The fluorescents in the hallway are dim and far apart. Angling the card to catch as much light as possible, he reads,

If you tell that child everything will be all right

Anna is writing even more quickly than usual, and by the time he looks back at her, she's already pulling out the second card and extending it. He can read it while it is still in her hand. It says: *you had better be sure you're telling her the truth.*

Some Sort of Long-term Solution

HE'S SO WEARY that he feels scooped out. He should go home,
but what can he do there? Fuss at Rose? He knows from long experience that when she's frightened she moves inward, becomes
remote and distant, as though she's wrapped in a brittle, transparent shell.

It seems better to stay here. And maybe *here*, at least, something can to be settled.

"I don't think it'll work," he says. Last time he looked into
Treasure's room, Dok and Chalee were asleep, Dok beside Treasure, and Chalee curled up across the foot of the bed, the drawing
of Sumalee crumpled in her hand. Treasure's eyes were open, fixed
on Chalee, and she had the abstracted air of someone who has just
been deafened by an enormous noise.

He and Boo have been joined by a young African-American
woman named Katherine who's representing Father Bill and First
Home. Boo is silent, letting Rafferty deal with Katherine. "I probably agree with you," Katherine says, "but why do you say it?"

"She doesn't have the social skills." He's once again sitting on
the corner of Boo's desk, with Boo in the chair behind it and Katherine on one of the chairs the children dragged in. "You weren't
there, in her house, I mean. She was brutalized on every level. He
slapped her, he punched her, he turned her into a ventriloquist's
dummy. Literally: he'd force her to sit on his knee with his hand

on the back of her neck and press hard enough to cause pain, and when she opened her mouth he'd supply the words. Just completely overrode her will."

"Why? Why would anyone—"

"Because he was a sick, evil fuck, and he *could*. She lived in that big, awful house with him and two Vietnamese servants, and her mother, who was in a haze all the time, just knocking over furniture, so that left Daddy. I think it's amazing that she lets Dok and Chalee anywhere near her—"

Katherine says, "She touched your hand."

"Almost. You saw that?"

"I was in the hall, looking in through the door."

"I had no idea what to do." Rafferty rubs his face with both hands. "And I'm not at my best. My daughter is missing."

Boo says, "It's only been a few hours."

"I know, I know. She'll be fine, she knows the city, blah blah. Still, it's one thing to know all that and another to have her back home."

"I'm sorry about that," Katherine says, "but you're an adult male, and she—reached out to you."

"I don't understand it any better than you do."

Katherine shifts in her chair. "I hate to compartmentalize like this, but we need to figure out what to—"

"I know. Okay, let me talk. I don't think Treasure can get along in a bunch of kids, much less sleep in a room full of them. Dok and Chalee are exceptional. But, you know, in a group, there are— conflicts. It could be dangerous for her, it could be dangerous for them. She's never been around people her own age. When her father wasn't slapping her silly, he was showing her how to plan terrorist attacks. I worry about what kind of behavior someone in a group, someone who's not as sympathetic as Chalee and Dok, might accidentally trigger. This is a girl who lit fire to her own house."

"We have to do *something* with her," Katherine says.

Boo says, in English, "He's thinking about it."

"I have a lot of money that, I suppose, belongs to her," Rafferty says. "I've been using it to try to get her mother sort of straightened up, but—" He puts his hands flat on the tops of his thighs and blows out a lungful of air. "But that's not going to work. She's past straightening up."

Katherine says, "You have her money? You've been *taking care*—"

He raises a hand. "I had it all worked out, I thought. Put Mama in an apartment, pay someone to keep her straight. Mama would be fine, Treasure would show up, everything would work out. It's so *American*. They'd all be sending out Christmas cards in a year or two." He yawns. "I feel like I should work for Hallmark."

"Then stop thinking about you," Boo says, still in English.

Rafferty sighs and rocks back and forth in his chair, which squeaks. Closes his eyes and sees floating red spots. "I've got to go home. Okay, here's where I am right now. Leave her where she is tonight. Tomorrow, if we haven't thought of anything better, let her sleep in here."

Boo looks around the room. "In my *office*?"

"Are you in here at night?"

"Well, no, but—"

"Then stop thinking about you. Put three cots in here and let Dok and Chalee stay with her. Find a way to close that door. Just temporarily."

Boo says, "We need to talk to Dok and Chalee first."

Katherine says, "They'll agree. Kids love to feel necessary."

"I know they'll *agree*," Boo says, in Thai this time. "I want them to suggest it to her. Tell her that they'll all have their own beds or something, that it'll be—I don't know—fun."

"Tomorrow," Rafferty says. "Leave them where they are tonight." He gets up and shoves a hand into the pocket of his jeans and works out a wad of money. "Here's twelve thousand baht. Get some new pads for those cots, new sheets. Pillows. She used to live in a nice house. Put something colorful on the walls. Magazine pictures of girls with friends. She had them all over her hiding place. I'll send you more money tomorrow morning. Buy Dok and Chalee whatever they want."

"She needs more help than two little kids can give her," Katherine says.

"Obviously, but she's *letting* them help. That counts for a lot. For now, anyway."

Katherine says, "She needs a long-term solution."

"Tomorrow," Rafferty says.

"It'll have to be—" Katherine says, looking past Rafferty, and then breaking off. "Who's this?"

Rafferty turns to the doorway to see Miaow, looking at him with no pleasure at all.

Miaow says, "What are *you* doing here?"

28

The Cord

"A KNIFE," HE says to Rose. "The son of a bitch had a knife."

Rose is occupying virtually all of the couch, sitting dead-center, her knees folded to the left, her long arms extending along the sofa's back. It's a position he's learned to avoid from across a room.

Miaow, who has paused behind him, apparently to judge Rose's reaction, pushes past him toward her room.

"If you go back there," Rose says, "you can stay there until your next happy birthday for all I care."

Miaow says, "He chased me with a knife, or didn't you hear that part?"

"I heard it. I would have chased you with a knife myself if I'd been the one who spotted you."

"Nice to be home," Miaow says, heading for her room again.

Rose brings her head forward a lethal inch or two. "I wasn't joking, Miaow. Go back there and close that door, and we'll have a real problem."

Rafferty says, "Rose—"

Over him, Miaow says, "What's a *real* problem? If he'd caught me, if he'd stabbed me out on Soi Whatever it was, would that have been a real problem?"

"*Here's* a real problem," Rose says. "The whole world is about you. The whole world and everything in it exists just so Miaow can tell us all whether it's good or bad. We all just wait, hanging uselessly from strings, for her to give us the word. She goes to a school most kids would give their teeth to be in, a school full of kids from all over the world, and it's all about Miaow. Andrew has a father who's got a head made out of rock, and that's all about Miaow. Poke and I are going to have a baby, and that's all about Miaow. My own *baby* is about Miaow."

"That's not fair. You didn't even—"

"I'll give you this, you had more class than Andrew's father. You were winning there for a minute while he was here, even though you've been a complete hairball for the past couple of months. But then what happened? You learned something that you knew made Poke and me happy—or leave me out of it, if you want, something that made *Poke* happy, Poke, who's turned himself inside-out for you—and what do you do? You make it all about Miaow and you storm out of this apartment. And I'll tell you, since I'm angry enough not to keep it from you—you humiliated us in front of that Vietnamese toy soldier who acted like he'd honor our home by shitting in the middle of the floor. You acted like the girl he thought you were. Just tell me, eye to eye, since I have to ask a question I never thought I'd have to ask, are you even the *tiniest* bit happy for us?"

Miaow's eyes fill most of her face and her shoulders are trembling.

Rafferty says, "I think that's enough, Rose."

"Do you?" Rose straightens her legs and puts her bare feet on the coffee table. "What I think is that this is a conversation between women, and maybe you should get some rest after chasing all over Bangkok to find the missing princess."

Rafferty says, "No," just as Miaow says, "Yes."

Rose says, "Two to one. Get yourself a beer and go into the bedroom." She looks over at him, and her face softens. "Please."

Rafferty says, "We do have to talk about the knife."

"We will. First, Miaow and I need to get some of the smoke out of the room."

Poke says, "Do you want something? Either of you?"

Rose closes her eyes and says with enormous patience, "We both know where it all is."

He has to say something, so he says, "Well, then." He goes into the kitchen, pops the cap on a Singha, and stands irresolute in front of the open refrigerator until Rose calls out, "Don't forget to close it, like some people do."

"Righty ho," Rafferty says, feeling as clueless as Bertie Wooster. "I have an idea," he says, going back into the living room. "You go talk in Miaow's room, and I'll watch a little TV."

Miaow is sitting on the hassock now, her legs crossed tightly beneath her, leaning forward with her hands on her knees, not a restful pose. The two of them give him identical looks, looks that make him feel like something they regret buying, and Rose says, "Goodbye, Poke."

When the door closes behind him, both of them wait until they're certain he's kept going, that he's not standing on the other side with his ear pressed to it. Miaow's gaze falters, and she looks down at her crossed legs.

"Let's begin," Rose says, "with me saying I know you're having a hard time."

Miaow blinks heavily, as though she's been slapped.

"This is a miserable time for a girl. I know nobody wants to hear this, especially not from her mother, but you'll live through it. If I lived through it, anybody can."

"You?" Miaow says. "You're beautiful."

"I was the town joke," Rose says. "I was too tall, I was all knees and elbows, I was half blind. I *squinted* at everybody. *Stork* is not a flattering nickname."

"I'm a dwarf," Miaow says. "A black dwarf."

Rose says, "Oh, shut up," and Miaow rocks back. "You're going to be beautiful. Go look at your eyes. Look at the shape of your mouth. Go suck in your cheeks, because those are going to disappear. Your nose is perfect."

"I barely have a nose."

"You act like there's a hole in the middle of your face. Listen to me. This isn't just about what you look like. You don't even know what you look like. This is about you not liking who you are, and I know *everything* about that. I was a tall, ugly child whose own father tried to sell her, and then I was a whore. Your turn, tell me what you've got to compare with that."

Miaow is using the tip of her index finger to write something invisible on the glass surface of the table. Rose can't see her eyes, and she's pressing hard enough to turn her fingernail white.

Rose says, "Do you actually think we don't love you?"

Miaow stops moving. Then she brings her knees up and wraps her arms around them and lowers her head until it rests on her knees. "I don't know."

"Yes, you do. We both love you more than we love anything else in the world. Every day, we wake up happy just because you're here. Both of us, we're only really ourselves when you're with us."

"When were—" Miaow begins, her head still down.

"When were—when were we going to tell you?"

"Yes."

"Miaow. I've only known for three days. I was only sure on the night before you and Andrew got into all that trouble."

"Is that true?"

"Do I lie to you?"

Nothing. Just the top of her head with its fading dye job, the chopped haircut growing out to the point where her natural center part is beginning to reassert itself. The shoulder seam of her angry-duck T-shirt separating a bit to show the brown shoulder beneath.

Rose says, "Do I?"

"No."

"No, I don't. And now," she says, lowering her voice, "here's the reason I made Poke leave. This isn't a lie I told him, it's just something I haven't talked about yet. That means you're the only person who knows about it. And you have to promise me that you'll let me be the one to tell him."

Miaow raises her head. When she sees Rose's face, she nods.

"This baby I'm carrying, this is the second."

Miaow's eyebrows come together in a question, and then her mouth opens and she looks quickly down at the floor, but Rose can see that she's listening all the way to her toes.

"The first one, when she was about three months along," Rose says, and grabs a breath, "she decided not to be born. I didn't lose her on purpose, she just didn't want the life I could have given her. I had a—a miscarriage. Until a few days ago, I didn't think I could have another child."

Miaow has knotted her hand in her hair and, apparently, forgotten about it. Her hair is bearing the entire weight of her arm.

"When I knew about the baby—*this* baby—I thought she was my first, coming back to be born."

Miaow says, "Maybe it is."

"No," Rose says. "It isn't. I worked out the time, Miaow, and I realized that it's you."

Miaow starts to say something, stops, and asks, "What is?"

"*You're* my first baby, Miaow. You came back so you could find your way back to me. To us." Her face is wet but she doesn't seem to be weeping. "It was *thirteen years ago*, Miaow," she says. "You found us all the way across this city. Like water running downhill." She blots her cheeks with the heel of her hand. "I've always been your mother. So, you see, this really is your little brother or sister. It can't come between us."

Miaow says, "I thought. I mean, I thought—there would be a cord between you and your baby, when the baby came out, and that cord would be there forever."

"Miaow," Rose says, "do you really think there's no cord between us?"

"It's obviously safe in here," Rafferty says from the doorway.

Rose has moved to the end of the couch, and Miaow is on her

side with her knees drawn up and her head on Rose's lap. Without looking up, Miaow says, "I love you, Poke."

"I know," he says, "but that doesn't mean I don't want to hear it. I love you, too."

Miaow says, "You don't have to tell me."

"Okay," Rafferty says. "What's a guy *supposed* to say?"

Rose says, "Is there any of that awful whiskey left?"

"Unless you drank it."

"Three glasses," Rose says.

"Are you sure?"

"This is a special occasion," Rose says. "Miaow's allowed."

"I wasn't thinking about Miaow," Rafferty says. "Miaow can have as much as she wants. It's you that—" He's started toward the kitchen but he stops so suddenly he might have reached the end of a rope. "You haven't been smoking," he says.

Rose says, "I thought you'd never notice."

"Well, that's amazing and I admire the hell out of you for it, but I still don't think you should have a drink."

"Is eating still okay? Breathing?"

"Anything in the world you want is okay except smoking and drinking."

Miaow says, "There's nothing left," and Rose laughs softly and smoothes Miaow's ragged hair.

"Two whiskeys," Rafferty says, "Coming up."

"If Rose can't have it, I don't want it, either."

"Well, I sure as hell don't want it. I was only drinking it to keep my twelve-year-old daughter company."

"Thirteen," Miaow says.

"Historians are divided on that."

Rose says, "Thirteen."

"We have a new source?" Rafferty says. "Something I don't know about?" Miaow smiles and snuggles in Rose's lap. "Well, okay, there's *always* something I don't know about. Since I've been spared the whiskey, I'll have a beer."

"Diet Coke for me," Miaow says.

"And how about you, little mother?" Poke says, suddenly feeling as happy as he ever has in his life. "A nice glass of warm tap water? I could scatter some powdered yeast over it."

"Nine months," Rose says. "I have to put up with you for nine months."

An hour later, with Rose and Miaow in bed, Rafferty sits at his cramped little desk, in the long rectangle of gloom cast by the television. All the lights in the living room are on the other side of the screen, so he's turned on the pinspots above the breakfast counter.

As soon as he was alone he allowed himself to give in to the waves of panic that had been lapping at him all evening, ever since he learned about the knife. What in the *world* can he do? He doesn't know who these people are, or where, or why they want to kill his daughter.

And then there's Treasure. Anna is right; if he promises something to that child, who's never been given anything but sorrow in her miserable life, he had better be one hundred percent certain he can make it happen.

And sustain it. She's not going to get up in a week, say, "I'm all right now," and apply to a prep school.

Just as he's feeling his smallest and least effective, a whole swarm of other concerns begins to swirl around him, dive-bombing like hornets. What he wants is another beer. What he does is open a drawer and pull out two sheets of paper and a pen.

What Arthit had said, about it being an illusion when problems swirl together into one, that's what he's facing. *Keep them separate*, Arthit had said.

Aloud, Rafferty says, "How hard is that?" He thinks he hits just the right tone of voice. Anyone who heard it would think he was confident.

He folds a blank sheet of paper in half and tears it. The very act of separating the two sheets eases his tension. On one half he writes *Miaow* and on the other he writes *Treasure*. Then he takes another sheet of paper and, without tearing it, writes, at the top, *The Baby*.

It takes him no more than a few minutes to create a list on the page headed *The Baby*. It begins with *Obstetrician?* and ends, on the other side, with *New apartment*. Just looking at it makes him feel productive.

He realizes that the page headed *Treasure* can also be divided in two, so he draws a line down the center to create a second column. He heads it, *Neeni*.

Even before he begins to fill it in, he gets up and goes to the couch. He pulls out the center cushion, turns it over, and unzips the white canvas cover. The bills he took from Murphy's house are all US hundreds, in stacks of twenty, and he removes twenty-five stacks. That'll take care of the fifty thousand he'd promised Hwa in exchange for staying in Bangkok with Neeni and trying to get her off the codeine.

He replaces the center cushion and removes the one on the left. Five more stacks will give Neeni ten thousand to take home to her village. That should keep her in codeine for a while. Any more will be stolen while she's out bumping into trees. He takes the money to his desk, snaps rubber bands around the two stacks, and makes two new notes in the Neeni column, *Bank account*, and beneath that, *Monthly transfers*.

Beneath *Monthly transfers*, he writes *Travel plans*. The two of them need to get home, Neeni to Laos and Hwa to Vietnam. Hwa can be trusted to arrange it, but she'll need more money. He goes back to the center cushion and pulls out another thousand, which he folds and puts in his pocket. That seems to take care of the *Neeni* sheet for the moment.

There's a slight easing around his heart, and he stretches his legs. It feels like days since he's slept.

Well, those are the easy ones, the baby and Neeni. He adds to the sheet about the baby, *Let Miaow name it?* He hasn't had a chance to discuss it with Rose, but he likes the idea.

So. The real problems.

Under *Miaow*, he writes, *Stay in touch with Arthit for info* and beneath that, he writes, *Let her go to school, yes or no?* and beneath that, *Some kind of guard?* And then, *Captain Nguyen*. Then, to the right, he writes *Miaow and Andrew* and draws an arrow to *Captain Nguyen*. Then he writes, *Andrew in danger?* And draws a second arrow to Captain Nguyen.

He looks at what he's written and realizes it's all reactive. In large letters, centered at the bottom of the page, he writes *AIM AND IGNITE*. He'd seen the words on the screen of Miaow's laptop when she was listening to a band called Fun. He doesn't know what the words mean relative to the band or its songs, but he knows what it means in regard to Miaow. It means, find a way to go on the offensive and then take it.

Someone chased his daughter with a knife. It's connected with this snarl of questions about the murders of Sawat and Thongchai. Enough of sitting passively on the sidelines with his fingers crossed: Time to aim and ignite. Aim *what*, aim it at *whom*, and ignite it with *what*; those are details. What matters now is the intent.

He goes back to the column headed *Treasure*.

Looks at it for perhaps a minute. Swears beneath his breath, and writes *Everything*.

29

Adrift

AT FIRST, ARTHIT blames the software.

He's cranky, stiff-backed, over-caffeinated, and jammed into a tiny, stuffy office in the dirtiest police station he's ever been in. He'd been forty minutes late, thanks to the kind of traffic jam that might result from it being the end of the world, and everyone knowing which direction the damage is coming from. His mood was not improved by three calls from Thanom, demanding to know where he was. After the third, he tossed the phone onto the passenger seat with enough force to make it bounce off the seat and onto the floor. Glaring down at it, he heard a horn behind him, looked up to see that traffic was moving, and accelerated.

Which sent the cell phone sliding beneath the seat. Out of reach.

So he was already well beyond the zone of calm reason when he limped into the station, his back having seized up again. He forced himself upright, aiming at bluff, masculine competence and knowing he looked like he was trying to walk in high heels. The thought *Poke would find this funny* didn't amuse him at all.

And now this. The software on the department computers gives him nothing.

If it's not the software, it's the data. If it's neither the software nor the data, it's either human error or intentional human omission.

So. Test things one at a time.

The software. He thinks back over the past four or five years, comes up with half a dozen murders he remembers in some detail, and enters the number of victims, sorting them into men, women, and children.

Gets hits on all of them.

Pushes back from the desk and thinks for a moment. Enters only the number of women killed.

Gets the ones he remembers and several others in which the same number of mature females were victims.

Okay. The crimes he's looking for are probably farther back in time than the ones he remembers.

He gets up and goes out to the reception area, where he finds the resident ancient sergeant sitting where he sits in virtually all stations, at the front desk. Arthit says, "I need a favor. Think back ten, twelve years and come up with a few murders. Just write down the number of victims—men, women, children—and the approximate year and give it to me. Multiple victims, or the results will be meaningless."

"My first year here," the sergeant says, "whole family, grandma, mother, father, four kids. Worst thing I'd ever seen. That would have been 1979." He pushes his lower lip out a surprising distance and looks at the desk. "The headman of a village in this district poisoned his wife, her mother, and her sister, the whole bunch of them. So that's three women." He writes it down. "Maybe 1987."

The database delivers both cases. The one involving two women, the father, and four kids comes up when he enters all the victims, when he enters *four children*, and when he enters *two women*.

So the database works.

He enters, for the fifth time, what was said when Sawat was killed, *Two women, three children*.

It isn't that there aren't any matches. There are half a dozen, but none that concerned Sawat or anyone close to him. One of them was only a few months ago and most of the others were after Sawat was suspended. Arthit supposes it's possible that Sawat had continued to operate after he was booted off the force, but he doubts that the cops who had protected him originally would allow it.

The same kind of results with the victims named when Thong-chai was killed: nothing that even *suggests* Sawat.

He gets up and wanders into the detectives' office. "Who's the computer genius?"

"Clemente," says the closest cop. He points with his chin to a young woman with dark skin, frizzy hair, and a flat, squarish face. When she hears her name, she looks up at Arthit through eyes so beautiful he immediately thinks they will probably drive some poor man to suicide, if they haven't already.

"The database," Arthit says. "What areas does it cover?"

"Geographic areas?" The eyes are a bottomless dark brown, laced faintly around the pupils with gold.

"Yes. For starters."

"Okay," Clemente says. She leans back in her chair and spins a pen across the tips of her fingers without looking at it, something Arthit has never been able to do. "The greater Bangkok metro-politan area and beyond, but not contiguously."

"Sorry?"

"It's mainly data from urban areas. So, for example, we have stuff from as far to the northwest as Kanchanaburi and as far north as Nakhon Ratchasima. East to Ubon Ratchathani and south to Pattaya and Ranong, southwest to Prachuap and Koh Samui, Koh Samet, the tourist areas in there. But there's lots of area in between that we don't have."

"Still, that's a big net. Is all that territory—is that the, what's the word, the default?"

"No," she says. "Bangkok metro is the default."

"Can you do me a favor? Can you widen it as far as you can for me?"

"Sure." She gets up, and every man in the office looks up and then down again, and Arthit is glad he's not a young female officer with gorgeous eyes. He follows her back to the little room that's got the monitor and keyboard in it, and when she's taken the only seat in the room and is banging the keys around, she says, "This used to be a closet."

"It's still a closet," Arthit says. "They could divert a stream through it and plant a tree, and it would still be a closet." He watches her work for a moment. "When you got here, was this work station in a closet?"

"No," she says. "But, you know. I'm smaller. I didn't need such a big space."

"Or as much air. Have you complained?"

"Lieutenant Colonel," Clemente says, "I'm happy just to be here. And, to be fair, I also have that desk out there."

"Where people can stare at you."

"Are you an *agent provocateur* or just nosy?"

"Nosy. It's always seemed counterproductive to bring women into the workplace and then make it difficult for them to work."

"The idea, I believe, is that if they make it difficult enough, we might go away. But you know what? Any woman who goes into police work knows she's going to be climbing a steep ramp."

"You ever think about working downtown?"

She looks up at him. "Are you making an offer?"

"It's not all lights and glamour," he says. "The closer you get to the center of power, the more politics there are."

"Just a different set of problems," she says. She gets up. "There. That should get you everything you need."

"Give me a couple of minutes more," he says. "Please. Just so I know I'm not screwing up. I'm looking for murders five to twelve years ago in which the victims included one woman and two children, and murders in the same time period in which two women and three children were killed."

"Children," she says, sitting down again. "Who could kill children?" She's tapping the keys, and results are swarming the screen, many more than Arthit's searches had produced. "When you talk to the ones who did it, they're usually so bewildered they're not even certain what they did."

Arthit says, "Evil's not hard to find."

"No," she says, "but it's usually the product of stupidity and pain." She hits *enter* again and sits back, and Arthit leans over her shoulder. "Here we go." She rolls the chair back, and it bumps him and he backs up. "Are you serious about a job?"

"Sure, if you don't mind a ball of snakes."

"What I've got here is a room full of blunt objects."

"Give me your card before I leave." He sits down and studies the screen. A few moments later he becomes aware that he's alone in the room.

He decides to make no assumptions and to check every one of the cases Clemente's search turned up, however improbable it may look. Almost two hours later, he sits back and rocks in the chair, his eyes on the screen but not reading anything. He didn't know what to expect, but he certainly hadn't anticipated this.

There's not a single likely case. Not one with rich victims, and all Sawat's victims were killed for money. None that fit the profile, with multiple eyewitnesses and an unimpeded conviction. And none of them was investigated by Sawat.

Not one. His first thought is that someone has pruned the database, but that's virtually impossible, since so many different police units contribute to it, and they'd be quick to demand an explanation if their cases suddenly went missing. There are simply no matches.

He thinks, *What the hell?*

He thinks, *Who in the world can I tell about this?*

AT SEVEN FIFTEEN that morning, just as Arthit is beginning to experience the impenetrability of the day's traffic jam, Rafferty's phone buzzes on the kitchen counter to announce a text message.

Rafferty lowers his coffee and regards the phone with mistrust. He doesn't text and he doesn't encourage texting. Pretty much the only person who ever texts him is Miaow, and she's sitting on the couch in shorts and the T-shirt she'd slept in, staring open-mouthed at the screen of her Mac Air. While it's certainly possible, he doubts she's texted him from across the room.

The text reads: *If you don't want Miaow to go to school today and you and Rose are busy, she could stay here. A policeman's house is probably safe.*

It's signed, *Anna*.

With his big fat clumsy thumbs he crunches out a thank-you and adds that Miaow and Rose are going to stay home with a guard, and watch their new TV. Says (although he's still ambivalent about her) that they should all have dinner soon. It'll be the first time, he thinks with a pang of loss, the first time the four of them have gone out together. He should have fixed this weeks ago.

A moment later, another buzz tells him she and Arthit would love to.

"Look at you," Miaow says. "Twenty-first century man."

"It's stupid and labor-intensive," he says. "Writing is one of civilization's great gifts, but it's no way to say *Hi*. It's as dumb as Twitter."

"I take it back," she says. "So why are you doing it?"

"Because Anna can't hear."

"Anna." She makes a face.

"How'd you sleep?"

She lowers the screen of the laptop a bit and gives him the tiny smile that means she's holding back a bigger one. "Best in days." Looking back at the laptop, she asks, in a tone that just misses being offhand, "What are you going to do today?"

"All sorts of stuff. I have to take care of some things about—about that girl's mother."

She lifts her face to him. "The girl in the bed? Treasure?"

"That's the one."

"She's—beautiful," Miaow says.

"If she is, it's the only thing in the world she's got."

She looks back to the screen, but he can see that she's not focused on anything. "Can you help her?"

"If I can figure out what to do."

The brown tips of her fingers, folded over the top of the screen, look like a kitten's paws. "Would you think about bringing her here?"

"No. I think we have enough going on already."

Miaow nods. "Is she dangerous?"

"Maybe. Probably."

"Poor girl." She swivels the screen up and down. "What else are you going to do?"

"I have to talk to Arthit about the guy with the knife and start to turn things around. And I have to talk to Captain Nguyen."

"You *need* to," she says eagerly. This is what she's been steering him toward. "He has to know that those guys could come after Andrew. When are you going to call him?"

"I already did, while you were in the shower. I'm going to go to his office at one."

"You already called him?"

"Yes, Miaow," he says. "I called him at seven."

"Sometimes you're actually cool," she says.

"God knows I try. What about you?"

"I'm always cool."

"I'm happy you realize it. What are *you* going to do today?"

"Fight with Rose for the remote control. She wants to watch shows where women talk about their lives and cry."

"Well, it's all yours until she wakes up. What do you want to watch?"

"Good acting."

"Try the Korean soaps. The acting is good, and women cry on them, too. Oh, you're going to have a guard today, so try to get him on your side."

Her brows pull together until they almost meet over her nose. "Who?"

"A cop named Anand. You've met him."

"He'd be cute if he knew how to cut his hair."

"I'll tell him you said so."

"Poke," she says, and her tone makes him look over at her. "I want to tell you something."

He says nothing, just looks at her.

"When I, I ran out of here, I—I know this sounds dumb—I realized that I didn't have any place to go."

He waits for a long beat to see whether she'll continue. The last thing he wants to do is assume anything, so he says, "Mmm-hmm." He feels an odd mixture of pride and sympathy: she's so strong and so vulnerable at the same time.

She shakes her head. "No, that's not it, really. It wasn't exactly that I didn't have a place to go. I sat on a curb on Sukhumvit and asked myself where I belonged."

"Doesn't sound dumb to me."

"I've been pretending to be someone, you know, someone different because I didn't feel like I belonged there." She lifts her chin in the direction of the sliding glass door and, beyond it, Bangkok. "At school, I mean. So I tried to be someone who would belong there, but it doesn't work. And then, after I learned about the baby, I didn't feel like I belonged here, either, and when I was on the sidewalk, I *knew* I didn't belong there. And I know there's a *way* I belong here, I already know that. But I belong here because you and Rose love me. And you made this place and you want me here. But where do I belong that's a place I made myself?"

He chooses the most neutral reply. "A lot of people ask that question their whole lives."

"Well," she says, "I think I know." She probably isn't aware how intense her gaze is. "I was there once. One time. Do you know where it was?"

"No," he says, although he thinks he does.

"When I was Ariel," she said.

He says, "You were wonderful."

"I *made* that. I had help from Mrs. Shin and, and you—"

"And Shakespeare."

She gives him a quick smile. "And Shakespeare. But I was the place, it was inside *me*, where all of that came together, does that make sense? The words and the movements and her—her spirit. For those minutes when I was on the stage, I was where all that lived. And I made that myself."

"You want to act."

She sits back on the couch for the first time since they began to talk. "I want to learn more about it."

"Do you want me to talk to Mrs. Shin? About places you might go for lessons?"

"Would you do that?" She's closed the screen on her finger, and she pulls it out without looking down.

"Will you try out for the play? For *Small Town?*"

She says, "I already decided to."

"Then of course I'll talk to Mrs. Shin. And you know, whatever your mother said to you last night when I wasn't in the room, whatever she said about loving you? It goes for me, too."

"Oh, *you*," Miaow says. "I've always known about you."

Ten forty-five a.m., and it already feels like it should be dusk through the window.

Thanom pushes the cup away so violently he almost upsets it. He's been told to cut down on caffeine, and his secretary, Taan, has been given charge of the effort by his wife. The steaming cup contains chamomile tea, which tastes, he thinks, like steeped mummy fingers. And instead of giving him the lift he needs to cope with the present situation, it *soothes* him.

He doesn't need to be soothed. He needs an edge. He's adrift on a fucking black ocean, without a light anywhere and rocks in all directions. He's no closer than he was on Friday to finding the killers of Sawat and Thongchai, and though he's almost certain that's not really the issue, finding them would at least placate the princeling in the white uniform, who could break him in half any time he likes.

He needs coffee.

He's thinking about seeing whether he can get someone to call Taan away from her desk so he can slip down the hall, fill a cup with the corrosive brew from the little kitchen, a brew that manages, even as it drips, to smell and taste half a day old, ancient and burned, with most of the water long evaporated. The way it should taste.

Taan buzzes him.

"Do you know someone named Arundee? Says he's your banker."

"Arundee? No. Which bank?"

"First Siam."

First Siam is one of the banks Thanom uses, but it's mainly for his wife's money, which is considerable. The idea that something might be wrong with one of his wife's accounts brings him straight up in his chair. "Line two?"

"Yes, sir."

He punches the button. "Thanom."

"Yes, Colonel. Sorry to bother you—"

"Is there a problem?"

"No, no, I wouldn't say a problem. More an opportunity."

"Are you calling to sell me something?"

"Not at all. It's just that, well, there's quite a bit of money in this account, and it seems to be inactive. I was wondering whether you'd thought about putting some or all of it into a CD with a better rate."

"You should be talking to my wife."

"Perhaps," Arundee says cautiously, "but since it's in your name, I thought—"

"In my name," Thanom says, and something heavy and formless

begins to assemble itself in his gut. "With enough money to consider turning it into a CD."

"Oh, yes. Almost two million baht."

He has to inhale twice to get enough air to speak. "And there have been deposits until—when?"

"Six months, more or less. The last one was five months and . . . twenty-six days ago."

"Almost two million."

"One million, nine-sixty. The rate on a CD that size would be—"

"And the last withdrawal?"

"Nine months, give or take."

"Wait, wait." He passes his hand across his forehead and then wipes it on his shirt. "Why haven't I been getting statements?"

"They've been going out monthly."

"Monthly."

"Yes sir. Same as your wife's accounts."

"But," Thanom says, feeling for the bottom and not finding it. "But not to the same address."

"Oh," Arundee says. "Let me look. That's right, a different address."

"What address?"

Arundee reads an address Thanom has never heard of.

"What is that?"

"I'm sorry?"

Thanom sits forward, hearing his wet shirt pull itself away from the back of his leather chair. "That address, what kind of address is that?"

There's a pause, and Thanom can almost feel Arundee sitting back in his chair. "Colonel, are you saying something is wrong?"

"No, no. It's just that—that there are a lot of accounts, and I don't recognize the address."

"Most of our best customers have multiple accounts and multiple addresses," Arundee says, sounding defensive. "Police officers, politicians, army commanders—"

"I understand." He covers the mouthpiece so the other man won't hear him swallow. "The bank has always been very—very discreet. Just refresh my memory."

"It's a post office box."

"Give me a moment here," Thanom says. "Hang on." He puts the receiver on the desk and uses his sleeve to mop his face. Then he draws three deep breaths, gets up, goes to the door, and opens it. "Coffee," he says. "And no argument."

Back at the desk, he says, "We do have a problem. And it might be a police problem. I need you to answer some questions. Official questions."

"But—I'm not the right person for this."

"I don't care. Answer the questions you can and make a list of the ones you can't, and get back to me with answers. Clear? Unless you want officers in uniform down there, I don't want excuses, I want answers. How much was the last deposit?"

"Umm . . . twenty-two thousand baht."

"And the one before that?"

"I have to bring that up." Thanom hears keys clacking. "Twenty thousand."

"How long before?"

"Six months. Before the last one, I mean, so that would be a little more than fifteen months ago."

"They've been every six months?"

"Just . . . a . . . minute. Pretty, um, pretty close. And recently they've been between nineteen and twenty-two thousand baht each. Average is about twenty thousand baht."

He sees a small piece of blue sky. "That doesn't make any sense at all. That would be something like a hundred deposits every six months. What's that, fifty years? They would have started when I was nine years old."

"I said *recently*. They were quite a bit bigger seven or eight years back."

He can't help himself: he echoes Arundee. "Seven or eight years."

"That's an estimate." He hears keys clicking. "But, yes, they got smaller a little less than six years ago. For the first two or three years, they were bigger."

"How *much* bigger?"

"Considerably. They vary, but they were in the hundreds of thousands."

"Hundreds of—" The door opens, and Taan comes in, her mouth a graphic of disapproval. She puts down the half-full cup harder than necessary and makes a straight-line exit.

"The biggest was a little more than two hundred thousand."

Thanom tries to blink away the little spots floating in front of his eyes, tries to slow his breathing. He sucks down half of the coffee and pushes the buzzer. "How were the deposits made?"

"I can't—I mean, I don't have that information. This was just an exploratory call."

"Find out." The door opens, and Thanom drains the cup and holds it out. "More. *Now.*"

When Taan is gone, he says, "I need to know how the deposits were made and by whom. I need a list of dates and amounts. I need to know what branches they were made to. I need to know what identification your people demanded and what it said. And anything else you can think of that might be helpful to someone who's just learned he has millions of baht in an account *he never opened,* and who's a high-ranking police officer. And I don't suppose I need to tell you this should be discreet."

"No, sir."

"Ten minutes. I'll wait ten minutes."

Thanom hangs up and exhales so heavily it catches in his throat. He gets up and goes through the door to meet his coffee halfway.

30

Question Time

RAFFERTY FEELS TIME at his back, like a wind. He has no idea what will happen next, but he knows that the trouble isn't over, that it's closing in from one side or the other, and he needs somehow to get out in front of it.

So his first exchange, with Hwa, is a pleasant surprise, if only because it goes by so quickly. She had met him at the door of the apartment she keeps Neeni in and accepted the envelopes without a change in expression, as though people handed her sixty thousand dollars every day, and said she'd already taken care of the tickets.

"Good, that's good." She starts to close the door, but he stops her. "Ummm, listen. I found Treasure."

Hwa says, "So?"

"Maybe if she saw Treasure, maybe—"

Hwa shakes her head. "You are good man," she says. "Have heart too much. But no."

Rafferty says, without intending to speak out loud, "Poor kid."

"Yes," Hwa says. "Poor kid." She purses her lips as though sealing off something she wants to say. Then she steps back and puts a hand on the door. "We go tomorrow."

"Fine. Well, if you need anything . . . " He lets it trail off.

"You do everything already." She closes the door.

* * *

ARTHIT'S CELL PHONE goes unanswered. Rafferty leaves a message, just thanking him for arranging for Anand to stay at the apartment, and calls Rose.

"This man you left here is very handsome," she says.

"Good. You can look at him and give the remote to Miaow."

"She hid the remote."

Rafferty tries not to laugh and fails. "What's she watching?"

"Something from England. Everybody's rich and they live in a big house and say awful things to each other."

"Could be anything."

"I want to look at Dr. Drew."

"Gosh," he says. "That's terrible."

"When do you come back?"

"You mean you miss me?"

"No, but maybe you can find the remote."

"I have to see Andrew's father at one. So that's, what, an hour and a half from now? Rose, let Anand answer the door. And neither of you should go out without Anand, and I don't want either of you in the apartment alone, either."

There's a moment of silence, and then she says, "That bad?"

"It could be."

"All right. Should I take Miaow to my mother's?"

"Maybe. If I'm right, the people we have to worry about are cops. They'll find you up there in no time."

"We could go to Fon's again."

Neither of these solutions makes him happy. "Give me a few hours. Maybe we'll all go up there."

Rose says, "We could take the TV."

"Fine," he says, "as long as the remote stays here."

BOO SAYS IN Thai, "Tell me you've called because you have an idea."

Rafferty had decided against a sixth cup of coffee and is instead dredging his way through some almost cosmically sweet coffee-milkshake-sort-of-thing that he has privately dubbed a *crappucino.* "Not yet." He's speaking English, which Boo understands much better than he can speak it. "I have money for First Home. A couple of thousand dollars now, with a lot more to come as needed."

"That would probably help. But there's nowhere here she'd be isolated from the other kids."

"How was it last night?"

"They were all there in the morning."

"That's something." A beep in his ear announces an incoming call. He glances at it, doesn't recognize the number, and ignores it.

"But she's not talking," Boo says. "Not even to them. She just sat on the cot until Chalee went and got Katherine, and then she stood up and allowed Katherine to lead her to the toilet."

"Well. I guess that's something. She trusts three people, to some extent."

"She trusts you most."

"I know, Boo, but it's not possible, not now."

"When?"

Well, Rafferty thinks, *that's the question, isn't it?* Boo has always cut to the center of things. "Maybe never. But I'll come up with something."

After a moment, Boo says, "This must be because you are American."

"What must be?"

"You always think you can make things work."

"I never think I can make things work," Rafferty says. "I just say that because it keeps me from giving up. Look, I'll bring the money by later. Maybe I should talk to Father Bill. It's his place."

"You have to. I think one or two days, that's all we've got. We have to find someone who knows how to take care of her. And a place where she can stay."

"Okay, okay."

Rafferty pushes the cold glass away, brings up the missed call and punches *return*. It rings eight, nine times, and he hangs up.

He's got more than an hour before he's due at Nguyen's office. Not enough time to do anything worthwhile, too much time to waste. A snip of time that's exactly the wrong size. If a day were a jigsaw puzzle, it would be a missing piece.

He tries Arthit again. Still no answer.

Okay. Question time. Why did anyone want the phone? What Arthit said, because their faces were on it? But that's pretty thin: with almost seventy million faces in the kingdom of Thailand, searching for one or two is like looking for a needle in a stack of needles. To narrow the field, you'd need a line to these people, a link to one or more of Sawat's victims.

But let's say that was the reason anyway. So with the phone in the hands of the police, why send someone after Miaow? They'd been seen by a dozen people when they trashed the vendor's stand. What harm could Miaow possibly represent?

Someone with a knife. Someone who meant to use it.

He's rubbed his finger on the wet side of his glass, and he's drawing question marks on the table. If it's not the pictures, what?

The cops have the pictures now. There are cops involved in all of this—Sawat's racket had to involve several highly-ranked officers. Arthit's boss, Thanom, is the most probable link to Sawat, but he's also the one who knows best that Miaow doesn't have the phone. So why would he send that man after Miaow?

It suddenly occurs to him that the man with the knife must have picked Miaow up at the apartment. Reflexively, he calls home and tells Rose that no one, not even Anand, is leaving the building until he, Rafferty, is back.

He's on his feet without even knowing he got up, standing next to the plate glass window and looking out at the heat of the day. *Andrew*, he thinks. Andrew had the phone overnight at his apartment. Maybe there's something *else* on it, something worth killing a child for. Maybe Andrew saw something without knowing it.

Thirty minutes left. He'll walk to Nguyen's office. That'll use up at least twenty.

The heat slaps him in the face as he steps outside, but it doesn't sap the coil of uneasy energy at his core. As livid as he is about the threat to Miaow, there's a new level of anxiety that's all about Rose's pregnancy. He hadn't thought in the past that the idea of something happening to her could be any more agonizing than it already was, but this is in a whole new language.

There are days when Bangkok strikes him as the world's biggest juicer, a giant, malevolent machine devised solely to extract perspiration from the defenseless. He's dragging his feet to stretch out the walk, and still he's practically squirting sweat as he approaches the high steel gate of the Vietnamese Embassy and heads for the closed door with the urgent-looking red sign on it. As he reaches out to open it, his phone rings: same number as before.

"Hello?"

"This is Nguyen. Where are you?"

"About to knock on the door or whatever the protocol is here."

"I'm not there," Nguyen says. He sounds agitated, more rattled that Rafferty can recall his being. "I'm at home. Something has happened. Please come here."

"Your apartment."

"Yes. I'm sorry for the inconvenience. Please come now."

Nguyen disconnects. Rafferty glares at the phone for a moment and then turns back into the heat of the day.

31

Hooked and Landed

THE LAST TIME Rafferty visited this apartment, his impression was one of precise control, an architectural equivalent to the way Nguyen oils his hair to paste every strand in place. The symmetry of the apartment—too rigid, too precious—made it feel like a diorama under glass.

Now it looks like the entire place was picked up, turned sideways, and given a good shake.

He pauses in the entrance to the living room, where the two blue couches are upside-down, their cushions slit and the stuffing scattered. Nguyen had greeted him at the door with a tight nod and then turned, leaving Rafferty to follow him inside. Over Nguyen's shoulders, two compact, fit-looking men give him challenging stares until he looks elsewhere.

One of them is short and broad-shouldered, with rapidly receding hair above a Pleistocene brow-ridge. The other is whippet-thin, with lips so narrow they look like they could draw blood. They both wear slacks and polo shirts and they put no visible energy into exuding charm.

"These are Chinh and Homer," Nguyen says without indicating which is which. "You have a policeman at your place. Can you trust him?"

"He's a friend. How do you know that I have—"

"I called. It was the first thing I did when I came home and saw this." Nguyen kicks some glistening white stuff, like the angel's-hair they used to put on Christmas trees, probably an element in the couch's stuffing. It drifts about a foot into the air and waffles down. "You called me to tell me someone chased Miaow with a knife," he says, "because you were concerned about Andrew. I called your apartment because I wanted to tell Mrs. Rafferty and Miaow that they might think of going somewhere else."

"Thank you."

Nguyen gives him a brusque nod and watches as the other two men straighten the room, looking under and into everything they touch. "I've noticed that you feel most comfortable when you think you're in charge," Nguyen says, turning to him. Rafferty searches for a hint of humor in the man's eyes but finds none. His face is stony with fury. "Would you like to ask questions, or should I just tell you about this?"

"Tell me."

"We'll sit at the table," Nguyen says, not bothering to make it sound like an invitation. A round table stands at the corner of the floor-to-ceiling windows that wall half of the living room. Beside it are four carved wooden chairs whose blue silk-covered seats have been sliced open. This was where Rafferty sat the first time he came here, eight or nine weeks ago, asking Nguyen to side with him in a war with a former American operative who had done a lot of damage in Vietnam. Nguyen had remained neutral.

Nguyen chooses a chair with its back touching the window while Rafferty, who's never been happy with heights, takes the one farthest away. Nguyen begins to talk even before Rafferty is seated. "My wife, as you know, has been ill for a long time. I tell you this again because it is related to what happened here this morning. Anh Duong—Andrew—and I took her to her doctor this morning at ten. That's the only time this apartment has been empty since we took her to that same doctor four weeks ago. It's a monthly appointment."

Rafferty says, "Maybe they were watching."

A sideways tilt of the head that's clearly not intended to express agreement. "Maybe. But I doubt it. I doubt it because the doormen say they saw nothing while we were gone. No one, they say, came in and went up to this floor. And the video surveillance disks are missing."

Rafferty says, "Ahhh, shit."

One of the hard-eyed guys makes a sound like a stopped-up snort.

"Chinh, Homer," Nguyen says. "Go finish in Anh Duong's room." He's speaking English, probably for Rafferty's sake.

When they've left, Rafferty says, "Homer?"

"His mother is a Classics scholar. He has a brother named Virgil."

"Okay," Rafferty says. "Only cops could operate with this kind of impunity. Scare your doormen into calling them when you leave, walk away with the video. Is the appointment always the same day?"

"First Monday of every month."

"And you were gone—?"

"A little more than two and a half hours. Plenty of time for this kind of search. If they'd wanted to be subtle it might have taken longer."

"But they didn't care whether they were subtle."

"No, they didn't," Nguyen says tightly. "And that was one of their mistakes."

"One?"

"The other was to chase Miaow with a knife. Destroying this apartment tells me they don't think they can be touched. Taking a knife to your daughter tells me that they would kill my son, too. And before we go any further, I want to say something personal. It's clear to me now that Miaow saved Andrew's life." He's sitting bolt upright in the shredded chair, his knees apart, and now he dips his head slightly. "I owe your daughter my thanks."

"I'll pass them along."

"I'll tell her myself. If you'll do what I suggest, I'll have lots of opportunity."

"What's that?"

"I'm moving Andrew and his mother into the embassy. Immediately. We would be honored to host Mrs. Rafferty and Miaow, too."

Rafferty is taken so off-guard it takes him a moment to make sense of it. He says, "The embassy," and then he laughs.

Nguyen doesn't laugh, but he looks like he remembers having laughed once, which is as close as Rafferty has seen him get. "Exactly," he says. "The Embassy is Vietnam. The Thai police have no jurisdiction there. They can wipe themselves on their badges."

"It's perfect."

Nguyen says, "It's going to throw Andrew and Miaow together."

"They'll both survive."

"It *is* important to me, Mr. Rafferty, that my son marries a Vietnamese girl."

"Mr. Nguyen—"

"Captain. Captain Nguyen."

"Sorry. *Captain* Nguyen. And it's important to me that my daughter falls in love with someone who deserves her."

Nguyen's mouth tightens.

"Nothing personal," Rafferty says, "not any more than the way you feel about Miaow is personal."

"We have responsibilities," Nguyen says, "filial and family responsibilities. As an only son, Andrew's is to honor his family. To do that, he'll have to marry a Vietnamese girl. This is something he needs to learn now, while he still does what he's told."

"You may be right," Rafferty says, making no effort to sound like he means it. "He's your kid. But I'll tell you what. The cops made *three* mistakes. The third one was pulling this shit in the week my wife discovered she's pregnant."

Whatever Nguyen is going to say, he bites it back when one of the hard-eyed men, Homer or Chinh, comes back in, followed by Andrew, who gives Rafferty a double-take and says, "Hello, Mr. Rafferty."

"Hey, Andrew. How you handling this?"

"I don't know. What's my choice? Is Miaow all right?"

"She's fine. She's got a cop—one of the good ones—babysitting her right now."

"Nothing more," Chinh or Homer says, and the other one comes in, too.

"There *isn't* anything more," Andrew says with a kind of condensed bitterness. "They got everything."

"Everything what?" Rafferty asks.

"Every computer and peripheral in the apartment," Nguyen says. "Mine, too, which is causing some excitement at the embassy."

"But it's Andrew's they were after," Rafferty says.

"Of course," Nguyen says. "They took everything he could conceivably have used to copy or store the information from that phone."

"All of it?" Rafferty says.

"All of it," Nguyen says.

"Andrew," Rafferty says. "Did they get all of it?"

Something glimmers in Andrew's eye, and then it's gone. He says, "Not unless they closed down Google."

His father says, "Google?"

"On the way home from buying the phone," Andrew says, his eyes watching for his father's reaction, "while Miaow was being carsick, I emailed everything to myself."

THANOM PUTS THE phone down and sees that the handset is smeared with his sweat.

He feels as though the back wall of his office, three stories in the air, has just collapsed, and two of the legs of his chair are dangling twenty meters above the street. His life is over.

He suddenly remembers the twinge of guilt he'd felt about implicating Arthit, and a hot wave of shame rises up to choke him. Not Arthit, he thinks. *Him.*

It's been him all along.

For years, they've been working on this. This is a ten-year plan, one the Chinese government would envy. It must have been put into place practically the day he received the promotion that put him in charge of Sawat.

Oh, no, he thinks. The promotion. The high point of his career. The only time his wife ever expressed any pride in him. For her, the marriage had been one long decline into unbroken disappointment until he was promoted. She had said, "Isn't this a nice surprise?" He hadn't told her exactly how surprised he was.

There had been two men between him and the desk at which he now sits, two people who were more likely choices than he, who could have argued that they were more deserving than he, who could have made a fuss, in fact, about the chain of command. And hadn't.

Both of them have done very nicely for themselves, he realizes, both of them have moved up and sideways, like the knight in chess. Like a piece of choreography.

And he'd been so complacent, so smug, so secure that his worth had been recognized and rewarded at long last. His career, which had begun slowly, had finally gotten the traction he deserved. His superiors had recognized him for what he was.

A fall guy.

The bank account had been opened about a month after he was promoted. Sawat was already active by then. The deposits had been cashier's checks and money orders, sometimes cash. They had been deposited by someone whose identification proclaimed him to be a police captain named Sawat.

There had even been occasional withdrawals, made by someone using his, Thanom's, name, just for verisimilitude.

It was so nicely designed, such a tight fit, he could almost respect it.

The person who made the deposits was in police uniform, unlikely to have been scrutinized by a low-ranking bank employee. There was some possibility, Arundee had acknowledged, in response to Thanom's frantic demand, that at some point the identification of the person who made the withdrawals might have been scanned and copied, but probably not. He was, after all, a police officer, and the police . . .

But he would look to see whether anything was there.

Hooked and landed, Thanom thinks. All they need to do is cook him, and they can do that any time they get hungry.

The Dancer. He knows some people in the department call him the Dancer. He'd taken a kind of pride in it, but that was when he thought he'd been leading. Now that he knows different, now that he knows he's been maneuvered, one graceful step at a time, to the edge of a cliff, he feels the lack of affection the nickname implies. He has no allies.

There must be *someone* he can trust. There must be someone with whom he can discuss this. There must be someone who can—

His mind stops, absolutely blank, until he can finish the thought. There must be someone who can *help*.

He jumps two inches straight up as the comm box on his desk buzzes. He pushes the button, and Taan says, "On line one, sir. It's Lieutenant-Colonel Arthit."

32

Teams

"I CLEARED THE browser on the phone," Andrew says. "Right after I sent the pictures to myself." He's sitting at the keyboard in an Internet cafe, and his father, Rafferty, Homer, and Chinh are gathered around him as though he were about to do a trick, which, Rafferty thinks, isn't completely inaccurate.

"But the browsing history can probably be unerased, right?" Rafferty says. "Miaow talks about how you can't really erase much of anything."

"Well, sure. I mean, what I did on the phone wouldn't stand up to anyone who knew what he was doing. But I sent them to a, a—" He glances uneasily at his father, licks his lips, and plunges in. "A secret account. It doesn't have my name connected with it anywhere."

Nguyen says, "How many of these do you have?"

"Just *one*," Andrew says with total, unblemished sincerity, wide eyes and everything.

"Why do you need one?"

"Everything you do online," Andrew says, a bit hurriedly, "it's like skywriting. Nothing is secret. I mean, confidential. Kids at *school* can get through most firewalls."

"What's the name on the account?" Rafferty asks, mostly to back Nguyen off.

"It's, uh, 13catlover@gmail.com."

"Catlover," Rafferty says. Andrew goes fire-engine red. "Bet I can guess the password."

"You probably can," Andrew says without moving his teeth at all.

"Well, let's take a look."

Andrew brings up Gmail. The password displays in asterisks on the screen as he types it, but Rafferty sees him hit the M, I and A keys before Andrew glances up and catches him. Andrew says, "Do you *mind?*"

Rafferty says, "I wouldn't be a kid again for anything."

Either Homer or Chinh says, "Me neither."

Nguyen silences them with a glance, and all of them go back to watching Andrew. In about eight seconds he sits back and says, "There's the download."

"Only one?" Nguyen says. "I thought there were a lot of them."

"I zipped it," Andrew says. "I grabbed an online utility and zipped it. And it's got a password of its own, so even if someone found it, they'd have to work to see what it is."

Nguyen says, and he's almost smiling, "What password?"

"Julie." Andrew waits, but no one asks.

"After the character in *Small Town*," Rafferty says.

Andrew mutters something that could just possibly be, "Shit."

His father says, "Anh *Duong.*"

"Yeah, yeah," Andrew says. He sticks a thumb drive into a USB port and copies the zipped file.

"Here's a thought," Rafferty says, a bit ashamed of himself. "You're our tech guy, and all your stuff just got pounded. How about we go buy you a new laptop? It was a Mac, right?"

Andrew's head snaps around, his eyes wide behind his glasses. "I'll need some image processing software."

"You got it."

"And a, uh, a new iPhone."

"My pleasure."

"Mr. Rafferty," Nguyen says.

"It's my daughter they went after. Anyway, the kid needs a phone."

"Fifty-fifty," Nguyen says. His eyes flick to Homer and Chinh, and then come back. "Since we seem to be a team."

Rafferty says, "A team."

Over him, Andrew says, "MBK Mall, you know, Mah Boon Krong. They've got competing shops." He pulls out the thumb drive, clears the browser, and gets up. "Top of the line," he says.

Rafferty says, "Of course. What else?"

"We can't stay on the defensive," Nguyen says. "That's what they're expecting."

Rafferty says, "Great." He extends his arm and sights down it. "Aim and ignite."

THE DESK BETWEEN Arthit and Thanom could be a mile wide and a mile deep. They regard each other across it like Korean soldiers on opposite sides of the thirty-eighth parallel. Coffee cools untouched in front of them.

Thanom moves things around on his desk until they satisfy him. "You called me," he says.

"And I'm having second thoughts." Arthit picks up his cup, blows on the coffee, and puts it down again. He sits back in his chair and regards Thanom for so long that the other man lowers his gaze. Arthit can smell his superior even over the scorch of the coffee, can see the wet cloth beneath his arms.

"This is unacceptable," Thanom says. He blinks a couple of times, tantamount to a cry for help. "Just tell me what you found."

Arthit tastes the coffee and glares at it. Putting it down again, he says, "We've reached a tipping point." He uses the English expression.

Thanom shakes his head as though he's being swarmed by gnats. "We've what? What's a tipping point?"

"We both know," Arthit says, "that this thing could bite us in half."

Studying the surface of his desk, Thanom says, "Don't you trust me?"

"Of course not."

Thanom says, "Ah."

"And you don't trust me."

"So," Thanom says. "How do we start?"

"With a goal," Arthit says. "What do you want out of this?"

"To handle the case properly," Thanom says. "And to—to protect the department."

Arthit says, "Right." He looks at his wristwatch and pushes his chair back.

"I want to survive," Thanom says, biting the words off.

Arthit says, "Now we're getting somewhere." He picks up his coffee, starts to sip it, and puts it back down. He says, "Can you get your pet dragon to—"

"Taan," Thanom says into his intercom, "get us a pot of fresh coffee and two clean cups." He snaps off the intercom and sits back, hunching his shoulders practically up to his ears. He swivels his spine right and left and then says, "It's me."

Arthit says, "I thought it might be."

"I'm the sacrifice. Here's how dumb I was. They told me it was you, and I believed them."

"Did you argue with them?"

Thanom shakes his head.

"Well," Arthit says, "I was pretty sure it was you, and I didn't worry about it much, either. They told you? They who?"

Thanom points at the ceiling and then says, "Higher."

"Name."

"Not yet."

"Why not?"

Thanom says, "Once I tell you that, what have I got?"

"What did you have when I walked in?"

"A few . . . moves held in reserve." He wipes his face with an open palm.

Arthit lets it pass. "So they told you it was me and now you know it's you. So tell me the truth. Was it?"

"No." The word hangs over the table as though it's tethered there, and then Arthit nods.

"I believe you."

"Just out of curiosity," Thanom says, "why do you believe me?"

"You're not that stupid. You might never be policeman of the year, but you're not stupid."

"The people involved in this are not stupid."

"Up there?" Arthit points at the ceiling. "They can be as stupid as they want. They're untouchable. How do you know you're it?"

Thanom gazes at the center of Arthit's chest for a moment, and then closes his eyes. "They've been building a bank account in my name. For years." He opens his eyes, looks at Arthit, and blots his upper lip with his cuff. "Opened by someone in police uniform, using identification that said he was me. With deposits made by someone else in uniform with identification that said he was Sawat."

"How much money?"

Thanom takes a deep breath and says, "At the moment, almost two million baht."

"Starting when?"

"About ten years ago. When Sawat was active."

"When did they stop?"

"Six months ago."

Arthit says, "Two million. They were serious."

"It feels serious to me," Thanom says.

"How frequent were the deposits?"

"Months apart. Why?"

"How do you know it was two men?"

"How do I know *what* was two men?"

"The one who opened the account and the one who made the deposits. How do you know it wasn't just one man?"

Thanom says, "Stands to reason."

"Not really. Someone opens the account in, say, February. Then, in April or May, he comes back with new ID, gets in a different line, and makes a deposit. Or uses different branches for deposits and withdrawals."

"But why—" He breaks off. "Right, I see. In the wrong hands, this—this information—is a gun to the head. If the relationship with the person who does the banking breaks down, the guy behind him is at his mercy."

"Has to be someone he trusts."

"Or owns."

Arthit says, "Trusts *and* owns. Probably not many of those around, no matter who he is. He'd want to keep the number as small as possible. Whose name on the withdrawals?"

"ID in my name."

The door opens and Taan comes in with a tray. "This is foolish of you," she says, putting it down. "I'm going home."

Reflexively, Thanom says, "Be careful." He takes a cup off the tray and, after a second's hesitation, politely hands it to Arthit and takes the second for himself. He waits until Taan closes the door. "She terrifies me," he says.

"Do you think she's a plant?"

Thanom says, "No more than yours is."

"Something to think about."

"I don't need something else to think about."

"So we're in a situation," Arthit says. He drinks about half of the coffee, which is scalding. "You know they're after *you*, and I'm not sure they won't come after me. They might just clean up the whole mess, get rid of all of us, put people in here whose memories don't go back that far. Why don't you tell me who it was who called you?"

Thanom says, "You first. Tell me what you found today."

And, after a moment of reflection, Arthit does. It takes him the rest of the coffee in his cup and most of another one to tell it.

When he's finished, Thanom looks past him at the wall. He says, "No such crimes?"

"None that might have involved Sawat."

Thanom pushes the coffee away as though it's offended him. "Let's go get a drink."

33

Lighter Than Air and Apparently Combustible

WITH HOMER—THE ONE with the brow ridge—standing guard, it takes Rafferty less than twenty minutes to get them all packed up and ready to go. A medium suitcase for each of them, plus Rose's pillow, which goes wherever she goes. He's pulled the money out of everywhere he can remember stuffing it and repacked it into Murphy's briefcase. Probing the depths of the couch for some stray hundreds, his fingers hit the remote.

Holding it up, he says to Rose, "This is the first place I'd look."

"Shhhhh," she says, with a glance toward Miaow's room. "Put it back."

An unmarked embassy SUV is waiting in the underground garage, with Chinh at the wheel and Andrew in the seat behind him, his face lighted from beneath by the glow of his new laptop's screen, like a figure out of some Asian Toulouse-Lautrec. Miaow almost stumbles when she sees him, but then she marches forward, throws her bag in the back, and sits on the same long seat as Andrew, against the opposite wall. Neither child speaks. The SUV purrs quietly, and they're whisked up the driveway to the street. Rafferty sits in front with Chinh; Miaow and Andrew occupy the middle seat, pasted to their respective windows; and Rose sits in solitary and queenly splendor in the back. Homer, when they last see him, is angling for a cab to the embassy.

As Chinh signals a left into the street, Andrew clears his throat and says to Miaow, "Hi."

After a long four or five seconds, Miaow says, "Hi." The car goes silent again.

Watching the darkened sidewalks through the tinted windows, Rafferty doesn't see anything out of place, but he says to the driver, "Take us around the block. If the guy is here, I want to see his face. Miaow, crack your window so you can get a better look."

"I can only see one side of the street," Miaow says.

"Well, we'll go around twice, and you can change sides."

She lowers her window and says, to the street outside, "When I change sides, Andrew will have to move."

Rafferty says, "He will," and simultaneously Andrew says, "I will."

Miaow says, to no one, "Okay."

Rose says, in her calmest voice, "I hope the bed is nice."

"Oh, Christ," Rafferty says. "A bed. I forgot."

"Forgot what?" Rose asks.

"A bed. I have to make a stop between here and the embassy." He says to the driver, "I'm sorry, Chinh. Let's go around the block twice so we can look for friends we don't want."

Rose says, "A stop where?"

"Where Treasure is. I have to see Boo for a second."

Andrew lowers his window, too, and Miaow says, "What are you doing?"

"Maybe it's one of the guys who chased us," Andrew says. "If it is—"

"You can't see across the street," Miaow says. "It's like a kilometer wide and there's the Skytrain and—"

"Having you look too is a wonderful idea, Andrew," Rose says, aiming it at Miaow.

"But maybe she's right," Andrew says, immediately defensive. "I mean—I mean—"

"We know what you mean, Andrew," Rafferty says. "You're both right. Now let's all shut up and look out the windows."

Traffic is moving at the eternal Bangkok creep, and Rafferty figures both kids are getting a good look. It gets more difficult when they turn into the traffic on Silom and confront the packed sidewalk. Since Andrew can't see the other side of the street, he slides over next to Miaow. Rafferty waits, but she accepts it.

They roll half of the block in silence. Twice, Miaow straightens and inhales sharply, but both times she sinks back, saying, "No."

A moment later, Andrew, looking back, says, "*That* guy? Loose dark shirt?"

"No," Miaow says, following his gaze. "I looked at him twice, too."

After another fifteen or twenty meters, Andrew says, "I'm glad you got away from the one with the knife."

Miaow doesn't reply. As they near the first crossstreet, Chinh hits the turn indicator, but Andrew remains next to Miaow.

Rose says, "Are we going to eat something any time soon?"

"After we see Boo," Rafferty says.

"I'm eating for two," Rose says. "I've been waiting all day to say that."

As they take the corner, Andrew says, "What does that mean?"

Miaow says, "She's going to have a baby."

"Oh," Andrew says. Then he says, "Jeez." At the same time, Miaow says, "*Slow down,*" and Andrew is thrown against the back of the front seat as Chinh brakes.

"That one," Miaow says, pointing to a man in dark pants and a dark long-sleeved shirt who's suddenly reversed direction to trot away, still walking, but putting some back into it.

Rafferty says, "You sure?" but he's already got his door open and he's on the pavement before she can say, "Yes." He's running almost weightlessly, buoyed up by an explosion in the center of his chest, something lighter than air and apparently combustible, something that feels surprisingly like hope: He's *finally* going to get a chance to wring someone's neck. All the fury and frustration he's been compressing these past few days is expanding into this strange bubble that's lightening him, pushing him forward so he's gaining on the man rapidly, but the man glances back and sees him, giving Rafferty a brief glimpse of his face. Instantly, the man is stretched out, streamlined as a whippet, taking steps that seem, to Rafferty, far too long for a man of his size.

The face, the *face.* As Rafferty pushes himself faster, he does an automatic short-term-memory ransack and comes up blank. It's a common enough face, dark-skinned, wide-nostriled, but with small, deep-set eyes and a low forehead that combine to give him an unusual foreshortened, thuggish look that, Rafferty thinks, is probably what made Miaow recognize him. The face's slightly brutish cast is not something she'd forget.

He's closed the gap to a couple of car lengths, but Silom is blossoming in front of him, and with one more quick glance back, the man disappears to the left, down the Silom sidewalk.

Rafferty is there a second or two later, just in time to terrify a Chinese senior citizen, one of forty or fifty strung out in a staggered squadron, three abreast. They're following a young woman in a bright yellow hat who's holding up an orange flag with Chinese characters on it. The woman he nearly knocked down is patting her chest like she's got the vapors, and all along the line behind her, there are small rear-end collisions as people are forced into the people in front of them by the people behind them. By the time Rafferty has dog-trotted an apology down the ranks, the man with the low forehead is long gone.

Poke leans against a store window, feeling the energy drain from his body as the Chinese seniors scroll by, probably off to take some cautious snapshots of Patpong. Feeling as bleak as a cinder, he turns and makes his way back to the cross street.

Miaow and Andrew are there on the sidewalk, Andrew's eyes wide and Miaow's faintly accusing. "Too many people," Poke says, fighting for breath. He heads for the car, the kids trotting behind.

"You move *fast,*" Andrew says, and Miaow sniffs.

"Yeah, but he's gone." He feels the constriction in his throat and recognizes it as pure hatred, so he turns away from the kids, opens the SUV's door and climbs in, saying to Chinh, "Come on, once more around, just to look for a tail."

Chinh says, "No tail."

Rafferty chokes back a spasm of rage and gets his breathing under control before he replies. "Well, okay, but we need to get going." To Miaow, he says, "We have to feed your mother."

RAFFERTY'S SO BUSY keeping an eye on the road behind them that he misses a left and gets turned around as they approach First Home. Fixing it requires them to backtrack for eight or ten unencouraging minutes through some of the grimmest streets in the most impoverished area of Klong Toey, the river gleaming darkly below them, glimpsed between slanting plywood shacks roofed with corrugated tin and sheets of plastic. Here and there the shacks have been razed to make way for windowless warehouses to receive the unending flow of goods from the port. There are very few streetlights. Now and then the SUV's headlights bring out of the darkness the figures of furtive children in outsize T-shirts or a shirtless man.

His face practically pressed to the glass, Andrew says, "Where *are* we?"

Miaow says, "Poor-people world."

Rafferty's phone rings, and he punches it up and says, "Hi. Yeah, we're coming. Got a stop to make first, and then we need to get something to eat." He listens for a moment, then turns around. "How are you, Andrew?"

Andrew says, "Huh?"

Rafferty says, "He's fine. He says to tell you *huh*. We're all together with Chinh at the wheel."

"My father?" Andrew says.

"Turn right here," Rafferty says. "This thing that looks like an alley, and go slow because the potholes will take your wheels off." Into the phone he says, "We're in Klong Toey. Up there, up there," he says to Chinh. "Visiting someone," he says into the phone, and then he closes it and calls back to Rose, "They've got food waiting for us at the embassy."

Chinh stops the SUV beside a featureless wall across from a low, mottled concrete building. The building has only a few windows, and most of those are cracked or broken and dark. Two of the windows on the ground floor are defined as rectangles of a faint, chalky glow, a chilly, damp-looking light that might be emitted by the phosphorescence of decaying wood.

Andrew says, "What kind of place is this? *Who* are we visiting?"

Rose, who's getting ready to climb out, says, "Miaow? Why don't you tell him?"

Rafferty, his door already open, angles the rearview mirror around to see Miaow leaning against the window, her eyes squeezed shut. As he gets out, he hears her say to Andrew, "Come with me."

34

Reading the Night

WITH POKE IN the lead, holding Rose's hand, they climb two crumbling concrete steps and pass through a wide-open double door into a big, airless room. A few stubby, cobwebbed fluorescent tubes flicker from the ceiling, surrounded by pairs of sockets designed to house others. About thirty cots stagger in random-looking rows across the concrete floor. Most of them are bare, but seven or eight have blankets folded on them and cardboard boxes shoved beneath them to serve as lockers. Three boys huddle on one cot, their heads bent over some kind of game on a cell phone. The boy holding the phone has four fresh, deep gouges, painted with Mercurochrome, running from his left eye to his jawline. Two other boys, possibly ten or twelve years old, lie on cots by themselves, three cots apart at a safe distance from the other boys, bringing their heads up to get a look at the newcomers.

The boys who are alone are filthy. Their skin is mottled with sweat and dirt, their hair and clothes oily and ragged. Both of them stare, and Rafferty thinks it's probably Rose who's drawn their attention, but when he looks more closely, he sees it's Miaow and Andrew. One of the filthy boys ostentatiously rolls over, turning his back to them, and makes a noise like a fart. Andrew swallows so loudly Rafferty can hear him. The boys hovering over the cell phone game glance quickly at Miaow and Andrew, and gather themselves into a tighter knot. Their eyes are sullen, resentful, and perhaps, Rafferty thinks, ashamed.

One of them clears his throat noisily and spits on the floor. Then the three turn back to their game. Only the second dirty boy, the youngest boy in the room, continues to look at them, and his eyes have a peculiar intensity, as though he believes one of these clean, well-dressed children will suddenly be revealed as his long-lost brother or sister.

Miaow chooses him and says, "Hi."

He says, "Hi." His voice has an odd foghorn quality, as though it doesn't get much use.

The boy with the gouged cheek says, "The zoo is over on Rama Five."

Miaow takes a deep, deep breath and says, perhaps a bit too loudly, "I know where the zoo is. I used to eat out of the trashcans there. Before Boo found me."

The boys all study her. Even the filthy one, who'd turned his back on them, sits up and stares at her. But the most intense gaze in the room is Andrew's. His arms hang so loosely, his jaw is so slack, that it looks to Rafferty like his body is empty and about to fold to the floor.

Rose says to Poke, "Let's leave them alone," and leads him, still holding his hand, across the room and through the gap in the partitions that forms the door to Boo's office.

THE SPACE IS as jammed with furniture as Rafferty's father's old garage, back in Lancaster, California. In addition to Boo's desk and his three chairs and the big whiteboard, three cots and three folding metal chairs like the ones in the makeshift hospital room have shouldered their way in. Two of Boo's chairs have been shoved against the partition on the right like wallflowers at a dance. Color pictures from magazines, mostly of teenage girls with enviable clothes, are taped to the walls. The place smells richly of garlic.

Sitting at the chair behind Boo's desk, with a heaping, apparently untouched, plastic plate of noodles in front of her, is Treasure. She's wearing a man's wrinkled, pale-blue shirt that looks enormous on her narrow shoulders. It's buttoned to the top, but it hangs loosely enough to bare her collarbones, still prominent after weeks of starvation. Her dark tangle of hair has been pulled back and secured, on top and off-center, by a bright red plastic clip in the shape of a heart, obviously a loan or a gift. Dok sits on the desk's nearest corner, next to the broken electric fan. He has a fork in his hand, heaped with noodles. Both of them turn quickly when Rafferty comes in, but the moment Rose follows him through the door, he might as well be invisible. Their eyes float to her and stay there.

"Hello, Treasure," Rafferty says.

She looks at him for a tenth of a second and then she lowers her head and her eyes drop to the plate in front of her, and then skitter over it before they slide back up to Rose's face and stay there.

Rose says, "So you're Treasure. He told me you were pretty," she says, coming the rest of the way into the room, "but you're not. You're beautiful. Your mother must be exquisite."

At the word *mother*, Treasure ducks her head lower, and her hand accidentally knocks the plate sideways. Dok catches the plate without spilling a noodle, as though he's done it all his life. He says to Rose, "Who are you?"

"I'm Rose. I'm Poke's wife. You're Dok, right?"

Dok grabs his lower lip between his teeth and then nods.

"Where's—" Rose makes a puzzled show of scratching her head. "Where's—"

"Chalee," Dok says. "She's getting more food."

Rose lifts her chin toward the plate and says, "Is that good?"

Dok nods, but Rose's eyes are on Treasure. "Do you like it, Treasure?"

Treasure closes her mouth tightly, and shrugs.

"Can I have a bite?" Rose says, "I've been hungry for hours."

Dok says, "She needs to eat," but Treasure silences him with a glance, and he says, "but Chalee is bringing more, so, uh . . ."

"Let's make a deal," Rose says. "Treasure can take a bite and then you take one, and then I'll get one. Is that all right, Treasure?"

Treasure yields up another tiny shrug, but Dok blows out a little puff of air, like someone who's just heard the answer to a puzzle he's been trying to solve for days.

"You first, Treasure," Rose says. She pulls one of the metal chairs around and straddles it, right in front of the desk. "Get her that piece of shrimp, too," she says, and Treasure keeps her eyes fixed on Rose as Dok swirls the fork around in the dish. Then Dok brings the fork up and Treasure opens her mouth without taking her gaze off Rose, and when Dok pulls the fork out, it's empty.

Rose gives Treasure a smile so wide the girl sits back a few inches, Rose says, "Dok's turn." Dok eats a minuscule amount and holds out a groaning forkful to Rose.

Rose says, "You have no idea how hungry I am." To Treasure, she says, "This is really yours. Is it okay if I eat it?"

Treasure's mouth opens, but then she closes it and nods. Rose cleans the fork, turns it around to lick the back, and gives it to Dok. Looks up at Rafferty, surprised. "It's *good*," she says.

"Boo's not going to give them slop," Rafferty says, and Chalee comes into the room, balancing a plate in each hand. She stops in the doorway, not even glancing at Poke, just staring at the group at Boo's desk.

"Who are you?" she asks.

"I'm Rose, and you're Chalee, and you're just in time, because Treasure and I are really hungry."

Chalee, still holding the plates, glances at Poke, and says, "Are those two kids in the other room yours?"

Rafferty says. "Sort of."

Chalee says to Poke, "You came back."

"That's what I do. I come back."

"Who's Rose?"

"My wife."

Chalee looks again at Rose, and the left corner of her mouth travels toward her ear in an expression of pure doubt. She looks back to Poke and shrugs.

"I know," Poke says. "I don't understand it either."

"Look," Chalee says. She watches with something like amazement as Treasure accepts a second mouthful, and whispers, "This is the most she's eaten, *ever*."

"Maybe she's getting better."

Chalee says, "Maybe, maybe not," and threads through the maze of furniture to put the other two plates on Boo's desk.

Rose says, "I'm eating *everything*."

Chalee says to Rose, "Are you really married to him?"

Rose says, "Amazing, isn't it?" and Treasure actually smiles, just long enough for Poke to doubt that he actually saw it, and then Rose is saying to Dok, "Treasure's turn," and Rafferty hears Miaow's voice, raised and tremulous, from the other room. He turns to see Boo standing in the opening, staring slack-jawed at the sight of Treasure eating.

Rafferty doesn't hear Miaow say anything more, so he waves for Boo's attention. "We need to talk."

Boo says, "You have no idea."

Following Boo back out into the big room, Rafferty sees Miaow sitting on the cot with the three boys who'd been playing with the phone, which she's now holding. The two filthy boys have changed cots to get closer to the group; now they're just one vacant row away.

Andrew is nowhere in sight.

Miaow gives him too-bright eyes and a smile that looks like a muscle exercise, and Rafferty looks again for Andrew. He raises his eyebrows in a question, but Miaow looks away and Rafferty can almost hear the metal door clang down between them. One of the boys on the cot says something and the other boys laugh. Miaow just stares at the cell phone screen. Boo taps Rafferty on the shoulder and goes out and down the steps.

Rafferty hesitates, but Miaow doesn't send him a signal, so he turns and follows Boo out into the alley. Sees the SUV parked there with Chinh at the wheel and Andrew back in his original seat, his cheek against the glass of the far window and his eyes wide open, apparently reading the night.

"I don't know how long we can get away with this," Boo says.

"I brought fifty thousand baht," Rafferty says. "Just to make it clear to Father Bill that I'm working on it."

"That's not the problem." Boo looks up and down the alley without even knowing he's doing it, and Rafferty knows it's instinctive, it's what he's been doing for years now: looking for the abandoned, the throw-aways. He does it everywhere he goes. "Dok and Chalee aren't in school, and they *have* to go to school, or they won't get into First Home. I'm only allowed to keep kids here for two weeks until they can be considered to move inside, and if they're not in school, as far as Father Bill is concerned, they're not here. I don't want to have to boot Dok and Chalee out. Father Bill is a good man, but he sticks to his rules. "

"He has to," Poke says. "These kids could scam Saint Peter."

"And he's not settling for the two of them taking turns and teaching each other. But *they*, Dok and Chalee, I mean, they know she can't be left alone. She needs care, someone who knows how to work with badly damaged kids, someone who can stay here with her, at least some of the time. And she needs a place."

Rafferty feels a physical wave ripple through him, emptying him out. The concrete beneath his feet seems to pitch from side to side. He recognizes it as the tidal pull of exhaustion and widens his eyes, prompting Boo to take a step back. "I'm working on it. I am, I'm working on it. And she looks better."

"She may look better," Boo says, "but today she laid open the face of one of the kids in the outer room."

"He must have—"

"He went in to *talk* to her," Boo says, and Rafferty sees that he's weary, too. "Dok and Chalee were both gone, for just a few minutes, and the kid thought she might be lonely. And, yeah, he was curious. The kids who have seen her talk a lot about her, about the way she looks. So he goes in and she's on her cot, with her arm over her eyes, and he gets closer than he should have and then he makes some kind of noise, trips on the furniture or something, and *bang*, she's up and her claws are out, and she swipes him straight down his face. Barely missed his eye."

"Are you sure he didn't touch her?"

"Seriously?" Boo says. "Of course, I'm not sure he didn't touch her. But, you know, there are other ways to handle being touched."

"Not for her."

"That's *exactly* what we're talking about."

"Well," Rafferty says, "yeah. Does the kid need a doctor?"

"He's seen one. Poke, I'm not trying to make your life difficult. But I've got to think about *all* these kids. I'm close to the edge here, and I can't just focus on one. She's had it rough, I know, but none of these kids grew up in a palace."

"Yeah, yeah, yeah. I'll talk to Father Bill. Tomorrow. See what I can set up." He pulls a fold of money from his pocket and holds it out. "For now."

Boo eyes it for a moment but then takes it. "Okay." He follows Rafferty's gaze to the SUV, where Andrew is now staring down at his lap. He hasn't even turned on his computer. "What's with him?"

"Oh," Rafferty says, suddenly furious, "who the fuck cares?" Boo's startled face brings him back to himself, and he says, "Sorry. This isn't my best week. I'll talk to you tomorrow. I'll talk to the whole goddamn world tomorrow."

He goes in to collect Rose and Miaow, and when they come out

Miaow cuts in front of him to climb into the SUV's front seat. Rafferty takes the seat she vacated, opposite Andrew, who doesn't even look up. As Chinh starts the engine, there's a knock at the window, and Rafferty lowers it for Boo.

"Forgot to tell you," Boo says. "Your friend was here today, after the fight."

"Which friend?"

"That woman," Boo says. "The one who doesn't talk."

Rafferty puts a hand on Chinh's shoulder to make sure he's not going to pull away, and says, "What did she want?"

"I wasn't here. A couple of kids told me she looked around, went upstairs and into my office. She had that little pad and she wrote on it."

"Great. Exactly what I needed."

"Problem?" Boo says.

Rafferty says, "Yeah. *Yeah*, it could be a problem."

35

They Repaired His Moral Compass

"WE'RE READY," NGUYEN says from the doorway. The room, like the other parts of the embassy they've seen, is an odd blend of institutional and traditional: bland wall-to-wall carpets, white walls, and recessed pinspots in the ceilings, offset by dark, ornate wooden doors framed in lustrous hardwoods. The small meeting room they're in has a mahogany table in the center that seats twelve, and when they arrived, the table was covered in food. Rafferty chewed on things, not even registering what they were, Rose ate with both hands, and Miaow looked down at her plate as though she was trying to warm it with her gaze.

She hasn't said a word since they got into the SUV outside Boo's refuge.

Nguyen turns away, saying, "Turn right. Third door on the left," and disappears. Rose has already risen, and as he pushes his chair back, Rafferty says to Miaow, "Coming?"

"I guess." She gets up with the underwater slowness only teenagers can manage, every muscle in her body arguing with every other. When they'd emerged from the thick silence that had filled the SUV and entered the embassy, Andrew had vanished at the first branching of the hallway. They haven't seen him since.

Rafferty has no energy at the moment for the Miaow-Andrew drama. He's on red alert about Anna. When he first met her, Poke was in a bad situation with one bunch of Thai cops, and Anna had secretly been on the other side. His distrust of her had driven the wedge between him and Arthit that's only now begun to disappear, and here he is again: back in a bad spot with the cops, and bang, there's Anna, appearing someplace that's tangled up in his life right now.

Bringing up the rear, with Rose in the lead, he looks at the stiffness of his daughter's neck and the neglected, fading dyed chop of hair, once so carefully tended, and sees her perform a quick little hitch-step to catch up with Rose and take her mother's hand for the first time in months, and through all the anger and the frustration and the exhaustion, he feels his heart crack open.

"You went to school in England," Thanom says. His hair, usually brushed straight back, hangs over his forehead, and his hands are clasped around his double Scotch as though he's prepared to defend it. He's almost shouting to be heard over the din. "This place, look at it. What's the thing with pubs?"

They're in one of the thousands of imitation British public houses that have sprung up all over Bangkok, and, like most of them, it's bristling with woozy *farang* and a few red-faced Thais, plus a conspicuous scattering of lissome beer girls dressed in body-hugging sheath dresses that improve the design of the can of beer they're hustling. They put most of their energy into the *farang* customers, who persist in believing the girls can successfully be hit on. The Thais know better.

"The English are serious drinkers," Arthit says. "Real burn-down-the-football-stadium drinkers. So they've invented this sort of theme park setting to do it in. Like they're sipping spirits in quaint, picturesque Merrie Olde England instead of pouring down enough to send them out to throw up in the street."

Thanom looks around the room, keeping his head down so as not to meet anyone's eyes, and says, "I've never been out of the country."

"I barely made it myself," Arthit says, feeling apologetic. "My father was crazy for education, and he piled up some money—"

"As a cop."

"Yes, he was a cop. Not a very good one, but eventually a pretty rich one. He did favors for anybody with weight. His money got me into an English university."

Thanom raises his eyebrows, just taking in the information, and drops his gaze to his drink. He rotates it left and then right, like a compass. "I don't think I ever told you how sorry I was about your wife."

"And I appreciate that you didn't," Arthit said. "It would have made me uncomfortable. We've never had that kind of relationship."

Thanom says, "But here we are."

Arthit leans in and lowers his head, meeting Thanom's eyes. "Tell me something. Why did your—whoever it was—think you'd buy the idea that he could stick me with being Sawat's guy in the department?"

Thanom tightens his lips and looks over Arthit's shoulder for a moment, obviously asking himself the question afresh. "Your— position, right next to Sawat in rank. The fact that the phone turned up in the hands of that kid, who's the daughter of a friend of yours."

"That's not even thin," Arthit says. "It's transparent."

"But it wasn't *me*," Thanom snaps, leaning in. "I've been waiting for that shoe to drop for years. He could have pointed at anybody and I would have bought it, as long as it wasn't me."

"That kid you just mentioned," Arthit says. "That little girl, twelve, thirteen years old? Someone tried to kill her last night."

Thanom picks up the glass, blinking fast, and knocks about half of it back. There's a little moisture on his brow. "She's okay?"

"Yes. But that's just because of who she is. No thanks to the police. I'm assuming cops were behind the killing of Sawat and Thongchai. They tried to kill that little girl, and they'll probably try to do it again, and kill the boy, too, although I don't know why. So that's your ally. And now they're coming after you, and you're talking to me, and you don't even know if you can trust me."

Thanom drinks again.

Arthit hoists his Jack Daniel's and pretends to drink. "I need to know what's so important on that phone. Why even now—now that the department has it—they're trying to kill everybody who looked at it."

"You won't believe me."

Arthit looks around the room, just giving himself a moment to figure out how hard he can push. Two *farang* at the bar are apparently in a shot-downing contest; each of them has six full glasses in front of him. At the count of three from the men around them, the two drinkers down in unison the shots they're holding and hand the empty glasses to the barmaid. A beer girl with one arm thrown familiarly around a customer's shoulder holds in her free hand a wad of baht, apparently the group wager.

Coming back to Thanom, Arthit shakes his head. "We're past that. We can trust each other or not, and we'll just have to judge, moment by moment, whether we want the conversation to continue. I can get up and walk away any time."

"I've got no idea what's on it. Honestly. The phone was out of my hands about two hours after I got it. I saw pictures of Thongchai and Sawat and some kind of stupid snapshots of two of the guys who chased the kids. I was going through it a third time when the call came in to release it." He tilts the glass, almost empty now, back and forth, watching the ice cubes slide. "Here's how touchy the big guy is about it. The Sikh who sold it to the kids has been in jail, incommunicado, since about two hours after the little girl was brought in. He's in the country illegally, and he'll be out of it by this time tomorrow."

Arthit says, "He has a family. Miaow—that's the *little girl* you keep referring to, Miaow—said he kept talking about his—"

"All of them, out. Waiting to be deported. Clean sweep."

A whoop from the bar announces that two more shots have been put into the past tense. "He's that powerful," Arthit says.

Thanom seems to be searching the tablecloth, but it's evident to Arthit that he's not actually looking at anything, and he hasn't reacted at all to the noise at the bar. He's relaxed his grip on the glass, and the fingers of his left hand tap the tablecloth in a pattern that might, on a piano, be a melody. He says, "He's a princeling."

"That pares it down," Arthit says. "But it raises a whole new set of questions. The kind of money Sawat was making—I mean, it's a lot for you and me, but for any of the three or four current princelings who seem most likely, it's shoeshine cash. Those families are drowning in money."

Thanom says, "I've been thinking about that."

"And what have you come up with?"

"That I need friends."

"That gives you two problems, then, doesn't it?" Arthit says. "First you have to be certain your new friends are on your side. And before we go any further with this, the only friends I can think of for you aren't cops."

"At this point, that's in their favor. What's the second problem?

"You need to bring something to the party. Something they need and don't have."

"And I've got it," Thanom says. "The name."

RAFFERTY FOLLOWS ROSE and Miaow into another meeting room, this one with a projection screen at one end. Seated at the end of the table farthest from the screen, next to his new laptop, is Andrew. He throws a glance at Miaow as they come in, but she brushes past and sits at the table three chairs away, her back to him, facing the screen. Rafferty and Rose sit on the other side, and Rafferty is surprised to see Chinh and Homer come in and stand at the back of the room.

"I've asked Andrew to connect his computer to the projector,"

Nguyen says. "Better than everyone crowding around, trying to look at that little screen."

Andrew fiddles with the keyboard, but he doesn't seem to agree that it wouldn't be better for everyone to crowd around. He looks at Miaow's back and his shoulders droop.

"Tell them, Anh Duong," Nguyen says.

"When I had these before," Andrew says. He's clearly keyed up by all the attention and Miaow's indifference or anger or whatever it is. He's tapping his first and second finger against the tabletop, fast. "When I had the phone, and before those cops took my computers, I messed with them. I used the imaging program you bought me today to, uh, make things clearer and, you know, um, make things . . . clearer."

"We understand," his father says soothingly. "You wanted to make things clearer."

"The resolution on the phone isn't the best," Andrew says, still tapping. "And there were lighting problems, you know? So I did some filling and contrast adjustments, and I also did some sharpening and stuff like that. So what I mean is, I did it on my old computer before, the one they bagged. I haven't had much time with this setup, but I remembered what I did before. These could be better, but this is what they are."

Poke says, "I'm sure they're fine, Andrew," but Andrew is looking at the back of Miaow's head.

Without taking his eyes off her, Andrew says, "And I know which picture they don't want anyone to see. I know why they tried to kill Miaow."

Miaow's head is coming around when Nguyen says, "Homer? The lights, please," and the pinspots dim and Andrew brings the screen to life. The first thing Rafferty sees is Sawat, wearing an expression that suggests that he's either just bitten his tongue or would like to bite someone else's. The two guys nearest him look like hired muscle.

"This is in Pratunam," Andrew says.

Rafferty says, "Do you know when they were taken?"

"This one was May sixth. It took three days to take them all," Andrew says. "The last one was May eighth, four days before the first man was killed. This guy."

He pushes a key, and there's Sawat again, one of the same hired biceps at his side. He's coming out of a department store, glaring at the world. His hands are empty, but the bicep is carrying several bags.

"See?" Andrew says. "He doesn't know he's being photographed. It was one of the first things Miaow noticed." He pauses, but there's no sign Miaow has even heard him. Andrew says, "Look here."

He pushes the key again and brings up a blur of motion, the world sliding sideways. "I think someone was about to look at the man with the phone, and he turned away. That happens again, five or six shots from now, but with the other guy."

"Thongchai," Rafferty says. "Sawat's coordinator. He put together the hits and paid the cops."

"Miaow said looking at the pictures was like spying." He brings up another: Sawat, on another sidewalk, giving someone a hard time on a cell phone.

"It is spying," Nguyen says.

Rafferty says, "Best anyone can figure, the pictures were for the killers, so they'd hit the right people." He rubs his eyes. "Although I have to tell you, now that I say that out loud, it doesn't make sense."

"Why not?" Nguyen asks.

"The guy who killed these two said something both times. He named a certain number of women and children. Because of that, everyone's been assuming that these are revenge killings. But wouldn't someone who's taking revenge know who he came to Bangkok to kill? Why would he need pictures?"

"It was a professional." Nguyen says. "The victims' families hired someone?"

"Probably. But then, it's odd that a pro, with no emotional involvement, would bother to deliver a parting message. Sure, *tell* the client you did it, but why waste the time to actually say it? It's not like the victim is going to contradict him if he fibs about it."

"They were on video," Miaow says.

The room falls silent. Andrew swallows.

"They showed it to us," she says. "At the police station. To see whether the guys who chased us—"

"*These* guys," Andrew says, flipping through the pictures fast: Sawat, Sawat, Sawat, Thongchai, Thongchai, another blurred camera move, Thongchai—

—two men in a room, an inexpensive hotel room from the look of it. There's a window with a lot of light coming through it and, sitting on a bed in front of it, two men. They're talking.

"The tall one," Miaow says, leaning forward. "That's the golden man. I mean, that's what I thought of him as. The other one was with him."

Another shot. This time, the men on the bed are looking at the camera, and the tall man has a hand up, palm out, clearly meaning, *Stop.*

"The third one," Miaow says, "the one who's taking the pictures, he's the one who chased me with the knife."

Rafferty says, his head spinning, "Of *course*, they were on video."

"I need to show you this one picture," Andrew says.

"You think they staged that?" Nguyen says. "Said it for the camera?"

"I think something is wrong with the way everyone is thinking about this. And we all know what the killers look like. What's so valuable about these pictures that someone would try to kill Miaow? Or trash your apartment?"

Andrew says, "Mr. Rafferty, look. *Listen* to me. Look."

He's paging back through several photos of Thongchai, and then he stops it. Thongchai, facing the camera three-quarters, laughing at something the man next to him has said. They're on yet another sidewalk, in front of a big display window.

"What are we looking at, Anh Duong?"

Andrew uses the cursor to describe a scribbly, off-center circle on the window. "That," he says.

Rafferty says, "Holy Jesus."

"It's not very clear," Andrew says, his voice cracking again, with excitement this time, "but here he is."

Reflected in the window, pale and semitransparent, a man holds up an iPhone.

"It's him," Andrew says. "The guy who took the pictures."

Rafferty's cell phone rings. He's fishing for it as he says, "I can't see him very clearly."

"That's what I've been *doing*," Andrew says, flipping through the pictures. "That's why I needed that software you—"

The phone says ARTHIT, and Rafferty looks at his watch. Well past ten.

"Hang on," he says to the room, as a new picture comes onto the screen. He accepts the call and says again, "Hang on," just as Andrew brings up a new photo.

"Who?" Nguyen says. "Who should hang—" He breaks off, looking at the screen. Says, "Anh *Duong.*"

Staring at the picture, Rafferty says into the phone, "Can I get back to you?"

"We're at your apartment and it's the middle of the night," Arthit says. "Are you all okay?"

"We're fine." To Andrew he says, "Well *done*, Andrew," and then, to Arthit, "Who's we?"

"Thanom and me. You need to know a few things."

"And you need to see what I'm looking at, but I don't want Thanom to. And I don't want him to know where we are."

"It's no problem," Arthit says. "He's been visited by three spirits, and they repaired his moral compass."

"I don't know."

"He needs help," Arthit says, and Rafferty hears a querulous voice in the background. "And he's reminding me that he's got a piece of information that makes his company worth it. Oh, and so do I. Have information, I mean."

"Well," Rafferty says, "that makes it unanimous." He looks at the screen, at the digital magic Andrew has done to pull a face from the almost-ephemeral image reflected in the window. "But I don't want to share mine with Thanom."

"Then don't. Where are you?"

"Give me a second." He mutes the phone and says to Nguyen, "Two cops. One is my best friend, and the other one isn't, but my friend says he's had his teeth pulled. And they both have something to tell us."

Nguyen says, "Here?"

"Unless you've got someplace better."

Nguyen looks at his watch and grimaces. "I'll get the kitchen to put on a pot of coffee." He stands and puts a hand on his son's shoulder. "Good work, Anh Duong," he says. Andrew closes his mouth so quickly he bites his lower lip. His low moan of pain brings Miaow's head halfway around.

But only halfway.

Part Four
AIM AND IGNITE

36

There's No Way They've Been Allowed to Go Anywhere

THE EFFECT, RAFFERTY thinks, is a perfect space for conspiracy.

Homer and Chinh have brought three brass student lamps with green glass shades into the room and positioned them on the table. With the lamps on and the overhead lights dimmed, the table and the chairs around it seem to have been carved from the darkness.

Rose and Miaow have been taken to the rooms that will be theirs for the duration, side-by-side bedrooms with a connecting door. The beds are all full-size, just a little larger than twins. Rose chooses the one farther from the door, sits on it, and says, "I like you enough tonight to share this."

Rafferty says, "The way it's going, I'll be lucky to be back by daybreak."

"But you're happier," she says. "You're doing something."

"That's true."

"Men are so much simpler than women." She turns her head and listens, apparently to something she hears in Miaow's room. "Represent me well," she says.

"We want the same thing."

"And I'll be here, faithfully waiting for you."

"Snoring all the while."

"Please," she says. "I'm sleeping for two now."

Rafferty says, "*How* many months does this take?"

*   *   *

"AT THE RISK of seeming unwelcoming," Nguyen says, sounding very unwelcoming indeed, "I want to remind you that inside this embassy you have no police power. You're in the Socialist Republic of Vietnam."

Arthit catches Poke's eye, and Rafferty looks down. The two police officers are framed in the doorway to the room, but Thanom comes further forward before Nguyen has finished speaking.

"We're here," he begins, and then he hesitates. "We're here to try to help you solve your problem." His face is flushed and his speech very slightly slurred.

Nguyen says, "It's a *police* problem."

Thanom says, "It is. And I was part of it, although I had no idea it would go this far."

"Really," Rafferty says, his longstanding dislike for the man welling up. "Where would you have drawn the line?"

"Attempts to kill—children," Thanom says. No one applauds, and he adds, "To kill anyone."

"What about tearing my family's apartment apart?" Nguyen demands.

"I had no idea," Thanom says.

"That's why we're here. We're avoiding your police force."

Arthit says, "So is Colonel Thanom."

Nguyen looks from Arthit to Rafferty, a silent question. Rafferty gives him a tiny shrug, and Nguyen takes a step back, yielding the room to them. "So it's your problem, too. Have some coffee. We have sandwiches and—what else do we have, Homer?"

"American cookies," Homer says. "They were for the kids."

"Have a cookie," Nguyen says. It sounds more like a dare than an invitation. He turns his back to them and takes a seat.

The screen and Andrew's computer are still in place, but both are dark. Andrew has been sent to bed, over much protest.

Arthit and Thanom pump coffee into thick mugs, and Thanom

piles oatmeal cookies on a napkin. By the time he turns around, Poke is sitting next to Nguyen on the far side of the table, and the cops automatically take the nearer side.

Sitting, Arthit says, "This feels faintly adversarial."

"Unintended," Nguyen says, without much energy. "So. Why are you here?"

"Before that, if I may," Rafferty says, "I think it would be nice to get our objectives on the table. Just to make sure they're the same. Mine is to figure out who tried to take a knife to Miaow, and who was *behind* that person, and either kill them or neutralize them permanently."

Everyone looks at everyone else for a second, and Nguyen says, "I'm not sanctioning killing, but I want this episode brought to a close, with appropriate penalties for those responsible, and iron-clad guarantees that it's over."

Arthit looks inquiringly at Thanom gets a nod, and says, "I want what Poke wants, and I wouldn't be upset by a death or two. I'm ashamed that my department has anything to do with creating the sewer of secrecy behind all this." He says to Thanom, "Colonel?"

Thanom picks up his coffee cup and puts it down without even glancing at it. "I was a passive part of what Sawat did. I knew about it and I kept my mouth shut."

"And you've had a change of heart?" Nguyen says.

Thanom's face tightens, and he clears his throat. "I'm being set up. I was the obvious scapegoat as Sawat's superior, and they're going to try to blame me for all of it." He looks at Nguyen and Rafferty in turn. "But that's not the only reason I'm here." No one responds, and he adds, "It's a moral stand, too."

"Good to hear it," Nguyen says.

Arthit says, "If they do in fact make it look like it was the Colonel here—and they've gone to a lot of trouble to create a convincing case—they'll be able to close the door on the whole thing. Everybody will walk away. All clean and shiny."

Rafferty says, "But they're still not going to feel safe until they've removed the people who saw the pictures on that phone."

Arthit holds up both hands to break in on Poke and says, "Okay. Recap. For the benefit of everybody in the room. A police officer set up a murder-for-profit operation within the department. They committed a number of murders, arrested suspects, got convictions, and wrapped the cases. They made millions of baht doing it. Then they got caught, at least unofficially, and when the rumors about that got out, the department sidestepped the public demands to take the case to court and the two men who were responsible, Sawat and Thongchai, were retired in disgrace, with no official admission that they were guilty. That was six years ago. Everything simmered under the lid until Thursday night, when Sawat was killed, and Friday morning, when they got Thongchai."

"Presumably in revenge," Rafferty says. "Except that it doesn't make sense."

Arthit says, "I'm getting to that. And on Friday morning, Andrew and Miaow buy a used phone, and all hell breaks loose. They get chased, then there's an attempt on Miaow's life. And you don't know this yet, but the Sikh who sold them the phone, plus his whole family, are sitting in custody as illegal immigrants, waiting for deportation and not allowed to talk to anyone."

He looks over at Thanom, who's slumped back in his chair, his arms crossed tightly over his chest, staring at the surface of the table. "And as I told the colonel here, I searched the databases today and there are *no murders* linked to Sawat that have the number of female and juvenile victims that Sawat and Thongchai's killer so carefully mentioned on those surveillance videos."

It takes Rafferty a second or two to make sense out of the sentence, and when he does, the back of his neck begins to prickle. He says, "Really."

"Nope. There were a few matches, but not linked to Sawat."

"Miaow was right," Rafferty says, trying to put things together in a way that makes sense, or at least isn't laughable. "The shooter knew he was on video. He said it for the camera."

Nguyen says, "But what does this tell us? Why wouldn't they use—how would you say this—a count from two of the real cases? If, as you say, there are really so many killings involving women and children?"

There's a silence. Arthit breaks it by saying to Nguyen, "This is just one of the things you don't know about."

Thanom says, "Before we go past this, let me suggest something. The plan was always to frame me. To stick me for all of it. If they'd used real numbers, maybe those would have pointed at a killing I couldn't have been involved in."

"How?" Rafferty says. "You're being framed as a conspirator, not a killer. I mean, alibis wouldn't matter, since no one is suggesting you were at the scene."

"I don't know, I'm just looking for an explanation, same as you. For this to be closed out as far as we—I mean, the police—are concerned, it has to be resolved with a sacrifice from inside the department. That's the only thing that will shut up the media and the political opposition. It has to look like someone inside the department, killing Sawat because he'd become a threat. Me."

He spreads his fingers on the table, hands flat, and looks down at them. "And let me also say that the men who actually killed Sawat and Thongchai are almost certainly dead by now. There's no way they've been allowed to go anywhere."

"I don't buy the explanation for why the murders on the surveillance videos don't fit," Poke says. "But maybe we can make them fit when we answer the real question, which is, if it's *not* you, who is it? Obviously, someone with a lot of clout, if the immigration people have been roped into it."

Thanom says, "I know who's behind the way the investigation is being run. But that doesn't necessarily mean he's behind the murders of Sawat and Thongchai or the attempt on your daughter's life. It doesn't necessarily mean he was the one who was shielding Sawat in the first place."

"Do you know who it is, Arthit?" Rafferty asks.

"I do," Arthit says. "And you've already had one dance with him, and nothing about him would surprise me." He turns to Thanom. "Colonel?"

"He's a princeling," Thanom says. "Came into the department near the top. His name is Ton."

"A few years ago," Rafferty says as he pours coffee, "I was put in the position of writing a biography of a guy named Pan."

Thanom's head comes up, his eyes fixed on Rafferty's face. "*That's* when we met," he says. "I remember your wife."

"Everyone does. Yeah, at that ridiculous fund-raising dinner he threw for that malaria charity, whatever it was called."

"Net Profits," Thanom says.

"It's interesting, considering why you're here tonight, that Pan described you back then as the cop who ran the murder-for-hire ring inside the department."

Thanom rests his chin on his hand and says, "Did he." He doesn't make it sound like a question.

"By the time you and I met, I had been threatened by two factions if I didn't write the biography. Problem was, they wanted diametrically opposite books. The more dangerous faction, one that managed to drive my wife and child into hiding, was headed by Ton."

"But you survived," Thanom says. "Here you are."

Rafferty looks at Arthit and smiles, although it feels more like a baring of the teeth. "That's right. Here I am, with my wife and child in hiding, *again*. And you know what? Now that I know who it is, it seems impossible to me that he isn't into it up to his eyebrows."

"In the investigation, yes," Thanom says,

Rafferty says, "All of it."

Thanom holds up both hands, asking for his minute. "You have no evidence that he's not running the case the way he is to protect—to *whitewash*—the department, avoid further embarrassment."

Arthit says, "In a way that's consistent with the plan to frame you. And you say that goes back a long way."

Thanom is nodding, but he looks like someone who's just been told he has ten minutes to live. "But—" Thanom swallows. "He's worth billions and billions of baht. Hundreds of millions of dollars. His family is one of the richest in the kingdom. Why would he be interested in the kind of money Sawat was pulling in?"

Rafferty says, "There are usually three reasons for crime, right, Arthit? Love, money, and power. Love is a non-starter, and maybe, in this case, so is money."

Nguyen shoots Rafferty a look and gets up, and the movement has so much energy coiled inside it that they all watch him cross the room to refill his mug, looking like someone walking an invisible line. He takes a sip and turns and leans against the counter. "Corruption is the infinite crime," he says. "It's the worst of all because there's literally no limit to how far it can go. Every successful act of corruption brings more power and more money. And it also gives the corrupt official more to defend, and more weight to defend it with. It's a terrible cycle. It's the way an obscure country doctor, like Papa Doc or Idi Amin, given ten or twelve years and the right opportunities, turns into the kind of national leader whose policies are implemented with machetes. It's the way some people pervert whole social and political structures to become rich. Everyone in this room has experience with corruption." His eyes go to Thanom and slide past. "Some of us from both sides of the line. Me, for example. I've put up with, fought against, and taken advantage of corruption all my adult life. And I agree with you, Colonel. The money is nowhere near enough to attract the attention of a man like the one you describe." He takes another sip. "But that doesn't mean he's not at the center of it."

Rafferty tilts his head back and closes his eyes, and it feels like the room has just stopped spinning. "We've been looking at the whole thing upside-down," he says.

Nguyen nods, but says, "What does that actually mean?"

"He didn't profit financially from the murders, at least not via Sawat. He didn't need the money. What he needed were the *murders*."

Thanom says, "What he needed were—?"

"He put Sawat in *business*," Rafferty says. He gets up, just needing to move a little. "I know, it sounds ridiculous, but look at it as a hypothesis. It explains everything: how Sawat chose his victims, how he was shielded for so long. Even how he kept living at that level after he was kicked out."

Arthit says, "And it would explain why he and Thongchai were killed. Look what they might have been threatening."

"Test it," Thanom snaps. "You're saying that a member of one of the richest families in the kingdom set up a police murder unit and chose its victims?"

Rafferty says, "That's what I'm saying."

Thanom shakes his head. "*Test it*. If you want to make a case, the first thing you need to do is establish motivation, and it would have to be *massive* motivation for someone like Ton to risk everything. And the phone, why would the phone—"

"Power," Rafferty interrupts. "Advantage. Money in the *long* run, enormous sums of money. The kind of money that comes with eliminating the competition." He's pacing around the table now, Arthit's head following his movement. "One of the most interesting things about the murders Sawat's gang committed is that—"

"Is that no one really looked at motive," Arthit says. "They convicted their murderer, the murderer had a plausible motive, usually robbery or getting even for something that was done to him or his family. And the case against Sawat never went to court. The department denied all of it, so none of the murders was reopened. All those motives are floating around out there."

"Perfect murders," Rafferty says, trying it on. "Committed for enormous stakes. Over a period of years. A long-term plan."

Nguyen says, "We need someone who's good with databases. We need to identify the possible motive for Ton killing each of these people."

"I've got the person you need," Arthit says. "I worked with her all day Friday. I'll bring her in."

"In here," Nguyen says. "We've got space, machines, and encrypted lines."

Rafferty says, "A cop?"

"And what a cop," Arthit says.

"And you trust her."

Arthit nods.

"Well, when she's finished juggling all that data, we need to find a way to present it." Suddenly he sees Andrew's graphic of the short and tall students, and he almost laughs. "A circle," he says. "I'd like her to come up with a nice, neat circle, really simple. A wheel with Ton at the center and spokes to each of the victims we know about, with a one- or two-sentence explanation of what he gained from the death."

"Sounds good to me," Arthit says.

"I stole it from Andrew," Rafferty says, glancing at Nguyen.

"We need more than a bunch of hypothetical motives," Thanom says. "We need a *connection*, something more than the possibility that he's just doing his job, running the investigation in a way that will protect the department. We need something real, a link, either to the earlier murders or to the killing of Sawat and Thongchai. Something tangible."

Nguyen looks at Rafferty, eyebrows raised in a question. Rafferty nods assent and says, "Andrew again. The kid's practically running things."

Nguyen says, "Please turn off the light nearest to you," and goes to Andrew's Mac Air. He brings the screen to life and the picture appears: the electronically enhanced image of a man holding an iPhone, reflected in a store window. "You want a connection," he says to Thanom. "We might have one."

37

I Don't Care If It's a Zebra

IT'S WELL AFTER three in the morning when Rafferty eases open the door to their room, but Rose says, "Here you are."

He closes and locks the door, which, since there's no window, reduces the room to almost total darkness. "What are you doing up?"

"Waiting for you, of course."

"Keep talking," he says, "so I can find you."

"I'm just wasting away all by myself," Rose says. "Wondering what I did wrong to be all alone in the middle of the night. Are you here yet?"

"The next touch you feel will be mine." He works his way up the side of the bed and reaches gently toward the space where he thinks the pillow will be.

She nips his finger. "That will be nice," she says. "But what I really *really* want is a cigarette."

"Not on the menu." He sits on the other bed and kicks off his shoes. "You've been doing so well."

"I know," she says. "Especially considering all that's going on. A week ago I'd have been smoking with both hands."

"We're going to be fine," he says with more confidence than he feels. "It's hard to believe, but all this started on Friday, and this is only Monday night. But you know what? We've got a big jump on the other side. We'll be all right."

"Life with you is too exciting. Working in the bar was more restful."

"This time, it isn't my fault."

"I'm just grumpy because I need nicotine. Aren't you naked *yet*?"

"Working on it." He undoes his belt and unzips his fly.

She says, "Do that again," and he zips and unzips it once more.

"My favorite song," Rose says. "I could get used to being here. You can't turn up the air-con."

"That's okay," Rafferty says, folding back the covers. "I've got this big ice cube to cuddle up to."

He slides in, and she slips an arm under him and tugs lightly on the hair on the back of his head. "You want to know what happened with Miaow tonight? Why all the silence between her and Andrew?"

"Sure."

"She talked to those kids for about thirty seconds about what it was like on the street, and of course, she was really talking to Andrew. And he walked out. Just turned his back on her and went out the door."

"You know," Poke says, "maybe he's just not the right boy for her. But the kid really did a job with that picture tonight. You can totally see the guy's face."

"Your daughter," Rose says.

"I'm *thinking* about my daughter. I'm thinking about the motherfucker who sent someone after her with a knife."

"Calm down." She takes his hand and puts it on her stomach, just below the navel, where his approximate grasp of female anatomy tells him is probably as close to the baby as he can get. At the thought of the baby, at the warmth and smoothness of her belly, the anger inside him melts a little. "This is nice."

She says, "Rub in small circles and don't press down too much."

"Press like this?"

"Just a little harder. It shouldn't hurt, but it shouldn't tickle, either."

"What we all want from life. Not hard enough to hurt, not light enough to tickle."

"This is going to be a valuable skill," she says. She puts her hand on his and guides the circles, and he relaxes his arm and wrist and lets her take over. It's so dark he can't actually see her face, but he has no difficulty imagining it. "Slower," she said. "Like that. Do you think he or she can feel that?"

"Oh, God," Rafferty says, and there are suddenly tears in his eyes. "I hope so."

"Me, too." She edges herself closer to him. "He or she?"

"He or she what? You mean, which do I want, or which do you think it is?"

"Which you want."

"Oh, Rose," he says. "I don't care if it's a zebra. I'm going to love it whatever it is."

"I think I'd prefer a boy," Rose says. She redirects his hand into a slow back-and-forth motion about six inches long. "Boys are important to families. They're the tentpole."

"You sound like Nguyen. The Asian sons syndrome."

"If I'd had a couple of older brothers," she says, "they would have been making money and my father probably wouldn't have had to sell me."

Rafferty says, "Ah."

She stops his hand and pushes her stomach out. "Will you still love me when I have a huge belly?"

"I don't know," he says, blinking in the dark. "Will you still love *me* when I have a huge belly?"

She says, "Absolutely not," and lifts her face to blow on the side of his neck.

And someone knocks on the door. "Mr. Rafferty? Mr. *Rafferty?*"

"Has to be Nguyen," Poke says. "Not many people call me Mr. Rafferty." He eases out of the bed and goes to the door, stark naked. Standing behind the door, he pulls it open a few inches and looks around the edge, but it's not Nguyen. It's Chinh.

"Sorry to bother you," Chinh says, "but the older policeman—Thanom?"

"What about him?"

"He was on the way out of the embassy, going home, when his phone rang. It was a maid at his house. She said that six uniformed policemen had kicked the door in and were looking for him."

Rafferty says, "I'll be right there."

He closes the door and says, "Looks like we haven't got as much time as we thought."

ONLY ONE LIGHT is on, but it's bright enough for Rafferty to see Thanom sweat. He's eating cookies without even looking at them, standing next to the food table. Nguyen, in a T-shirt, slacks, and white socks, is back at the coffee pot.

Rafferty says, "Arthit?"

"Coming back," Nguyen says. "We got him on his cell."

Thanom says, "They took my wife."

"You said she's from a good family," Nguyen says. "They'll let her go when you don't show up for work tomorrow. They're just holding everybody to keep them from tipping you off."

"Where am I going to go?" Thanom looks down at the cookie in his hand and drops it onto the table as though it were red-hot.

"Nowhere." Nguyen looks at Homer and flicks a finger at the coffeepot, and Homer trots over and picks it up. "You'll stay here."

Rafferty says, "How many people can you put up without causing a problem?"

"As many as I want," Nguyen says. "I have a certain status here."

Rafferty says, "I've been wondering about that."

"Good," Nguyen says. "It'll give you something to do." He calls something in Vietnamese after Homer. To Thanom, whose face had crumpled with suspicion at the sound of words he couldn't understand, Nguyen says, "I told him to bring some tea, too." He lifts both hands like a magician clearing his cuffs and says, "That's all."

There are voices in the hallway, and Arthit comes in. "Sooner than I thought," he says to Rafferty.

"I was just saying the same thing. How early can you call your database cop?"

Arthit says, "Now. I offered her a job downtown, so she gave me her home phone so we could discuss it without everyone listening as I raid their talent." He starts to punch up a number.

Nguyen says, "Wait. Write the number down and use my phone. Here, give me yours. All of you, turn off the cell phones. Pull out the batteries, if it's even possible. We've got dozens of phones, all unregistered." As Arthit goes into the hallway, Nguyen smiles at Thanom, not a very friendly smile. "The Thai government has big ears."

"The man in that reflection," Rafferty says. "He has to be close to Ton. I'm betting he's related. He's not going to trust anyone else. One thing on our side is that Ton's family is still at the level where they get photographed for the newspapers. They haven't quite made it into the stratosphere where no reporter would dare to point a camera at them. I'm going to spend the day at the Bangkok *Sun*, going through the social pages."

"His family," Nguyen says. "We need a chart of his family."

"I can give you that," Thanom says. "My wife—" He stops, staring at the center of the table. "My wife knows everything about those families. She's—educated me."

"Why don't you make a list?" Nguyen says, and Rafferty is surprised at the gentleness in his voice. "I'll get you some paper. Do a family tree. And tomorrow, you can call your wife and review it with her over the phone. And we'll figure out where everybody is in the family's businesses." He looks at Rafferty as Arthit comes back in, phone extended to Nguyen. "That might tell us quite a bit."

Arthit says, "She'll be here at ten. Her name is Kwai, last name is Clemente. Her father's a Filipino. And I just called home."

At the word "home," Rafferty remembers his question about

why Anna had been at Boo's place, but he can't think of any way to ask it. Arthit has picked up something, though, and his eyes come to Rafferty's face.

"Was Anna at your house?" Rafferty says, just to ask something. "Everything okay?"

"No problem," Arthit says. He turns to Nguyen. "Got room for one more?"

Nguyen says, "Does she prefer coffee or tea?"

38

It'll Have Holes Worn in It in Twenty-four Hours

FOUR HOURS AFTER he finally climbed into bed, Rafferty sleepily follows Rose to the meeting room where they'd first gathered, and finds Arthit, Anna, Thanom, and Andrew sitting around the table, silently eating breakfast. The embassy kitchen has put out Thai and Western food, plus bowls of steaming *pho*.

Eight places have been set, and at each of them, positioned beside the knife and spoon, is a generic cell phone and a shiny Ziploc bag.

Rose goes straight to Anna and starts talking as though she's resuming a conversation that was interrupted only minutes ago. Anna keeps her eyes on Rose's mouth. At the coffee pot, Rafferty takes advantage of the conversation to look for some evidence of nervousness in Anna, but she seems occupied in following the stream of Rose's chatter. Thanom is eating rice with an egg broken on it, and the hand with the spoon is shaking so badly he's scattered grains of rice all around the bowl and on the front of his uniform. He seems to have aged ten years overnight; he's unshaven and his head trembles very slightly as he raises the spoon to his mouth.

Andrew continues to stare at the doorway after Rose and Rafferty have come in, and Rafferty says, "She's asleep, Andrew. She's not much on breakfast." To Arthit, he says, "Look at this spread. Our host has some clout."

"Optay eyespay," Arthit says with his mouth full.

"Gesundheit."

"He's using Pig Latin," Andrew says, just barely not curling his lip. "So I don't know he's calling my father the top spy in the embassy."

"Is he really a spy?" Rafferty says. "That could come in handy."

Arthit says, "Caught by a mere child." He smiles. "You're very impressive, Andrew."

Andrew says, "Me, impressive? I'm a jerk," and then he gets up and stalks out of the room. His napkin clings to his jeans until he's at the door, and since Rafferty's standing, he goes after the boy and picks it up.

"He is kind of a jerk," Rafferty says, refolding the napkin without knowing he's doing it. "Or at least, he was last night, at Boo's place."

Thanom says, "We—we need to get started. We need to do something."

"Kwai will be here in an hour," Arthit says.

"And we have a room set up for her." Nguyen comes in, wearing a dark, beautifully tailored suit. He looks like he slept ten hours. "After what you told us last night, I gave her a window."

"She'll like that," Arthit says.

"Colonel Thanom, your wife is still with the police, but they've begun to release the servants, so it shouldn't be long. Unless they hold her to threaten you."

Thanom spills some rice, and he glares down at it and then releases an enormous sigh.

"I don't think they will," Nguyen says, watching him. "Not with her family background. What else, what else? Oh. Each of you should take the phone next to your silverware, and that's the only one you can use. If you need to download phone numbers or other data from your own phone, let Homer or Chinh know, and they'll take you into a shielded room, where the signal can't be detected. Otherwise, please put your own phone into the Ziploc bag and drop the whole thing into the basket on the table. The police already know most of you are here, but let's not keep notifying them."

Thanom says, "But what if someone calls us? There could be important calls from—from—"

"Every ninety minutes or so, one of our drivers will take the basket out in the car. A few miles away, he'll stop and power one on, check for incoming, turn it off again, and drive a few more miles, doing them one at a time until he's got them all. Then he'll use his own phone to call whoever got a message."

Rafferty says, "You've done this before."

Arthit says, "How do you know that the cops know where we are?"

"It's obvious that my family would come here," Nguyen says. "And almost all of you have your phones, which are signaling away. But mostly, I know because we've got four in plainclothes watching the embassy."

Rafferty says, "Well, hell."

"It's more psychological than anything else. They can't come onto the grounds, and they'd be risking an incident if they stopped and searched an official embassy vehicle, so that's what you'll go in and out in, when you have to go in and out. And they probably don't know we've spotted them, which is an edge. Perhaps the two of you," he says to Arthit and Thanom, "would like to look at them on video, see whether you know any of them, whether you can figure out who might have sent them. And Mr. Rafferty, could you please come with me? We need to talk for a minute."

"Sure. You want some coffee?"

"Oh, why not. Black." Nguyen turns toward the door and waits for Rafferty. As he takes the cup, he says to Thanom, "Don't worry too much. This is going to be a very full day."

RAFFERTY TRAILS NGUYEN as they track down one hall and then another, leading into an area of the embassy Rafferty hasn't seen yet. It's obviously for the top echelon and their visitors: the carpets are thicker and paintings line the halls. Outside a dark, heavily grained double door, Nguyen stops and turns. "You want to get out of here today, right? To go see your reporter friend at the *Sun?*"

"Yes."

"Fine. Let's get the cops really worked up. You and I will go out in an embassy limousine, complete with the flag flying on the fender, with Chinh driving. They'd be apprehensive just to see you go into a newspaper office, but we'll crank it up. We have an early lunch reservation in a very nice restaurant, at a window table, with the paper's business editor. My official title here is business liaison, so I know him quite well."

"You and me and the business editor. That'll be an acid reflux moment for Ton."

"Then we'll walk in plain view, with Chinh and my bodyguard, Tuan, flanking us, straight to the newspaper. I'll go into the building with you and do some work of my own while you go through the pictures."

"It could take hours."

"The longer the better. Gives them more to worry about." He surveys Rafferty's jeans and T-shirt and shakes his head. "I guess you have your own inimitable style. But stand up straight, okay?"

Rafferty sips his coffee and says, "Do I slouch?" but Nguyen is already opening the door.

They enter an anteroom with carpets of a regal red on which floats a wide teak desk that's been claimed by a fearfully groomed Vietnamese woman in her mid-thirties. She smiles at Nguyen, glances at Poke, then says to Nguyen, "Go right in. He's expecting you."

Rafferty snags Nguyen's arm. "He who?"

"Secretary Tran." Nguyen puts his cup on the desk, and the woman immediately opens a drawer and puts a frilly white coaster beneath Nguyen's coffee and another beside it for Poke. "He's the ambassador's executive assistant, and for the purposes of this meeting he *is* the ambassador."

"Got it." Poke drains the cup and puts it on the coaster. The woman re-centers it.

Nguyen takes one last regretful look at Rafferty, sighs, and goes through the door, with Rafferty trailing along like a chastened Labrador Retriever. The room into which Nguyen leads him has the kind of volume that's meant to impress. Thick midnight-blue carpets match heavy woven drapes, and vermilion walls rise at least fourteen feet to culminate in a ceiling of dark, highly polished hardwood. Pinspots set into the ceiling pick out gilt-framed watercolors, impressionistic views of scenery that Rafferty supposes is Vietnam.

The desk is half the size of Rafferty's kitchen. Standing behind it, all ten of his widespread fingertips touching its surface as though Nguyen and Rafferty had caught him at the apogee of a pushup, is a thin, very sleek man in his fifties with a steel-gray military brush-cut, cheekbones that jut like elbows and tight, dry eyes that announce an unwillingness to be entertained. There's almost no upper lip, but the lower plumps out like a bumper, and for a second Rafferty thinks it's expressing disapproval of his clothing.

But then the man smiles, just a tug at the corners of his mouth, and the lower lip stays out there. He says, "Captain. Mr. Rafferty."

Nguyen says, "Sir."

"Your Colonel Thanom," Tran says without any warm-up. "How bad is he?"

Rafferty waits a beat to give Nguyen a chance, but when it's clear that the question is meant for him, he says, "Pretty bad."

"Is he—was he—involved in the murder ring?"

Rafferty says, "Sure, he was." Tran's eyes dart to Nguyen just long enough to cause frostbite, and then resettle on Rafferty, who picks up the thread. "Sawat's operation took a lot of cooperation. Cops had to be evaluated in advance to make sure they'd play.

They had to be pulled from duty to free them up for the hit. Time cards showing they were on their regular assignments had to be forged and entered into the system. Other cops had to be brought in to cover for the cops who were otherwise employed, et cetera. On and on. And, of course, all those secrets had to be kept, so money flowed. Thanom was Sawat's immediate superior, and there's no way he wasn't on the pad."

"On the pad," Tran says.

"Getting paid for odds and ends, for keeping his mouth shut. Maybe twenty thousand, thirty thousand baht at a time. Not often, just enough to keep him hoping for more. So, yeah, he was involved. Was he running it? No."

"You're certain."

"I'd bet the farm on it."

"And how big is your farm?"

"Not very big. But it's the only one I've got."

Tran nods. "That's the better question, isn't it? Not how much the other person will lose, but how much he'll have left." He steps in front of the high-backed chair behind the desk and sits. "In order for me to allow you to move ahead with this—"

Rafferty says, "Excuse me?"

"Your *plan*, whatever it is, undoubtedly calls for my offering your little flock a sanctuary. It presumably includes the continuing participation of Captain Nguyen."

"It certainly does." Rafferty ignores Nguyen's warning glance. "And they're not my little flock, beyond my wife and child, and I've taken care of *them* without your help in the past."

"Well, let's try not to put you in that position again. If I'm going to be involved, I need to know two things: first that we're not shielding an embarrassing villain; and second, that you—the two of you—are after the right man. Ton has business interests in Vietnam, and it would be counterproductive to disrupt them for no good reason."

"We'll know absolutely by the end of the day," Nguyen says.

"And until we're completely certain, we won't do anything that would have a permanent effect."

Rafferty says, "He's the guy."

Tran looks at him long enough to memorize him. "This isn't theoretical," he says. "We've received a formal request to hand Colonel Thanom to the Bangkok police, and I can only stall them for so long. And, relative to the size of your farm, I need to know whether Ton will still have the resources to cause problems when you're done with him."

Nguyen says, "We're going to strip him stark naked and flay him alive in public."

Tran pulls the corners of his mouth together, perhaps at the imagery, and says to Rafferty, "And you?"

"Exactly what *he* said," Rafferty says. "But he forgot the salt."

"So I stall," Tran says. "Thank you. That'll be all."

"Just out of curiosity," Rafferty says, "How will you stall?"

"I'll tell them that we've taken their request under consideration." He blinks and pauses, and Rafferty has the sense that he's reviewing what he's just said to confirm that it's the right course of action. He gives himself a tight, stiff-necked nod. "That will hold them a few hours."

"We need more than a few—"

"And when they come back to us," Tran says, without raising his voice, "we'll inform them that one more importunate query will lead us to issue a public statement that Colonel Thanom sought refuge here voluntarily, and that we believe that a situation involving certain elements within his department poses a threat to the sovereignty of the Socialist Republic of Vietnam and the personal safety of its diplomatic representatives and their families."

Rafferty starts to speak, but Tran raises a hand. "And bearing in mind the long friendship between our respective countries, et cetera, et cetera, we'll promise to expedite our investigation of the particulars of the case—particulars, I have to say, just between us," he says, looking at Nguyen, "that are in scarce supply. And that we'll act according to our discoveries. Oh, and it's also come to our attention that those same certain elements within the police department are holding Colonel Thanom's wife without a legal basis, and we will be petitioning for her release." He gives Rafferty the ghost's smile again.

Rafferty says, "My, my."

"As solid as that sounds," Tran says, "it'll have holes worn in it twenty-four hours from now. So *settle* it; make absolutely certain you've got your man and that you can take him all the way down. In no more time than that."

"Yes, sir," Nguyen says. "We will."

"You understand, Colonel, you wouldn't even have twenty-four hours if it weren't for the assault on your family."

"Yes, sir."

"And now," Tran says, "if it's all right with you, Mr. Rafferty, that'll be all."

"We'll just let ourselves out," Rafferty says, and when they leave the room, he's in the lead. They pass the perfectly groomed woman in the outer office without a detour to get their cups. In the hallway, Rafferty stops when Nguyen touches his arm. Before Nguyen can speak, Rafferty says, "We'll be certain within twenty-four hours?"

Nguyen says, "The salt?"

"It seemed like a colorful touch."

Nguyen nods and then breaks into a smile. "You must have Vietnamese blood," he says.

"Filipino," Rafferty says, "but thanks for the compliment."

"So it's time at last," Nguyen says. It's the kind of smile, a tight-edged baring of the teeth, that probably gives his enemies the night sweats. "Twenty-four hours, and not a minute more. What was that phrase you used? From some song?"

"Aim and ignite," Rafferty says.

Nguyen says, "If not now, when?"

39

The One Wearing Hand-Me-Downs

THE RESTAURANT BUILDING used to be a bank, complete with the requisite picture window, and they get the number-one table, dead-center behind the big pane of glass. They get a hard, hot slab of morning sun, yellow as butter, through the window. They get service that seems to begin before they walk in: a maître d' pulling the door open when they're still several steps away, complimentary appetizers. They get offered specials that are, they're assured, available only to certain valued patrons. They get to watch a bottle of champagne—a gift of the house—be borne toward them in a sweating bucket from the open bank vault.

They get a beefy man in a red baseball cap passing the window and glancing in at them. Two minutes later they get the same beefy man going the other way, wearing a yellow cap.

And, ten minutes after they sit down, they get James Kalmenson, in whose name the reservation was made: a fiftyish, balding, very closely shaved, pink-faced man whose broad jowls and tiny mouth give him a permanent expression of petulance and who has no obvious shortage of self-regard. The moment he walks in, the reason the entire staff is on its knees to them becomes apparent.

Kalmenson is a finger-snapper, a man who points at people across the room and crooks a finger when he wants them, a man who indulges in the kind of imperious post-colonial behavior that makes Rafferty feel apologetic for being a *farang*. Within a moment after sitting down, Kalmenson refers to the Thais as "these people" and makes it clear that he holds each and every one of them personally responsible for the sorry mess the country is in.

"Compared to what other country?" Rafferty says, leaning across Nguyen, but Nguyen steps on Rafferty's foot and agrees that the Thais certainly seem more interested in having a good time than in running a tight ship, and Kalmenson takes a corrective stance, because, Rafferty can see, Kalmenson takes a corrective stance on everything.

"Not your boy Ton," he says. "Not the boy you're here to talk about. The exception that proves the rule and so forth." He sips his red wine, the second bottle brought to the table after he waved the first one off. "Of course, he's mostly Chinese, all the good ones are, but my Lord, he's a pistol. He could make it in the States."

He holds up the wine glass and tilts it, sighting through it, and Rafferty bets himself one hundred and seventy million baht that Kalmenson will say something about *legs*, and he says, "Nice legs. It's a little thin on the tongue, but got a nice viscosity to it." To Nguyen, he says, "Ton was the runt of the litter, of course, third son and all. Real Medici family: oldest brother in government, second in the Army, Ton in police, all of them using their positions to shovel whatever business they can into the family vault. Not much fondness among them. You're broadening your relationship with him?"

"We're considering modifying it," Nguyen says. "We're beginning to see him in a new light."

"He's quite the emerging boy," Kalmenson says. "You could do worse. You'll keep me abreast of matters as they progress."

"You'll learn what we learn," Nguyen says.

"Tit for tat." Kalmenson looks up, irritated, as a shadow falls on the table, but when he sees the menus in the waiter's hand he smiles.

He demands and gets the list of specials, orders something that there are only two servings of—it could be pheasant feet, Rafferty thinks, and he'd still order it—and strongly recommends something to each of them. Nguyen accepts his suggestion, and Rafferty says to the waiter, "Whatever you'd order."

"Give me an overview," Nguyen says. "The family business as it stands now."

"Not a lot of change in the past year. Overall, they're in construction—roads *and* buildings—and communications: they control one of the not-quite-top cellular networks. They're in rice milling and export, they're massive landlords—probably control several million square meters of business, residence, and factory space in Bangkok alone."

He pulls another roll out of the bread basket. "But the current jewel in the crown," he says, "is all Ton's: the Northeast Farmers' Trust." Rafferty's ears ring with the name and he sees Chalee's drawing of her sister as Kalmenson pours his third glass of red wine. "I told you, he's already got milling operations and rice export networks, and he's got some influence on price-setting. He controls about fifteen percent of the national crop, worth I can't even guess how much. So tell me, what's the pebble in the rice bag?"

Nguyen says, "Farmers."

"You Viets," Kalmenson says approvingly. "You've got the instinct. All that Chinese blood."

Rafferty says, his voice sharp in his ears, "What *about* the farmers?"

"Who needs them?" Kalmenson makes an expansive sweeping gesture with the back of his hand, just missing his wine glass. "They're a mess. They have too many kids, so farms that once were decent size have been carved into dozens of tiny plots, all brothers and fathers and cousins, squabbling night and day. A nightmare to deal with. So here's the deal. These people are already living at subsistence level, right?"

Rafferty, whose wife's bankrupt farmer father tried to sell her into the sex trade, swallows and says, "Right."

"It's a classic squeeze. As a miller, you lower the price you pay for their unmilled rice, and you increase the price they pay for the milled rice they eat. Say they're making two hundred baht per kilo for unmilled rice, but they're spending three for the rice they live on. And you restrict the kind of seed they use and double the price. The farmers are in a deeper hole every year. Beauty, huh?" He pulls the bread basket over to him, peeks in, then raises his hand to catch a waiter's eye and points at the basket.

"Typical," he says as the waiter takes the basket. "So, so, so—right, right—he sets up the Northeast Farmers' Trust, Ton does, a little bank with no purpose except to lend money to farmers who aren't making it. No interest, just a balloon payment at the end of the year. And you map the village, mark out the pieces each family uses, and when it comes time to collect and they can't pay, you foreclose. The first ones you take are the ones around the perimeters, create a wall around as many paddies as you can. Deny people the right to cross your paddies to get to theirs. Put rural cops—here's where being an opera cop, with that fancy uniform, pays off—to enforce the *no trespassing* edict."

Rafferty says, "What happens to the families who get foreclosed on?"

"He keeps them on at first, pays them a little to work their old land. But when you've got ten or fifteen plots, you give all but one or two of the families the old heave-ho and leave the others in charge. Then, when you've made it really difficult for people to get across your land to their family plot—good one, *family plot*, because that's what it turns out to be—you offer the others sixty cents on the dollar to sell. Pretty soon, you own a village. Do it often enough, and you'll own the rice business from seed to feed and everything in between. And he does. About fifteen percent, like I said."

Rafferty's throat feels like there's an iron band being tightened around it. He says, "What a guy."

"So if you're thinking of doing new deals with him," Kalmenson says to Nguyen, "jump at it. Just keep your hand on your wallet."

"All this sounds very rosy," Nguyen says. "But tell me. Is there any reason he might be feeling some pressure?"

Kalmenson's expression, as he regards Nguyen, goes remote. "Why do you ask?"

Nguyen pours wine into Kalmenson's glass and offers some to Poke, who shakes his head. He pours a bit into his own glass. "I have a preference for choosing successful people as my—I mean, my country's—partners. But I also want to know that my partner has some real skin in the game. I want to know that the business will matter to him in the long run, because that's how I think, long run. He's the youngest son, and he's obviously doing well. But he's got older brothers who can probably overrule him. How do I know he'll still have his shoulder to the wheel in, say, five years?"

Kalmenson eyes him blankly for a moment and says, "Where's the food?"

Nguyen says, "Coming," and settles comfortably in his chair.

"What you want," Kalmenson says, rubbing his hands together, "this new topic, that's a little beyond just information. It's judgment. That makes it more in the nature of a personal consultation."

"How much?"

Kalmenson purses the little mouth in thought. "A thousand, American."

"Do you have that much on you, Poke?"

Poke says, "Sure," and reaches into his pocket. "Hundreds okay?"

"I'm sorry?" Kalmenson says. He pushes out a smile and then turns it off. "I've missed something. What's your role in all this?"

"Mr. Rafferty represents some special interests," Nguyen says. "I can't tell you more without compromising the nature of my business with Ton."

Kalmenson says, "American interests?"

"And Thai," Poke says. He holds the money out. "Sorry to be

so gauche, paying in the open like this. I know you'd be more comfortable getting it under the table, where the whole world can't see it, but I can't reach you under the table."

Kalmenson stretches out a hand and palms the money. "Rafferty, right?"

Nguyen says, "Of the Philadelphia Raffertys."

"Fine." The money disappears into a shirt pocket, and the man in the baseball cap who's been looking in through the window decides it's time to go elsewhere. "Funny we haven't bumped into each other."

"Mr. Rafferty operates very privately," Nguyen says. "But I'm interrupting. You were about to tell me why Ton has so much skin in the game."

"The *long run*, you said." Kalmenson brings the tips of his fingers together into a tent and regards them with satisfaction. "A business is like a building," he says. He raises his hands several inches above the table, fingertips still touching. "Roof beams," he says. "A company needs a good foundation, which Ton's family's company has: several generations of experience, lots of working capital. But it also needs roof beams. And in an Asian family business, roof beams are sons."

Nguyen blows out a little air, and Rafferty is sure he doesn't know that he did it.

"The family is short on sons," Kalmenson says. "His older brothers, between them, produced four daughters and one son, but the son races motor cars, uses drugs. Useless, in and out of trouble."

"And Ton?" Nguyen asks.

"Two daughters, one son, who got himself killed climbing some damnfool mountain, about fourteen years ago. But before he died, he and his wife had two sons. Ton's grandsons."

Nguyen says, "Ahhhh."

"Yes," Kalmenson says. "They *bear the name*. They're eleven and twelve, I think, but they're the only ones with the family name who will be in line to inherit. It's a wonderful irony, don't you think? Being the runt all these years, the one wearing hand-me-downs, and all of a sudden you see the future, and it's all yours. Or, at least, your grandsons'. Since the first one was born, Ton has been making deals left and right. Almost got a personal candidate into the running for Prime Minister."

"Pan," Rafferty says.

Kalmenson blots his lips with his napkin, as though he's tasted something unexpectedly greasy. "You're well informed. But Pan was a peasant whose head got too big, and he got himself shot. Ton will try again, though. So that's your skin in the game, Captain Nguyen. He's going to do anything and everything to make sure that company goes to his sons—sorry, grandsons—and that it's thriving when it does. The long run that you mentioned. He's in it."

Nguyen says, "Sons."

Rafferty says, "Grandsons," but he's certain Nguyen doesn't hear him.

40

Overcoat of Rage

RAFFERTY FEELS AS though he's wrapped in a thick overcoat of rage as they push down the crowded sidewalk. All he can think about are Rose and Miaow—and Chalee, her sister hanging in that empty house. Thousands of children, thrown onto the streets of Bangkok to live any way they can, footnotes to some spread-sheet of gain and loss in the rice trade.

Kalmenson is nattering on to Nguyen in the over-emphatic, contentious manner of a bad drunk, as Nguyen nods and interjects the occasional sentence fragment. To Nguyen's left, between him and the traffic, is Tuan, his bodyguard, whose military experience advertises itself in his walk. Since there are too many of them to walk abreast, Rafferty is a couple of steps behind, with Chinh to his right, his sport coat—conspicuous in this heat—suggesting he might be packing.

From behind, Kalmenson carries his head in a way that seems to announce, *here's a guy you might want to punch.* He walks with a penguin's waddle, his toes turned out and his upper body tick-tocking slightly from side to side, like a metronome. Rafferty is pleasurably lost in loathing when Chinh touches his arm, and Kalmenson, at virtually the same moment, says, "One of yours?"

Ahead of Rafferty, Tuan turns to his left, his spine straight as a ruler, one hand going to the small of his back, beneath his loose-fitting shirt. At the curb, moving slowly to keep pace with them, is a black town car. Its dark windows are all the way up.

Rafferty hears a scuff on the pavement and turns back to see Chinh, his right hand creating some misery at the pressure points on either side of a neck. The neck belongs to the man with the baseball cap who'd passed their window so frequently while they were eating, and now he's almost hanging from Chinh's hand, his shoulders all the way to his ears, his face the mask of tragedy, mouth wide, eyes shut.

Approaching them purposefully from the other direction are two uniformed policemen.

"Let him go, Chinh," Nguyen says. He gives the town car a small wave. "One of theirs," he says to Kalmenson. Then, to all of them, "Come on, the office is just up here."

Seeing Mr. Baseball fade back into the crowd, turning his head left and right with some difficulty, the cops slow, looking a bit directionless. Nguyen leads the group briskly toward the policemen, chattering to Kalmenson about the Thai government's rice stock-piling program, and when one of the cops takes a sidestep to plant himself in Nguyen's path, two taps from the town car's horn back him up again.

Rafferty follows obediently behind, feeling useless and out-classed.

RAFFERTY'S ACQUAINTANCE, a reporter named Floyd Preece, is mercifully out, although the reek of old cigars marks the cubicle as his. A note on the computer screen announces that all Rafferty will have to do is swipe the touchpad, and he'll find himself in the database. Then he can just tab from item to item.

You said your guy was in his mid-thirties, the note reads, so I set you up to start about 15 years back. Too bad you don't have a name, but you got one break. A society reporter here is doing a big picture book about the clothes of Bangkok society and she's been working for years on pulling out the pieces that have pictures with them. I'll be back about four, and you can tell me how this story is going to win me the Pulitzer.

"Wasn't that pleasant," Nguyen says, pulling a chair from the adjoining cubicle, one of many that seems to be empty.

"The lunch or the little dance on the sidewalk?" Rafferty removes from his hip pocket a printout of Andrew's enhanced photo of the reflected man and smoothes it out on the desk, studying it. Then he taps the computer's touchpad, and up come three ladies with Imelda Marcos hairstyles, frozen hovering over their dinners by a flashbulb. He sees no one he recognizes, hits the tab key, and is presented with a line-up of eight or twelve people, dressed in the kind of clothes he's never seen in person, the men looking like Daddy Warbucks and the women holding bouquets.

"Both," Nguyen says. "By now, there are probably fifteen people on the phone lines in and out of Ton's office. Which reminds me, I think we need reinforcements." He pulls out his phone and switches to Vietnamese and a more peremptory tone, and Rafferty recognizes the name "Homer" and what sound like several other names.

More matrons, more shiny material that seems to be satin. The photos are dreadful, just flat flash on heavily made-up skin and lacquered hair. Many of the eyes above the smiles look tired or jaded or both; being a rich Thai man's wife is not an unmixed blessing. Every now and then a much younger second wife, her hair still allowed to obey gravity, looks at the camera in pleased surprise, glad to be there. About two hundred pictures in, Rafferty says, "This may not take a long time, but it's going to *feel* like a long time."

Nguyen says, "If he's even in there."

"If he's not," Rafferty says, paging through, "all we'll have done is waste a big chunk of the twenty-four hours Tran gave us."

"Nineteen hours now." Nguyen sits back in his chair and closes his eyes. "If you see something, say my name. I wake up easily."

Rafferty says, "You're kidding," but gets no answer. Ten or eleven clusters of women, thirty-five or forty tuxedos, and twelve hundred dead flowers later, Nguyen's breathing deepens and evens out.

He glances at his watch: 1:44. Up pops a wedding, which gives way to a charity ball, which gives way to some debutantes, which gives way to a long line of rigid-looking women lined up for an audience with Princess Sirindhorn, which gives way to another wedding, then an event in a museum, then wedding announcements with photos, then . . .

Then he's falling off a cliff. He sits bolt upright, blinking at the screen, which is now in color, apparently a Sunday edition, and he has no idea how many days he snoozed through, just reflexively hitting the tab key. Checks the date: he's covered five months so far. Okay, change rhythm. He gets up, edges past Nguyen, and goes to a vacant cubicle, where he phones Arthit.

"How's your pet cop doing?" he says. "She at work yet?"

"It's . . . slow," Arthit says. He sounds tense and stopped-up, as though he'd prefer to be shouting.

"Not compared to what I'm doing, it's not."

"She has to pull up each case, get the victim's name, and then search five or six indexes to build a picture of their business interests. What they did, names of their corporations, all that. Then she takes all those corporate and personal names and searches the business sections of three newspapers in the eight to ten weeks preceding their death."

"At least she's got names. I've got ten thousand women in satin, a lot of people with the same names as minor cities, and a photographer whose flash should be taken away forever."

"She hit one interesting bit so far. The second victim we know of was in a bidding war for a big fat slice of cellular geography. The only company against him belongs to Ton's family, which already controlled some surrounding territory. Ton was arguing economies of scale—doubling up on existing cell towers and so forth—and the other side was arguing that they'd provide better service because they *wouldn't* be doubling up on cell towers."

"Maybe my job isn't so boring after all," Rafferty says.

"More than a hundred million US a year at stake," Arthit says. "When the victim was killed, in what was supposed to be an attempted robbery, Ton's guys argued that the other side no longer had experienced leadership. They won the contract."

"That's our boy. Wait'll I tell you some of the other stuff he's up to."

"Lieutenant Clemente is waving at me," Arthit says. "I've got to go."

"Don't forget my chart," Rafferty says. "The wheel with Ton in the middle."

"You'll get it."

"How's Thanom?"

"Falling apart. Got to go."

Rafferty wanders for a couple of minutes, girding his loins before re-entering high society. Then he edges past Nguyen again, careful not to touch him or wake him.

Without opening his eyes, Nguyen says, "Everything okay back home?"

"Got one possible murder with motive, if a hundred million US sounds like a motive."

"Get back to it. What year are you in?"

"1993."

"Skip to 1995."

"Why?"

"The man in the reflection isn't very old. Unless his family is more prominent than Ton's, he's not going to be on those pages until he's more than just a promising college graduate."

Rafferty takes another look at the printout photo and bangs his way through the database until he hits January of 1995. Instantly, he notes positive fashion trends: better hair on the women, more business suits and fewer tuxes on the men, a general sense that people have stopped getting embalmed as preparation for an evening out. The events are the same, though: more charity balls, some product launches—businesses of the rich and famous—and these draw a lot of people, so they slow him down a little, more people awaiting royal audiences, more weddings, more weddings, more—

—and there he is. The proud groom beside his beaming bride. Rafferty's eyes go back and forth between Andrew's blow-up and the newspaper shot; the man on the computer screen is younger than the one reflected in the window. The newspaper photographer's flash swallows up some detail, so he can't be entirely certain, and it's not until the fourth or fifth time he looks at the wedding photo that he even registers the bride's father.

He says, "Captain Nguyen."

"Right here," Nguyen says, and he is. He leans past Rafferty to look at the screen. Then he starts to laugh, very softly. "The son-in-law," he says.

Rafferty says to the picture of Ton, smiling happily on the screen beside his daughter and her new husband, "Gotcha."

BEFORE HE'LL STEP into the street, Nguyen makes a short call and speaks very brisk Vietnamese. Then he slips the phone into his pocket and says, "Thirty seconds."

A few seconds early, Homer pushes the door open and says, "The other side is at the curb. Black car."

"How many do we have?" Nguyen asks.

"Counting the two of you, seven."

"Fine." To Rafferty, he says, "Stay close to me, and I mean that."

Homer backs out, Nguyen and Rafferty following, into the late-afternoon heat, their shoulders almost touching. Waiting for them are Chinh, Tuan, and two other Vietnamese men, blunt-faced, with the seen-everything eyes of cops. In the time it takes Rafferty to pull the door closed behind him, they've formed a phalanx with Nguyen and Rafferty at the center and are moving up the street, against the flow of the crowd.

To Rafferty's right, a horn sounds, and someone shouts

something. He turns to sight past Chinh and another man, and sees the black town car again. As Nguyen murmurs, "Don't even look," the window goes down, and the man in the passenger seat puts his head out and smiles at him.

It's the man Miaow spotted the previous evening, the thuggish-faced man, the man who'd gone after her with a knife. Rafferty stops cold, and the Vietnamese man behind him bumps into him, and the man in the car grins more broadly and slowly raises his middle finger.

And then Rafferty takes off, but he hasn't gone two feet before he's yanked back by a hand inside his collar, and the next thing he knows, Homer is marching him down the street like a marionette, and Nguyen is laughing and talking to him as though nothing in the world is wrong, and Rafferty registers the men in police uniforms scattered here and there among the pedestrians.

He gets control of his feet and tries to walk normally, his heart pounding so hard he's certain it must be visible. He forces a smile at Nguyen. "That was the man who tried to kill Miaow."

"Really," Nguyen laughs as though Rafferty has made a joke, but he takes a quick look back and then he says, "Keep walking. Don't even spit on the sidewalk. You're okay unless you give them a reason. They know we won't let go of you unless you give them legal cause to take you, and even if they do have cause, they know we'll follow you to the station, calling lawyers as we go. But it would cost us hours, so do *not* give them a reason. Okay?"

"Okay."

"That man will be part of our bargain."

"What bargain?"

"The bargain we make to end this thing. And don't look at me like that. Smile."

"*Bargain* is kind of a soft word," Rafferty says through his smile.

Nguyen says, "You and I together, Mr. Rafferty, we're going to make the bargain a genuine, unadulterated, unimprovable motherfucker."

*   *   *

"WE'VE HAD A call," Arthit says, "from the embassy guy who takes our original phones out for a walk every few hours."

"Hold on," Rafferty says. "I want to put this on speaker for Captain Nguyen."

"Where are you?" Arthit asks, and the last word emerges tinnily from the phone's speaker.

"A couple of kilometers from the embassy, moving very slowly."

"Well, turn around. Thanom got a message from a Mr. Arundee at First Siam Bank, saying he's located the snapshot, whatever that is, of the last withdrawal from Thanom's mystery account. They only keep them for a year, so a few months from now, it would have been untraceable."

"Can't he email it to you?"

"He won't. He doesn't want it logged in on the bank's email system."

"But he'll release it physically to someone other than Thanom?"

"If Thanom calls and gives a name, and the person who shows up has identification."

"Tell him I'll be there in—" He stops because Nguyen, who is seated beside him in the backseat of the embassy car, has put his hand over the phone. Rafferty hands it to him.

"This is Captain Nguyen," he says. "I don't want Mr. Rafferty to get out of the car again. We have company, and they want an excuse to grab him."

Rafferty pulls the phone toward him and says, "He's right. And I don't know what a snapshot is in bank jargon, but if one of us goes in there, Ton is going to know that he's looking into that account, probably looking for the person who did the deposits and withdrawals. Suppose he makes that person disappear before we can get to him?"

Nguyen says, "I should have thought of—"

"Is there someone out here you can send, Arthit? If any of you leave the embassy, you'll have followers."

"Anand," Arthit says, Rafferty straining to hear him with the phone in Nguyen's hand. "He hates princelings. I'll get him over there. And we're finding more links between the victims and Ton's business deals. We're four for seven now, and still looking."

"We're building the box," Nguyen says. "And, just to put a lock on it, Mr. Rafferty discovered that the man who took the pictures with that cursed phone is Ton's son-in-law."

"His full name is Jaruk Pratchuwan," Rafferty says, checking his notes. "Ask your database wizard to find out where he works."

"And lives," Nguyen says. "Home address is essential."

"I'll get Anand moving right now," Arthit says. "Bank's closing soon."

Rafferty disconnects, and they ride in silence for a minute or two, and then Nguyen says, "There's something I need to say to you. Miaow saved my son *twice*. If she hadn't gotten away from the man with the knife, he probably would have come after Anh Duong. And Anh Duong would have been . . . easier to kill than Miaow."

"I don't know," Rafferty says. "He's quite a kid. I think he could surprise all of us."

41

The Best Scene in the Play

"GOOD LORD," RAFFERTY says to Arthit. "That woman has the most beautiful eyes I've ever seen."

"I have to agree," Rose says. "Amazing." Embassy or no embassy, she's wearing shorts, a T-shirt, and red patent-leather sandals. It's a little after five P.M., and they're all gathered in what Rafferty thinks of as the Food Room. Arthit and Thanom have followed Rafferty in to find more cookies on the platters, soft drinks afloat in an ice tub, and a pungent fragrance coming from a restaurant-size coffee machine. In Rose's honor, a jar of Nescafé squats beside the coffee-maker. One door away, in the adjacent room, Officer Clemente is at work on a computer with an enormous flatscreen monitor.

Miaow comes in, heads for the cookies, grabs two, and turns to Rose. "Mama," she says, in English, "am I pretty?"

"*Mama?*" Rose says. "And I thought we'd settled that."

Arthit says, "You're *very* pretty, Miaow, and you're on the way to being beautiful."

Miaow, looking a little surprised, says, "Thank you, Arthit." She breaks a cookie in half and says, "Who knew I was acting?"

Rafferty says, "You're always acting."

"That's from *Small Town*," Miaow says. "That's Julie, the character I want to play. She gets to die."

"Everybody gets to die," Rose says.

"*And* she gets to come back."

"Everybody gets to come back," Rose says.

"Not like *that*, not like karma. She comes back as herself and gets to say goodbye to everyone and everything she loves. It's the best scene in the play."

"When I played Ned," Rafferty says, "I thought the part where she and Ned talk about the future was the best scene."

"It is, for Ned," Miaow says. "Julie mops the floor with him."

Figuring *the hell with it*, Rafferty says, "Is Andrew going to try out for Ned?"

Miaow breaks the other cookie and says, "Who cares?" She leaves the room, ostentatiously stepping aside for Andrew, who's coming in. She gives him so much space he could be riding an elephant. He turns to watch her go and a moment later they hear her say, from halfway down the hall, "Oh, *excuse* me."

"You did it, Andrew," Rafferty says, pulling the printout of the reflected man from his pocket.

"Did I ever," Andrew says glumly.

"No, I mean, look—" Rafferty opens the picture and waves it at him. "You're the best detective in the room. This guy? We know who he is now, and without you, we'd never have figured it out."

With the expression of someone who's just located a match in the middle of an endless night, Andrew says, "Is it important?"

He looks so hopeful Rafferty has to fight the impulse to hug him. "It's the most important thing any of us has done. It might be what gets us all out of this."

Andrew says, "Will you tell Miaow?"

"Don't be a sap. Go tell her yourself."

"You saw. She won't even stay in the same room with me."

"Well, as much as I hate to say this, that's your problem. Go fix it."

Rose says, "You walked out when she was trying to tell you who she was. She was pretending to talk to those kids, but it was really for you, and it was one of the bravest things she's ever done. And you turned your back and walked out."

"I had to," Andrew says. He shoves his hands into his pockets, so hard his jeans sag. "She was talking about—eating out of trash cans and running away from men and not having *shoes* and—and I started to cry. I couldn't let her see, but I couldn't stop, either. She would have *killed* me."

"Oh, baby, come here," Rose says, opening her arms. Andrew drags his feet and studies the carpet all the way across the room, but ultimately she's got her arms wrapped around him, and the boy lowers his head and Rafferty, seeing the little knob at the top of his spine, wonders how it can possibly look that sad.

"This is almost perfect," Rafferty says.

He's at the table in the Food Room with Arthit, Thanom, and Kwai Clemente, whose glorious eyes are red and fried-looking from squinting at the computer screen all day. In front of each of them is a chart: a wheel with a photo of Ton in the middle, surrounded by small circular pictures of six of the victims of Sawat's murder squads. Beneath each picture is the name of the victim and the dates of his birth and death. Spokes radiate out from the picture of Ton to connect him graphically to the victims.

"What I'd like to see," Rafferty says, "is the name of the victim's company in between his name and the date. Just three lines of type: name, company, death date. You can lose the birth date, but before the date of death, put the words *Murdered on.* And then I want you to break the spoke between each one and Ton with a really quick summary, something like *Competitor for cellular phone contract. Estimated gain for Ton: $100 million US annually.*"

Clemente says, "Easy."

"And I want you to make a second chart, exactly the same except you put Andrew's picture of the son-in-law, Jaruk, in the circle with Ton. We have to think of the two of them as a single entity, because we're not just after Ton for the murders all those years ago; we're going to nail both of them for killing Sawat and Thongchai."

"And probably the men they hired to do it," Arthit says. "It's hard to believe he'd leave them alive."

Thanom says, sounding fretful, "Where's the man you sent to my bank? He should be here by now."

"Don't worry," Arthit says. "You're off the hook."

"You sound like Ton is just going to roll over," Thanom says. "He'll say, *Oh, please, run over me, of course, I did it all*. He was born to power. He's got resources we can't even imagine."

Arthit is used to Thanom, but the look Clemente gives him makes it clear that her first impression isn't a good one. Thanom glances at her and then looks back at the chart. He still has the tiny tremor in his head, but at least he's shaved. He says to her, "Don't you have something to do?"

"She's doing it," Rafferty says.

"I think I've got another one," Clemente says. "It's not quite as clear, because it didn't happen while he was competing for a specific contract, but he and Ton had gone head-to-head for years."

"How long ago?" Arthit says.

"Eight years."

"Look at the biggest deals Ton made in the two or three years after that death. See whether the dead man would have gone up against Ton on any of those."

Thanom says, "It's hard to believe no one put this together before."

"The murders were spread over years," Rafferty says. "Someone was convicted for each of them. Ton made lots of other deals, and all the victims made lots of other deals. And who's going to speculate publicly about Ton doing something like that, unless he's got a hell of a case?"

Arthit picks up the chart and flicks it with his index finger. "This is a pretty good case."

Thanom is shaking his head. "It's not proof."

"We don't need proof," Rafferty says. "We're not going to court."

"We're not?" Thanom demands. "Then what are—"

Homer comes into the room, followed by Anand.

Anand is in his early thirties, with the slender body the police uniform was designed to show off: broad shoulders, narrow hips, flat stomach. Clemente looks up at him, rubs her eyes gently with her fingertips, and looks at him again.

"Got it," Anand says, waving a half-sheet of paper at them. "Oh, hello."

"Hello," Clemente says.

"Anand, this is Kwai Clemente," Arthit says. "Officer Clemente, this is Anand. Now that you two know each other, what does it say?"

"I don't exactly know." Anand pulls a chair out and sits, his eyes going to Officer Clemente again, and says, "Arundee was starting to explain it to me when someone told him he had a phone call. When he came back out, he was almost running, and I felt like it was a good time to leave."

"Ton?" Thanom says.

"Probably." Rafferty reaches for the paper. "Checking up after they saw us this afternoon. But that doesn't mean he knows anything. Would *you* tell Ton that you've just given this away?" He looks down at it. "How far did he get with the explanation?"

"Here." Anand leans across the table and a big index finger lands on the page. "This symbol means transaction, and this means withdrawal. So, the transaction, on *this* date and at *this* time, was a withdrawal. This is the amount—"

"One million five hundred thousand baht?" Rafferty says. "That's fifty thousand US. This late in the game, why do I have the feeling Ton doesn't know about it?"

Thanom says, "Keep going, keep going. Where does it say who it was?"

"Well, it doesn't, not exactly. Here's the teller's name and her number, and this note means the money was withdrawn in cash."

"What do you mean, *not exactly?*" Thanom says.

"Well, it says it was you."

Thanom sits back so hard his chair squeaks.

"But we know it wasn't," Anand says. "And this scramble at the end was what he was going to explain to me. It's the information that got registered when they swiped the magnetic strip on the back of the ID the man presented."

"*This* number," Clemente says, putting a tangerine-colored fingernail on the page, next to Anand's brown finger. "This is—or could be—a badge number. Right number of digits, right place for the dash. If the man was pretending to be the Colonel, he would have presented a police ID card."

"Is that your number, Colonel?" Arthit asks.

"Not even close." Thanom swipes his nose with his index finger and sniffs. "Where's the picture? These cards have pictures."

"Not encoded on the strip," Clemente says. "But—"

"Then what fucking good is it?" Thanom says.

"*But*," Clemente says, "I can access this on the police database, and the picture should be part of the record. They use those records to print the cards."

Thanom says, "You mean, you think the card is real?"

"Sure, it is," Rafferty says. "What could be easier for someone in Ton's position? They probably changed one character in your name, or your birth date, and assigned the card an unused number. They knew the bank would run the strip to verify the card. If it bounced, there'd be no transaction."

"Shall I?" Clemente says. She gets up, and Arthit and Rafferty get up, too. After a moment, during which he seems to be translating what he's just heard, Thanom pushes his chair back. He has to put a hand on the table to rise.

Anand gets up, too. "Can I come?"

Arthit says, "Could we stop you?"

About three minutes later, Clemente says, "Here he is. This guy is everywhere."

In a nice, clear, recent photo, full face, Ton's son-in-law, Jurak, looks out at them.

Rafferty says to Arthit, "How would you feel about sending Anand, if he's willing to go, and two or three other uniformed cops to pick *Khun* Jurak up and put him on ice somewhere? Some minor station where they can register him under a fictitious name for a few hours? Get him into an interrogation room, show him this picture and the shot from the phone. I don't think he'll have much fight in him."

"How would I feel?" Arthit says. "I'd feel constructive. I'd feel decisive. I'd feel like a cop for the first time in days."

To Thanom, Rafferty says, "The case just got a lot stronger. And we still don't need proof."

IN THE HALLWAY, he's working his way through three or four possible ways to use the information to maximum effect and simultaneously congratulating himself on getting out of harm's way everyone who could be used as a pressure point against him. And then he stops in the middle of the hall.

There *is* a person out there who could be used as a pressure point: Treasure. The moment he has the thought, he relaxes because, he thinks, there's no way for Ton or Ton's men to know about her.

And then he realizes who he hasn't seen since he came back to the embassy.

42

A Different Magnitude of Darkness

BEING JAMMED INTO the trunk of an Infiniti G-37 sports car is even less pleasant than he'd thought it would be. He's bent so sharply, in so many places, he feels like a clothes hanger. The air is unpleasantly warm and as dark as a torturer's soul.

But it's the smallest car in the embassy compound, and it seemed to him, during the brief and frantic time he had to think about it—after Boo failed to answer two panicked calls—that the trunk of a weensy car would be less suspicious than a big one. From the moment he learned that Anna had been driven to Klong Toey to the time they closed the trunk on him and the car wheeled through the gates and onto the street, it's been less than twenty minutes, which makes it about 5:30.

"We've got one," the driver says. He and Rafferty are connected by cell phone.

"Well, I'm glad. I'd feel like an idiot, going through all this with nobody following us. Let me know when the first stop is coming up."

"Just a minute or two. I'll be turning into a *soi* to park."

"Got it." The idea, if it even qualifies as an idea, is for the driver to run several very ordinary, very boring errands, leaving the car empty so the followers can get up close and confirm that no one is cowering in the backseat. The hope is that the followers will go away. If they don't, two other cars wait behind the embassy gate, engines running, to supply a diversion.

"Office supply store," the driver announces, and the car swerves into its turn. A moment later there's a gristly grinding of gears as the driver botches the shift into reverse, and they stop. "They just went past," he says, and the door opens, the car rises as the man gets out, and the door slams. The car makes the little *boop* that announces it's locked.

The driver's shoes scuff the asphalt. Rafferty settles in and waits, doubting every decision he's made in the past few hours. How could he have forgotten about Treasure? Why hadn't he kept tabs on Anna?

All the questions disappear as he hears the footsteps. Someone tries the driver's door, and then there's a line of light around the back of the fold-down seat he'll use to get out of the trunk. Someone's using a flashlight.

"It's empty," a man says in Thai, probably into a phone. "Driver went into that Staples a kilometer from the embassy. Left the car at the curb." There's a pause, and the man says in response to someone, "Okay, whatever you want." The footsteps recede and then stop abruptly, and Rafferty figures the man is standing there, watching the car, and then there are more footsteps, fading away this time.

The next errand is a liquor store, and this time the footsteps stop some distance from the car, and Rafferty imagines the man hanging back and waiting to see whether anyone emerges from the trunk. The next thing he hears is the driver, coming back.

"The one who just left was keeping an eye on the car," the driver says as he starts the engine. "There's another one driving."

"Well, let's see what happens now."

"If this stop doesn't do it," the driver says, "nothing will."

They park relatively close to their destination, and Rafferty can smell hot fat and charred meat, smells that bring back Lancaster fast-food joints when he was a kid, spreading their plume of cooking oil through the clean desert air. Almost immediately after the driver leaves, there's a scratching at the trunk, and a voice says, "Locked. And there's no keyhole. You have to open it from inside."

Footsteps, and then another man says, "He's getting takeout."

"Did you hear that?" the first man says. "He's getting hamburgers. Got to be for the Americans back at the embassy. This is a waste of—" Then he says, in English, "Yeah, okay."

"What?" says the other man.

"He says fine, follow him back to the embassy and we can wait there again."

"This is stupid," the other man says. Then Rafferty hears nothing until the Infiniti's driver says, "Scoot back as far as you can." He manages to wriggle a few additional inches farther from the trunk lid. The driver pops the trunk and puts several big bags of food next to Rafferty, and then it's dark again.

A moment later, the driver says, "Don't eat any of that."

"I'd like to get farther away from it. Are they still back there?"

"Don't know. It must have looked like the trunk was empty."

"Okay." He feels a fizz of anxiety behind his breastbone. He'd hoped they would have peeled off by now. "Call Homer and tell him it's showtime. Just put me on hold, I'm not going anywhere."

A moment later, another call comes in on Rafferty's phone, and Rafferty puts the driver on hold and says, "Yeah?"

"Where are you?" It's Nguyen.

"Hard to tell, since I'm in the trunk, but we've finished at the fast-food place."

"This is a bit labor-intensive. You're tying up one of my drivers, and two more are racing their motors just inside the gate."

"Those are my reserves."

Nguyen says, "You spread yourself too thin."

Rafferty can't disagree, so he doesn't argue. Instead, he resorts to explanation, "It's about exposure. I need to make sure the kid I told you about is all right, because if she's not, she could be used as a lever against me. Truth is, if I got a call saying someone has her, I don't know what I'd do."

"Well, I'm not happy about it," Nguyen says, "And you didn't give me much time to argue. I could have sent men with you."

"If I show up with an army, I'll tip off Anna that I don't trust her. What I need to do is to get to a point where I can walk in casually, with nobody following me, and say 'Hi' and figure out whether I've got to snatch the girl myself." He puts Nguyen on hold and says to the driver, "Still back there?"

"Maybe not."

"Well, keep your eye on the mirror in about sixty seconds. Nguyen is about to loose the lions." To Nguyen, he says, "The cars that are at the gate, they're SUVs with tinted windows, right?"

"That's what you asked for."

"Okay, good. Then, please, just tell them to leave. Out through the gate and into traffic, going as fast as they can."

"And the people who are watching will follow them," Nguyen says. "According to you."

"And since the car I'm in is coming back with all this American food, I'm hoping they'll call our tail off and put them into the game, too. And then I can get out of this damn trunk and flag a cab."

"Very devious," Nguyen says.

"Thank you. Please tell those cars to go."

"Count to ten." He closes the connection.

"They should be going any minute," Rafferty says to the driver. "Keep your eye on the mirror."

They hit a pothole, and Rafferty's head emphatically meets the roof of the trunk. He's still rubbing the sore spot when the driver says, "Four cars back, somebody just made a very fast turn into a *soi*."

"If you had to bet, would you say yes or no?"

"Yes, but—"

"Okay. Turn into the next one-way *soi* and slow down. Keep your eyes on the mirror."

The car sways as it turns left, and Rafferty pulls the lever that folds down the backseat. In less than a minute, he's curled up on the folded-down backs of the seats.

"No one back there," the driver says.

"Find a parking space and turn off the interior light, and thanks for everything."

With the car stopped, the driver says, "Still no one."

Rafferty pushes the back of the passenger seat forward, opens the door, and a moment later he's sprinting up the sidewalk.

He gets out of the cab half a block from the alley. The moon is down, and in this run-down part of the city, with few streetlights and with the vast, unilluminated expanse of the river just blocks away, the darkness seems as concentrated as smoke.

He waits at the alley's mouth, listening. The alley curves to the left, so he can't see Boo's building, only the walls of the structures on either side of the narrow passageway, blackened brick with small windows and a few old tin roofs. There are no lights in the windows. As dark as the street is, the alley is a different magnitude of darkness.

But, of course, that works both ways. If anyone is here, they won't see him, either. It'll be a blind date.

He chooses the wall on the right so he won't be visible coming around the bend, and keeps a hand against the filthy brick as he moves. Involuntarily he thinks of Miaow, at four and five, negotiating alleyways like this, barefoot, alone, with no way of knowing what was waiting a few steps ahead. Not only Miaow: Boo, Chalee, Dok, and all of Boo's charges. Thinks of Andrew, smart, coddled Andrew, hearing Miaow's story for the first time and bursting into tears.

Thinks of Treasure, flaming with fever, collapsed in an alley like this one for Dok and Chalee to find. Chalee, running from her suicide-stained family to these alleys. Dok, small for his age and defenseless, on whatever miserable path led him to Boo's shelter.

At the turn, he pauses. For all he knows, there's a crowd waiting for him around the bend. He presses himself against the wall to reduce his profile and takes the curve slowly, studying, as it comes into view, each slice of the dead end containing Boo's building. The building plugs the alley except for a supernaturally dark strip to the left, just wide enough to allow two people walking abreast to reach the next street.

Only one panel of the double door into the boys' dormitory floor is open. The same dismal fluorescents are dispensing their miserly, arctic light. No figures in the doorway.

Just stroll in casually, someone who drops by every day. So he takes a last look around and walks toward the building as though it were the most normal thing in the world. Hi, how you doing, and what a surprise, Anna, to see you here.

He takes the two steps up and into the big room. Two of the cots are occupied by boys, the same newcomers as the night before, still dirty, but now on adjoining cots. When he comes in, their eyes snap to him, but until the moment they became aware of him, both had been looking to his left, toward the corner that houses Boo's impromptu office.

He turns, too, and sees five children, boys and girls, pressed into and around the gap between the partitions, looking into the office. A moment later, he hears laughter—eight or ten kids by the sound of it. The children with their backs to him join in.

It takes him a few seconds to carve a passage, very gently, between the children at the door, smelling the essence of kids, the scent of hair and skin in need of a washing: the first smell he associated with Miaow. As the last children give way to let him by, he leans forward and looks into the room.

There are now nine chairs, both the metal ones and the rickety wooden ones Boo had been using. They're all occupied; a handful of kids Rafferty hasn't seen before, plus Boo and Chalee. In the front row is the boy with the scratches running down his face. Sitting in a corner, on Boo's one good chair with her two friends between her and the rest of the room, is Treasure.

She's almost smiling.

The laughter ceases the instant he comes in, and Anna, at the front of the room with Boo's whiteboard behind, stops writing and turns to him. She communicates something in sign language, her hands flying, and then in her flat, uninflected voice, says, "We have a visitor."

He knows how sensitive Anna is about the way she sounds when she speaks, and here she is, doing it in front of a room full of people.

Her eyes are shining, her face transparent with happiness. "Chalee and Dok and Treasure already know *Khun* Poke," she says to the children, speaking the words as she signs them. "*Khun* Poke is a famous writer. One day he'll come back and talk to you all about writing. We all need to read and write well, isn't that true, *Khun* Poke?"

Children turn to look to him, so intently it makes his ears ring, and he says, "Absolutely."

Anna signs his answer and asks, "And why is that?"

"For—uhhh—joy?" he says. Feeling foolish, he smiles and points to the corners of his mouth. "And, and having a better life and even making money."

"*Khun* Poke and his wife," Anna says, "adopted a daughter from the street, and now she goes to a good school and when she's grown up she'll be able to be anything she wants, isn't that right?"

"Anything," Poke says, and his voice is unexpectedly fierce in his ears.

"Because she's learned to *read* and *write*," Anna says, signing away. "And you, *all* of you, can do the same. Remember, each and every one of you: you don't have to live in the street. You can be whatever you want. You can have whatever you want."

Dok says, "Can I have a computer?"

"You can have two of them, if you work hard enough. Chalee?"

Chalee sits up, startled.

"Can you pass out some of your paper? Does everyone have a

pencil? Let me see the hands of anyone who didn't bring a pencil."
No hands go up. "While I talk to *Khun* Poke, you copy three times
the characters I wrote on the board, and then we'll play a game
with them. Ting?" A boy nods, and Anna begins signing and then
says, for the benefit of the hearing students, "Ting will go to the
board with Chalee and make the signs for *mother, father, brother,
sister,* and *hello,* and Chalee will draw them on the board. We'll try
them when I get back. Remember," she says to the children, "the
best way to understand each other is to talk to each other."

The kids at the door part as Rafferty and Anna come through.
None of them is looking at Rafferty. The two newcomers on their
cots watch Anna, too, but when she smiles at them, one looks
down and the other turns his back. The one who looked down
looks back up a second later.

Rafferty says, "I'm, um, amazed."

"I talked to Father Bill yesterday," Anna says. She's gazing at
him with such intensity he feels as though his reaction could
decide her fate. "They've got seven non-hearing kids inside the
compound, and they're having trouble teaching them. I used to
teach—I mean, back before—before—"

"Before they fired you," Rafferty says, "because you didn't tell
the cops everything you knew about what I was doing."

"Back then," Anna says, and her discomfort about that time in
their lives makes her blink rapidly and look down. "Father Bill
said, if I can teach them at the same time I teach Treasure and Dok
and Chalee, then Boo can keep Treasure here. We still have to
find her a different room, but Boo will let the three of them sleep
in the office for a while, and—well, who knows? Maybe she'll
make progress. Those two are angels."

Rafferty is simultaneously delighted and ashamed of himself.
He says, "This is better than anything I could have hoped for."

"And for *me,*" Anna says, "for me, it's like being let back into
paradise. I'm back, I'm back working with children again."

"Do they know Treasure's story?"

"Not yet." She clasps her hands in front of her chest as though she's about to sing. Her face is more open than Rafferty has ever seen it. "We're all going to write our stories, as soon as they can begin to scratch the first words. They're all ashamed. Even here, with each other, they're still ashamed. So first they'll talk to each other and then they'll write to each other, and when the secrets are out, they won't be ashamed any more."

Rafferty lets the words echo in his head for a moment, thinking of Miaow. He says, "You're going to work a miracle."

"That's a teacher's job," she says.

"I need a minute with Treasure."

"Out here?"

"No, if it's okay with you, I'll go in and talk with her. Just a few seconds."

"Fine. So she can hear you over the kids, we'll start with the signing. Chalee should have drawn them all by now."

As they go back into the room, they find everyone turned to face them, except Chalee and the boy called Ting, who are still busy at the whiteboard. Rafferty edges between the chairs toward Treasure's corner. Passing the chair Chalee had vacated, he sees on top of her stack of recycled paper another drawing of Sumalee, her sister. On impulse, he moistens an index finger and slides it off the stack, folding it into quarters. He slips the picture into his hip pocket and kneels down beside Treasure's chair. When their heads are level, she pushes her chair back a few inches but holds his gaze.

"Anna can help you," he says.

She looks down at the floor as though the words are an enormous disappointment. When her eyes come up, they go past him for a split second and then return to his. She says nothing.

"I have something I have to do. I should be finished tomorrow, maybe even tonight. Then I'll come back. I'll come every day."

Her lips move silently, as though she's making sure she has the sounds right, and she says, "I stay here?"

"Can you?" he asks. "For now? People here care about you."

Her eyes dart past him again, looking at whatever she glanced at before, and then they come back, and she nods.

"See you tomorrow. I promise." He gets up, wanting to touch her but afraid to violate the distance between them, and she extends a finger and snags the sleeve of his T-shirt as he rises. She allows the weight of her arm to hang from it for a second, and lets go. He reaches to pat her hand but pulls back, still not sure whether to touch her.

Turning to go, he sees the boy with the gouged cheek staring at him and he realizes who Treasure had been looking at. The boy avoids his eyes until Anna says, "Say goodbye to Mr. Rafferty, everybody," and then the boy gives Rafferty the deep-dredged look he has seen from so many of these children, the look that says, *So you're not my adult, either.*

43

Gravel in a Clothes Dryer

IT ISN'T UNTIL he's dragged his regrets around the bend in the alley that he hears the men behind him.

He turns. Two figures saunter into sight and stop. They're not particularly big and they're not particularly powerful-looking, but there's a kind of compressed violence in the way they face him. The smell of cigarette smoke makes them feel closer than they are. The one who's smoking shifts his weight rapidly from foot to foot with an energy that might be chemical.

Rafferty backs up against the wall, putting the men to his right. Something in his gut crumples at the thought that he led them there, straight to Treasure, because he doubted Anna. Because he couldn't trust the judgment of the best friend he's ever had, who loves her. It takes an effort, but he pushes the despair aside and does a quick survey of the terrain. To his left is the mouth of the alley, the way he entered. Even with his eyes on the two to his right, he still sees, in his peripheral vision, the other two as they come in from the street.

One of them is the brutish-looking man who had tried to use his knife on Miaow.

Rafferty has nothing, not so much as a butter knife. His Glock is in the apartment. He's wearing jeans, a T-shirt, and a pair of running shoes. And a belt.

At a signal he doesn't see, all four men begin to move toward him.

If he goes right, he'll have to get past the two he saw first, and he'd be leading them back toward Treasure, Anna, and the children. To his left, the alley leads to the street, to the occasional car, to the possibility of watching eyes, even allies.

Not a hard choice.

They've advanced four or five steps toward him now, and he sees what they want to do: they're trying to form a semicircle, pushing him against the wall. As the brutish man pulls out his knife, the decision becomes much simpler.

Rafferty puts a steadying hand on the wall, trying to look irresolute, and his other hand goes to the heavy buckle of his belt. It takes one snap to unfasten it. He angles right, his back to the street, as though he's going to try to run back to Boo's. When he's facing away from the man with the knife, he tugs the belt, sliding it out of all but the last couple of loops on his jeans.

They're about three meters from him at this point, and he knows he needs all that distance to work up some speed, so he pushes off the wall with his free hand and whirls, yanking the belt free and breaking into a run, sliding his hand down to the perforated end, leaving the heavy buckle hanging free. One of the men shouts a caution, but he drowns them out with a scream that surprises even him, and he swings the belt in a blurred, whirring circle over his head and leaps toward the man with the knife.

The man jumps back, but Rafferty is already leaning into another long stride, and then he swings the belt buckle down at a 45-degree angle, slashing it the full length of the man's face.

Instinctively, the knifeman brings his hands up to his face, which is already pouring blood, and the other man takes a step back. Rafferty closes with the knifeman, grabs his hair with the hand holding the belt, yanks the man's head up, and drives a straight, short left to his unprotected throat. Then he shoves the man straight at his partner, and while the knifeman is still making the cramped, agonized sound that's probably supposed to be a scream, Rafferty is between him and the wall, running full out for the street.

He hits the sidewalk and sprints right, not thinking about anything except covering ground. He hears them behind him, at least two pair of feet, but he doesn't want to turn and look. Coming up is a yellowish streetlamp, the only one on the block, throwing a jaundiced light that brings the buildings' corners into sharp relief and reveals nothing in the way of help, not a pedestrian, not an open door, not a lighted window. He passes the light and, twenty meters ahead, he sees another lane, sloping down toward the river, on the other side of the street—the lane Chinh used to get here after they got lost—and he takes the diagonal, leaping off the curb and risking a quick look back. He sees three of them behind him, and then he's across the road but he snags his toe on the opposite curb and almost goes down, fighting his own momentum and windmilling his arms to stay upright. He doesn't fall, but they close half the distance, and Rafferty, still off balance, manages at the last moment to turn enough to slam his left shoulder against the brick, and at that instant he hears a sound that seems to punch him in the ear and something whines past his cheek and blows a cupful of brick from the wall.

His face is stinging. He knows he's bleeding from sharp-edged brick fragments. He can't outrun the gun, so he turns and lets his arms drop to his sides and watches them come.

The yellowish streetlight is behind them, stretching the men's shadows toward Rafferty so that the dark imprints of their heads and shoulders extend almost to his feet. The man holding the gun is in front. The other two are slightly behind him, about two meters away from him on either side, deployed as though they expect him to try to run. The man on the right talks into a cell phone.

The one with the gun says, "Don't move an inch."

The one to the left says, in English, "And drop your belt."

"*Drop your belt?*" Rafferty says, letting it fall at his feet. "That's heroic dialogue."

"The hero," says the man with the gun, "is the one who wins."

"Can I move now?"

"If you want me to shoot you."

"I actually don't think," Rafferty says, "that your boss wants you to kill me."

"Yeah?" the man with the phone says, putting it away. "Think again."

A sound like gravel in a clothes dryer, but full of rage, makes the man with the gun look over his shoulder. The knifeman, his face and shirt black with blood in the sodium-yellow light, hobbles out of the alley, one hand at his throat and the other holding the knife. The man with the gun says, "He's got a problem with you."

The three of them are standing in the street, too far from Rafferty for him to move on them, but close enough to shoot him. The knifeman drags himself along, one eye swollen closed in the canyon gouged by the belt buckle, his bared teeth the only light in his face. The other men fan out to give him a wider passage and, perhaps, to get away from the knife.

An absolutely blinding tide of rage—this piece of *gutter shit* chased Miaow with a knife—washes through Rafferty, sweeping away his lifelong dread of knives, and he says, "Come *on*, motherfucker."

The man with the knife leaps.

"*Hey*," the man with the gun says. It's a warning, and the one with the phone shouts something to echo it, but his voice is drowned out by the roar of a motor, and out of the lane leading down to the river comes a black SUV, angling right and cutting the corner so tightly its wheels bounce onto the sidewalk and down again as it surges past Rafferty, scattering the men in the street like bowling pins. The vehicle clips the man with the gun and sends him spinning and then accelerates straight at the knifeman, blocking him from Rafferty's view until he hears a kind of wet impact he knows immediately he'll never forget, and the vehicle backs up, away from the thing crumpled in the street, and one door opens wide with Chinh at the wheel, and Nguyen says, "Get in."

44

He Can't Shelter Them Indefinitely

"I WOULD HAVE been there a little earlier," Chinh says, "but I got lost again."

"I think it timed out nicely," Rafferty says. He hears the vapidity of his reply, but he's in the grip of an elation—*I'm alive!*—that even the sight of his bleeding face in the mirror can't douse. From the moment he saw the knifeman dragging himself into that street, he'd figured it was over.

But now, he'll be here for the birth of his child. He'll be here to do for Miaow and Rose whatever they'll let him do.

"This was, if you'll excuse my saying so, stupid," Nguyen says from the backseat. "As close as we are now, you could have endangered all of it."

"I know it was. I led them here, thinking that Anna—"

"You assume responsibility somewhat promiscuously," Nguyen says, and Rafferty realizes he's hearing the tone that's shaped Andrew. "You weren't followed. Your friend's woman was. She didn't tell her driver to check. And at the risk of wrenching us back into the present, twenty minutes after you got out of that Infiniti, Ton left his house. He hasn't come back. And it's—what?—almost two hours now. He's out of sight, we have no idea where. Let's just suppose those idiots had captured you instead of trying to kill you. Let's just suppose you and they and Ton were in a room somewhere right now, and your friend with the knife was whittling at your answers."

"But I'm here," Rafferty says. He leans closer to the mirror, which is on the back of the passenger-seat sunshade. There's a sliver of brick protruding from the skin beneath his right ear. "How do you know he left?"

"Obviously," Nguyen says, and from the sound of his voice, his teeth are clenched, "I had someone on the street. If you'd stayed where you belong—"

"I'm a member of your *team*," Rafferty says, turning around to face him, "not a hand puppet. Get over it. Oh, and here's a present, the reason Arthit couldn't match any of Sawat's crimes to the victim counts mentioned on the video. Ton chose crimes that had nothing to do with him. Sawat's murder would still look like a revenge killing, but no one would be led back to any of the murders Ton profited from. Nothing would point to him."

"Could be." Nguyen sighs, probably his version of relaxing, Rafferty thinks, and sits back for the first time.

"I need to yank some stuff out of my face," Rafferty says to Chinh. "Can you pull over for a minute?"

"At the hotel," Nguyen says. "We can't go back to the embassy until this is over." He looks at his watch. "We've only got until the embassy opens tomorrow, when Secretary Tran will have to back off."

"What happens then?"

"Whatever Ton can get away with. Probably starting with the arrests of your friend and Colonel Thanom. I'm going to be fine one way or the other," he says. "My family and I are shielded. But everyone else is just hanging in the open. Your man Ton has a lot of power."

"And Tran will stick to that deadline."

"He's not the president of Vietnam," Nguyen says. "He's a diplomat. He can't shelter Thai citizens like Arthit and his woman and Thanom from the authorities indefinitely. And you, you're a floater. You could make a run for the American embassy, but I doubt Mrs. Rafferty and Miaow could get in."

"We're going to get him," Rafferty says, "and we're going to do it before your fucking deadline."

They drive on in a thick, pressurized silence.

IT STRETCHES INTO the longest night of Rafferty's life.

Since they can't go back to the embassy, they trek from hotel to hotel until they find one that still has a fax in a guest room, and then they move again when the fax is out of order. They end up in a suite big enough to sleep eight very wealthy people, but the fax is right there on the desk, and the test page Clemente sends comes in just fine.

"Both versions of the chart," Rafferty says. "The one with just Ton in the middle and the one with Jurak in there, too, and mock up the phony police ID card, make it look like yours, with Jurak's picture."

"Already done," she says on the other end of the line.

"Great, great." He yawns, more nerves than exhaustion, and checks his watch. Almost 2:30. "Listen, just send everything you've got." He gives her the number.

"Fine," Clemente says. "Anything else?"

"Wake Andrew up. I need another hard copy of the picture from the iPhone. Send me that, too, best resolution you can get. And anything else you think might be interesting."

"Done," she says. "Your wife has come in three times to ask if you're okay. Said she didn't want to bother you."

"Tell her I'm in the lap of luxury. Arthit is right about you," Rafferty says. "You're ready for the big time."

He hangs up and looks across the room at Nguyen, who is on the other phone, talking for perhaps the twentieth time to the man watching Ton's mansion. Nguyen feels his gaze and shakes his head, then cuts off the call.

"A famous Vietnamese soldier once said that waiting was worse than fighting," he says. "I never knew what he meant until now." He looks at his own watch, and his phone rings.

He holds the phone to his ear for a moment or two and then closes his eyes in what looks like resignation. Into the phone, he says, "How long can you hold him?" Shakes his head at what he's hearing. To Rafferty, he says, "They're going to have to cut Jurak loose pretty quick. Either that or book him formally."

"They can't book him," Rafferty says. "If it gets into the computer system, someone will call Ton within ten minutes." He looks at his watch again; it's been three minutes. In seven hours or so, Tran will lift the protective blanket. "Do they have a fax at the station?" he says, as the fax in the hotel room whirs into action.

"Hold on." Nguyen repeats the question into the phone and says, "They've got one."

"Get the number and ask them to stand right at the machine in about five minutes. Maybe the fake ID cards will scare him into talking." Rafferty gets up and checks the fax machine as the first of the two charts begins to slide out. "Where the *hell* is Ton?"

Half an hour after the last of Clemente's faxes arrive and the phony police ID card with Jurak's picture on it has been sent off to Arthit, Poke goes into one of the big bedrooms and lies down, feeling as rigid as a two-by-four. There are no comfortable positions, and his eyelids won't stay down. He's about to add *sleep* to the growing list of things he's not good at, but then he's gone.

NGUYEN'S TOUCH BRINGS him to a full sitting position even before his eyes are open. Through the window, he sees the first paling in the eastern sky. Nguyen says, "It's five eighteen. Ton has just pulled into his driveway."

45

The Light in the Window

IT TAKES THE man at the gate almost ten minutes to allow Rafferty in. In that time, the triangular fragment of paper Rafferty gave the guard has been passed to an elegantly dressed servant—a butler of some sort, probably—and carried into the house, mostly dark at this hour. Rafferty and the guard share the warming dawn in silence, while around the corner, the SUV ticks as the engine cools and Nguyen cools too, livid at Rafferty's insistence on going in alone and convinced in the end only by Rafferty's repeated reminder that it was his child Ton had attempted to kill.

He catches himself patting his hip pocket for the third time. The items in it feel thin and flimsy, nowhere near substantial enough to do what he hopes they'll do to Ton's life.

He has no backup plan if Ton won't see him. He's never wanted to take it to court. It's possible that the case isn't strong enough for court, given Ton's prominence. So if the butler calls from the house and tells him Ton has no interest in seeing the rest of the page the triangle was cut from, Rafferty figures he'll be running for his life, and everyone else will be tossed out of the embassy by 8:30. And if that's the way it plays out, he and Rose and Miaow might have to find a way out of Thailand for good. As a drifter with no diplomatic armor, he could be killed and no one would make a huge fuss. And Miaow and Rose? A street child and a former prostitute? Wouldn't even make the papers.

The house is big, white, and vaguely American-Southern. Give it some pillars and an oak tree or two, and a Thai Scarlett O'Hara would look right at home, fanning herself or patting talcum on her neck as she sips a Mekong. There's a big window to the left of the door, dimly lighted. Rafferty's guess is that it's the living room and that the light is coming either from the entrance hall, which had looked quite bright when the butler came out and went back in, or from a room behind it: a dining room, perhaps. Above the front door, but staggered to the right, are two mullioned windows. They look as though the room they open into is halfway up the stairs Rafferty glimpsed in the entrance hall.

The lights behind those two windows had snapped on a moment after the butler took the piece of paper into the house. Now, as the stars disappear overhead and sweat begins to prickle the back of Rafferty's neck, he hears movement behind him and turns to see two of the men from the alley, one of them the man who'd had the phone. They're coming at him slowly but with obvious intent. They plan to beat him to death.

"Hey," Rafferty says to the guard, backing up a step. "Did you know these guys were coming?"

The guard looks past him and says to the men, "Stop. I gotta call about this," and reaches for the phone. At that moment, it rings. The guard picks it up, listens, and says, "Yes, sir." He turns to Rafferty. "You're in." The gate begins to glide inward. "Don't get him mad."

Rafferty says, "I'll do my best." The other two men eye him like waiting vultures as he walks through the gate.

HE FOLLOWS THE servant through the door into the bright hallway. White polished marble on the floor, a ballroom-size chandelier dangling overhead, and, in the relative dimness of the living room, heavy brocades hanging on the walls like paintings.

"Please," the butler says in English, inviting Rafferty in. He leads Rafferty to the stairs, and Rafferty follows, consciously slowing his breath and trying to locate a center of calm. For an instant he wishes he were better dressed and immediately abandons the thought: as if there were any proper dress for an occasion like this one. He counts the stairs to quiet his mind, to sharpen his sense of the moment.

Halfway up, the stairs broaden into a landing with a door to the right. The butler puts his hand up to knock, but instead looks directly into Rafferty's eyes. For three or four seconds, the two men gaze at each other, and then the butler lowers his eyes and knocks. Without waiting for permission, he opens the door and steps aside.

Ton is sitting behind a polished black wooden desk, in the circle of light thrown by a porcelain lamp. The only object on the desk in front of him is the triangle of paper Rafferty gave to the guard.

Rafferty hasn't seen him in person since the party at Pan's house all those years ago. Their interaction—and there had been quite a bit of it, mostly threats—had been through intermediaries and on the telephone. The man who regards him through gray-tinted glasses looks like he's aged double-time, although Rafferty thinks he's probably one of those people whom time skips for years and years and then catches up to all at once. He'd been smooth-faced and strong-jawed then, but now the skin beneath the jaw is looser, the lines around the sharp-cornered mouth more deeply engraved, the hair too black to be natural.

Ton says, "You know what time it is."

Rafferty says, "Yes."

"I'll give you ten minutes." Ton touches the piece of paper with an index finger, pushing it partway across the desk. "Starting with this."

"If you're going to give me ten minutes," Rafferty says, "they're mine to use as I want, and I want to begin with this." He takes the folded papers from his hip pocket and opens the top one. He turns it right-side up for Ton and puts it on the desk. In the eternal half-light of that penciled window, Chalee's sister gazes up at Ton.

"Her name was Sumalee," Rafferty says in English; Ton's is as good as his. "She lived in Isaan."

"Really," Ton says. His tone says he's humoring Rafferty, but not for long.

"I'm going to begin this conversation with two little girls," Rafferty says, "because I can't think of a better way to convince you of the depth of the malice I feel toward you. And you need to understand just how much I hate you if you're going to believe that I mean what I came here to say."

Ton passes a hand over his hair, sighs, and says, "So. What was her name again?"

"Sumalee. It means *flower*."

"I know what it means," Ton says.

"Sumalee." Rafferty tows an ornate chair over to the desk but doesn't sit. "The picture was drawn by her sister, Chalee. Sumalee was fourteen when Chalee first drew the picture. She draws it over and over now."

"I can hear the clock ticking."

"I said she lived in Isaan, right?"

Ton glances at the drawing again and then, to signal he's finished with it, turns it around so it's facing Rafferty once more. "You know you did."

"About a month after Chalee drew that picture for the first time, her family lost the plot of land they grew rice on. To a foreclosure mill called the Northeast Farmer's Trust. One of your companies."

Ton spreads his hands but says nothing, but his eyes are on Rafferty's.

"And Sumalee's father decided that the only way to pay the debt was to sell Sumalee into the sex trade. Sumalee hanged herself. So I guess she's fourteen forever."

Ton shakes his head. "There are people who can't manage money. It's regrettable, but—"

"I feel terrible about Sumalee," Rafferty interrupts, "but—man to man? It's sort of . . . theoretical. I know these things happen— hell, part of it happened to my own wife. Her family raises rice, too. But here comes something that isn't even remotely theoretical."

"You really are idling through your time."

"This is the *other* little girl," Rafferty says, putting a photograph on the desk. "My daughter, Miaow. You sent a man to kill her several days ago."

"Nonsense. If someone injured your daughter, that's regrettable, but I had nothing to—"

"My guess is that you don't get interrupted much," Rafferty says over him. He puts a foot on the arm of the brocaded chair and watches Ton's face stiffen. "But here I am, interrupting you. You sent the man who tried to kill my daughter, and *that* I take very personally indeed. This evening I think I crushed his larynx, a couple of minutes before some friends of mine ran over him. But that's nothing compared to what I'm going to do to you."

Ton pushes his chair back and opens the desk drawer. In it is a Sig Sauer P226, blunt and black and ugly. "Just so you know," he says, resting a hand on the gun. "And this conversation is tiresome."

"The gun's not going to help you," Rafferty says. "I can't think of a weapon in the world that would help you. You're as helpless right now as Sumalee was when her father told her he was going to sell her."

"So far, I haven't heard anything that's raised my pulse rate."

"One girl dead and one you tried to kill. One of them my daughter. Just keep that in mind as I put the rest of the cards on the table." He unfolds a standard sheet of paper with a piece cut out of it. Then he reaches across the desk and slides the triangular fragment into place and turns the sheet around for Ton.

Ton looks at it, then lowers his head to study it more closely. Rafferty hears the change in his breathing: shallower, a bit quicker. "Interesting," he says, "but entirely conjectural. And its implications, I mean the implications you're suggesting, aren't even conjectural. They're fictitious."

"Who's in the middle of that circle? The one who profited from all those murders?"

"You know perfectly well that I am."

"Well, gee, I'm sorry. That's an early draft." Rafferty pulls it back and puts out another sheet. He pushes it across the desk and watches Ton's face go completely still. "This is more up-to-date. The man next to you in the circle is Jurak." He pauses for a moment and adds, "The father of your two grandsons." He looks over at the color pictures on the wall. "Nice-looking boys, by the way."

The eyes Ton gives Rafferty are, for the first time, the eyes he expected when he first stepped into the room, the eyes of someone who could kill for years without ever getting blood on his cuffs.

"All those deals," Rafferty says, drawing a circle in the air above the chart. "All those murders. All for your grandsons. A business empire built one killing at a time, a lifetime's worth of revenge on your brothers. It will be your grandsons who inherit everything. Or it might be."

Ton's hand is flat on the diagram, as if to obscure it, and now he makes a fist, crumpling it. "This is nothing that would persuade a prosecutor. Anyone could—could draw this up. The murders and the little lines and the, the sums of money, well, yes, it's suggestive. Just graphics. But you have nothing that actually links either me or Jurak to any of this."

"Well," Rafferty says. He unfolds another piece of paper. "First, I have no interest in prosecutors. Second, have you noticed that kids can do things instinctively with computers that would take you or me—well, me, anyway—days to learn? A thirteen-year-old boy managed to pull this image off a crappy cell phone picture of a reflection in a store window, and I don't know how—"

Ton has snatched the page from him. He glances at it and slaps it facedown on the desk.

"—how he got it to read so well," Rafferty says, "but he did. And it's been cropped a bit, but the whole frame shows Jurak quite clearly taking a picture of Thongchai with the same phone that was given to the men who killed Thongchai and Sawat. The phone that started all this."

"It's a fake," Ton says. "The phone is gone."

"We have all the pictures. Even without the phone, they tell a story: shots of the two murder victims, a self-portrait of your son-in-law photographing one of them, even some happy snaps of the men who killed them. All, by the way, date-stamped and sequenced."

Ton's tongue explores the right-hand corner of his mouth.

"And then there's this," Rafferty says, unfolding the last piece of paper. "Did you know your son-in-law withdrew almost fifty thousand US a few months ago from the bank account you and he set up to frame Colonel Thanom? He used this as ID."

Ton says, "He withdrew—"

"Around a million and a half baht. I'm sure you knew about that."

"From *what* account?"

"You know, the one you and he—wait, listen, you and Jurak really ought to get your stories straight. Why don't you call him? See if he can clarify things."

Ton's eyes are everywhere in the room, as though he's taking inventory on the fly. "Call him?"

"You know." Rafferty mimes a phone, thumb and little finger extended at his ear, and watches as Ton lets his gaze settle on the copy of the police identification card. "Unless you think he might not be there. Unless that's where you've *been* for most of the night, looking for him, because you're afraid the cops have—"

Ton starts to push his chair back. "I've heard enough. Your time—"

"—because you're afraid the cops have already picked him up. Because you're afraid he's already talking to them. Settle the issue. Call him. See who answers the phone."

Ton stares up at him with a new kind of loathing, one that has apprehension behind it. Rafferty says, "Or, if you don't want to come up on Jurak's caller ID, since who knows who'll be looking at it, wherever he is, why not use my phone? Here."

He holds out the phone. Slowly, Ton takes it and pushes the

first four digits. He pauses and then, very quickly, hits the rest of the buttons.

Rafferty hears Arthit say, "Hello?" and Ton punches the key to disconnect as though he's afraid something will come through the receiver. He puts the phone dead center on the desk and stares down at it like it might begin to move on its own.

Rafferty picks it up and slips it into his pocket. "To settle the issue, I can tell you that he is. Talking, I mean. When I left the room he was talking so fast the stenographer had to ask him to slow down."

Ton has put his hands against the edge of the desk to push his chair back, but he stays there bent awkwardly at the waist, the chair half a meter from the desk. He's looking down, into the open drawer with the gun in it.

"It will do you no good to kill me," Rafferty says. "It'll just make things worse for you. This is too far underway, and too many people are already involved. All my death would do is put you—*finally*—in the same room as someone you've killed." He takes his foot off the chair, turns it around, and sits. "So, just by way of recap. Over a period of years, you set up Sawat's operation to kill people who were standing in the way of your business interests. We've got it all documented, eight deaths and two more being researched. You and your son-in-law, Jurak, created a ghost bank account to incriminate Thanom. We've got the ID cards he used to do both, one with the name *Sawat* on it and the other with the name *Thanom*, and both with Jurak's picture. You hired three killers to have them take out Sawat and Thongchai. Jurak helpfully took Sawat and Thongchai's pictures first. We have the photo of him doing it. And right now he's talking about all this, and much more, to a circle of cops. When I left, he was on the verge of telling them how you killed the men you hired to get rid of Sawat and Thongchai." Jurak had done nothing of the kind the last time Rafferty spoke to Arthit, but by now, Rafferty thinks, he probably is.

Ton raises a hand as though to speak, but lets it fall again.

"And you did it all for your grandsons. In the long run, every-thing you built up, and everything your brothers built up, would go to your grandsons. You would have triumphed. Over time, over family, over your own son's death, over your rotten relationships with your brothers."

Without looking up, Ton says, "What do you want?"

"Let me back up just a step or two," Rafferty says. "There *still* might not be enough to convict someone of your stature of a capital crime, although I doubt it, but by the time Jurak finishes talking there will certainly be enough to disgrace you forever and to put Jurak away for life. And if you think your brothers are charitable enough to let your business, and theirs, pass to the grandsons of a disgraced brother and the sons of a convicted mur-derer, you have a higher opinion of them than I do."

Ton says, thin-lipped, "They'd adopt first."

"Pretty much my thought. So, you see, even if you somehow stay out of prison, which you won't, you've lost everything. Now and in the future."

Ton says, "We must be able to work something out."

"Just what I was going to say. Suppose no one ever found out about any of this? Suppose it all just went away?"

Ton straightens up and sits back in his chair. He seems to be working something through, and when he finally looks at Rafferty, his eyes are speculative. "How could you do that?"

Rafferty shrugs. "What matters is that I can."

Ton turns away and looks at the photographs on the wall. "How much do you want?"

"What if I said ten billion baht?"

"Then I'd need to know how you're going to do it and what my security is. I'd need something ironclad. A handwritten and wit-nessed document acknowledging that you knew about all of this and conspired to cover it up, for profit."

"Well, I don't actually want ten billion baht. What I want is free. Doesn't cost anything."

"What's that?"

"I want you to kill yourself."

"You're," Ton says, and takes a new breath. "You're joking."

"I went to some lengths at the beginning of this chat to let you know how deeply I loathe you. Would you like me to tell you again?" With one hand in his pocket, he presses *send* on his phone, the signal he and Arthit agreed on.

Ton says, "This is ridiculous."

"It's just another decision," Rafferty says. He disconnects and looks at his watch. "But it's one you'd better make quickly."

The phone on Ton's desk rings. He looks at it and then up at Rafferty.

"That'll be the guard at your gate, telling you there are some uniformed cops downstairs, asking to come in."

The phone rings again.

"Answer it," Rafferty says. "Don't take my word. Talk to one of the cops."

Ton picks up the phone, says, "Yes?" and listens for a second. Then he hangs up. He's chewing on the inside of his left cheek.

"You might be asking yourself," Rafferty says, "how you can trust me and those cops down there not to put your son-in-law on trial anyway, once you're dead. Well, you can't. All I can say is that what you *should* be wondering about is why it's me up here with the cops downstairs instead of the other way around. We've reached an agreement, the cops and I. I have nothing against your grandsons and no reason to want to ruin their lives, and all the cops want is for this scandal to go away quietly. That's why I'm the one sitting in your nice chair. They *certainly* don't want this flap to involve one of the highest-ranking people in the department, putting the whole force under suspicion and probably ruining dozens of careers. So they'll leave Jurak alone, if you give them a chance to do it."

He gets up, goes to the window, and looks down at the gate, feeling Ton's eyes on his back and listening for the sound of the gun being lifted from the drawer. Down below he sees Arthit, Thanom, Clemente, Anand, Kosit, and two others. "Six or seven of them," he says. "That makes it your call: lifelong shame and scandal, probably prison, your son-in-law in jail as an accessory to murder and for murder itself the minute we find the bodies of the men you hired. Your grandsons disinherited. Living in the street, for all I know. It's unlikely, but there would be certain poetry in it.

"All of that on the one hand, and on the other, you're dead. A headline: PROMINENT POLICE OFFICIAL KILLS SELF. You get the big funeral, you get the honor guard and the sad speeches. Your family can hold its head up. Your wife's not disgraced, the grandsons will still inherit. The next day, life goes on just as you planned it. Minus you."

The phone starts to ring again.

He starts to move toward the door. "Don't want to answer that? I wouldn't either. One last thing. I know that right now, somewhere in your mind, you're searching for a way your family's power can save you. Well, don't bother. If you're still alive past my deadline, you're going to set Phase Two in motion. At eight this morning, less than three hours from now, police officers with copies of all these—graphics, you called them—will make calls on ranking members of your victims' families. As you can imagine, there's going to be a lot of interest."

With one hand on the doorknob, he turns to face Ton directly. The gun is still in the drawer. "As much influence as your family has, they'll be outweighed and outclassed. Taken as a whole, if what we've learned so far is accurate, your victims' families control more newspapers, more radio and television stations, more government ministers, and more elected legislators than your family does. And let's not forget, they still run businesses that compete with yours. Some of them," he says, "even have princelings in the police department who would advance in your absence."

The phone, which had stopped ringing, begins again, but Ton doesn't appear to hear it. He seems twenty years older to Rafferty than he had a few minutes earlier. He's looking down at the surface of his desk, with the litter of paper and pictures on it, and one of his eyelids is lower than the other, as it might be after a stroke. Rafferty isn't sure the man is even following what he's saying.

"So here's the deal," he says, opening the door a foot or so. "The light from this room can be seen from the street. I'm going to leave and give you ten minutes. I'm sure you have some things to write down, details to take care of. Before the ten minutes are up, you'll turn off this light and then you'll use that Sig Sauer on yourself. The police will come in because they heard a gunshot from inside the house, and if they don't hear a gunshot they'll say they did and come in anyway, and you'll be arrested and those visits to the families will be made, and you can deal with all that."

The phone isn't ringing now, although Rafferty couldn't say when it stopped. He can hear Ton's breathing.

"They'll be bringing up a car to break through the gate," Rafferty says. He comes back to the desk and picks up all the pieces of paper. "They'll be watching for the light, so don't forget to turn it off." He refolds the papers and shoves them back into his hip pocket. To Ton, who now seems to be studying the color photos of the boys on his wall, he says, "Ten minutes. Up to you."

He goes out and closes the door. At the bottom of the stairs, he says to the butler, "He'll call you if he wants you," and lets himself out.

Eight minutes later by Rafferty's watch the light in the window goes out. Before he's drawn three breaths, the police charge in at the sound of the shot.

46

A Lot Here We Wouldn't Want to Lose

"FURNITURE IS GETTING moved around on the top floors," Arthit says. "There may be a great public silence since the suicide, but behind closed doors people are wheeling desks from place to place. Pictures are being hung."

He and Rafferty are knee-to-knee at Rafferty's desk, shoehorned into the space behind the big flatscreen. Rose is watching something that features a great many women speaking English, and once in a while she laughs. It almost tempts Rafferty to listen to what's being said, but only almost. Miaow is in her room, rehearsing the speech from *Small Town* she wants to read for her audition. It was going to be a scene between Julie and Ned, but at the last moment Andrew called to say he couldn't come.

"Thanom's going to get a promotion." Arthit takes a healthy slug of the Crown Royal Poke had poured. Rafferty's bottle of beer sweats on his thigh, where he's put it to keep from making a ring on the top of the desk. His jeans are wet. "It's more a lateral than a forward pass, but he seems to be happy."

"*Seems* to be?"

"Our friendship has cooled. He's found a way, since the department just wants to close the door on everything, to keep the money in that phony account. So he's better off financially, he's got a higher rank, and he knows he fell apart in front of me in the embassy. He doesn't need me any more."

"Well," Rafferty says, drinking. "We certainly need you *here*, if you ever have time to spare . . ."

"And Miaow?" Arthit lowers his voice. "Happy ending in sight?"

"Not even close," Rafferty says. "Because Nguyen and I talked to that financial reporter Kalmenson about Ton just before the suicide, the ambassador is pulling him out. They may already be on their way back to Vietnam."

Arthit says, "I'm sorry."

"Andrew called about two hours ago. He was supposed to come over and rehearse a scene from the play for the auditions, but when he called he was in a car on the way to the airport."

"How is she?"

"In her room. I think she'd already given up on the relationship, but you know."

Arthit says, "One thing I've learned is that letting go of a relationship is a solid-gold bitch."

The two of them sit in silence for a moment, until they're brought back to the present by someone emoting from the flatscreen, with a British accent since Rose hasn't officially found the remote yet and Miaow left it on the English Channel or something.

Arthit regards the long high rectangle of the television, its cables trailing across the carpet to the wall. "This is an interesting decorating effect," he says. "It's like rebuilding part of the Berlin Wall in your living room."

"Rose spends a lot of time in front of it," Rafferty says, raising his voice. "She's watching for two."

Rose says, as though she's been saving it up, "The baby already speaks English."

"The baby," Arthit says. He grins. "The baby."

Rafferty feels himself grin back. "Yeah. The baby."

Rose says, "Poke is a wonderful father."

Rafferty says, "Are you eavesdropping?"

"Shhh," Rose says. "The good girl is starting to cry."

Rafferty puts a finger to his lips, and Arthit drains his glass and puts it down. "I actually had two reasons to come over," he says softly. "First is to tell you that we found the bodies of the men who killed Sawat and Thongchai."

"How?"

"A tip." He shrugs at Rafferty's expression. "Well, the tip came from Jurak, but as far as the world knows, they were killed by Bangkok police in the name of duty. Their deaths close the case. The story is, they took revenge and got caught, and the names of the victims they were avenging are being kept confidential to protect the innocent members of the victims' families, who have been through so much, et cetera. Jurak is going to live under a microscope for the next few years, but no one will charge him with anything because it would open up Pandora's Box. It's all over, case closed. Ton will get a full police funeral."

"It all sounds so tidy," Rafferty says. "An orderly, grammatical paragraph without a true sentence in it anywhere."

"'Truths would you teach, or save a sinking land?'" Arthit says. "That's Alexander Pope, smug as always."

"Sometimes I think the land should just be allowed to sink. Something better might rise in its place."

Arthit tilts his head in Rose's direction. "There's a lot here we wouldn't want to lose. Which brings me to the second reason I'm here. Anna wants to know whether you think it would be a good idea for you and Rose and Miaow and her and me to cross our fingers and take Treasure out to dinner."

"Gee, I don't know. I mean, Treasure's not—" He stops. Having to deal with Treasure might make it easier for the four of them to go out for the first time.

Arthit picks up his empty glass and puts it down again and says, "And Dok and Chalee."

"We'd love to," Rafferty says. "We'll be like a buffer zone between Treasure and everyone else. The Balkans."

From the other side of the screen, Rose says, "That would be ripping."

"Anna's so happy," Arthit says. "What she needed in her life was kids she could teach. She's in heaven."

Rafferty says, "If I knew what to do about Miaow, I'd be pretty close myself."

LATER THAT NIGHT, Rafferty sits beside Rose on the couch and watches Miaow, in front of the dark television screen, perform Julie's farewell to the world. She stops and takes a shaky breath before the final goodbye, and what he sees in her face brings tears to his eyes. When she's done, he applauds and goes into the bedroom before they spill over and give him away.

He's sitting on the bed, trying to think of an explanation for fleeing the room, when Miaow comes in. He says, "You're going to be wonderful." Then he's blinking again.

She sits next to him on the bed. In the living room, the television comes back on. She says, "You're a crybaby."

"I've always been a crybaby," he says. "I cry when someone bites into a carrot."

She sniffs and glances at him out of the corner of her eye. "Do you remember," she says, "when you used motorcycles in traffic to explain geological strata to me?"

"Yes. I mean, I suppose so."

"Well, I remember it. It was a cool explanation."

He looks over her, but she's gazing into her lap. "Thanks."

"I've thought of the name for the baby. Remember, you said—"

"I remember."

"If it's a girl, I mean."

"Great," he says. "What is it?"

She says, "Angelina. You know, because Angelina Jolie is so—"

"Right," he says, without even knowing he's interrupting.

"—beautiful and everything, and she adopts all those kids and stuff."

Time has pretty much oozed to a stop as far as he's concerned, so he has no idea how much of it has managed to shudder past by the time he says, "Great. That's—*great*. Just, you know, tell your mom about it."

"Okay," she says, and she gets up and leaves.

He sits there perched on the edge of the mattress, thinking, *nine months, we have nine months to find a way around this*, and then, from the living room, he hears Miaow and Rose burst into laughter. Not polite, discreet laughter, but choking, gasping, nose-running laughter. One of them says, "Shhhh," and then it starts up again, Miaow carrying the high violin line and Rose the cello.

It goes on for quite a while, and as long as it lasts he sits there and listens to it.

Afterword

WHEN PEOPLE ASK (at bookstores, usually) what the Poke Rafferty books are about, I often say they're about a travel writer who was searching for a home and found it in, of all places, Bangkok. Then I say something about how the books' real protagonist is a family of three who all see each other as a final chance for happiness. This last response frequently has the advantage of shutting down that line of inquiry for a while.

But if the questions continue, I say that when the series is finished, it'll tell Miaow's story from the time she was adopted to the time she leaves the nest Poke and Rose have created for her. Privately (at least until now) I've always hoped I could continue to write the books from the time the family forms, in *A Nail Through the Heart*, until it's reduced from three to two with Miaow's inevitable departure. The very thought makes me misty.

Some time ago, I emerged, blinking in the sunlight, from the cave in which I isolate myself while I'm writing, and I went to a fan convention called Bouchercon, that was being held in some midwestern city. *The Queen of Patpong* had just come out, and my publishers at the time thought it would be a good idea for me to, you know, get some sun, eat some solid food, and talk to a few people.

So I went, and it was one of the greatest experiences of my writing life. I had person after person grab me to talk about the books, and one theme emerged: a *lot* of people were skipping to the end of each book before they read the beginning. And why was that?

They wanted to make sure that nothing bad happened to Miaow.

This took me completely off guard. I knew *I* loved Miaow, but I had no idea that so many other people felt the same. Several people who had read *Queen*, which was mostly about Rose, asked when I'd write a book about Miaow. So this is it, I guess—the *first* book about Miaow, anyway. I hope those people I met in (I think) St. Louis enjoy it. I hope you do, too.

Those of you who have gotten this far in the other books in this series know that I usually talk about the music I listened to as I wrote. This time around, many of the artists who supplied the soundtrack were relatively new to me. Probably more of it was written to Fun.

than any other artist. *For the Dead* was often difficult to write, and the two albums by Fun. gave me energy and a perspective that carried me over many miles of muddy road. Miaow has been listening to them at the beginning of the book, and the section titles are all taken from songs by Fun except for "Drowning Girls," which is a misheard phrase from the song "Benson Hedges." Imagine my surprise, after writing about 150 pages with the image of drowning girls before my eyes, when I looked up the lyric online and realized I'd gotten it wrong; it's actually "Holy Ghost." How *embarrassing*.

Fun's members decided on an eye-catching way to spell the band's name: fun.—complete with lowercase "f" and a period. On a page of manuscript, it looks like a typographical sneeze, so we've used "Fun" throughout the book, knowing we ran the risk of outraging purists.

Most of the other music was by female artists: Lindi Ortega, Amanda Shires, Tegan & Sara, Mindy Clark, First Aid Kit, Kacey Musgraves, Aimee Mann, Jenny Lewis, Carrie Rodriguez, Joan Armatrading, Alexis Krauss (of Sleigh Bells), the ever-essential Emmylou Harris, and a dozen more. If there seems to be a lot of country music in there, it's because adolescence is essentially a country song.

A few of the artists I played (Lindi Ortega, for example) were recommended to me by readers who contacted me through my website, www.timothyhallinan.com, to suggest music. Please, if you have music to suggest, let me know.

Thanks to all who helped out with this book, including the phenomenal crew at Soho: editor extraordinaire Juliet Grames, whose contribution was substantial and even educational; widely-read marketing maven Paul Oliver; paragon of efficiency Rachel Kowal; and, riding herd, publisher Bronwen Hruska.

Special credit, as always to my amazing wife and first listener, Munyin Choy-Hallinan, whom I still don't deserve; my agent, Bob Mecoy, who offered cheerleading when cheerleading was necessary. The type was scanned six ways from Sunday by Everett Kaser, Alan Katz, and Marie Orozco, who caught many errors, large and small.

Brett Battles, one of my favorite writers, helped out immensely by reminding me several times that I always think every book is my last. Now that this one is finished and I'm writing the next, I realize how much I needed that perspective.